W9-BXM-717

3 5674 00580308 6

DETROIT PUBLIC LIBRARY

BL

DATE DUE

AFTERMATH

A NOVEL

BY HANS HABE

NEW YORK · THE VIKING PRESS

1947

COPYRIGHT 1947 BY HANS HABE

FIRST PUBLISHED BY THE VIKING PRESS IN OCTOBER 1947

PUBLISHED ON THE SAME DAY IN THE DOMINION OF CANADA
BY THE MACMILLAN COMPANY OF CANADA LIMITED

TRANSLATED BY RICHARD F. HANSER

PRINTED IN U.S.A.
AMERICAN BOOK—STRATFORD PRESS, INC., NEW YORK

PART I

Germany today, shown through the experiences of two men: Peter Olden, who leaves his American wife for an earlier love and devotes his time, after the war, to redeeming Germany, and Major Stroud, who finds, when the time comes, he must choose between mistress and wife.

WHEN the first American troops entered Paris Captain Peter Olden had been in the city three days. Going in ahead of invasions and liberations was an old story to him. In North Africa he had lived among the Arabs for weeks before the invasion began; he had parachuted down behind the little town of Battipaglia just ahead of the Salerno landing; in Naples he had come close to disaster when he was inspecting the city while the Germans were still packing their bags; and he had greeted the first of Bradley's patrols to reach Cherbourg.

Compared to these events his entry into Paris was tame. Dressed in civilian clothes, he had mounted a bicycle in Rambouillet and had simply pedaled through the German lines. Now, as the American vanguard poured through the Port d'Orléans and LeClerc's lead tanks went clanking past the Luxembourg, the invasion of Paris was three days old for him.

He had selected the most luxurious room in the Hotel Scribe for himself, before some colonel or general could occupy it. His experience with colonels and generals in this respect had not been happy; they usually turned up tardily and demanded the choicest apartments. Peter Olden sat in the bathtub, smoked a cigarette, and gave himself over to a happy contemplation of the gleaming laundry and the meticulously ironed uniform laid out on the bed. He had incautiously brought along laundry and uniform in a bundle, because he hadn't liked the idea of receiving the Americans in Paris dressed in his shabby civilian clothes, like just another member of the liberated mob.

He dressed slowly and with great care. Below, on the boulevard, the people of Paris surged and shouted. The first jeeps, coming from the Opéra, crawled along in the direction of the Madeleine. The throng had overpowered them. Eight or nine girls, sometimes more, their thin summer blouses and skirts fluttering in the August breeze, were mounted on every jeep. The soldiers sat in their vehicles, grinning speechlessly, their faces smeared with the mingled dust of the highway and the lipstick of the Parisiennes. The buttons had been torn from their OD shirts, and wi   their bare, sun-browned chests they looked like invading India   From the Place de la Concorde came the monotonous rattle f machine guns.

Captain Peter Olden had the whole day before him. Colonel Whimsley, to whom he was to report, would not arrive before six o'clock. General Donovan, "Wild Bill," probably would arrive in Paris during the night too. Until then Peter had eight or nine hours to himself. Eight or nine hours in Paris, on August 25, 1944, the day of liberation. He drained a glass of champagne from the bottle presented to him by the hotel management as a small courtesy to the first American tourist and prepared to go out.

Meanwhile the tired splendor of the Scribe lobby had given way to a wild and deafening turmoil. A British major was attempting, above the din, to explain to the manager how to run his hotel according to military rules. On the long desk of the *portier* bottles of cognac were being set up as on a bar. Whores with upswept hairdos stumbled over mounds of musette bags and bedding rolls. The first correspondents milled about inquiring for telephones, and redheaded H. R. Knickerbocker of the *Chicago Sun* was already returning from sending off his description of the liberation of Paris.

Peter kept an eye out for his command car, which Dirty Thompson had been ordered to drive into Paris. T/5 Dirty Thompson had been a Chicago taxi driver in civilian life. He had earned his nickname from an implacable aversion to water. Peter would not have traded him for any other driver in the entire United States Army. Dirty drove through blacked-out nights as if the brightest sun were shining; he was afraid of nothing, and he worked around the clock. Once a month he got moderately drunk, but otherwise he made no more demands on the world than a Trappist monk. Thompson had promised Peter to be in front of the Scribe on the morning of August 25 between nine and eleven. He was in Europe for the first time; he had never been to Paris before. At nine-thirty o'clock, on the morning of August 25, he was sitting in the command car in front of the hotel.

The Captain did not find him at once. Thompson and most of the command car were hidden from view by a swarm of beautiful Parisiennes. They sat on the hood, on the fenders, on Thompson's lap. His face, which always reminded Peter of Wallace Beery, seemed to be bleeding from a dozen lipstick wounds. His stubby arms bare to the elbows, he was scribbling on slips of paper that were being thrust at him from all directions. He was signing autographs.

"Hey, Clark Gable!" Peter called.

"Hello, Captain." Thompson grinned.

"Have a good trip?"

Thompson smacked his lips and his grin widened. "You got any cigarettes?" he asked. "I gave 'em all away."

"Mine too?"

"Yours too."

They laughed. Now the girls threw themselves upon Peter. He was a head taller than most soldiers, with chestnut brown hair slightly bleached by the sun, and cool, gray, wholesome eyes. He wore no helmet, and in his clean khaki shirt he looked as if he had been fighting the war in a bathtub. "*Mon premier Américain!*" cried the girls, who had already kissed hundreds of Americans, and the freshly laundered shirt had its first smears of red.

It required some gymnastics for Peter to free himself and take his place in the driver's seat. "Let's go," he said, starting the car. "Otherwise we'll never get out of here."

"Where we goin'?" said Thompson, as if he were in Chicago asking a fare for the address. He was standing upright in the car, holding on to the windshield with one hand, and with the other waving to right and left in response to the exuberant cheers and shouts of the people in the street. "Just like Hitler in the goddam newsreels," he said admiringly of himself. Then he asked again, "Where we goin'?"

"I think we'll do some shopping," said the Captain.

Thompson was teetering, on the verge of falling out of the car, as he grasped the hand of a passing beauty who did not want to let him go. Even so he did not lose his infallible sense of the practical. "All the shops are closed," he pointed out.

"We'll just have to open them then."

"Okay." Thompson was thinking of a kind of shopping that requires no money.

They were held up on the Place de la Concorde. From the roof of the Crillon a group of snipers were firing on the crowd. A machine gun returned the fire from the Tuileries. A time bomb exploded near the obelisk, and for a moment the area was fogged in smoke. Under the whining bullets the women lay flat on the ground, and their summer dresses formed a festive carpet over the Place de la Concorde. It was as if the square had suddenly burst into blossom. The women were laughing; only the men cursed. A half-grown youth who had clambered up a statue was hit and pitched to the ground. From his throat a widening stain spread upon the pavement, and two painted girls tried to bind his wound with handkerchiefs. Several small tanks stood in the middle of the square, their drivers uncertain what to do. A French lieutenant was senselessly making some sort of signal with a flag.

Thompson reached for his carbine. "I'll go up there and shoot the sons-of-bitches," he said, outraged. He was bursting with bravado.

"Stay out of it," said the Captain. "That's none of our business. Since when are we infantry?"

The firing stopped. The square again teemed with life and movement. The laughter of the women wove a bright ribbon of sound through the humid August morning. The command car turned into the Champs Elysées.

"There it is," said Peter. "The loveliest street in all the world."

"Just like Michigan Boulevard in Chicago," said Dirty Thompson. "Only no traffic."

It was as though a gigantic broom had been pushed down the street, sweeping it clean. Not a single vehicle was to be seen all the way to the Arc de Triomphe. It will never be this lovely again, the Captain mused. In the fifteen years he had known the city, he had never seen the avenue stretching out before him completely clear and unobstructed. Usually it was a churning flood of automobiles, people, bicycles, and horses, which washed away the perfection of its architecture. Now the Champs Elysées lay there like the terrace of a summer hotel in the morning, freshly washed, untouched, flooded with sunlight. If only Patricia could see it now, he thought.

He pulled up before the great white front of Susy Perin's *haute couture*, jumped out of the car, and attempted to open the heavy glass door. It was locked. He began to rattle it violently. Behind the door a marble lion stared at him. When rattling and shouts and more rattling brought no response, Peter returned to the car.

Thompson was standing on the seat, pointing his rifle at the roof of the building, furiously trying to translate the word "bastards" into French.

"What's up, Thompson?"

"Snipers," said Thompson without looking away from the roof.

Peter's hand went automatically to his holster. Then he noticed the two men leaning over the railing of a balcony. They were obviously not snipers, but peaceful citizens who were trying to convince Thompson of their good intentions. He could not make out what they were saying.

The men finally decided to do what Peter had come to expect of Frenchmen who are at a loss. They summoned a woman. A flagrantly artificial blonde appeared on the balcony.

"Who are you?" Peter shouted at the top of his voice.

"I'm Susy Perin."

"Come on down and open up."

In a few minutes the glass door was opened. The blonde, no longer young and with overdone make-up, stood in the empty marble hall.

"Just what do you want, Monsieur?" she asked. She did not yet know the American rank insignia.

"My name is Peter Olden," the Captain said. "And I want to buy a dress, of course."

"But, my dear fellow," said the woman, "the shop is closed. Don't you know there's a war on?"

"Madame," he said gallantly, "you certainly don't look as if there was still a war on."

The ice melted perceptibly. Madame ventured a smile. Even the lion seemed to relax. Peter closed the door behind him.

"You are the first woman in Paris," he said, "who hasn't given me a kiss."

Madame smiled again, put two bare arms around his neck, and kissed him patriotically on both cheeks. Then she accompanied him upstairs.

Two or three mannequins appeared from somewhere. They stood in the big blue silk salon with the little white stage, which, with its indirect lighting, was supposed to give the effect of a Grecian temple. From the Place de la Concorde came the sound of shooting.

"I'd like to send my wife the first gown from liberated Paris," said Peter. He felt that he ought to apologize.

"Do you know the measurements?"

"No. But a few years ago when we were in Paris we bought one or two dresses here. Mrs. Peter Olden. You must have the size."

"What sort of a gown are you looking for?"

He didn't know. Just a dress bought in Paris on August 25, 1944. It really made no difference whether it was an evening gown or an afternoon frock.

Madame Perin vanished, and the mannequins began to parade up and down. The dresses were implausibly short. "For bicycle riding," said one of the girls. "Everyone in Paris rides bicycles now." The evening gowns were cut implausibly low. For this the girl had no explanation. Peter liked a long white evening gown with discreet gold embroidery around the décolletage. He had it shown to him twice.

Madame Perin had meanwhile found the measurements. She apologized because there was no saleslady on duty.

They were interrupted by the abrupt appearance of Dirty Thompson in the middle of the show room. Thompson bumped against a girl in a blue silk costume, who swayed back and forth under an absurdly tiny parasol.

"Captain," he said, "there's something going on over there." Thompson spoke calmly and deliberately to avoid making a fool of himself over snipers a second time. He pointed to the open window.

On the roof of the building across the way two men were locked together in wordless combat. One was an American soldier—whether an enlisted man or an officer Peter could not tell. The other was in civilian clothes. The fight must have been going on for some time, since both men, like tired wrestlers, showed signs of near exhaustion. They were completely entangled with one another; it was as if neither man knew any longer which arms and legs belonged to him and which to his opponent. On the street below a crowd was gathering.

"Should I go over there, Captain?" Thompson asked.

"No. It's too late for that."

The Captain had drawn his pistol, but was uncertain what to do with it. The two men were a single mass. It was impossible to draw a bead on the civilian alone. Their struggle was bringing them closer and closer to the edge of the roof, where there was nothing to prevent the plunge to the street below. The faces of the fighters were not visible.

"Should I shoot?" asked Thompson. "I'll get the son-of-a-bitch."

Peter shook his head. Only now did he perceive the grotesquerie of the situation. At his right stood Thompson, his carbine half raised and his face covered with grime and lipstick. At his left, frozen with fright, was the girl in the blue silk costume, her tiny parasol still held daintily above her head. Somewhere behind him Susy Perin was trying to calm two hysterical mannequins. In the Grecian temple a fourth girl in a new gown stepped out upon the stage, unaware of the whole episode.

On the roof the two men released each other for a moment. The soldier reeled, caught himself. If either of the men had a weapon, it apparently had been lost earlier in the struggle. For a moment Peter could see the American's head—a longish head with gray hair—and then the two seized each other again. Now each seemed to be straining not to throw the other off the roof, but merely to take the other with him. They clung to each other with the desperation of lovers who, having turned on the gas, await death together. In the crowd below a woman screamed.

The civilian, younger and stronger, succeeded in thrusting the soldier from him. Again the soldier staggered back. This time he was obviously too weak to resume the fight. The civilian crouched back against a chimney, gulping in air, preparing to spring again.

The instant the civilian gathered himself for his lunge, Peter seized Thompson's carbine. He did it swiftly and silently, thrusting his pistol at the same time into Thompson's hand. The shot was hardly audible; it was as if somebody had knocked on a door. Nothing happened. Again Peter raised his weapon, aimed with deliberation, and fired another shot. The man on the roof in civilian clothes twisted convulsively and tottered. There was a howl from the crowd. Somebody leaped aside in horror. A bloody, pulpy heap lay on the pavement.

Peter turned quickly to Thompson.

"Go and get that soldier," he said. "He'll need help. Bring him up here. Don't talk to the people outside. We'll have to wait until they disperse."

"Okay," Thompson answered, and added appreciatively, "Nice shootin', Chief."

Peter sat down and lit a cigarette. His hand shook. The mannequins were twittering like startled birds. One of them was giving Madame Perin a glass of water.

It seemed a long time to Peter before Thompson returned. With him was the soldier, from whom the crowd had torn the last buttons and his rank insignia. He was covered with soot and soggy with sweat. The smile he attempted was a rigid grimace.

He stretched out his hand. "Major Stroud," he said. "John Stroud." Each word was an effort.

"Sit down, Major," Peter said.

A mannequin brought a glass of water.

"Cigarette?"

"Yes. Thanks."

The Major was about fifty-two or three. But now he looks older, Peter thought. What is he doing rampaging around the rooftops of Paris?

Stroud seemed to know what Peter was thinking. "I spotted the man shooting at passers-by from the roof. I went up. That's how it all started." He tried to clean his face with a handkerchief. "Probably one of those German officers that stayed behind."

"The city's full of them."

The Major held the handkerchief to his eyes for a moment. "Excuse me," he said, "but I haven't thanked you." He extended his hand again. Then he asked the question for which Peter had been waiting, the question every American in the war asked every other American within five minutes of meeting—in foxholes, in airplanes, or behind machine guns.

"Where are you from, Captain?"

"I live in New York."

The Major hesitated. "That's not your native city, is it, Captain? You have an accent."

The Captain smiled. "I'm not from New York originally. I have a foreign accent in all languages." To get off the subject he said, "Where's your home?"

"Spokane, Washington."

For the first time the Major seemed to notice his singular surroundings: the little blue chairs, the indirect lighting behind the silk drapes, the Corinthian pillars, the girls in their oddly assorted costumes, the glaringly blond Susy Perin. He edged closer to Peter. "What kind of place is this?"

"A fashion salon," said Peter, amused.

"What are you doing here?"

"What one usually does in a fashion salon—buying a dress."

Peter went to the window to see if the crowd had dispersed. A little group still stood around the corpse. "We'll have to go down and tell the police what happened," he said. He took a deep breath. Through the window came the heady sultriness of the August day.

As he went out with the Major, he said to Susy Perin, "I'll be back shortly. And I'll take the white one with the gold embroidery."

≫ 2 ≪

THE last days of September, 1944, were unusually warm in Europe. The General's room was nevertheless overheated. Through the little narrow windows high in the wall sifted the pale yellow rays of the evening sun. The General—Major General Joseph T. Lowell—sat on a folding camp chair behind an ordinary wooden table.

In better days the General's workroom had been a weapon hall. Rusted old pistols hung on the walls, and colored coats of arms had been let into the wainscoting. Family portraits of warriors in armor and elegant courtiers in periwigs were also built into the paneling, which was why the owner of the castle was not able to remove them. The furniture had been removed; the French count to whom the castle belonged trusted neither German nor American invaders.

General Lowell was a man in his sixties whom it was easier to imagine in a periwig than in a suit of armor. He was small and haggard, with the intelligent, shortsighted eyes of a scholar. The only thing military about his face was its taut leanness; he somehow suggested the dried fruit of the field ration.

"Sorry to keep you waiting," said the General to Major Stroud across the table. "We ran into some mortar fire. We've taken Luxembourg, and we're right up against the West Wall." The General paused, waiting for Stroud to say something. Only the buzzing of flies broke the silence. The General went on. "How do you feel, John? Pain still bothering you?"

"No. The wound's all healed. I don't even feel a change in the weather any more." He thought, I won't do him the favor. If he wants to send me home, he'll have to begin it himself. I'm not going to make it easy for him.

"John," said the General, "I've got good news for you. General Bradley has awarded you the Silver Star. It will appear in Special Orders tomorrow. The day after at the latest." The General was accustomed to impatience in soldiers when a decoration or a promotion was in the offing. But the Major seemed completely indifferent.

"Thanks, Joe," he said.

"Don't thank me. You've earned it. First that incident in Paris and then the attack on Ste. Menehould right after it." The General cleared his throat. "But that isn't all."

The Major was not surprised. He wouldn't be the first to receive his walking papers on a ribbon. Emily would be happy to have him home again. She had argued from the first that this war was none of his affair. It occurred to him, too, that his practice urgently needed him; clients had been slowly falling away from his partner. He couldn't be sure how his daughter Eleanor's marriage was turning out. And in a few days Jim would be getting his wings. But all this evoked no emotional response. Home seemed very far away—much farther than the six thousand miles between Verdun and Spokane.

"I'm sorry as hell, John," the General continued finally, "that you have to leave your battalion. I know how strongly you feel about it. But, after all, you've been wounded twice in one year. Give somebody else a chance to do something."

"You mean I'm getting old," said the Major. He managed a smile.

"Old? Why, I'm three years older than you are." The General chuckled. "No, it's simply that we've planned something else for you."

"I know."

The General's eyebrows went up. "What do you know?"

"I'm supposed to go home and see that nobody gets too drunk in the Davenport bar."

The General was annoyed. "Hell!" he said. "What kind of a fool do you take me for? I wouldn't think of sending a man like you home. Unless—"

"Unless what?"

"Unless you really want to go—"

"No," said the Major quickly.

The General leaned back as far as he was able in the camp stool. "The thing is this. Every day the number of prisoners we're taking gets bigger. Eight thousand yesterday alone. It's impossible to ship them all to America. We plan to set up a big PW camp in Germany. A kind of model camp." He paused, then said hurriedly, "We want you to command this camp."

"In other words, you want to make an MP out of me."

"That's ridiculous. The commandant of a camp with ten thousand men is no MP."

"Ten thousand Sad Sacks behind barbed wire."

"That's the wrong way of putting it. You don't understand what's involved here. Let me explain it to you." The General leaned forward and offered Stroud a cigarette. This was unusual, for the General detested smoke. The Major declined. "Headquarters conceives of this as a test camp, a sort of laboratory. We have to determine what can be done with the Germans—if anything. A project like this offers an unprecedented opportunity to experiment with them—with their souls, if you like. Or to establish that they haven't any—of which I personally am convinced. You will have an absolutely free hand. Run the camp the way you want to. We'll give the Provost Marshal and G-2 directives to leave you entirely on your own." He leaned back again. "What do you think?"

"Very interesting," said the Major. "But why pick me?" He thought suddenly of the zoo in San Francisco. He saw himself as a small child, watching a keeper throwing chunks of raw meat through the bars to the lions and tigers. The keeper was a round little man with a big round face. I don't want to toss raw meat to animals, Stroud thought.

"We need a man with law experience," the General continued. "Someone familiar with the rules of justice. But that isn't all. We need a man with some understanding of psychology. On top of that, you know Germany and the Germans. You were in the occupation army in the last war. You've been back to Germany three or four times. You speak German fluently. Just show me somebody else who has all those qualifications."

"And is unfit for field duty besides," said the Major.

The General did not reply. The rays of the sun now fell across the table between the two men. The Major looked up at the window. Remarkably like a prison window, he mused. Millions of tiny dust particles danced in the sunbeams. I'd be better off going home, he thought.

"No," he said. "I don't think I'm suited for this job. I don't like seeing people behind barbed wire. Not even enemies. I've never been able to bring myself to hate them, really."

"That makes you doubly suited for the job."

But the General knew that they would arrive at no result today. He could, of course, have given the Major an outright order. But they had been friends too long for that, and he knew also that a sulky and discontented commandant for the camp was out of the question. He got up from his chair.

The Major also stood up. "Thanks for your confidence in me, Joe," he said. Thanks did not commit him to anything.

They were standing under the family portraits. Something else occurred to the Major. "Joe," he said, "remember the favor I asked you when you visited me in the hospital? Did you find out anything more about Captain Olden? Captain Peter Olden?"

"I remember," the General answered. "That's the man who saved your life in Paris. I had him looked up but didn't learn much about him. He belongs to the OSS. General Donovan's cloak-and-dagger boys. Here—" He turned to his desk, leafed through some memos, found a notation. "A writer in civilian life. Born in Germany, 1910. He married Barbara Draper's daughter. Apparently that's all. You know how Donovan is. To find out what goes on in his secret service we'd have to organize a secret service of our own."

He extended his hand to the Major. "Think it over, John. I won't try to talk you into anything. It's an important and worthwhile assignment. But I can't blame you if you prefer to go home. I'd like to go myself. Give my best to Emily and the kids when you write."

"Thanks."

At the door the Major turned around. The General was already bent over his papers again.

"Is there any chance at all of returning to my battalion?" asked the Major.

"No," said the General. "None at all."

⇛ 3 ⇚

I T HAD been raining two days. The early March sky was gray and sullen, as if it might snow at any moment. The man who came walking along the highway toward Trier was wearing a light coat. He had no hat. His shirt stuck to his body, and water trickled down his collar. He whistled softly to himself. He always did when he was afraid.

Evening was descending across the Moselle. Its coming was almost indiscernible, for the whole day had been dark. From the west came the muffled, rolling sound of artillery. Somewhere a town was burning: the glow of the flames soaked into the sky like red ink on a blotter.

He looked at his watch. It was six-thirty; it would be dark in an hour. There was nothing comforting in the thought. He had learned long ago that it was not any easier to cross the lines at night. Darkness, of course, had a certain advantage. The rain, too, would discourage patrols. But all this meant only that it would be less difficult to cover the last two or three kilometers.

He had hoped to cross the Sauer at Wasserbillig that afternoon. He knew a little bridge there that wasn't blown. At least it hadn't been blown three days before as he came out of the American lines into unoccupied Germany. But it was always easier to get behind the enemy's lines than to make one's way out of them again. A great deal could have happened in three days. Just the same, he could swim the Sauer if necessary. He shivered a little

at the thought, but at the same time he would have been glad
to be at the river. The rain had delayed him. He was still two
kilometers from Trier. Then thirty more kilometers to Wasserbillig. No vehicle would take him along now. He would have
to stay in Trier.

Two German soldiers on bicycles pedaled toward him. Involuntarily he ceased whistling. They paid no attention to him and rode
on. When they had passed he resumed his whistling. Under a tree
he stopped and tried to light a cigarette. The wind and rain extin-
guished one match after the other. If only I had brought along my
Zippo, he thought; but one has to be careful. Finally he succeeded in
lighting the cigarette. He noticed that his hands were shaking. I'm
more nervous than usual, he told himself. Why? Forebodings? He
dismissed the idea. No, it was simply that he knew that this was his
final mission. What he had seen in the last three days in the
Rhineland had convinced him. The war could last only a few
weeks more. It would be senseless to get himself killed now.

Whether it was at this moment that he thought of Maria was
never clear to him later. But all at once it was as if he had been
thinking of Maria all day long, as if the thought of her had been
slumbering within him for weeks, somewhere deep inside. Now
he also knew why he had chosen the road leading through Trier,
instead of bypassing the city.

At the same time he was aware of the foolishness of what he
intended to do. He had last seen Maria twelve years ago, before
he had left for America. They had parted from each other in
Trier. At first, for a year or two, he had written to her. Then had
come the curious letter from their friend Eric, telling him not to
write any more if her life meant anything to him. For two or three
months he had continued to receive letters from her. He had not
answered. He had heard nothing from her for ten years.

He hastened his steps. The rain had stopped. Great heavy drops
fell from the trees. The earth gave forth a fragrance, strong and
narcotic. Little patches of vapor rose from the fields and scurried
across the highway like startled does. He passed the first bombed-
out houses.

How old would she be? Thirty-five, of course. They had been
the same age. He smiled. It's hardly likely that she remained
twenty-three. Her daughter must be seventeen now. What was the

name of her husband? She divorced him not long after she went
into the theater. She was hardly twenty then. Hoffman or Hoffen-
reich or something like that. Had she married again? Probably. It
did not occur to him that she might be dead. Yet Trier was a badly
bombed city. And who was to say that she had remained in Trier?
The last letter had been from Berlin. Berlin had been bombed.
All German cities had been bombed.

The first hastening pedestrians came past. Mostly soldiers. The
population of Trier had long since been summoned by the authorities to abandon the city. Only the stubborn remained behind, and
on their own responsibility. Why should Maria be one of them?
He stood for a few minutes in a doorway. He was breathing hard,
and his wet clothing steamed. I'll step out of this doorway, he decided, and if the first person I see is a soldier, I'll try to find her.
If I see a civilian first, I'll forget all about it. The game he played
with himself was hardly fair: the chances were far greater that it
would be a soldier. The first person he saw was a woman. That
doesn't count, he thought. He began looking for the way that led
to her house.

Maria had lived in a villa on the western edge of the city. There
he had spent the last evening before leaving for France. The closer
he approached the street, the more he hoped that the house was
no longer standing. He was fully aware, now, of what he was
doing. What if she had become a fervent Nazi? Most German
women were. Wouldn't she turn him over at once to the police?
To the Gestapo? With a full description of his background? He
thought, one either knows a person, or one doesn't. People don't
change—not in ten, or twenty, or thirty years. And suppose she
isn't a Nazi? What if she gives me shelter for the night? Wouldn't
I be exposing her to the worst kind of danger? He decided to stay
for one hour only. In his mounting fever to see her again his conscience had let him down. Anyway, the house would no longer be
standing.

The house stood, one of the group that had escaped complete
destruction. It was dark. He clambered over the rubble. He stumbled against a twisted furnace grate, stopped to rub his leg, and
listened. He heard no footsteps. Only the rolling mutter of cannon
continued to come from the Moselle.

He stalked cautiously around the house twice. The windows had

DET PUB LIB

no panes; they were covered with wood; no light seeped through the cracks. Finally he knocked at the door.

He heard footsteps, shuffling, tired footsteps. A woman's voice asked, "Who's there?"

He knew at once that it was not her voice. "I," he replied. He had no better answer ready.

"Who is 'I'?" asked the woman.

He hesitated. Then he said, "Is Maria here?"

The door opened. In the light of a small blue lamp he saw an old woman. He did not enter.

"Don't stand there in the doorway," said the woman. "The light is showing." And, when he had stepped in she asked again, "Who are you?"

Again he answered with a question. "Is Maria here?" Only when the woman failed to reply did he add, "I'm an old friend of hers. From the theater."

At the same moment a door inside was opened. A stronger light fell into the narrow corridor.

"Peter!"

"Maria!"

They stood facing each other without speaking, neither able to move. They did not know how long they stood there wordless, motionless.

Then she said, "The way you look!"

"It's been raining," he said.

"Come in," she said. "You must dry yourself."

He stepped into the room, which had not changed in twelve years. The old woman shuffled off through a door at the back of the corridor.

He sat down at the table. A bread basket, a pitcher of water, and a plate with a few slices of cold sausage were on it. Here, too, the light was so weak that the wires were visible in the lamp bulb.

"You must be hungry," she said.

His stomach was so empty it hurt.

She saw that he hesitated. "I've already eaten," she said.

She put several slices of sausage on a plate. He began to eat hurriedly.

MORNING came, and they were still sitting opposite each other. She had given him a dressing gown; his clothes were hanging in the kitchen to dry. All through the night he had not noticed that it was cold; now he shivered. She sat holding his hand. He no longer knew exactly when she had taken it; probably they had been sitting that way for hours, hand in hand.

They did not speak in coherent sentences. He asked a question; she answered; then she asked a question. They did not begin with the day he left, and they did not finish with the day of his return. But before the dawn broke, they had asked each other a hundred questions and had given a hundred answers. He learned that she had not appeared on the stage since he left Germany. She had made hats, done walk-ons in films, sold her jewelry, gone to Poland and France as a Red Cross nurse, made hats again, and sold more of her jewelry. For two years her life had been devoted to following her daughter from place to place. Peter had remembered rightly: Helga was seventeen. Two years ago she had been drafted into Hitler's labor service. She had worked with the peasants in Pomerania, welded cables in an airplane factory in Schweinfurt, and had been assigned to an anti-aircraft unit in Berlin. Maria succeeded in saving her from flak duty, and Helga was now in Bavaria assigned to more farm work.

"Tomorrow you would have found me gone," said Maria. "My knapsack is packed again. Tomorrow I'm going to start out for Bavaria, if I can get through." She coughed. She coughed often, softly, barely perceptibly.

"Have you a cold?" he asked.

"No," she said. "I've had this cough a long time."

Now, in the gray of dawn, her face seemed changed. At first he thought that the last twelve years had left no mark upon her. The darkish blond hair was the same, and the deep hazel eyes. The eyes still had the same subdued shimmer, as if there were a golden coin, old and worn smooth, behind each pupil. Around the mouth, with its oddly identical lips, there were no new lines, and the impertinent little nose—"like a Czech peasant girl's," he used to say—still took from her face any vestige of gravity. But in the dim morning light that trickled through the slits of the boarded-up windows, he saw that her cheeks were sunken below the strong, almost Slavic cheekbones. It used to be that her cheekbones swelled gently from her face like little waves on water; now they stood out like rocks in a pool. Peter suddenly felt the necessity of holding on to the memory of her earlier face; if he were to leave now, the two faces would merge and blur, and neither of them would remain with him.

She started as if at a sound, held herself tense, and in her throat a little pulse began to beat.

"What's the matter?" he asked, for he had heard nothing.

"Planes," she said. "This is the time for the Americans."

Then his ears, less attuned to the sound, also detected the distant droning of motors.

"No sirens?" he asked.

"No," she said. "They stopped sounding sirens long ago."

The first bombs fell.

"They're still a long way off," she said. "Four or five kilometers."

"Do you want to go to the cellar?"

"No. We gave that up long ago."

Somewhere near by a bomb crashed. The earth shook with the reverberating thud of it, and the walls of the house quivered. It seemed as if the planes were circling over the house. The droning of the engines ceased only when the bombs exploded, and one almost wished that more bombs would fall to blot out the droning.

"It would be strange," she said, "if a bomb hit the house now."

"That kind of thing happens only in novels," he replied.

She was silent a moment, and he felt that she was no longer thinking of the bombs.

"Have you a picture of your wife?" she asked suddenly.

He nodded, stood up, and went into the kitchen. After a few minutes he returned, dressed. She was still sitting in the same position in which he had left her. She looked up, startled.

"What's wrong?" he said. "My things are dry. I got dressed."

"Yes," she said. "I didn't think of that. You'll have to be going soon."

She held the photograph of Patricia in her hand. Patricia was wearing a simple, unadorned dress, as she often did. But in contrast to the simplicity of her costume, her hair was arranged in precise, crown-like waves over her high, aristocratic brow. She was holding her hands with a kind of relaxed grace in her lap. The fingers were long and sensitive, and like the brow, had a quality of fragile transparency. Her whole aspect, however, was dominated by the long, delicately poised neck, which her dress in no way hid. It was a neck that looked somewhat naked without two or three strands of pearls.

"She is very beautiful," said Maria.

Peter took back the picture with a quick motion, and as he did so he could not tell whether he was shielding the woman who was with him, or the other.

The planes withdrew gradually. From time to time it seemed as if they were returning, like a storm that passes off slowly, rumbling as it subsides. Through the cracks of the window boards came the smell of burning.

"Do you have to go back today?" Maria asked.

"Yes."

"Strange," she said pensively. "Why do you do it?"

"Do what?"

"This thing you're doing—I don't know what you call it. Spying. Or sabotage behind the lines. Or whatever it is."

A warning signal sounded within him. "I'm an American," he said. "An American officer. I do what I'm told."

"No," she said, "that's not true. I know that much about war. I was in Poland and France. Nobody is ordered to do that kind of thing. You volunteer for that."

"What's the difference," he asked, "whether you huddle in a foxhole with a gun in your hand, or go wandering about behind the enemy lines? It comes to the same thing."

She shook her head. "You must have misunderstood me," she said. "I wasn't thinking about Fatherland, or loyalty, or childhood. I understand all that—" She paused, then continued hurriedly, "At least I try to understand it. What I don't understand is—" She stopped again. Then she said, "This woman is so beautiful. Are you happy?"

"Yes."

"Then I don't understand."

She smiled, and her face of today vanished. He saw her again as he had so often remembered her during these twelve years. He saw her as they strolled side by side along the wooded path that led from the little inn to the top of the mountain. Somewhere or other in Austria, that was. She was wearing a dirndl with a gay apron. They were both deeply tanned, and in the sun her hair seemed lighter than usual. "We'll go drink Enzian," she had said. "The peasants up above have Enzian."

She stood up and went into the kitchen. He heard her busy herself at the stove and followed her. She had started the fire and put coffee on. He held his hands over the open fire; the warmth went through him in gratifying ripples.

"Today there's real coffee," she said.

The strong, wholesome fragrance filled the kitchen. She had patted some powder on her nose, and around her disordered hair was a bright silk scarf. Czech peasant girl, he thought. Weariness seemed to have fallen from her, and he watched with amazement as she whirled about the kitchen like a girl.

"Can I help you?" he asked.

"No," she said, "you'd only drop everything."

She put out a tray. Suddenly she said, "Do you know what's lacking?"

"No."

"Think hard. What was it we always used to drink with our coffee?"

He laughed. "Enzian?"

"Yes, Enzian."

She spread a little white cloth over the tray. He looked at the clock. It was seven. He would have to be over there, in Luxembourg, by ten at the latest. Luxembourg seemed infinitely farther away than it had last evening.

⋙ 5 ⋘

IN PARIS delirious mobs sang and shouted. The city was dressed in flags, and in the streets there was dancing, as on a July 14. Women in Alsatian costumes laid wreaths at the foot of the Strasbourg monument on the Place de la Concorde. In London shops were hastily closed, and the busses stopped. Men stood on top of the tall taxis and sang "God Save the King." In New York a blizzard of confetti fell on Fifth Avenue. Policemen and taxi drivers forgot their deadly enmity and shook hands. In Times Square soldiers and sailors were almost crushed lifeless under embraces and kisses.

In Bad Nauheim, the little resort town near Frankfurt, May 8, 1945, was a day like any other. Major Stroud and Captain Olden sat on the red plush sofa in the old-fashioned lobby of the Hotel Bristol.

"These last ten days," the Major was saying, "are probably unique in history. The death of Mussolini, Hitler's suicide, Göring's arrest. And today the capitulation. It really went fast, once it started."

"Yes," Peter replied, "but it's remarkably quiet here."

"It's probably the tiredness that comes after tension."

"Maybe it's not yet clear what it does mean. No more danger of death. No more fighting. No more blackout. It's still hard to grasp. We've become accustomed to war."

"Maybe peace falls flat for us," Stroud speculated, "because the war meant so little to us."

From the bar came the sound of laughter and the chunking of a cocktail shaker.

"Well, they're celebrating in there," said Stroud.

The Major puffed slowly on his cigar. He asked, "Are you going home, Peter?"

The Captain gave an almost imperceptible start. "I feel as though I'd just got back. I was there for a month, you know. What I'm going to do now, I don't know," he said. "General Donovan says there'll still be plenty to do here." It sounded like an apology.

"It'll be especially hard for you," Stroud observed. "The war was more exciting for you than for most. It will seem pretty tame to you now, after the way you've lived the last few years."

Peter did not want to talk about himself. "How about you, John?" he asked. "Aren't you in a hurry to go home?"

"Not any more. I've gotten myself too involved in this new job. The prison camp is being transferred to the Munich area. But the experiment is just beginning. It's a great thing to experiment on human beings."

"The Nazis said the same thing."

"Yes, but we don't inject typhus germs into our guinea pigs."

"Psychologists don't work with typhus. Do you think your injections are any better?"

The Major smiled indulgently. "Psychology never killed anybody yet."

"Psychology has killed more people than typhus."

The Major leaned forward. "You don't understand, Peter," he said. "I'm experimenting on myself. Or at least, on what I believe. I don't believe in innately evil people. Not evil Germans, evil Americans, or evil Chinese. I believe that we all have a great deal of bad in us, but that none of us likes being wicked."

"That sounds a little too simple."

"I just want to explain to you why the experiment appeals to me so strongly. At first it repelled me. I don't know to this day why I took the job."

"Maybe you simply didn't want to go home."

Stroud looked shocked. Then he said, "You may be right. There was a war on. It seemed so petty to go home and defend pickpockets and insurance companies and child abductors. It begins to look as if I stumble into one job after the other by accident. I didn't want to be a lawyer, but a doctor. Then my father wanted me to study law so that I could take over his practice. I did it for his sake."

"How do you feel about it now?" Peter asked.

"It was all right, once I got over my distaste for the whole idea of practicing law. At first I thought it was contemptible to defend criminals, just to get paid for it. But then I discovered that most of the time it was possible to find out why a crime was committed. And then I usually had no further hesitation about defending the man who committed it."

"Are you religious?"

Stroud looked up. "No, not especially. I seldom go to church."

They stood up and went into the bar. It was early afternoon, but the bar was overcrowded. Victory marches came from the radio. From time to time details of the capitulation in the schoolhouse at Reims were announced. Nobody listened. The German bar-keeper, with his bald head, chilly eyes, and bulging chest, looked like a disguised colonel. His face had congealed into an unwavering smile as he mixed one "victory cocktail" after the other. He churned the shaker with a precise, measured movement, always in the same direction, as if he were loading shells into a cannon. Young officers stood at the bar, disputing about who would be the first to go home. Stroud and Peter sat down in a corner near the radio. They ordered cognac.

An Air Force lieutenant, blue-eyed and dark-haired, left the group at the bar and came up to Peter.

"Hello, Pete."

"Hello, Bob."

He was Patricia's brother, a boy of twenty. He had come to Bad Nauheim the day before and had spent the previous evening with Peter. Fresh from his aviation training, Bob had arrived in Europe two weeks before. He had made one observation flight, and the war in Europe was over. He was expecting to be transferred to the Pacific, but meanwhile he was going about the business of celebrating V-E day.

"Sit down with us, Bob." Peter introduced him to the Major. "My wife's brother," he added.

"I can only stay a minute," said Bob. He had a glass in his hand. He turned to Peter. "Do you know yet when you're going home?"

It was a natural question, and Peter could not tell why it annoyed him. "No," he said. "How could I?"

Bob continued his babble. "Say, you ought to have a fine time over here. You know the language and all. Have you visited your old home yet?"

"What do you mean?"

"I mean, have you been to Berlin?"

"I'm not from Berlin," said Peter. "I was born in Düsseldorf."

"Düsseldorf?" said Bob. "Never heard of it."

The Major asked how long Bob had been in Germany.

"Only fourteen days. I figure they'll send us to the Pacific now. How long do you think it will take with the Japanese?"

"Seven, eight months, I'd say."

"The shorter the better. I hope I can stop off at home on the way." He laid his hand on Peter's shoulder. "I'll bet I get home before you do."

"That's possible." Peter leaned slightly away, dislodging Bob's hand.

"Watch yourself with the *Fräuleins* over here, Pete!" Bob laughed. "I don't want to turn in any bad reports on you to Pat."

There was nothing malicious about this remark either, but it irritated Peter into giving an abrupt answer. "Just take care of your own affairs, will you?" he said. Bob had drunk too much to notice. He left and went back, not quite steadily, to the bar.

"Looks like a happy reunion," Stroud said.

Peter remained silent, looking with a studied expressionlessness at his glass.

"By the way," the Major continued, "I think I must have met your wife a few years ago. Isn't she a Draper from Philadelphia?"

"Yes. She was Patricia Draper."

"Have you been married long?"

"Nine years."

"Any children?"

"No."

Stroud was thoughtful, trying to remember. "I think I know where I met Mrs. Olden. Didn't she speak a few years ago in Spokane, before some kind of meeting in behalf of the children of criminals?"

"Very possibly. She's all taken up with that kind of work. You and she would get along very well together, John. She doesn't believe in the evil in man either." He laughed shortly, but there was no amusement in his voice.

The Major had a more sensitive ear than the young lieutenant. He heard the bitter undertone and said no more.

The bar was now full of smoke. Sweat glistened on the brow of the disguised colonel. At the next table four officers began a poker game. Two captains made a bet on who would be the first one home. At the bar the officers stood arm in arm and sang "It's a long, long way to Tipperary." It was the only tune that occurred to them. Out of the Second World War no song had come.

6

PETER was depressed as he left Bad Nauheim and headed for Braunschweig, where he believed his father to be. On the previous evening he had attended a conference of officers who were to be sent to various German cities as Military Governors. Most of them had already received training in the United States for their new jobs. They had an exact knowledge of the sewer system, the electrical facilities, the garbage disposal, and the water supply of the cities they were going to govern, and they possessed minutely detailed maps whose only drawback was that the streets and buildings designated on them no longer existed.

The discussion of the Military Governors had concerned itself principally with three questions: the problem of living quarters for the Military Governors; whether it was proper to shake hands with German officials; and whether German soldiers in uniform should be required to salute American soldiers. There was complete agreement that the Military Governor should invariably occupy the best house in town, but on the other two questions opinion was divided. The debate was especially heated on the problem of saluting. Should German soldiers be required to salute American officers only, or enlisted men as well? After two hours of lively controversy the question remained unsettled.

Peter's command car made slow progress on the highway to Braunschweig. Heavy tanks, cannon, and anti-aircraft guns moved in endless columns toward the west—the unmolested withdrawal of a victorious army. Discipline had given way to lighthearted relaxation. Gaily painted garden chairs, mattresses, red comforters, and cases of cognac and champagne were piled on the trucks next to rifles, helmets, and tent poles. In the turret of a lumbering Sherman stood a tank driver with a top hat set jauntily on his head and a huge cigar cocked upward in his mouth. With magical speed war had turned into carnival.

The long columns of tanks and guns were broken at intervals by convoys of trucks taking home German prisoners of war and bringing liberated slave workers another stage along the long road to their native lands. French, Polish, and Russian flags, stitched clumsily together from scraps of colored cloth, waved from the trucks.

The German prisoners stood jam-packed in the trucks, dressed in tattered winter overcoats, field-gray Wehrmacht caps pulled down over their ears. They jostled and maneuvered to gain a place close to the side of the trucks from which they could look out at the passing German landscape. They had not shaved for days, their eyes were sullen and hostile, filled with an unwavering look of dull amazement at a war irrevocably lost.

"The supermen," said Dirty Thompson. "I'd like to know why we're breakin' our necks to send those bastards home right away." He was having trouble trying to weave the command car in and out of a convoy of prisoner trucks.

Peter didn't know either, but it occurred to him that he could easily have been one of those men who were now traveling toward homes which were no longer there. He had been born in Düsseldorf, a border city over which the air of freedom blew from the other side of the Rhine. His father had owned, first in Düsseldorf and then in Braunschweig, an estate of medium size, which he ruled in the high-handed and self-willed style of a feudal prince. Peter remembered his mother as a consumptive little woman with great, gentle eyes and thick blond hair, which she wore wrapped around her head in heavy plaits. From his childhood there remained the memory of a succession of domineering maids who were his father's mistresses and who ruled the household even while his mother was still alive. He remembered one especially, a tall, dark girl with red cheeks and sensuous lips, who was his father's favorite at the time his mother died. Shortly after the funeral the maid gathered up all pictures of his mother and stacked them on the attic floor. Peter, who was ten, used to sneak up into the attic to dust off the pictures. Later he stood them up along the wall and sat in front of them, studying his lessons. His memory of his mother was hardly that of a living being, but rather of an eternally youthful woman posed motionlessly behind glass.

Like many people left to bring themselves up alone, Peter was stricter and less indulgent with himself than the sternest guardian would have been. He was very like his mother. At the time of her death he was a delicate, lonely boy, lost in dreams and fairy tales and given to soft conversations with flowers and animals. His father, whose natural children lived on the estate—he abandoned his mistresses one after the other, but he cherished his own blood in his bastards and kept them near him—hated the pale little boy who always evoked the memory of his dead wife. During this time Peter did everything in secret. He swam in the ice-cold brook that ran through the estate, he rode horseback for hours over the roughest terrain, and on winter nights he slipped out of the overheated mansion to sleep in the open. He was afraid of the cold, of the shadows, of being alone, but a stubborn sense of chivalry drove him: he felt himself the champion of the lonely lady in the attic, who had no one else to protect her.

Then came a turning point. One day in the yard he fell into a dispute with one of his half-brothers, a youth of Peter's own age, but sturdy, broad-shouldered, and with the beginnings of a beard. In spite of his fifteen years he shared all the pleasures of the hired men, drank like a groom, and cursed like a peasant. The argument turned into a fight, and soon the stable-boys, servants, and maids gathered around to enjoy the spectacle of the weakling taking a beating. But the fight had barely begun in earnest when the astonished onlookers saw Peter charge in, clamp a hold on the head of his strapping opponent, and squeeze until the bigger boy cried out for mercy. As the outcome became certain, the servants began urging Peter on until he wrestled his half-brother around the yard with such violence that he finally left him helpless on the ground, crying and panting.

From then on Peter's status changed, not only among the servants but in his father's house, where Richard Olden began to court the favor of his son. And now when he was being admired for his strength, Peter had no more respect for it than he had had when he was the victim of strength in others. The single triumph he permitted himself consisted in hanging the pictures of his mother in their former places, with the exception of his favorite, which he left in the attic. When his father silently submitted to this unheard-of presumption, it seemed to Peter that he had fulfilled his mission. In the big house, which had never seemed like home to him, he felt more of a stranger than ever.

He was sixteen when he left his father's house. He studied at Bonn and Heidelberg, earning his way by tutoring. He studied languages with an intensity born of an inner compulsion to break his chains—chains of home, of family, and also of his mother-tongue. He wandered on foot through France and Italy, and he was richer in experience when he returned to Germany, but no happier. He published his first groping verse in a Munich newspaper, became a journalist in Berlin, took part in the political turmoil of the early thirties, and at twenty-one began to work on his first novel. He was never able to resolve the contradiction of his early youth. Though something invariably drove him to come to the aid of the weak, he was never able to feel any community of spirit with them. He felt no conviction that the meek would inherit the earth; he was sure that only the strong could oppose themselves successfully to strength. As the Weimar Republic struggled for its life, he didn't know which disgusted him more—the blatant brutality of the Nazis or the weakness of the wavering republic. The basic causes of the battle between German and German were vague in his mind, but in a street fight on the Alexander Platz he killed a young Nazi without the smallest qualm of conscience.

In 1933 he went to America. He felt that no choice remained open to him; he had to go. He felt that he could no longer write in Germany. He suffered from the same sense of oppression that had embittered his childhood. All Germany had suddenly become like his father's house. One could no longer breathe. The streets rang to the rhythmic stomp of the Brown Shirts. The face of the man he killed was now multiplied a millionfold, and his name was not unknown to the new rulers of Germany. The young Nazi whom he killed had been one of the coming leaders of the party. Peter had not known that. He had merely known, as they stood opposite each other in the brawling mob, that one of them would not survive the fight. It was not only a matter of You or I because both of them had weapons in their hands. It was something else too. Peter had known that face of old—on his father's estate and at the university, in newspaper offices and on streetcars. Written on the face, in which everything was flat—the brow, the nose, the chin—was stupidity and an animal brutality, a new war and another kind of world. You or I: it had become much more than that; it was a struggle between two worlds.

7

THE command car nosed its way through the rubble-heaped streets of Kassel. The town had been completely destroyed in a single bombing attack. Not enough walls were standing to block the flood of cheerful sunshine, and in the springtime brightness the ruins looked doubly unreal. From the east came a light breeze, and it seemed as if the walls of the skeleton houses swayed with every gust. The two men in the command car had acquired such a precise knowledge of destruction that they could tell at a glance when the town had been destroyed—ruins, like people, show unmistakable signs of their age. These were almost antique, three years old; wild flowers and shrubbery were growing on the rubble—little dots and patches of pink, yellow, and violet on the dead gray hills of devastation. But the people had come back. Everywhere were hurrying pedestrians, mostly well-dressed men in somber suits, with severe hats, and almost invariably with a brief case under the arm or a little leather bag in the hand. They all seemed a little insane, these earnest figures scurrying through the ruins; it was as if they were playing at being busy citizens, going through the motions of city life in a city that was no longer there. Everyone carried or shoved something with a hurried, furtive air, as if wishing to conceal what was being carried or shoved: one with his entire worldly possessions jammed into a bursting suitcase, another with an illegal head of cabbage hidden under an empty potato sack in a pushcart. Young women went striding past in immaculate white blouses, their breasts thrust forward, their thighs straining against tight skirts. Almost all of them carried flowers, great bunches of varicolored wild blossoms, and as they hastened toward homes long since destroyed they too contributed to the mad implausibility of the scene.

"Where in hell do all these people live?" asked Thompson.

"In cellars probably," said Peter.

"They should have given up sooner," said Thompson philosophically.

"The Germans never give up in time," said Peter, as if to himself. "They're always infatuated with their own mistakes."

At the same time he was aware that he felt a sympathy for

these men and women. It came over him like a warm wave, and it frightened him. No, it was not compassion and pity for what had happened to them; it was sympathy, and a kind of understanding. He did not grieve for them because they lived in cellars and squinted in the sunlight like convicts in a prison yard; but he respected the invincible diligence with which the men dug a half-broken chair out of the wreckage, and he warmed to the women who brought home wild flowers to decorate their cellars, and he was moved by the spotless white blouses which offered defiance to the heaped-up dirt of the streets.

There was a traffic jam on the road leading out of the city. The tanks stood in long rows with their noses pointed to the west. The trucks with the prisoners of war stood in long rows with their noses pointed to the east. The American soldiers passed the time in calling out cheerful obscenities to the passing girls, who did not understand them. At the most the girls understood a few words and phrases: "Hey, Fräulein!" and "Was ist los!" and "Schlafen mit mich, Babe?"—the only German words the soldiers knew. The German prisoners looked on, glum and sullen; their faces brightened only when one of the girls drew near to offer her hand and an encouraging smile. Thus the two armies confronted each other once again—enemy columns face to face, with white blouses between them.

It was late afternoon when they drove into Braunschweig. The sun was going down, and the dying day wrapped the devastated center of town in fading red and purple. All that remained of the city hall and the other municipal buildings were isolated towers and walls, as random and unrelated as the building blocks of children on a playroom carpet.

Peter did not want to drive unannounced to his father's estate. He had not seen the place for more than thirteen years, and he suddenly asked himself why he had come at all. The lieutenant in charge of the town records found the address of Richard Olden without any trouble. Anyone who had anything to do with Braunschweig was familiar with the name. Richard Olden, now sixty years old, had been mayor of the city from 1942 to 1944. He had participated in the defense of Braunschweig against the Americans, and it was he who issued the usual desperate Nazi order, "Hold out to the last man!" after the Kreisleiter had fled and the previous mayor had committed suicide. Richard Olden's address was now the temporary municipal jail in the Brabantenstrasse.

Peter considered. Wouldn't it be best simply to turn around and go back to Bad Nauheim? But he felt that to do so now would be running away. At the jail in the Brabantenstrasse he showed his AGO card and asked permission to see the prisoner Richard Olden.

"Your names are the same, aren't they?" the captain in charge of the jail said. "Is that a coincidence, or what?"

"The man is my father," Peter replied.

The captain was startled. "I'm sorry," he said, and it was hard to tell whether he merely meant to be polite, whether he was refusing Peter permission, or whether he was actually expressing sympathy.

A half hour of telephoning through channels to the highest command in the district followed. Then the fact that Peter belonged to the OSS had its usual magical effect. With OSS men you couldn't be sure what reasons they had for acquiring fathers who were leaders of Nazi movements.

The prisoner entered the high-ceilinged, dimly lit room which had once been the Gothic study of a Braunschweig senator. An MP followed him and sat on a stool at the door, a rifle between his knees. The MP had obviously been given orders not to move out of the room during the meeting of father and son.

Peter was standing at the window, looking out at the ruins. A towering pillar soared into the evening sky. Once it had supported a huge balcony; now it stood there like an Atlas robbed of his globe. Peter turned around.

The old man knew him at once. "So it's you," he said.

"Yes," said Peter, without moving.

Richard Olden looked older than Peter had expected. The rumpled gray suit, the blue shirt without collar or collar button, and the white hair, sparse and uncombed, made him look like a man past seventy. He had the wrinkled, pinched face of an old peasant woman. Peter, looking at him, felt no sympathy, but he felt no satisfaction either.

"What do you want here?" the old man asked.

The rudeness of the question was unexpected.

"I wanted to see if you needed anything," Peter answered after a pause.

"No," said Richard Olden. "I have all I need. Food, drink, and a tooth brush."

There was a silence. Then, to make talk, Peter said, "I hadn't known that you were mayor."

"Yes. And also the last defender of Braunschweig." He laughed hoarsely. "You can tell that to your children. Have you any children?"

"No."

"That's what I thought."

There was another silence. The MP, puzzled, looked at the two men who were silent more than they spoke. The older man asked, "Were you one of the attackers?"

"How do you mean?"

"I wondered if we fought against each other."

"Not here in Braunschweig. But naturally, as an American, I fought against you."

"So you're an American?"

"You can see that."

The old man smiled. He used to smile in the same contemptuous way when dismissing a groom who was too weak and incompetent for his job in the stable.

"American?" he repeated mockingly. "One doesn't become an American just by putting on a uniform."

Peter did not want to reply. Anger surged up in him, but he checked himself. He glanced at the soldier with the gun. After all, he thought, we're not evenly matched now, my father and I.

"What became of the estate?" he asked.

"It probably belongs to you Americans now. You can have it for yourself. You don't even have to wait until they hang me."

"Thanks. I don't need your estate."

His father didn't hear the answer. "I hope it won't injure your standing as an American"—he emphasized the word "American"—"if your father is hanged as a war criminal."

"Have you been charged with being a war criminal?"

"Yes. I defended German soil. That is now a war crime."

"No, it isn't," said Peter. "What you did was continue the defense of the city long after it had ceased to make any sense."

"Heroism doesn't have to make sense."

"So you're a hero?"

"I'm a German." And after a pointed little pause, "And not just because I pulled on a uniform, either."

Peter's teeth clenched. Why did I come here? he asked himself. But he merely said, "Why did you become a Nazi at your age?"

"There weren't any young people left," his father said, evading the question. "They were all dead. Do you remember Walter Stein? Killed at Stalingrad. And Lambrecht Leberecht? You went to school with him. He died at Palermo. You were once in love with Oskar Guenther's sister. He was a fighter pilot and won the Ritterkreuz. Shot down over the Channel. They're all dead. None of them became Americans."

"All that still doesn't mean that you had to become the Nazi mayor of this town."

The old man hesitated. Even in the half-darkened room in which they stood opposite each other, without having moved a step closer together, Peter saw the face of his father twist into a malevolent grimace. With a shock Peter recognized again the cold, despotic face that he had feared throughout his childhood.

"Did they send you here to cross-examine me?" asked Richard Olden.

"No. I only want to understand you. But it makes no difference."

"I'll tell you," said the old man. "I took over the city after one of your bombing attacks on women and children. That was the specialty of your side—bombs on women and children."

"Who started the war on civilians? You seem to forget London and Coventry and Rotterdam."

"Those were military objectives."

Peter felt tired. Why am I staying here? he thought again. Why don't I go away? He said, "Military objectives? Were the six million Jews you killed military objectives too? And the tens of thousands of political opponents you wiped out? And the Poles and the Dutch and the Belgians your Führer attacked without warning? You Nazis made it a shameful thing to be a German."

"So you've become a Jew-lover too," said Richard Olden. "It's good I didn't know that, on top of everything else. But you always were a disgrace to me—" He broke off. "If you're having trouble now on account of me," he continued, "just remember that it's mutual. I've had enough of that kind of trouble on account of you."

"When?" asked Peter, astonished.

"When you became a murderer. When you killed the Storm Trooper Krafft. I assume you're very proud of that now."

Should I bother to answer at all? Peter wondered. He said, "Proud? No. The man was too unimportant for that. I should have used more discrimination when I killed. But if you want to know whether I regret it—no, of course I don't. I'm only sorry I didn't stay longer and kill more like your Storm Trooper Krafft. All of us who realized what those men were up to should have shot them down before they had a chance to plunge Germany and the rest of the world into misery." Even as he spoke he felt the futility of what he was saying, but he continued in the same tone. "Then maybe things would never have reached the point where you found yourself parading around as 'the defender of Braunschweig.' "

Richard Olden had listened with mounting fury. "I don't have to listen to this," he said. "I didn't want to see you, and I won't listen to you any longer." He went to the door.

The MP jumped up, stood in the doorway, and waited for a sign from the Captain. The Captain nodded. The prisoner and his guard disappeared into the darkness of the hall.

For a long moment Peter stood motionless at the window. Night had come. The blackout had long since been lifted, but no light burned in the ruins of Braunschweig. He took hold of himself and went out of the building with long, firm strides.

They drove slowly through the city. Thompson, who knew that Peter had been visiting his father, said nothing. Is it possible, Peter asked himself, that blood means nothing after all? That I have no feelings whatever for this man? That it makes no difference to me whether they hang him or not?

"It's getting cold," said Thompson. "Better put on your trench coat, Captain."

The car stopped. Peter wriggled into his coat.

As the car started again and Peter still remained silent, Thompson said, "It must have been rugged, Captain."

"Yes," said Peter. "It was rough."

He said nothing more. Thompson's sympathy made him feel more miserable than before. He shivered.

8

THE early June afternoon was hot and dry. Every passing auto
sent a rolling fog of dust across the camp. Naked to the waist,
the prisoners lolled sluggishly before the barracks. It was Sunday,
and they could have been playing soccer or handball, but it was
too hot.

As Major Stroud came by the prisoners jumped up and stood at
attention. The Major returned their salutes, and with rapid steps
continued on his way toward one of the barracks. Over its entrance,
in letters as painstakingly neat as only a German with nothing else
to do could make them, was the word *Bibliothek*.

The Major entered. The sergeant who first noticed him cried,
"*Achtung!*" A dozen men sitting at the tables reading leaped to
their feet and slammed their heels together.

"Sit down," said the Major. Then he asked, "Who is the librarian here?"

A German soldier stepped out from behind one of the homemade bookcases. He was young, and on his small, sharp nose was
a pair of rimless glasses. He had acute, darting eyes, which readily
became arrogant when he assumed a soldierly attitude. He gave the
impression of a postal clerk whom one would hesitate to ask for a
stamp.

"Corporal Horst Hanusch, librarian," he announced crisply.

"Everybody come over here," said the Major.

Fourteen or fifteen men left the tables and shelves and grouped
themselves around the Major. They all stood at attention.

"*Weitermachen!*" said the Major, a little embarrassed.

The men extended their left feet and crossed their arms behind
them.

"Which of you were present at yesterday's incident?" asked
Stroud.

No one answered.

"You know exactly what I mean," the Major continued, looking
directly at the librarian. "I mean the book-burning."

The librarian stepped forward. "I was present, sir," he said. "I
ordered the books to be burned." He looked around. There was a
triumphant glint behind his rimless glasses.

"Who else?" asked Stroud.

Before anyone could answer, the librarian said, "I alone am responsible for the burning of the books. I'm the only one who gives orders in the library."

Stroud was a little taken aback by the answer. "We'll see about that," he said. "How do you account for your conduct?"

"Literature hostile to Germany was forced upon us. We selected fifteen books and burned them." He corrected himself quickly, "I selected them."

"I've seen the list," the Major said. "There were no political books among them at all. They were mostly novels. For example, you burned Franz Werfel's *Forty Days of Musa Dagh*. What was anti-German about that?"

"A Jewish author," the librarian answered. He looked around again, as openly as he dared under Stroud's gaze. Several of the prisoners smiled.

The Major sat down and took a cigarette from his case. Two or three prisoners sprang forward with matches. The librarian did not move.

"Now, listen," said Stroud. "You know very well what would happen to an American prisoner of war who burned books in a German camp."

"*Jawohl,*" answered the librarian. "He would be punished."

"Right. And naturally I can punish you. But I want to talk it over reasonably."

"*Jawohl,*" said the librarian. Even his assent sounded like a challenge.

"You burn books merely because the author is a Jew, or because you've heard somewhere that it's 'subversive literature.' You do not try to form an independent opinion about them. I try to understand you, but I can't. It's just too idiotic. Look. In America there are two major political parties, the Republicans and the Democrats. I am a Democrat, but when I hear that a leading Republican has written an important book, I buy it. I read it carefully. I try to find out whether the man is sincere. But let's say that, after all, I find the book has nothing worth while to say to me. The author is completely wrong. Do you know what I do then?"

He waited for an answer. "No, sir," said the librarian.

"I put the book in my library," Stroud continued. "After a few months or a year I take it down again. Often I find that my views have changed somewhat, or that I get a new understanding from a second reading. It does a man good to admit being wrong once in a while."

"*Jawohl!*" said Corporal Hanusch.

For the first time Stroud was irritated. He looked up. "Don't keep saying '*Jawohl*' like a fool when you don't mean it."

"*Jawohl!*" said Corporal Hanusch.

Stroud gave a little sigh. "Let's say that this or that book is 'subversive literature,' or whatever you want to call it," he began again. "Don't be afraid! Read it anyway. If your convictions are as unshakable as you believe, such books can't harm you any. But at least you'll find out what the opposition thinks. That's reasonable, isn't it?"

"Yes, sir. But—"

"Go right ahead."

"I could safely read such books," the librarian declared. "But not everyone is as firm as I am. For others, such books are poison. If I had the time I might read all these books. But I can't leave them on the shelves of the library. Here they will fall into the hands of the unfit."

"Whom do you call fit?" Stroud asked.

The librarian reflected. He seemed to be seeking some phrase as pat and useful as "subversive literature" and "Jewish author." The others stood expectantly around him. Next to the librarian was a thin little man with tired eyes and small red spots on his cheeks. His eyes, attentive and amused even in their weariness, looked with faint derision at the librarian. I've got an ally, thought Stroud. Even if I have only one ally it's worth while.

"Well," he said, "whom do you call fit?"

The librarian had found his answer. "Those who are politically educated," he said.

"In other words," Stroud retorted, "those who are crammed with political preconceptions. So you're afraid, after all. Maybe not for yourself. But you're afraid that someone who hears the other side might thereby make up his own mind. You don't want to give him a chance to do that. In America we call that 'unfair.' Political education with us consists precisely in giving everyone the chance to hear both sides. We believe that everybody is entitled to make up his own mind. We don't believe in 'little people' who have to have everything predigested for them." He was now speaking chiefly to the prisoner with the red-rimmed eyes.

He stood up. That's enough for today, he thought. He addressed the librarian, "You seem to be fairly intelligent. You may continue as librarian. For the time being at least. We'll replace the fifteen burned books. Everyone who took part in the burning will pay his share of their cost. I don't want to know who they were. You will see that the money is collected. Understand?"

"Yes, sir," the librarian answered, hesitating again. "But—"

Stroud turned at the door. "Yes?"

The librarian looked fleetingly around. The prisoners were again standing at attention for the Major's departure. They were like a wall behind the librarian. He took the plunge.

"Propaganda literature," he said, "violates the Geneva Convention."

Stroud thought, Geneva Convention? The law in the hands of the barbarians. Geneva Convention. Executed Allied fliers. The gas chambers of Auschwitz. Slaughtered American prisoners at Malmédy. He paused a moment. But he said only, "Don't talk nonsense. Novels are not propaganda."

⇛ 9 ⇚

S TROUD was more or less satisfied when he returned to his office. Still, it was a relief, after looking into the foreign faces of the prisoners, to see the beefy, good-humored countenance of Master Sergeant Parker smiling at him as he entered. He did not even notice that a girl sat waiting in Parker's room.

Parker followed him to his desk. "There's a girl here wants to talk to you, Major."

"What about?"

"She's a Pole, sir." Parker was holding a slip of paper in his hands. "She wrote her name down for me. A DP from the Munich camp. She's a pretty spunky little tomato. God knows how she talked the guards into letting her through. Claims she's a lieutenant in the Polish Army. I couldn't do anything with her. She says she has to talk to you in person."

Stroud took the paper. The name was written on it in bold letters: "Wanda Komarnicki." The Major was not fond of people who insisted on seeing him personally. He was convinced that there was nothing that Parker could not safely dispose of himself. But something about the handwriting, even more than Parker's description, aroused his interest in the girl. The handwriting was energetic and headstrong, but also very feminine. "Send her in, Parker," he said.

The girl stood in the doorway. She was barely of middle height, and she wore a gray-green dress that had obviously been made over from a uniform. A beret of the same material sat slantwise on her thick, bluish-black hair. It was difficult to judge whether her face was attractive or not. It was a narrow face, white and grave. With a long rest and plenty of good food, the face would be different: rounder, livelier, younger. The gravity, the pallor, the sunken cheeks, seemed somehow inappropriate. Her eyes, untouched by the alteration that surrounded them, were too big and too blue for her face.

The Major noticed that she was carrying a tiny red-lacquered handbag. It was a child's handbag, an extremely cheap one, such as are sold at fairs, intended as playthings for little girls and not for any practical use. In the hand of this young woman of perhaps twenty-four or five it moved Stroud in a way he could not define.

At his invitation the girl sat down. She spoke in a melodious voice, deeper than he expected. Her English was faulty but easily understood. She had an agreeable Slavic accent, and had obviously learned her English from Englishmen, not from Americans. "I am most grateful to you that you have received me," she said. "I live in the Polish DP camp at Munich. I am in search of an SS officer. I would like to find out if he is here."

"What is his name?"

"That I do not know."

Stroud looked at her in surprise. "I'm afraid you'll have to tell me more about it."

"I was in the Polish Army," she said. "The Army of General Bor. I fought in the Warsaw uprising. After the fall of the city I was taken prisoner by the Germans. They brought me here. I was liberated by the Americans—that is, I thought that they had liberated me," she added bitterly. "Instead, they put me in a DP camp. That, of course, is against every international agreement. I am a soldier."

Those international agreements again, thought Stroud. He was annoyed. We're the only ones who pay any attention to them, and we're the ones everybody accuses of breaking them. "What's that got to do with the SS officer?" he asked.

"An SS officer murdered my family before my eyes," the girl said. "My father, my mother, and my two brothers. Me he raped. The corpses were still lying in the room." She said it simply, without emphasis, without dropping her eyes. Only her hands played nervously with the toy red handbag. "What his name is I don't know. But I would recognize him."

Stroud looked away. To pass over the subject as quickly as possible, he asked, "And what if you found him?"

"I would kill him."

Stroud looked at her. He said amiably but decisively, "I appreciate your frankness, my child. But you can hardly expect me to go around the camp with you until you find this man so you can shoot him."

"Why not?"

"It would hardly be legal."

She laughed. It was a short, shrill laugh. "Was it legal that he murdered my family?" she asked. "You Americans have peculiar ideas."

"Perhaps," Stroud answered. Without transition he asked, "How old are you?"

"Twenty-one."

Stroud glanced at the photograph of his family on his desk. His daughter was now twenty-four, but the picture was two or three years old. It had been taken about the time that Eleanor, against his will, had married Tim Cook, who was now raising enough chickens to make him rate as a farmer and thereby dodge the draft. In the picture Eleanor was wearing an evening dress with an orchid at the shoulder.

"Tell me more about yourself," he said. "How did you come to be a soldier?"

The girl answered indifferently, a little reluctantly. "It was in the summer of 1944 when the Russians were at the gates of the city. General Bor organized an uprising. You know that, of course." It sounded a little contemptuous, as if she meant to say, "Even you know that." "He needed soldiers. My two brothers and I volunteered. One of them served as a doctor, the other with the engineers. I was in a machine-gun company. The Russians didn't come. Instead, the Germans came."

"Didn't you know it was hopeless?"

"In all the sixty-three days of the uprising I never once thought it was hopeless."

"How did it happen that you were home when the end came?" Stroud probed further. He was not sure that the girl was telling him the truth. He felt himself on the defensive against believing her.

"The Germans split the city into two halves. There was no longer any communication between the old town and the new. A few of us were given the task of maintaining some sort of contact. The only way was through the sewers. You went down into them not far from the Café Napoleon, and came up again near Krasinski Square. You had to crawl through filth and you stank of the sewer. It made me sick at first. But at least it had the advantage that once in a while I could get back to the new town. My parents were there, and my two brothers. They defended one of the last positions near our house, in Ulica Staszica. Through this last corridor out of the old town I was able to get home sometimes and wash a little. It was useless, of course. The filth had eaten into my skin. And then it happened—" She spoke rapidly, like someone satisfying the troublesome curiosity of a stranger.

Stroud noticed it. "I didn't want to force these memories on you," he said apologetically. "I only wanted to know more about you. What did you do before the war?"

"Before the war?" she repeated. "I don't remember much about that."

"What did you want to be?"

He did not know why he asked. All this was none of his affair—the Warsaw uprising, the stinking sewers, the dead brothers, the girl herself. But he was suddenly afraid that she would go before he knew all about her. "What did you want to be?"

She smiled for the first time. He could imagine now how she had looked—before Warsaw, before she had lain behind a machine gun, before she had waded through human excrement, and before an SS officer had torn her skirt from her body. She was almost beautiful when she smiled.

"I wanted to get married," she said.

"Was your fiancé killed too?"

She was still smiling. Her hand lay quietly on the toy red handbag. "No," she said. "I had no fiancé. I just wanted to marry. What else is there for a girl to do?"

He offered her a cigarette. He also was smiling. "Do you still feel that way?" he asked. He could no longer repress the curiosity that impelled him to keep asking questions.

"Certainly. Why not?"

He forced himself to break off the conversation, which was in danger of becoming more and more personal. He should have asked how she managed to get into the camp at all, but he had no inclination to. "I'd like to help you," he said. "Not to shoot the man, but nevertheless to find him and bring him to justice. By the way, have you a gun?"

She looked at him steadily. "That is none of your business."

"All right. There are no officers in this camp. No SS men at all, in fact. But about sixty miles from here, near Reichenhall, there is an SS camp. I know the commandant. I could arrange for you to visit the camp. How would that be?"

"Would you really do that?" she asked. "That is more than I hoped for."

He felt the red mounting in his cheeks at her gratitude. Am I going to blush in front of this child? he asked himself. He stood up hurriedly. "How can I get in touch with you?"

She wrote her name, the designation of her camp and its location, on his desk pad. Again he admired the firmness of her handwriting, the curious mixture of delicacy and harshness.

"I'll come and pick you up," he said.

He accompanied her through the room where Parker worked and through the door. In front of the barracks stood the only trees in the camp. They were two tall shade trees, whose heavy foliage hung so low that he bumped his head against a branch. Beyond the wire fence, in the distance, the contours of the ruins of Munich were visible. In the sunset the sky over the city was a faint, fading pink.

He mumbled a few parting words. He did not extend his hand.
Then he walked quickly back into his office.

»» 10 ««

WHEN Peter reached Munich his first stop was at the prisoner-
of-war camp to visit Stroud. During the rare meetings possible between two officers in different services in the European
theater, words and silence alike had strengthened and deepened the
friendship between the Major of fifty-three and his much younger
companion.

Stroud sat reading on the little terrace of his living quarters,
which were set somewhat apart from the prisoner barracks, on this
August afternoon as the dusty command car with Dirty Thompson at the wheel drove through the high wire gate of PW Camp
Special B. Official regulations provided that the living quarters of the
commandant must be located outside the prison area, but General
Lowell had kept his word, and Stroud was able to make his own
laws in his domain. He regarded it as improper to live outside the
camp.

Stroud stood up, slammed his book shut, and went toward Peter.
"Haven't seen you since you got back from your last trip to America," he said. "It's good to see you again. You're surely going to stay
overnight?"

"No," Peter answered. "We have to move on. But I'd love a
scotch and soda with plenty of ice. It's damned hot."

"Yes, but at least it cools off some evenings. How'd you find
things at home?"

A prisoner of war, wearing a white jacket with his Wehrmacht
pants, brought the drinks. Peter stretched out his legs, looking out
from the terrace across to the prisoners' barracks. When the prisoner had gone, he asked, "Well, how's the great experiment coming?" He ignored the Major's question.

"Not bad," Stroud said. "You always seem to expect something
to go wrong. Do you really believe that the whole thing is nonsense?"

"Not entirely," Peter replied, lighting a cigarette. "But it's too mechanical. It overestimates experience and underestimates people. You take ten thousand men and prove something with them. When you've proved it, you imagine it also applies to other ten thousands. But the next ten thousand are entirely different. They are made up of other men, and they react differently on one another. We put too much stock in surveys in America."

"Maybe. But how else are you going to learn about people?"

"By using your imagination. You can't judge by what they do or what they say. Most of what people do and say, they do and say to conceal themselves from others. It's damned difficult to ferret out their various hiding places. Even children don't always hide behind the same easy chair."

"Well, according to your view," Stroud replied, "one would have to give up dealing with people at all. One would simply conclude that it was a hopeless riddle."

"Not at all. Just don't let so-called facts prevent you from looking a little deeper. The American adoration of the fact is sheer hypocrisy anyway. There is no such thing as a pure fact. Facts are merely our interpretations of the sum total of our notions about things, which we then claim to be fixed quantities. Americans go searching for facts and congratulate themselves when they think they have found them. But facts ought to be the beginning of our thinking, not the end. We ought to put more trust in our imagination. Imagination without facts is sometimes accurate. Facts without imagination never are."

"You seem unusually critical of American ways of thought today, Peter. Anything go wrong when you were home?"

Peter stared moodily at his cigarette as he answered, "Nothing really any different from usual, I guess."

Stroud did not pursue the subject. He asked, "Were you so contemptuous of facts when you left Germany twelve years ago?"

"I don't know. I was twelve years younger. One doesn't look at things very clearly at twenty-three. Then, too, I was more inclined to ascribe all the blame to one nation because I wasn't acquainted with enough nations. National character is bad, John."

"Which national character?"

"The character of all nations."

Stroud smiled. The skin ran together in crinkles around his deep gray, somewhat shortsighted eyes. When Stroud smiled, he always reminded Peter of Woodrow Wilson. Most Americans, Peter had often thought, look like Charles Lindbergh, Woodrow Wilson, or the Uncle Sam of the posters.

The sun was going down. Over the camp, with its rows of identical white barracks, was a soft, pinkish haze. Even the dust, which always hovered over the area, took on a rosy coloration. Smoke was coming from the kitchens. The prisoners were clustered around the water hydrants.

"Can't you stay overnight, after all?" Stroud asked. "Do you have to go chasing off after your mysterious documents? It's good to have you here. Sometimes I feel like a doctor in a lunatic asylum who gradually goes crazy himself. I'm slowly becoming a prisoner."

"Sorry, I can't stay, John. And I haven't even got the documents for an excuse. I'm on my way to Maria."

Stroud knew at once what Peter was talking about. When they had met in Germany in the last weeks of the war—for the first time after the episode in Paris—Peter had told him about Maria. He had spoken of her again when they had met on the day of the capitulation. Then Peter had been summoned back to America by General Donovan. Now it was almost six months since Peter had entered the lonely house in Trier.

Peter expected a question. When it did not come, he said, "It's all right to ask me why I keep looking for her, John. But I can't give you the answer."

"Do you know what will happen when you see her?"

"Yes."

"Do you want it to happen?"

"I don't know. I only know that for six months I haven't stopped thinking about her—where she is, what she's doing, if she has enough to eat, what her daughter is doing. Things that shouldn't concern me, really. But they're important to me. Sometimes it seems as if nothing else has been important to me for fourteen years."

"Maybe nothing else has been important to you."

"Nonsense," Peter retorted gruffly, but as if he were trying to convince himself. "Patricia has been as important as hell."

It did not sound quite genuine.

"When did you last hear from home?"

"Yesterday."

Peter pulled a letter out of his pocket. "Here. Do you want to read it?"

"Do you want me to?"

"Yes."

Stroud put on his glasses. With the round pince-nez over his discerning, somewhat too small eyes, he suggested Woodrow Wilson more than ever. The precise, narrow, up-and-down handwriting of the letter looked almost like some foreign script. He read:

Dearest,

I believe I wrote you that I was going to Philadelphia to help Mother with the charity bazaar for Canadian prisoners of war. It was a great success. I sat next to the Canadian ambassador and we talked about the two Ravineau girls from Montreal, with whom I went to school. He knows them very well. Renée Ravineau married the counsel of the French Legation, a man named Debussy. I think he is related to the composer. Do you know him?

The next morning I went back to New York. The train was terribly crowded; it's really unbearable traveling these days. Mary and I actually couldn't get seats in the same Pullman. From the train I went right to Brooklyn to talk to a boy whose father was sentenced to life imprisonment last week for a hold-up murder. The name is Brenton, you probably read about it in the papers. The whole family sat around and cried. There were at least eight people in the room, and I couldn't carry on a sensible conversation with the boy at all. I tried to explain the problem to the mother and to tell her that crying did no good and was bad for the youngster, besides. The boy mixed in and said his mother wouldn't be crying if she had some money. He is only eight years old and I ask myself if he isn't perhaps criminally inclined too. Do you believe criminal tendencies are inherited? I always forget to ask you. I helped the mother clean up the room—I think everything is easier to bear in clean surroundings, don't you?

In the afternoon I had to wait for hours at the hairdresser's. Charles sends his regards. He wants to give me a new hair-do, but I can't make up my mind whether to let him go ahead or not.

In the evening Senator and Mrs. Hooper, Mrs. Fauville, Colonel Roberts, and Helena and Robert Ricks came to dinner. You know only Helena and Colonel Roberts, but the others are all charming too. Catharine sent her regrets at the last minute, which caused the usual difficulties with the seating arrangements. She's very inconsiderate, really. Colonel Roberts has just returned from England, and he says the stories in our papers about food shortages there are much exaggerated. Is that true?

Next week I go to Washington. I hope I'll have time to write to you from there.

I send you my love,

Patricia

Stroud handed the letter back without saying anything. They sat in silence for a while and sipped their drinks. From one of the barracks came a melancholy song; a group of prisoners were singing "Lili Marlene." Stroud toyed with his glasses. He cleared his throat. "What do you want me to say? That it's not an especially heartwarming letter? That there's not much in it for a man sitting here surrounded by barbed wire, looking at the ruins of the city over there? Apparently that's what you want to hear. Perhaps it's true, perhaps it isn't. What was it you were saying before, Captain Olden? One must have imagination."

"Yes," said Peter. "You need plenty of imagination reading letters like that." He stood up.

Stroud arose also. The Major laid his hand on the shoulder of his friend, who was a full head taller than he. "I've gotten hundreds of letters like that during the war," he said earnestly. "They're perfectly normal. The abnormal things are over here, our surroundings. The wretchedness, the ruins, the blood and hate, the human beings locked up in a zoo, and locking ourselves in with them. And not being able to get used to living without danger."

He accompanied Peter to the car. Dirty Thompson sat in the driver's seat, whittling. He greeted the Major like an old friend. Stroud watched as the car rolled with illegal speed past the guards and out of the camp.

As soon as they had reached the *Autobahn*, Thompson asked, "How far we goin', Captain?"

"To a little place near Berchtesgaden," Peter answered. "We ought to make it in two hours."

"Then we'll make it in an hour and a half. That's if too many MP's don't cross us up. You seem to be in a hurry." He grinned at the Captain and stepped on the gas. Hunched over the wheel, his arms crooked in steering, he looked more like a gorilla cradling its young than a man driving a car.

The August evening was huge and silent. The sun had gone down, but one knew that it was still there, on the other side of the mountains, like a lonely climber going down the path leading home at the end of the day. The heat of the afternoon had given way to caressing coolness. The little Bavarian farmhouses, half stone and half wood, squatted peacefully in the dusk. The cows came ambling from the meadows in long rows. When they reached the yard to which they belonged, they took two clumsy steps and fell out of line. Their bells clanged. They knew they were home. In the distance, somewhere yonder in Austria, the violet outlines of the snow-capped peaks melted into the violet sky.

Peter breathed deeply. It seemed familiar to him, all of it: the mountains, the cows, the air. His lungs expanded. For a moment there seemed nothing within him but a great exultation. It was as if, at one stroke, everything fell away and everything was forgotten: the ship to America jammed with immigrants, the first grim years, the first successes, the strange and beautiful women, the war, the leap from the plane into the burning Italian town, the screams and the death, the cold, impersonal letters. He felt as if he must fly on ahead of the car, which was not rushing onward fast enough.

The speedometer showed sixty.

"I'm traveling as fast as I can," said Thompson, who, besides being a taxi driver in civilian life, must also have been a mind reader. Then, with great earnestness, and without looking at Peter, "Brother, being in love must really be something!"

$\ggg$ **11** $\lll$

PETER had met Patricia during his third year in America, just before Christmas of 1936. He was twenty-five then, and Patricia a year younger. His first published book had appeared shortly before, and since it almost immediately became a best-seller he had found himself in demand everywhere as a lecturer. It seemed that the American public refused to believe an author actually existed unless they could see him.

He had delivered a lecture in Philadelphia and afterward had been bundled into an immense limousine and whisked off to the home of Barbara Draper. It was almost a municipal ordinance in Philadelphia that visiting celebrities, literary lions, and nine-day wonders of the art world had to submit to the hazing that passed for hospitality in the grandiose mansion on Rittenhouse Square. The house of Barbara Draper was operated like an embassy for prominent visitors to the city, and they were expected, like travelers in a foreign land, to avail themselves of its services and protection.

Everything about the party in Peter's honor combined to confuse and unsettle him—his own sudden fame, which he found exaggerated and a little absurd; the glittering swirl of strangers around him; the huge, museum-like house, in which he could not imagine anyone's leading a reasonable existence; the majestic bearing of his hostess, who must have studied all available portraits of Catherine the Great and who, he was given to understand, was the widow of one of America's wealthiest women's-wear tycoons.

He fled in a kind of panic to the side of a slim, pale girl, whose fragile beauty had struck him the instant he entered the drawing-room. There was a hint of sickliness in the whiteness of her face and shoulders, but she had the kind of beauty he had adored since childhood. One could imagine her in wimple and flowing train, the high-born mistress of a medieval castle; or as the heroine of a tale of chivalry, with knights in plumes riding next to her coach; or, again, as one of those Parisian *beautés* of Zola, who on rainy afternoons flitted noiselessly through the doorways of elegant bachelor apartments.

Peter soon found himself attracted to her not only by her beauty but by her talk. His novel had been the story of a man who had spent fifteen years in prison for a crime he had not committed. "Rehabilitated" by prison authorities, he had been given his freedom again and promptly became an actual criminal. The delicate young lady in Barbara Draper's drawing-room disclosed an amazing knowledge of crime and criminals.

They had been chatting half an hour when she said, "I feel guilty keeping you from the rest of the party. Everybody here wants to meet you."

"Let's just stay where we are," he said. "I don't feel like wasting an evening on strangers."

"But I'm a stranger too."

"You were half an hour ago."

A little while later he said, "Look. I'd like to see you again. I could easily say that I want to talk to you some more about criminology and books. But I really don't give a damn about criminology, and the only thing that interests me about books is my next one. It won't have a word in it about crime or criminals."

"What will it be about?"

"About love."

"Well, what do you want to talk to me about next time?"

He smiled. "The theme of my next book."

To his surprise she blushed, like the storybook heroines she resembled. "I'm afraid that's a subject I don't know much about."

"I'm not looking for expert opinion. I just want you to listen to me."

Before the evening was over she agreed to go to the theater with him in New York. "Pick me up at the St. Regis," she said.

"Do you know," he said as he was about to leave, "I don't even know your name."

"I'm Patricia Draper."

He was so dismayed that she had to laugh. "Yes, I'm Mrs. Draper's daughter. Does that upset you?"

"Oh, no. I'm just trying to remember whether I said anything terrible about this house of yours."

"Is it such a terrible house?"

"It looks like a museum. I keep expecting the man from Cook's to come in and announce when the next tour begins."

They met again in New York, and after their first theater date their engagement was understood between them without the subject's having been mentioned. They dined at Twenty-One, the one good restaurant that Peter knew. Later they went to the quiet Penthouse Club on Central Park South, with candles on the table, a fire in the open hearth, the lights of New York outside the window, and a Yugoslav at the piano who sang with the air of a man ready to commit suicide afterward.

"This is the only night club I've been to in New York," said Peter.

"I haven't been to one since the year after my debut," she replied.

"Don't you like them?"

"Not much. People in night clubs never behave normally. The young ones want to be older. The old ones try to be young. I like normal, simple people."

"Do you know any?"

"Yes. I meet them in my work."

Poor girl, he thought. She's so tired of the people she knows that she has to look for normality among people who have robbed banks and murdered their wives. He said, "Do you think I'm quite normal?"

"I don't want to classify you," she said almost tenderly.

She was silent and for several minutes stared absently into space. "Peter, I must tell you something."

"Yes?"

"I'm married."

Again he was surprised, as he was by most things that she said. This time his surprise came not so much from the fact that she was married as from the solemn, portentous tone in which she confessed it.

"Is it a secret?" he asked. "You still use your maiden name "

"I'm really Mrs. Luce Holborn. I married Luce Holborn five years ago."

She spoke the name as if she were mentioning a Nobel Prize winner or the president of General Motors.

"And who is Luce Holborn?" Peter asked. "I'm an ignorant man."

"He's the best polo player in America."

"I don't play polo," he said, and added to annoy her, "My only sport is lawn bowling."

She laughed indulgently. "We haven't lived together for four years, but until now I haven't thought of getting a divorce." Peter heard with a stab of delight how she stressed, almost imperceptibly, the words "until now."

It was a month later that she went to Reno.

During the weeks of their tacit engagement Peter lived in a silvery fog. The outside world barely penetrated. He thought of Patricia the instant he awoke, and her image stayed with him uninterruptedly until he fell asleep again at night. The rest of the world became merely a conspiracy of 2,169,868,000 people all bent on keeping the two of them from being alone together. He took an absurd and childish pleasure in picturing his love affair in fairytale terms. The Draper mansion on Rittenhouse Square became a fortress in which an infinitely lovely Cinderella was being held captive. It was up to Prince Charming to set her free. Luce Holborn was the incarnation of wickedness, and in Peter's fantasy Holborn appeared on a polo pony, as beautiful as Phoebus Apollo but with two horns sticking out from under his polo cap. Playing polo seemed to Peter the most contemptible of all human activities, but when he read Luce Holborn's name on the sport or society page of his morning paper his whole day was ruined.

He used to meet her regularly at the St. Regis for their evenings together. She waited for him in the drawing-room of her suite, and she then went into the adjoining bedroom to put on her hat while he finished his Daiquiri. She had a way of calling to him through the half-open door—something completely trivial and commonplace—which made the most extreme physical intimacies he had previously experienced with women seem feeble and colorless in comparison. There was something sweetly marital about these conversations, called through the half-open door as she sat in her bedroom adjusting her hat or powdering her nose.

One evening she was not in the drawing-room when he entered, and she called to him to come into her bedroom. She lay in a bed covered with rose-tinted satin, but she was wearing a cambric jacket whose simplicity touched him strangely. She coughed. "I've caught a cold, Peter," she said. "Do you mind having a light dinner right here?"

He didn't mind at all. It was obvious that the maid who usually opened the door for him had been sent away, and he was able to perform for Patricia the little page-boy services which delight men in love: he brought her a handkerchief from a dresser drawer, and he went to the bathroom to bring her a glass of water.

She submitted wordlessly when he sat next to her on the edge of the bed. As he took her small body in his arms, she gave herself up without a sound to his caresses. She did not respond overtly to the play of his lips, but he could feel her mouth burning on his. Even today, as he thought back to it, he could savor the taste of her mouth, a taste that made him think of grass that grew in a hot sun. Her submissiveness, and the fact that she had arranged that they should be alone in her apartment, encouraged him. He kissed her shoulders, and his hands and then his lips found her breasts. When he sought her mouth again, he was surprised to see that she was lying back with wide-open eyes. But he found nothing shameless or obscene in her seeming detachment; in her great, clear eyes there was the amazed curiosity of a child.

He went through the whole ritual of seduction which men have used for centuries not so much to overcome the resistance of women as to induce that feeling of languor and weakness which makes it possible for them to abandon resistance. While he tried with his kisses to give her an excuse not to know what his hands were doing, his fingers slid over the firm, smooth bulge of her hips. It was then that Patricia seized his hands and gripped them firmly. He knew at once that this was not merely the usual womanly invitation to ruthlessness, the resistance that courts seduction.

"Don't you love me?" he asked.

She answered, "I love you, darling. But, remember, I'm Luce Holborn's wife."

He had to leave it at that. He could not tell why she had seemingly offered herself to him, only to withdraw with a virtuous reference to the marriage that had meant nothing to her for four years.

After their marriage they took possession of an old but fashionable house wedged between skyscrapers on Fifth Avenue. It was one of the several houses belonging to Barbara Draper, who had many addresses but no home. He hated the idea of living in a house owned by his mother-in-law, but Patricia had persuaded him with endless practical arguments, whose force he could not deny. Why should he spend his savings establishing a new house or apartment when mother's Fifth Avenue home was empty and available to them?

They settled down, as far as this was possible in one of Barbara Draper's houses. The cellar turned out to be too small for all the Venetian vases, Velasquez imitations, bric-a-brac, satin lampshades, Morocco rugs, and gilded French furniture that had to be removed to make space for living. When the transformation was completed, it turned out that none of the rooms was suitable for Peter to work in. A little parlor, next to Patricia's bedroom, was finally converted into a study, but it was so full of feminine tables and fragile chairs that Peter was never able to feel at home in it. In addition, Patricia habitually slept until eleven, and the clacking of his typewriter would have disturbed her. Peter said nothing. She had personally supervised the furnishing and decoration of his study, and he didn't want to hurt her feelings. But every morning he went to the Hotel Plaza to work, and his new novel was begun on hotel stationery.

Peter was completely happy during the first four or five weeks of their marriage. Patricia seemed to have overcome all her inhibitions; she gave herself up to him and to her love for him without restraint, and Peter was almost grateful that she had assumed that attitude of virginal reluctance which had puzzled him in the weeks of their engagement. But as soon as the honeymoon was over and they returned from Mexico to live in the Fifth Avenue house, Patricia's attitude changed.

From then on he had to go through the motions of seducing her if he wanted to possess her. At first he imagined that she merely wanted to heighten the excitement of their love play, but he soon found that she was not pleased with his willingness to overcome her resistance. What stirred and satisfied him most in their amorous relationship only puzzled and amazed her. Sometimes, lost in his lovemaking, he would suddenly discover her looking at him, unmoved, with calm, appraising eyes; and when he, almost ashamed of himself, broke his mood and pulled himself back to reality, her gaze seemed to be asking, "Poor boy, what is it that sweeps you away so completely?" He had always observed a code of lovemaking which required that the male defer with tact and gallantry to the amorous inclinations of the female. He now gave up this delicacy, since it was apparent that anything which prolonged their lovemaking was merely irksome to Patricia. Had he married a frigid woman? Even now he did not know whether what had, at times, driven him half mad had been a true frigidity or only a more challenging thing—a lack of specific desire for him. But even this explanation failed to account for the complexity of her reactions. For there were times when Patricia gave rein to her erotic impulses and incited him to excesses of lovemaking which he would otherwise never have dared to attempt. On such nights he believed that, at last, he possessed her fully. He soon discovered that her passion was not directed toward him, but was passion for its own sake; her intensity of emotion ran parallel with his, but did not merge with it. The fact that she was capable of experiencing passion misled him over and over again into attempting to channel it toward himself. The result, however, was never harmonious satisfaction, but only a constantly renewed challenge.

On his most recent trip to America she had invited a number of guests for his first evening home—some friends of his and some of hers, but mostly people he did not know. He sat in a corner and felt that he was in the way. One or two of the guests came over and sat down next to him, spoke admiringly of Patricia, and wanted to know when he expected to be leaving again. Someone asked him if he were permanently stationed in Washington, and if he wouldn't prefer to go overseas. He felt that no one spoke of him in this house, that his name was never mentioned while he was gone. He was suddenly homesick for Europe, for the mud, for field rations eaten with comrades in a tent in Normandy, for the curt, vital exchange of words with a pilot just before the leap into space. As for Maria—he fought desperately to keep thoughts of her out of his mind. He wanted to get drunk, very drunk. He went upstairs to bed. For hours he continued to hear the noise of conversation and the clatter of glasses below. Finally he heard Patricia come upstairs and tiptoe to her room so as not to disturb him. He could hear her moving about as she undressed. He made no move to go in to her.

The next night he went to her room, but he was uneasy about approaching her, and they passed a silent, unsatisfactory night. Patricia seemed disturbed by the stormy impatience of his love-making.

"You're hurting me," she whispered. "I have to get used to having a man again."

Toward two in the morning he went to his bedroom across the hall. He felt empty, and a little ridiculous.

There was a series of lunches and parties for him, at all of which he felt himself the least important person present. He did not go into her bedroom again, and she gave no indication that she thought this in any way strange. But in the car on the way to the airport she leaned her head on his shoulder. "The days went so quickly," she said. "We hardly had time to be alone together. The next time you come we'll get away from all those people. We'll go up to the mountains and be all, all alone. Oh, darling, I love you so!"

He saw how she had stood for a long time on the runway, following with her eyes the plane that was carrying him away. He saw her slim and delicate figure standing out in sharp relief against the airfield as the airplane climbed toward the clouds.

»» 12 ««

I T WAS midnight. Everyone in the little peasant house on the mountain slope had gone to bed. Helga, Maria's daughter, was asleep upstairs in the attic room. Thompson had withdrawn hours ago, nobody knew where.

Maria and Peter sat on the balcony. No moon was shining, but the sky was full of stars. The glow of their cigarettes punctured the darkness.

"I knew you would come," Maria said.

"Since Trier?"

"No. For twelve years."

"I didn't know that I would come."

"The one who goes away never knows that he will return," she answered. "Only those who wait know." For a moment there was silence. Then she continued, "That's why I told Helga so much about you. Ever since that night—"

"What night?"

"It was in Berlin. I was at the home of friends, across the way from us. The raid came suddenly, before the sirens had a chance to sound. I wanted to rush out of the house to Helga. She was in our house, alone. The bombs started falling before I could get out. The house caved in. Helga knew I was under the wreckage. For eighteen hours she worked with the rescue squad. As she worked her way closer and closer to me, she heard my voice. I was calling, 'Peter! Peter!' She thought I was out of my mind. They found me unconscious an hour later. For weeks she didn't dare ask any questions. Then one day, at breakfast, she said innocently, 'Mommy, who is Peter?' And so I told her about you. I told her you would come again."

A soft wind came from the Alps.

"Are you cold?" Peter asked.

"No. Are you?"

"No." He drew on his cigarette. In the sudden flare of its glow he saw the face he had been seeking for six months. It was her face of twelve years before. "We talked so much in Trier," he said. "But all the important things only came to me later."

"Is there something you want to know?"

"Yes. Why did I have to stop writing to you?"

"When your first articles began appearing in America, the Gestapo arrested me. They found all your letters. They held me eight weeks. Then they let me go. That's when Eric wrote you. I didn't know about it. He told me a year later."

"Why did you think I didn't answer?"

"I don't know. I thought you loved someone else."

"And you kept writing anyway?"

"What would that have to do with it?"

He threw his cigarette over the railing and took her hand. It was slightly rough and hard. When he buried his face in it, he smelled the fragrance that he had carried within him for twelve years. Now it seemed strange that this fragrance was again coming to him from outside. It was a sharp, country-like smell: something of hay was in it, and mowed grass, and the starch peasant girls use in their petticoats.

"Come," he said. "We're going inside."

They did not turn on a light. They did not put their arms around each other, did not even walk close to each other. They did not whisper. She went quietly through the darkened room. He felt his way and bumped against the bed. For a moment he stood still and listened. He could not hear what she was doing.

They undressed without speaking, without haste, in a curious, ritual-like solemnity. In the darkness now he could tell that she was taking off her clothes; he could tell, too, that she was not throwing them from her, but was laying them carefully on a chair. He slowly began to take off his boots. He also painstakingly put his clothes, one by one, on a chair. A chill passed over his naked body. There was in him a singular fear, a fear he had not known since he was sixteen and had for the first time taken a woman.

As he approached the bed he knew that she was waiting for him.

13

THE August heat of the late afternoon shimmered in the office of the lieutenant colonel who commanded the SS prisoner-of-war camp near Reichenhall. The colonel was unusually young for his rank. His collar was open, revealing a sun-coppered, muscular neck. With his short, bristly black hair he looked like a college fullback.

"It won't take long to look them over," he said. Stroud and Wanda were sitting opposite him. "We have several thousand SS men here, but only a hundred and twenty officers. I've had them formed up for you outside." And as he saw that Stroud was about to arise, "Take your time, Major. Let 'em roast in the sun for a while." He took out a cigarette and lit it. He spoke to Stroud as if Wanda were not present. "I hope you find your man. Even if it does cause a lot of snafu around here. Why we don't just put the whole bunch of these bastards against a wall, I'll never know."

The girl involuntarily looked at Stroud, but he said nothing.

"How you get any satisfaction out of your job is beyond me," the colonel continued, addressing Stroud. "I see you fought these animals in the infantry. So did I. That was okay. But why we should bother to house and feed them now—"

"Well, we can't just shoot them all down," Stroud said.

"Then I'd turn 'em loose," replied the colonel.

"But think of the damage these people could do!" Stroud exclaimed.

"Damage? Where? No place but in Germany. And what in hell do we care about that?"

He pressed a buzzer, and introduced to Stroud the lieutenant who responded. "The lieutenant will take you around," he said. He looked at Wanda for the first time. "The one thing that pleases me about your visit is that you're a woman," he said. "Most of these guys haven't seen a woman in five, six months. Not close up, anyway. Breathe right in their faces, sister! The more they dream about women, the better I'll like it. I know how it is. Once at the front I didn't have a woman myself for five whole months. All on account of these goddam krauts."

The lieutenant, who was considerably older than the colonel, smiled dutifully. Stroud did not know what to say. In his embarrassment he went through the door ahead of Wanda.

The camp was in faultless order. Stroud admired the immaculately scrubbed streets between the barracks, the whitewashed stones around the entrances, the spotlessly clean bulletin boards. The SS men sitting in front of the barracks sprang up as the two officers came past and stood at attention until they were out of sight.

They had to go through a wire gate to enter the officers' enclosure. The one hundred and twenty SS officers stood in rows of ten in the center of the parade ground. The lieutenant shouted a command, and they instantly snapped to attention.

The lieutenant remained standing opposite the group while Stroud and Wanda began to walk along the first rank of prisoners.

They were mostly young, between twenty and thirty. Their uniforms were worn and shabby, but still exhibited excellent cut and tailoring. In their eyes—mostly blue—was neither fear nor hate nor surprise. There was nothing but rank, staring lust. None of them looked Stroud in the face. Their gaze crawled slowly over the body of the girl, lingered on the curve of her hips, seized upon the V of her bodice.

Stroud was suddenly sorry he had brought her to this place. It seemed to him that all the prisoners were reaching out for her. The scene in her Warsaw home, which she had mentioned so briefly, now appeared to him in horrifying clarity. He saw each of these men thrusting a hand between her blouse and her skirt, seeking with brutal impatience for the fastening, to open it and undress her. He tried to force the picture from his mind. Involuntarily he stepped closer to her, as if to protect her.

She went calmly along the rows of prisoners, stopping briefly before each one. She was smaller than the prisoners. But as she stood before one after the other and looked into their faces, they lowered their eyes. Insolent smiles froze, and the corners of mouths that had twisted down with desire or contempt twitched upward as if two fingers had suddenly yanked them back into place.

Wanda remained standing before one officer longer than she had before the others. He was tall and blond, with surfeited, cunning eyes that were catlike in their secrecy. His skin was covered with pockmarks, which, curiously, did not deform his face, but gave it a leathery, manly look. He withstood Wanda's gaze longer than did the others. Stroud could not tell whether there was recognition in his eyes or merely fear concealed behind aggressiveness. The man and the woman measured each other for several minutes.

Stroud felt hatred against this foreigner rising within him. Hate was for him a strange and unknown sensation, like the onset of a new disease. Then the girl passed on.

When she had gone down the whole row she turned back again to the pockmarked prisoner. She pulled Stroud aside and asked him to question the man.

"On which front did you see action?" Stroud asked.

"In Italy, Belgium, and France," the officer answered reluctantly. "Last in Holland."

"Were you ever on the eastern front?"

"No."

"In Poland or Russia?"

"No."

"What outfit did you belong to?"

"The Seventh Waffen-SS Division."

"All the time?"

"All the time."

Stroud indicated Wanda. "Do you recognize this former Polish officer?"

"No."

Wanda continued to stand in front of the man. The tips of her shoes almost touched his. Stroud's glance fell on the gleamingly polished boots of the officer and on the worn shoes of the girl. The hate grew stronger in him. Then he heard her whisper, "No. He's not the one."

The day was still bright when they left the prison camp. The little Bavarian houses nestled snugly in the green of the meadows. As they drove along the highway, it was hard to believe that only a few weeks before battles had been fought here. Now and then they passed the wreckage of an airplane lying in the woods at the edge of the highway. The Germans had used the highway as a runway for their fighters. Now the gutted hulks of the planes lay abandoned under the tangled branches of the woods.

Stroud mentioned the futility of their expedition.

"I don't know what to do now," he said. "There's an SS camp

in Mannheim, and another in Nürnberg, but I haven't any connections with the commanders. Maybe your man is long since dead. Or, more likely, he's a prisoner of the Russians."

"If I only knew his name, or at least his regiment!" Wanda said.

"Then, of course, we could track him down in short order."

Thereafter they spoke little. But the closer the command car approached Munich, the more certain was the Major that he wanted to see Wanda again. He had never probed very deeply into himself or given much thought to his motives and impulses, and even now he did not analyze his feelings for Wanda. It was only that, when he was with her, he thought again and again of his daughter Eleanor and of the difference between the two girls, who were almost the same age. Oddly it was Eleanor who troubled his conscience rather than Wanda. It seemed to him that he had never in all his life felt such fatherly solicitude for his own daughter as he now felt for this foreign girl. He looked at her sideways. As he watched her narrow face with its large eyes, which looked attentively but at the same time distantly at the rushing landscape, he was overcome again by the emotion he had felt when she had sat opposite him in his office, fumbling with her toy red handbag. He had never known a great deal about his own children; less about Eleanor, even, than Jim. He admitted to himself that he had never made much of an effort to get to know Eleanor, but now he felt a compulsion to learn more about the girl beside him, about her past, what she planned for the future, and what she was really like.

He heard himself saying, "Shall we have a beer before I take you back?"

"Gladly."

They stopped at a tavern in a little village. As they crossed the empty taproom it occurred to him that American soldiers were forbidden to enter German taverns. He could not remember any other occasion on which he had deliberately violated an official rule.

They sat down at a table in the deserted beer garden. The sun burst out from behind a cloud and was bathing everything in a buttery yellow. Overhead there was a rustling in the branches of the shady chestnut tree.

"The later I get back to camp, the better I shall like it," the girl said.

"You'll be going back to Poland soon, won't you?"

"No," she said, "not before Poland is liberated."

"But Poland is liberated."

"Not as long as the Russians are in Warsaw."

"Why do you bother your head about politics?" he asked.

"I don't bother about politics," she answered. "I don't understand anything about them. Freedom has nothing to do with politics."

"You must hate the Russians because they didn't come and help you in the uprising."

She hesitated. "No. That's not it, although we have every reason to hate them for that. Only, I just don't want to be forced into believing anything. Neither by Germans nor by Russians. I believe in the dear God above, and that's enough."

"Do you still have relatives in Warsaw?" he asked.

"I don't know," she answered.

"Would you like to go to America?"

"I don't know that either. It isn't so important to me where I go."

"You're a very courageous little girl."

"Why?"

"You ask why, after all you've done?" He drank his beer slowly. "What I mean is that you are brave because you're not afraid of being alone."

"I was always much alone," she said. And after a slight pause, "Many people don't help one get over being lonely."

"Wanda, I could learn a lot from you."

He had never before used her first name. She did not appear to notice. She looked into her glass, but she did not drink the beer.

"Are you hungry?" he asked quickly.

"No."

He knew she was lying. He touched her hand as it lay on the table. "Do they give you enough to eat at the camp?"

"Yes, of course."

"How would it be if I brought some chocolate one of these days?"

"Chocolate?" she repeated. "Chocolate would be glorious." Her face lighted with the joy of a little girl of twelve. "I haven't seen any chocolate for years."

He looked at his watch. "I must take you home now," he said.

He paid, and they went out through the garden. She walked on ahead of him, and he watched her down-at-the-heel shoes scuffing through the grass. She's got to have new heels for her shoes, he thought.

As they climbed into the car, he saw that she was smiling. "Why are you smiling?" he asked.

"You said 'I must take you home now' like a cadet in the Poniatoffsky Dancing School in Warsaw." And she told him about her carefree days before the war. "We all went to Poniatoffsky's Dancing School in Warsaw. I'll never forget Poniatoffsky. He was a former cavalry officer. He had terribly bowed legs and a ridiculous mustache. I'm sure he colored it black with shoe polish. We always went to his classes, even though nobody ever learned to dance there. He demonstrated the steps for us but he danced himself as if he were still riding a horse."

"What happened to him?"

"He defended his dancing school like a fortress. It was on Marzalkowska. There was much fighting there. The Germans killed him."

They hardly spoke at all on the rest of the journey. At the DP camp she got out of the car and offered him her hand.

"I'll come by soon and bring you the chocolate," he said. Then he drove off so quickly that she could not reply.

PART II

14

THE British Secret Service had established the fact that on the night of April 28, 1945, one Ernst Argonaut, an SS officer, had been in the air-raid shelter in the Reich Chancellery in Berlin with Adolf Hitler, and that, shortly before Hitler's death, Argonaut had been commissioned by Hitler to take certain personal papers—perhaps final instructions for secret resistance against the occupying armies—through the Russian lines to an unknown destination. Since the day when the *SS-Standartenführer* had put the documents in his pocket and left the air-raid shelter, no trace of him had been found.

The British Secret Service learned, further, that Argonaut's wife was living in the Bavarian village of Hof. It could be assumed that Argonaut would get in touch with his wife. The Third United States Army, then the occupying force in Bavaria, was asked to take up the search for the vanished SS officer. The Third Army, aware of the damage that might be done by these papers while an idolatrous aura still surrounded the name of Adolf Hitler, turned the job over to the OSS. Colonel Whimsley in turn gave the assignment to Captain Peter Olden.

The Argonaut house was an agreeable villa on the edge of the little town, set in the middle of a large, rambling garden. Until 1937 it had belonged to a Jewish doctor, who had since died in a concentration camp.

Peter decided to pay a midnight call on Frau Argonaut, unconventional as the hour might be for an unannounced visit to the home of a stranger. Under cover of darkness Peter swung himself over the garden fence and chose an observation post behind an ancient oak from where he could observe the entrance to the house as well as was possible in the darkness. There was a light in one of the windows of the house, but a tightly drawn curtain prevented him from seeing what was going on inside. He settled down to wait.

Peter was used to waiting. He remembered other long hours of vigil in the night—the slow, heavy-footed passage of minutes and hours until the moment for action came. At those times he had passed the hours making plans for the future. Now, for the first time, he could not tear himself away from the present.

It had been raining for days, and the garden gave off a strong and heady odor of wet earth. The air was clear and the sky seemed measureless, sprinkled everywhere with stars that shone as if the rain had washed and polished them. One or two lights, competing feebly with the stars, gleamed on the sides of the mountains. Peter thought of Maria and of the night in her house. Something piercing and sweet, like the smell of the earth, went through him. He knew then that he had made plans for the future only because the present had meant nothing to him. Now the future was here— as real as Maria's embrace, as living and immediate as the pulsing of his heart.

The light on the ground floor had gone out. For a moment a window on the second floor brightened. Then the whole house became dark. The church bell tolled twelve. The strokes rang out deeply and melodiously. It must be a very old bell, he thought. It occurred to Peter that he could not remember ever having heard church bells at night in America.

Automatically he took the safety catch off his pistol, but even as he did it, he thought, what do I need a gun for? To put a woman through a police grilling? He felt no excitement, and hardly any interest in his task. All this had been much simpler while the war was on. You risked your life, but you didn't think much about it one way or the other. It wasn't easy to accustom oneself to peace.

Just as he was about to approach the house a light appeared again on the second floor. The first light had been in the third window to the left. Now it went on in the fourth window to the left. He waited until the light went out again. Only eight minutes had passed.

He went up to the door of the house and rang the bell twice. There was no response. When there was no answer to his third ring, he began to hammer on the door with the barrel of his gun. Now he could hear footsteps on the stairs inside.

A woman's voice called out, "Who is it?"

"American Military Police. Open up!"

A light went on and a woman wearing a satin dressing gown over her nightdress opened the door. She tried to look like someone who has just been awakened from a sound sleep. Peter could see that she had not been sleeping.

"Good evening, Frau Argonaut," he said, putting his foot in the door.

"What do you want?" asked the woman.

"Wouldn't it be better to talk inside?" Peter asked, and entered without waiting for a reply.

They were in a large room, pleasantly furnished in Bavarian peasant style. On the light paneling of the walls hung bright peasant dishes with painted mottoes and proverbs. Pewter jugs stood along the walls. Over the fireplace was a large, square spot several shades lighter than the surrounding area. A nail, glaringly obvious in its uselessness, protruded from the spot. That nail hasn't been unemployed for long, thought Peter; a little while ago it had a job to do—I wonder where the Führer's portrait is now.

He stood in the middle of the room so that he could watch the stairs to the second floor and the entrance to the house at the same time. "My visit is probably not wholly unexpected," he said. "The hour is a little unusual I'll admit. I'd like to talk to Herr Argonaut."

"My husband is not here."

He scrutinized her closely. She was a woman of about forty, and except for the tight pinched lines around her lips she was not unattractive. Tiny lines ran from all directions to her mouth, like little rivers pouring into the sea. I won't have an easy time with her, Peter thought.

When he spoke again he raised his voice and talked in the direction of the stairway. He judged he could be heard by anyone upstairs or in an adjoining room.

"The house is surrounded," he said. "There's no use trying to get away."

"My husband is not here," the woman repeated.

"When did you last hear from him?"

"Before the collapse."

"When was that? Try to remember exactly."

"About eight weeks before the collapse."

It sounded well rehearsed.

"Where was your husband at that time?"

"In Berlin."

She patted her hair nervously. She's not very good at acting, thought Peter. My questions can't be making her that uneasy. It is something else that's bothering her. He had the feeling that something was occurring in the house. He felt like a man who enters a dark room and senses, without seeing, that someone is there.

"Do you live alone here?"

"Yes."

"Are there guests in the house?"

"No."

Peter waited a moment and then said, "Tell me, Frau Argonaut— what do you know of the relationship between your husband and Hitler?"

She hesitated for a fraction of a second. "I don't believe my husband knew Hitler personally."

"Then you don't know the nature of the papers your husband sent you for safekeeping?"

She looked puzzled. "Papers?" she said. "I don't know anything about any papers."

Is she better at acting than I thought? Peter wondered. But then she gave her hair another uneasy pat and pulled the cord of her dressing gown tighter. The bodice of her nightdress was cut low, and Peter could see her limp, deflated breasts.

"If you'll excuse me for a moment," she said. "I'll be right back. I hardly look presentable. I was sound asleep when you knocked."

That was a lie. Peter remembered the lighted windows. "No," he said. "Stay here."

He was about to ask another question when he heard a noise upstairs. He paused and listened. Someone was apparently moving around in an upstairs room. There came a sound as of someone bumping against a piece of furniture. The woman heard it too and moved as if to place herself between Peter and the stairway. Peter paid no attention to her. He took his automatic from its holster and bounded up the stairs. At the top he stood for a moment in the darkened corridor and tried to get his bearings. A slit of light was escaping through a crack in a door at his right. Peter thrust the door open, his gun ready, his body sideways in the doorway so as to offer the least possible target.

In the middle of the room stood a man in blue-striped pajamas, holding a shoe in one hand. He had long, dark hair that fell into his face. Peter could not make out his features clearly.

"Don't move," Peter said in German.

The man looked up. He could not have been more than twenty-four or five. His eyes looked at Peter vaguely, without any marked interest and with no alarm. After a moment he turned away and began putting on his shoe.

"Don't move," Peter ordered again.

The man looked at him in the same vague, indifferent way.

"Talk English if you want me to understand you," he said finally. He began fumbling with his shoelace.

Peter lowered his automatic. The absurdity of the situation was instantly clear to him. All the tension went out of him. He felt tired and ridiculous.

"Get dressed and come downstairs," he said in English.

"Okay, Captain," the man replied peevishly.

The woman was standing in the doorway, looking from one man to the other. On a chair next to the double bed with its rumpled covers was an American soldier's uniform with sergeant's stripes on the sleeves.

➤➤ 15 ◄◄

DOWNSTAIRS Peter sent the woman out of the room and sat down alone with the soldier. He lit a cigarette and offered him the pack. "Well," he said. "What about it?"

"What about what?" answered the soldier.

He was obviously not going to be co-operative. "Suppose you tell me what you're doing here," said Peter.

"I'll give you three guesses, Captain."

The soldier reeked of whisky, and his whole attitude suggested that if the Captain wanted to get tough, that was all right with him.

"Do you know who this woman is?" Peter asked.

"Her name is Argonaut. So what?"

"How long have you known her?"

"Listen, Captain," the soldier said truculently. "All that is none of your business. I know, non-fraternization and all that crap. But I really go for this dame, see? I'll pay my sixty-five bucks, or you can throw me in the can for a couple of weeks, for all I care. But I'm not going to sit here and answer a lot of damn fool questions." He stood up. "My name is Gerald W. Mackey, and my outfit is the 601st Anti-Aircraft Battalion. And that's all."

Peter stood up and began pacing up and down the room.

"I didn't come here to pry into your love life, Sergeant," he said slowly. "For all I care you can sleep with this Argonaut woman from now until you go home."

"Aren't you an MP?" the soldier asked.

"No, I'm not an MP. What I want to know is, have you any idea who this woman's husband is?"

"Some German soldier or other."

"Do you know why this woman is sleeping with you?"

"Hell, all German women sleep with American soldiers."

Peter paused in his pacing. The sergeant's answer, he could not tell why, sent a stab into his heart.

"Do you know that this woman's husband was a high-ranking SS officer?"

"So what?" asked the sergeant. It appeared to be his favorite expression.

"You don't seem to know what that means: a high-ranking SS officer. How long have you been overseas?"

"Three months."

"Have you ever heard of the SS? Do you know what the SS did?"

"They were against the Jews, I suppose."

"And that's all you know about it?"

"What do I care about the SS?" said the sergeant irritably. "I sleep with the woman because I'm nuts about her. That's all there's to it."

"Are you married?"

The soldier did not reply at once. He finally said, "That's none of your business either."

Peter sat down, crossed his legs, and said nothing for a while. Then he began in a conversational tone, "Sergeant Mackey, I'll talk reasonably with you. I've already said I'm no MP and as far as I'm concerned you can bat around with German women as much as you like. But this case is a little different. You're badly mistaken if you think you can get away with this one for a sixty-five-dollar fine or a few weeks in the guardhouse. You're apt to find yourself in a particularly tough spot if you decide that you don't want to talk. I'm not trying to scare you. I'm just trying to make you understand that you've got to stop acting like a damn fool kid. I haven't any time to waste. When and where did you meet this Argonaut woman?"

"At the end of May, here in town."

"Did she invite you to her home soon afterward?"

"Yeah. So what?"

"You knew you weren't supposed to consort with German women. Why did you do it?"

"I'm not made of wood, am I?"

"Sergeant Mackey," Peter said amiably, "I was born in Europe. I know something about German women. Are you sure this woman isn't putting something over on you? Are you sure she isn't just using you?"

Peter seemed to have struck a responsive chord. The soldier leaned forward, and there was urgency in his voice when he spoke. "Yeah. She never asked me for a thing. You know yourself how most of these *Fräuleins* are. Chocolate and cigarettes. You can even have them for Kleenex. But Grete is different. She never took a thing from me. When I brought my rations here she cooked them up for me and insisted that I eat them alone. When I came here evenings, she'd have a bath ready for me. She'd put out my slippers, right here by the footstool. Captain, I'm telling you, I didn't know there were women like that."

"Weren't you happy with your wife, Sergeant?"

"In a way, I guess. But this is something different."

"How different?"

"I was a goddam fool, Captain. I only got wise to myself over here. I always thought that a man had to help his wife around the house, wash the dishes, take his mother-in-law automobile riding on Sundays, and push a chair under his wife's fanny whenever she wanted to sit down. I thought the husband had to hang up the curtains in the house, and there was hell to pay if I slept late

Sundays instead of getting up to cut the grass or shovel snow off the sidewalk. And when we came home from a party my wife was always tired and wanted to go right to sleep, instead of—you know what I mean. Grete won't let me raise a finger around the house. That's a woman's business, she says. When I have my day off she even brings me breakfast in bed! A couple of times I got off duty at two A.M. and came here. She got up and made me coffee. And she was never too tired either." He looked pointedly at the Captain and grinned in a way that left no doubt as to what he had in mind. "Grete is okay," he said.

Peter went to the window and opened it. "Didn't she ever say where her husband was?"

The soldier pretended he hadn't heard the question. Peter turned around. "Look here, Mackey. The SS is a criminal outfit. Your girl friend's husband is a major criminal. If we find him we'll most likely hang him. Where is he?"

The soldier stood up. For a moment he stood there in silence, then he spoke rapidly, as if what he was saying was distasteful to him. "I can tell you where he is, if you promise that nothing will happen to Grete."

"I'll do my best."

"He's hiding in an insane asylum."

"Where's the asylum?"

"About sixty miles from here."

"Were you ever there?"

"Yes," Mackey replied. "I went there twice. I took some papers to him."

Peter called Frau Argonaut. She had gotten dressed and combed her hair. She looked younger; her greenish eyes regarded Peter with frank malice. She gave Mackey a questioning look. Had he talked? Peter stood alertly between them. He said he would take the soldier back to his billet.

"And you," he said to the woman, "will not leave the house until further notice. The house is being watched."

She made no reply, but when the men moved to the door she accompanied them. In the doorway she touched the soldier's arm. "Take care," she said. "It's getting chilly out. Don't catch cold."

THE first prisoner died on the evening of August 30. On September 2 and 3 two other deaths occurred. Corporal Heinrich Schur, the first to die, was a man who had kept pretty much to himself, taciturn, steady, and without known enemies. Nevertheless, he had been murdered. The second victim, Karl Weiss, a corporal, had described himself as a Communist and deserter. It did not appear that he had taken part in any political agitation in the camp. Nor was there anything about his personality that offered any clues in the investigation.

The only one of the three whom Stroud could call to mind was Sergeant Eberhard Helletsberger, a merchant from Westphalia who spoke fluent English and was known as an anti-Nazi. Stroud had first used him as an interpreter, and later Helletsberger had worked on the camp newspaper. Nothing extraordinary had occurred in Helletsberger's life in camp until the third of September, when he reported to the hospital with violent stomach cramps, expressing the fear that he had been poisoned. He died in excruciating agony an hour later. An autopsy established the fact that he had died of arsenic poisoning.

The only known facts that gave any direction to the investigation were that all three of the prisoners ate in Mess Hall 4, and all had evidently been poisoned at breakfast. But no trace of the poison was found in Kitchen 4 or in any of the barracks. No other prisoners had been affected, which eliminated the possibility of an accidental or deliberate mass poisoning by a random distribution of arsenic in the food. The three victims had obviously been singled out for death.

The first break in the case came when Master Sergeant Parker pushed his considerable bulk through the doorway of Stroud's office and, instead of standing there and delivering his message, as he usually did, waddled up to the Major's desk.

"Major," he said quietly, "I think we've got something. The guard just off duty on Compound 12 reports that a PW came up to him as he was leaving and slipped him this note."

Parker laid a piece of folded paper addressed to Stroud on the desk. It read:

Can give you important information but am being watched. Have me called to your office on some plausible pretense. Corporal Paul Langhoff, No. 7821-D.

Stroud sat thinking for several minutes. "Did we find more letters hidden in the prisoner packages in today's mail?" he asked.

"As usual," Parker answered. "I've got four of them on my desk."

"Good. Call those four men into your office, and this Langhoff with them. See that as many people as possible know that we've found more forbidden letters in packages from relatives. Dispose of the four men one at a time, and take Langhoff as the last one. When you've got him in your office alone, send him in to me."

"Right, Major."

Stroud immediately recognized the man who entered his office an hour later. He was the little prisoner with the tired, red-rimmed eyes whom he had singled out as an ally during his questioning of the librarian in the book-burning affair. The prisoner's oversized uniform hung limply from his meager shoulders, like a suit on a clothes hanger.

"Sit down, Corporal Langhoff," said the Major. "We're more or less acquainted. I saw you recently in the library."

"That's right, sir," Langhoff replied.

He looked slowly around the room. He seemed to be listening for something.

"You can talk without fear, Corporal," said Stroud. "Nobody will hear what you say but me."

"I have come because I know something about the murders, Herr Major," he said.

Stroud decided not to launch too abruptly into his interrogation. "Have a cigarette," he said. "Suppose you begin by telling me something about yourself."

The prisoner lit his cigarette and inhaled greedily. "I was a high-school teacher," he began. "I was active in the Social Democrat movement. When Hitler came to power in 1933 I organized a resistance group. They uncovered us in 1935, and I was sent to a concentration camp. I was released in 1939, but they marked me 'unworthy to serve in the armed forces.' I worked in a brick yard and a leather factory. When they began drafting everybody they could get hold of in 1943, I was called up too. The first chance that came along, I deserted."

He spoke hurriedly, in short, direct sentences, like a man who has no time to lose. Stroud remembered the gleam of amusement and derision that had brightened the man's tired eyes that day in the library. The gleam was gone now. There was nothing in his eyes but fear.

"What do you know about the three deaths, Langhoff?" the Major asked.

The prisoner dropped his voice. "Not a great deal," he said. "I just know that all of these men were friends of mine, and that I'm going to be next."

"You'll have to explain that more fully, Corporal."

"A few of us decided to help the Americans. Not because we love Americans, but because we believe in a new Germany. Schur and Weiss and Helletsberger were in this group."

"What do you call 'helping the Americans,' Langhoff?"

"I could give you plenty of examples. For instance, you organized a school here, Herr Major. But after a few weeks you turned it over to the prisoners to run themselves. The prisoner who taught history immediately began giving lectures on the significance of Frederick the Great. You gave the camp a newspaper, but there were no guards in the print shop. So right away, along with the newspaper, they began printing pictures of Hitler for distribution among the prisoners. You allowed gifts from the German Red Cross to be given out. You also put a prisoner in charge of that. Only reliable party members ever received any of those Red Cross parcels. We set ourselves to oppose all that. We protested in the history lessons. We tore up the Hitler pictures. We threatened to make a scandal out of the Red Cross affair."

"Very good, Langhoff. But you were helping yourselves, not us."

"Yes, we were helping you too. The Americans want to prove that it is possible to work together with the Germans so they can send their soldiers home sooner."

Stroud pondered. "What I don't understand," he said, "is why you've kept silent until now. Why didn't you report those incidents?"

The prisoner gave a little sigh, like a man who feels that he is not being understood. "I'm no informer, Herr Major," he said. "We tried to organize resistance to the Nazis here on our own, those of us who were active in underground movements before. We'll have to continue underground work if we're to accomplish anything."

"That's obviously not so," said Stroud, somewhat irritated. "You now have our support."

The prisoner lost the restraint with which he had begun the interview. "We don't have your support, Herr Major," he said. "The American idea of democracy is to find out what the majority wants and thinks. We regard that as a waste of time. We think the Americans shouldn't worry so much about the majority, but instead give all possible backing to the good Germans."

His voice had grown louder, but he lowered it suddenly as he concluded. He looked at the clock on the Major's desk and shifted uneasily in his chair. He took his glasses from his nose and began polishing them nervously. His hands were trembling. So it's as bad as that, Stroud thought. The man is terrified by the thought that he may be staying too long in the camp commander's office.

"But you don't really believe that these men were killed for the trivial reasons you have mentioned, do you?"

"Murders come easy to us, Herr Major," Langhoff answered. "Human life doesn't mean much to us."

"Then you can't have much real hope for your country, can you?"

"One always has hopes for one's fatherland, Herr Major. But democracy can't be delivered to a people like corned beef. You can't just pack it in cans in America and ship it for consumption over here. It has to grow out of our own soil."

"Can't we at least sow the seeds?"

"It's foreign seed you're trying to sow here, Herr Major."

Stroud was a lawyer by profession and versed in the methods of cross-examination. He said suddenly, without transition, "Who put the arsenic in the food?"

But he had underestimated his man. The tired little eyes betrayed nothing. "I don't know, Herr Major."

"You don't know, or you don't want to say—which?"

"I don't know, but I wouldn't tell you anyway. I came here merely to tell you what's going on in the camp and I've told you. If I'm found dead tomorrow morning you'll know why. But as long as I'm alive I'll try to handle the thing myself. This is a German matter."

"Does that mean you'll try to kill your enemies before they kill you?"

The prisoner shrugged his shoulders. "I believe in nonviolent methods," he said. "As long as possible."

"Do you eat in Mess Hall 4?"

"Yes."

"Aren't you afraid of continuing to eat there?"

"I'm not worried about the food. They know that's being watched now. They'll try other ways next time."

"I'm going to see to it that there'll be no next time," said Stroud.

There was doubt and a good deal of scorn in the prisoner's smile. He stood up and brought his heels sharply together. He stood for a moment at attention, and the sleeves of his coat slid down over his fingers. Then he about-faced stiffly and marched out of the room.

➳ 17 ⤆

PETER had been summoned to headquarters in Frankfurt to make a report on the recovery of the Hitler documents.

It was a strange establishment in which he had found the *Standartenführer* Argonaut. The clinic Dr. Wilhelm Leibl had operated for years under the Hitler regime had served as a kind of sieve for various extermination camps. Dr. Leibl experimented with a new method of electrical shock which he believed would cure certain forms of insanity. If his electric shock cured his patients, they were dismissed from his institution after a short stay. If the shock brought no improvement, an ambulance came and took them to Ohrdruf or Auschwitz, where they were put into chambers whose gases were far more effective than the electrical impulses of Dr. Leibl.

When the capitulation came Dr. Leibl's asylum served as a hideout for fleeing Nazi notables. It did not occur to the Allies, who regarded all Germany as a madhouse, to look for vanished pillars of National Socialism in an obscure little insane asylum. Ernst Argonaut was admitted to Dr. Leibl's sanctuary under the name of Ernst Müller. He announced loudly whenever anyone was within hearing that he was the emperor of China, and he took his meals in the doctor's villa, which was in a little wood near the asylum. The Hitler documents were found in this house, following Peter's interview with Sergeant Mackey in Frau Argonaut's living-room.

Peter was now staying at the Carlton, the officers' hotel in Frankfurt. He had made his report and planned to leave for Munich the following day. But the next morning Dirty Thompson was missing.

Peter had given Thompson the previous evening off and had instructed him to be ready to leave at six in the morning. When the command car did not appear before the hotel at six-thirty, Peter went to the garage to find out what was wrong. The car was in the garage, but there was no sign of Thompson. He had left the car there at seven o'clock the evening before and had not been seen since. Peter went to the billets of the enlisted men and found that Thompson had not reported there at all. Dirty Thompson had gone out into the night from the garage and had vanished. Peter decided to check informally with the MP's, and to conduct his own search if they knew nothing, so that he could save Thompson from a charge of being AWOL.

Nothing was known of T/5 Ralph Thompson at the MP station. No Ralph Thompson was listed at the local military hospitals. Peter returned to his hotel, hoping that meanwhile Thompson might have turned up there. Nobody at the hotel had seen him, but Peter ran into a soldier who was the driver for an OSS major and a pal of Thompson's of long standing.

"Have you seen Dirty around anywhere?" Peter asked.

The soldier grinned knowingly. He seemed disinclined to say much, but he finally admitted, "I saw him at midnight, Captain, but he was so stewed he didn't know if his name was Thompson or Greta Garbo." The driver had left Thompson at a disreputable

German café called the Blue Pearl, about two miles south of the city.

The Blue Pearl was empty when Peter entered it. The owner looked like a Neanderthal man who had just emerged from a barber shop. He claimed that he had seen nothing of an American soldier of Thompson's description and that, naturally, his place was not patronized by American soldiers at all.

Peter saw that he would get nowhere with polite inquiries. "Listen, you," he said. "I'm not from the Military Police. I'm looking for my driver who got drunk here last night. He was seen here at midnight. You know damn well you're not supposed to serve American soldiers, and besides that you're supposed to close at ten o'clock. I'll forget the whole thing if you co-operate, but if you try to hand me any more malarkey I'll have this joint shut up for keeps."

The ultimatum gave the pug-like proprietor pause. Peter offered him a cigarette. "I'll give you about thirty seconds to make up your mind," he said.

"Would the *Herr Hauptmann* perhaps care for a glass of *schnapps?*" the German asked.

Peter was getting annoyed. In his flawless German, which, coming from an American officer, added to the proprietor's confusion, he replied, "The *Herr Hauptmann* does not care for a glass of *schnapps*. But the *Herr Hauptmann* is going to be extremely unpleasant unless you start telling him what he wants to know, and damned quick."

This was the kind of talk that the host of the Blue Pearl understood. With frequent interruptions to explain his own innocence in the matter, he reported that a soldier answering Thompson's description had come into the café shortly after seven the night before and had ordered six or seven glasses of brandy in rapid succession. He then demanded a whole bottle. The host, assuming that the soldier intended to take the bottle away with him, sold him the brandy in the hopes of ridding his establishment of a drunk who might soon become troublesome. But the soldier insisted on emptying the bottle at his table. Meanwhile, other soldiers had come in, and the host asked them to persuade the solitary drinker to leave. Thompson brushed aside all efforts to lure him away and allowed nobody to join him at his table. Shortly after midnight, when his bottle was empty and all the other guests had gone, Thompson demanded female companionship. The host explained, so he said, that he was running a respectable place, but Thompson emphasized his demand by laying a revolver on the table.

"Did he pay for the brandy?" Peter interjected.

"Strangely enough, he did," the host answered with a shade of sarcasm in his voice.

Good for you, Thompson, thought Peter, whose sympathy for his wayward driver was mounting when military discipline required that he feel increasingly indignant. "Go on," he said to the host, "and don't cover up anything."

"Shortly after that," the man continued, "a girl just happened to come in. She visits one of my waitresses from time to time. The soldier finally went off with her, after forcing me to sell him another bottle of brandy. He could hardly stand up. I was glad to see him go, so I could close up the place."

Peter refrained from pointing out that the story of the girl who "just happened to come in" was a little thick. His concern was for something else. He changed his attitude. He pulled two packs of cigarettes out of his pockets and laid them on the bar. "For the address of the girl," he said, holding his hand over the cigarettes.

The Chesterfields worked their usual magic. The host hesitated, went into a back room to confer with his wife—"I have to see if my waitress knows the address," he said—and finally gave Peter a street number in Frankfurt. All he knew about the "friend of his waitress," he vowed, was that her name was Rosa.

Peter had trouble finding the address, and at first he feared that the host of the Blue Pearl had misled him. The house was not a house, but merely a façade. Its front door led from vacancy on one side to vacancy on the other. When Peter went through the door he found himself on a heap of bricks, mortar, broken furniture, and twisted stove pipes. Then he noticed that a narrow path led through the debris to a rear section of the house which was still standing, an oddly isolated survival amid the ruins.

Fräulein Rosa was the only inhabitant of the three-story remnant of the house. What was left of the structure was on the verge of collapse, and apparently no one else dared live in it. The windows were boarded up, and the rooms were littered with plaster fallen from the buckled ceilings. Ascending the wobbly stairs was like going up a mountain path which drops away on one side into nothingness. The only usable apartment left seemed to be hanging in the air.

A girl in a dirty Japanese kimono opened the door at Peter's knock. She was of indeterminate age and everything about her seemed to hang—her nightdress, her hair, her breasts, and even her gray, flabby skin. A cluster of gold teeth dominated her generous mouth.

To Peter's surprise, she admitted at once that there was an American soldier whose name she did not know sleeping in her apartment. In fact, it soon appeared that she was greatly relieved that someone was going to take him off her hands. She told Peter that she had managed to get Thompson, protected by the god of drunks, up the wavering stairs and into her room, where he had insisted on drinking another half bottle of brandy. He had then vomited repeatedly and fallen into the bed. She had not been able to rouse him since.

The air in the miserable room was unbearable. It reeked of unaired bed linen, remnants of food, alcohol, and vomit. Thick dust lay on the scanty furniture. In the high, brown bed, over which hung cheap religious prints, lay Dirty Thompson, snoring. There was nothing restful about Thompson's snores; they did not come from healthy sleep. It was as if his dreams were tormenting him and he were trying, like a snarling dog, to drive them away.

"Open a window," said Peter.

Without saying anything the girl indicated the only window in the room. It was boarded up. Peter began pounding on the boards to knock them loose. They splintered. The girl protested loudly.

"I'll see that your wood is replaced," Peter told her. He managed to remove two of the boards, and the glaring light of midday flooded into the room. It played over the pasty, swollen face of the man on the bed. Under his puffy eyelids there was a slight movement. The rattling and rasping in his throat grew louder.

"Help me get his shoes off," Peter ordered.

The girl obediently set to work. The laces were loosened, and the heavy army boots thudded to the floor.

"Get some water," said Peter.

The woman left the room and returned shortly with a pot full of water. She did what she was told eagerly and quickly.

Peter dipped a handkerchief into the water and began to bathe Thompson's brow and temples with the wet cloth. Thompson groaned. Peter put the pot next to the bed, handed the cloth to the woman, and said, "Keep on."

He began undressing Thompson. He loosened his tie and opened his collar. Thompson's dirty neck did not now remind Peter of the countless times he had made cutting remarks about his driver's aversion to water. The veins in the neck stood out, and it was impossible to tell the streaks of dirt from the thick blue veins. What had happened to the guy? Peter wondered. He strained to lift the heavy body so as to be able to pull the pants down over hips and thighs. The girl was meanwhile dipping the handkerchief repeatedly into the water, wringing it out, and then passing it with short, almost tender strokes over Thompson's face.

Peter tried to arouse him with sharp little slaps. He himself felt a little benumbed from the odor in the room. The warm summer air that came through the window at first tended to strengthen the stink. The long-dormant dust swirled up through the room and clogged the air.

While Peter struggled to get Thompson's shirt off, a letter fell out of one of the pockets. Peter did not know afterward why he decided to read the letter immediately. Maybe it was because a penetrating reek of cheap perfume came from the bright blue envelope, or maybe because of habit acquired in secret service work. At any rate, he knew at once that the key to Thompson's behavior was in the letter.

"Go downstairs to my car," he said to the girl. "There's a musette bag on the seat. Please bring it up."

He sat in the creaking plush easy chair with its dirty lace antimacassar, like those formerly seen in first-class railway compartments. The letter was written in a large crude hand. It read:

Dear Ralph,

I'm sorry I have to write you this letter, but it isn't easy for me either. But I think it is the right thing to do to tell you that I want a divorce before you hear about it from somebody else.

When we got married I thought everything would be all right and we would be happy together. Well, I can't really blame you Ralph be-

cause you always took good care of me. The first year you were away it
was not so bad even if it wasn't so easy on me. But then I met this
man at the factory and right away I knew, this is it. I did not want to
write to you about it right away but now you say you might be coming
home soon and I don't want you to be disappointed when you get here.

Dear Ralph, I guess you will not want to live in Chicago when you
get back so I talked to your Mom on the telephone and if you want I
can send your belongings to Cleveland next week. Norah is driving to
Cleveland next week anyway. It is too bad you gave away your civilian
clothes because they are hard to get now. The kitchen things belong to
you too but your Mom has got her own, hasn't she? Write to me if
you will sell them to me. Especially iceboxes are impossible to get now.

I have not said nothing to the Prizodas and the Whites yet, they'll
find out soon enough and will make a lot of gossip and scandal out of
it. You know how they are. I am glad now Ralph that I never wanted a
baby, you always wanted one but now you see I was right after all.
Please do not be too mad at me, you know you always said you wanted
I should be happy. That is why I am sure you won't be mad at me and
you will soon forget all about me.

Your Doris

PS Please write me and tell me what happens about the allotment.
Doris

Peter looked up. The woman had come back and was standing
silently before him, the musette bag in her hand. "There's a bottle
of rubbing alcohol in it," he said.

She took the bottle out and began to use it with the assurance
and efficiency of a nurse, pouring drops of the alcohol on the handkerchief, rubbing it on Thompson's temples, holding the bottle
under his nose from time to time.

"He's coming to," she said.

"Yes," said Peter. "He'll be awake in a minute."

He poured some of the alcohol on the palm of his hand and
rubbed Thompson's chest with it.

"Maybe you could hold him up while I rub his back," the girl
said.

Peter watched her as she busied herself with Thompson's back.
He noticed that she had deep, almond-shaped eyes. In the sunlight
she looked older but somehow less repulsive than she had in the
semidarkness.

"Did he talk to you at all?" he asked.

"Very little. He was too drunk." She was rubbing Thompson's back with firm, steady strokes. "But don't do anything to the poor fellow," she urged. "He must be terribly unhappy."

"How do you know?"

She shrugged. "Men who come to us drunk are usually unhappy."

"Do many soldiers come to you drunk?"

"Yes. Many soldiers are unhappy."

Peter wanted another handkerchief with which to rub Thompson's stomach. He looked in Thompson's pants for one. Out of the pockets fell keys, a K-ration can opener, a squashed pack of cigarettes, and a crumpled wad of money. She has taken nothing from him, Peter thought.

Thompson had ceased making rasping noises. He was breathing through his open mouth, heavily and with effort, but the raucous snoring had stopped. He opened his eyes and looked around in bewilderment. He yawned. He stared fixedly at the ceiling, but seemed to see nothing.

"Hello, Thompson," said Peter.

There was no reaction. Peter took the round head with its GI haircut in his hands, and looked directly into Thompson's eyes as he lifted the head slightly from the pillow.

"Hello, Thompson," he repeated.

"Hello, Captain," said Thompson. His gaze was dull and clouded, and his voice weak.

"How do you feel?" Peter asked.

Thompson stared at him stupidly. Movement came back to his eyes, and they fell on the girl. "Where am I?" he said. He reached for his head. "I got a headache, Captain." It sounded like the complaint of a small boy.

It took almost two hours before Thompson was completely himself again. Once he began to recuperate, his recovery was rapid. He was able to dress himself, and even expressed a desire to wash.

After giving the woman money, cigarettes, and an authorization for wood, Peter took Thompson to his hotel room. There he gave him aspirin, made him lie down under protest for further rest on the couch, and set about cooking him an omelet of powdered eggs on a spirit lamp.

"I been actin' like a pig, Captain," said Dirty Thompson.

"Everybody does once in a while."

"But you ought to be on the way to Munich."

"We'll leave early tomorrow."

They were silent.

"What was eating you, Thompson?" Peter asked cautiously. He thought, unhappy people are hard to deal with. Some find relief by talking, but it makes others feel worse than ever. Hardest of all are robust characters like Thompson who don't know what it means to be unhappy. Unhappiness takes training too.

"My wife's been unfaithful, Captain," said Thompson. "She's divorcin' me."

Peter's back was turned to the couch, but he knew that Thompson was taking out the letter.

"I've read the letter," Peter said.

Thompson did not seem to be surprised. "What'll I do, Captain?"

"Do you love her?"

"I don't know."

"Could you forgive her?"

"Maybe, if she'd ask me. But I'd murder the guy. I don't know who he is. I don't know anybody at the factory where she works."

Peter brought him the omelet. Thompson insisted on getting up and eating it at the table. He took pains to walk steadily.

"You got another aspirin, Captain?"

"Later. Eat first." He poured a small glass of cognac. "Drink that. A hair of the dog."

Thompson ate hungrily.

"We were married four years," he said abruptly. "Two years of that I was overseas." It sounded like an apology. "She's a good girl, Captain. I knew her when she was seven and I was nine. Then I moved away and didn't see her for a long time, until we were both grown up. And then I married her. We were awful happy. I was, anyway." He took a little swallow of the cognac. "I should never of gotten drunk," he said.

Peter stretched himself on the couch. He was tired. He did not know what made him ask, "And what about you, Thompson? Were you always faithful?"

"No. Not since I came over here. But I only went to bed with whores. That don't count."

"Why not?"

Thompson looked at the Captain in surprise. "Why, it don't mean anything. Anyway, the girls over here don't count. I would never have given up Doris. She was a good kid. Sweet and clean, and wonderful around the house. You can tell that from her letter, the way she worries about the kitchen stuff. Goddam it, it's all my fault!"

"Your fault?"

Thompson tried to smile. His mouth slipped sideways like a badly knotted tie. "You know how I am for looks, Captain. She never enjoyed goin' out with me much. When we went to the movies she always made like we wasn't really together. And then I worked too hard, Captain. I'd come home pooped every night. Drivin' a taxi in Chicago—that ain't like drivin' along one of these highways over here. The traffic is tough, the passengers drive you nuts, and the competition's somethin' fierce. I was good and tired nights, and when I got home I'd read the funnies, see how the Cubs were doin', and go to bed. Then come the war and I had to leave."

"You certainly couldn't help that, Thompson."

"Makes no difference. I was gone, and the other guy was there. Naturally, he took her out, and maybe she was proud bein' seen with him. I know Doris, Captain. It wasn't her fault."

"Would you like to go home, Thompson? You've got enough points. Almost eighty, isn't it? It could be fixed up pretty easily."

Thompson shook his head. "No," he said. "Where would I go? I don't feel like goin' to live with Mom in Cleveland. I ain't been to Cleveland in years." He stopped talking and stared vacantly. "If I went to Chi all my stuff would be gone. And if I saw the two of them together, Captain, I'd murder the guy. That's for sure."

"Killing people doesn't get you anywhere," Peter said.

Thompson did not answer. He went with his heavy, shambling tread to the window and looked out. "It'll rain tomorrow," he said. "I'm sorry we didn't get off today, Captain."

18

Paul Langhoff was not, as he feared, the next victim in PW Camp Special B. Six days after the third victim of arsenic poisoning had died, thirty-six-year-old Private Helmuth Gerecke was found dead near one of the latrines. He had been stabbed from behind with a knife about six inches long.

Prisoners had been forbidden to leave the barracks at night without permission. If they had to go to the latrine they were supposed to approach the guard, who paced back and forth between the barracks, and ask permission. Gerecke, whose bed was in Barracks 2, had done this. But shortly after the murder became known, the guard assigned to the area between Barracks 2 and the near-by Barracks 3 made a significant report: on the night of the murder another prisoner had left Barracks 2, without asking permission. He had apparently chosen a time when the guard, leaving Barracks 2, was walking off in the direction of Barracks 3. The prisoner would have succeeded in returning unobserved to his bed if the guard had not happened to hear a suspicious noise in the vicinity of Barracks 2; he returned ahead of time without completing his patrol to Barracks 3 and caught the prisoner slinking along the wall toward the barracks door. Asked to account for himself, the prisoner said he had been seized with violent cramps and had no time to wait for the guard's return before going to the latrine. Such excuses were not unusual, but the guard had taken down the prisoner's name anyway.

He was a tall, gaunt man named Emil Teitinger, whose flesh was drawn tautly over his angular face, like papyrus stretched over a death's-head. Stroud had Teitinger brought to the office. Pretending to be absorbed in some papers on his desk, Stroud let the suspect stand for several minutes without paying any attention to him. Then he looked up. They were alone in the room.

"Well," said Stroud. "Do you want to make a confession?"

The prisoner said nothing.

"Very well," said Stroud. "You want to make things difficult for yourself. Tell me, Teitinger, how long have you known Private Gerecke?"

"Not long. A few days, I guess."

"Did you have much to do with him?"

"No."

"Were you a party member, Teitinger?"

"Since 1934."

"Why did you become a National Socialist?"

"Because I believed in the Führer."

"Do you still believe in the Führer?"

"Yes."

Stroud riffled through the papers on his desk. "Would you care to tell me what happened that night?" When the prisoner did not reply, Stroud continued, "I want to know about your leaving your barracks without permission."

"Nothing special happened," the prisoner replied. "I had a stomach-ache. Cramps. I couldn't find the guard right away and went to the latrine. As I was returning the guard stopped and questioned me."

"Did you notice that Gerecke had left the barracks shortly before?"

"No."

"How many beds are there between yours and Gerecke's?"

"Three or four."

"How long was it between the time Gerecke left the barracks and the time you got up to go to the latrine?"

The prisoner did not fall into the trap. "I don't know," he said. "I didn't see or hear Gerecke leave."

Stroud took another tack. "Why didn't you ask the guard for permission? I mean, why didn't you wait the few minutes it would take him to return?"

"I had violent cramps."

"Hmm. How long had the cramps been going on before you decided you couldn't stand it any more and had to go to the latrine?"

"I don't know for sure. Maybe ten minutes."

The byplay between the two began to stimulate Stroud. It reminded him of his legal duels in the courtrooms of Spokane. Suddenly he asked, "Are you hard of hearing, Teitinger?"

The question came as a surprise. "No, sir," said the prisoner.

"You've put your foot in it, Teitinger," Stroud said. "You just told me that you had cramps for about ten minutes before you got up. So you were awake. Do you mean to tell me that you didn't hear a man getting out of bed a few feet away from you? The guard comes back to your barracks every four minutes. So you left your barracks not more than three minutes after Gerecke."

For the first time the dark eyes of the prisoner wavered. They were eyes in which it was hard to read anything, for the black of the pupils seemed to run together with the brown of the iris. But Stroud had seen fear in too many eyes not to recognize it. When people were afraid it was as if they saw something not visible to others. Stroud knew that the time had come to make a decisive thrust.

"All right, Teitinger," he said, standing up. "Do you want to tell me where you got the dagger with which you stabbed Gerecke to death in the latrine?"

"I didn't stab Gerecke."

But Stroud felt that he had won the first round. The prisoner's voice had wavered. It was the hoarse voice of a desperate man whose life is at stake. Now, thought Stroud, the thing is to smooth the way for a confession. Pacing up and down, he said, "Listen, Teitinger. We know well enough that you are not the instigator or the leader of the conspiracy behind these killings. You're only a tool. Your one hope lies in a full confession. Who ordered you to kill Gerecke?"

"No one. I didn't kill him."

There was a sharp knock on the door. Stroud turned in annoyance. He had given orders that he was not to be disturbed for any reason during his examination of Teitinger. The door opened and Parker walked in. With a gesture of apology, but also with a triumphant smile, Parker handed the Major a note and a dagger with the handle wrapped in a clean handkerchief. It had been found a few minutes before in a refuse barrel that stood between Barracks 2 and the latrine. The prisoner, standing with his back to the door and to Stroud, could not see what was going on.

Stroud decided to bluff. After the door had closed again, he remained standing behind the prisoner. With no change from his previous tone he said, "Did you own a dagger, Teitinger?"

"No, sir."

"Never?"

"Not since I was made prisoner. Everything was taken from us."

"You had no dagger with you when you went to the latrine that night?"

"No, sir."

Stroud paused to heighten the effect of what he was about to say. Then he rapped out, "How does it happen, then, that your fingerprints were found on the murder weapon?"

There was total silence in the room. It was as if ice water were trickling from the walls. Stroud, observing the man from the rear, felt rather than saw how the long, bony neck of the prisoner stiffened. The muscles on his hairless neck tightened. They twitched as if the man wanted to turn around to fend off an attack. But he did not dare.

Still standing behind the prisoner, Stroud said, "Come, Teitinger. Speak up!"

This time there was no defense. Only silence. Stroud went around the prisoner to confront him face to face. Somewhere in the back of his brain flashed the questions: Since when have I learned to hate? Since when have I become a prosecutor instead of a defender? He stood now before Teitinger, who seemed to have become more rigid than ever. The dagger was in Stroud's right hand.

"Where did you get this weapon, Teitinger?"

The whole body of the prisoner jerked. His hands—long, big-knuckled, and thin, almost like a skeleton's—shook, and he could not suppress their trembling. He pressed his bloodless lips together as if forbidding them to speak. Murderers are all the same, Stroud thought. They have less fear of conscience than of the weapon that calls their deed to mind. A weapon, unlike a conscience, cannot be soothed, pacified, silenced.

"Who gave you this dagger, Teitinger?"

The narrow lips remained closed. The Major was a head shorter than the prisoner, but the German seemed to be sinking into himself. The head sagged between the high, pointed shoulders.

"Speak up!" Stroud ordered. "It's no use trying to lie. We've got your fingerprints."

"I didn't do it!" Teitinger cried desperately. "I didn't do it!"

Stroud now had the feeling that it was not so simple to explain the terror of the prisoner. The man was not only afraid because he had committed a murder. He was afraid of something else too, something that Stroud could not immediately grasp. But the Major was not given time to consider what method to try next to evoke a confession.

For the second time Parker disregarded the order not to come into the room. He went up to Stroud and whispered in his ear, "General Lowell has just arrived."

Stroud broke off his examination and had the prisoner led away. As soon as Teitinger left, the Major went to greet his guest.

"Hello, John," said the General, extending his hand.

"Hello, Joe."

"I was in Munich," said the General, sitting down, "so I thought I'd drop by and see you."

It was supposed to sound offhand, but Stroud knew that the visit was far from casual. The General, too, dropped the pretense and came to the point. "How's the investigation coming, John?"

"I think we're finally on the right track. The man they just took out of here is the one who committed the last murder."

"Has he confessed?"

"Not yet."

The General got up and began walking up and down.

"John," he said, "I don't know whether you realize how serious this situation is. We've got to clear it up, and soon. The press is beginning to show an uncomfortable interest in what's going on here. We simply can't afford any publicity for this camp of yours."

"Why not?"

"Because we didn't ask permission of the War Department to set up this kind of camp in the first place. It was my idea and I proceeded without specific authority. I'm not so sure now that it was a good idea."

Small and shrunken, the General went up and down the room with quick, agitated steps. In breeches and riding boots, the gray little man gave the effect of a mouse in uniform. He was pale, and he looked a good deal older than when Stroud had last seen him. The Major thought involuntarily of the fear shown by the prisoner who had been in the room a moment before. Stroud asked himself, is everybody afraid of something? But what he asked the General was, "Have we got anything to hide?"

"The public doesn't like the idea of murders being committed in our camps."

"I don't like the idea either," Stroud said. "But this camp is supposed to resemble a typical German community. In a German community murders are sometimes committed."

"Maybe so. But the public insists on order. People back home demand that our Army be able to maintain order."

"Hitler kept order too. Order is something completely negative."

The General stood still. "My God," he said, "you talk like an anarchist."

"Not at all. I believe that order is necessary, of course. But it's not a be-all and end-all. When somebody talks about order as his sole objective, then he hasn't anything else to offer."

"That may be true, John. But we live in a democracy. We've got to take the public into account."

The Major tried to check himself, but it slipped out. "What are we—soldiers or movie actors?"

"For the public there's not much of a distinction. The American public doesn't want any complicated answers. We want either to damn our enemies to hell or forgive them everything. Trying to understand them is too much trouble." The General's pacing brought him to the door. "I'd like to take a look at your camp, John," he said.

They went through camp followed by a retinue of officers. Sudden, unannounced inspections were rare and against Army custom. The General seemed favorably impressed by the cleanliness of the barracks, the sanitary arrangements, the kitchens, the modern equipment in the hospital, and the neatness of the prisoners themselves. Then he abruptly requested to see all the latrines, the enclosed ones as well as the open, and especially the latrine where the murder had occurred. He remained standing at that latrine, looked around, and muttered to himself. Stroud knew at once that something had put him into a dangerous mood. Not until they were alone again in Stroud's office did the General say anything.

"The camp is in good order on the whole," he said, by way of introduction. But he was now no longer Stroud's personal friend; he was Stroud's superior officer. "Nevertheless, my fears have been confirmed. I found just what I thought I would find."

"What do you mean?"

"The regulations specifically state that on all corners of the prison area, guard towers are to be erected and equipped with searchlights." He sounded like a talking manual. "After dark these searchlights are to sweep the camp area at regular intervals throughout the night. If these regulations had not been disregarded, the most recent murder could not have been committed."

The Major felt like a schoolboy being rebuked by his teacher. But he was an old soldier, and he knew that soldiering meant reverting to the status of a schoolboy. He said, "I am aware of the regulations you mention, General. I considered installing the towers and searchlights and decided against it."

"With what justification?"

"The basic idea behind the establishment of this camp was that these men were to be given, as far as possible, the illusion of freedom. Human beings cannot react and behave like free men when all day long the barrels of machine guns are pointed at them, and when all night long searchlights shine through their windows."

"Your so-called free men poison and stab each other."

"Other free people do those things too, you know." Stroud refrained from mentioning that the General had promised him a free hand to run the camp as he saw fit. The Major knew that in the Army one is given a free hand to bring glory to one's superior not to create difficulties for him.

"I don't want freedom to be interpreted in that way," the General said. "The guard towers are to be erected at once. They are to be constantly manned and equipped with searchlights."

"Yes, sir."

General Lowell got up and prepared to leave. At the last minute he hesitated and offered his hand to Stroud. "I'd like to have a report on the investigation by tomorrow noon," he said. "And I'd like to have that confession tomorrow too."

Stroud saluted. The General left the room so rapidly that Stroud could not accompany him. Left alone, he sank back into his chair. On his desk was a sheet of white stationery. He took up his pen. Pictures came tumbling into his mind, one after the other, one crowding the other: the prisoner Teitinger . . . guard towers . . . arsenic sprinkled on food . . . Eleanor wearing orchids . . . Wanda . . . the SS camp . . . searchlights . . . a dagger . . . Spokane . . . and again Wanda.

He put down his pen. No, he thought, I did not desert during the war. One does not desert in peacetime either.

19

T HE summer night poured in through the open window.

"Are you sleeping?" Peter whispered.

"No. I can't sleep, darling. I've been lying still so as not to wake you."

"Shall I draw the curtains?"

"No," she replied. "It's good that I can't sleep. I can feel you near me."

His arm was beneath her. Now she turned toward him. In their every movement was the great, silent affirmation of their bodies, the yearning that is never stilled, the fulfillment that signifies a new beginning. There was never any struggle between them; they conquered each other without having fought. There was no need for one to overcome the reticence of the other; where something still restrained them, it was the same restraint—and together they overcame it. Neither dominated the other; in the triumphs of their bodies, each was the victor and neither suffered defeat.

"I love you," he said. "Do I say it too often?"

"No. Not often enough."

Her knee touched his knee, her hands his chest, his hands her breasts. The way they invariably answered a caress with an identical caress was like a strange, mute agreement of which they themselves were not aware. What prompted them was not mere lust, but a selfless impulse in each to make the other happy. When he felt the tenderness of her hand upon his body, he laid his hand tenderly upon her body. In the rich reciprocity of their lovemaking, each wanted to be the bestower. And because both wished to be givers, both became recipients.

They seemed to retain no memories of what had occurred between them twelve years ago. The past flickered up in their conversations and in some of their emotions for each other, but from their bodily love there remained no recollection of gestures, touchings, and whispered words. Everything was young, new, and fresh. He kissed her throat with closed lips, almost shyly. Every approach had, for them both, the quality of the first approach. It was only the supplicating kiss itself that they felt, not the nakedness of their bodies. But at the same time they celebrated over and over again the thousandfold feast of recognition, the joyous assurance of a familiar bygone melody that swells up anew.

In the whole gamut of their lovemaking, neither could say which one was the challenger and which took up the challenge. When his head lay upon her breasts, her lips went lightly over his ear, and when he kissed the little hollow inside her elbow, her fingers softly stroked his back. In the web of their love play there were no individual strands; only threads woven together into a completed pattern.

Without realizing it they came to scorn the uncertainty they had always regarded as essential to the excitement of love. This was perhaps the loveliest, the most breathtaking discovery of their being together: that the certainty of what would happen took nothing from the joy of what did happen. She knew how he would respond when she let her little finger glide back and forth between his teeth; he knew that her knees would open to the slightest pressure of his hand. They no longer understood why resistance had once seemed enticing—now an unsuspected delight flowed out of submission without resistance.

They did not seek to discover and did not want to discover the secret of their love. Otherwise they would have known that their utter unrestraint, the mingled tenderness and wildness of their passion, the purity at the core of their shamelessness, the solicitude for one another simultaneous with losing themselves in the enjoyment of each other, was as simple as the day: the love of their bodies was indivisible from the love of the hearts which pulsed inside their bodies. That was the great, incessantly rejuvenating interplay of their relationship—that their everyday talk and the serene association of their days was crowned and climaxed in the night, and that the singing harmony of their nights merged imperceptibly with the commonplaces of their talk and feelings of the morning. There were for them no days and nights: only hours that flowed together.

In the ultimate union of their joined bodies he would bury his face between her neck and shoulder and kiss the soft little hollow formed by her collarbone.

Then it was as if they were no longer in possession of their own bodies. She no longer knew where her body ceased, and he no longer knew where his began. They no longer had any awareness of merging into each other; they lost their sense of exultation in each other. Nothing remained but total oneness. They sometimes experienced an almost painful sensation of being one whole, the two parts of which had been forcibly torn asunder. Over and over again the two parts strained to come together and complete the whole. In every fulfillment an impulse toward renewal, in every ebbing of emotion a new desire for the flood, in every exhaustion a new yearning.

But their tenderest words were spoken as they lay side by side in the sweet weariness of completion. Then each felt a need to thank the other. Sometimes there were eager, rushing words, whispered admissions and confessions; sometimes she lay on his arm and sang, and he, hesitantly and softly as if not to disturb her, joined in her melody. Sometimes there was only silence, and the soundless room was filled with the delicate texture of their gratitude for each other.

He propped his head on his hand, looked at her, and said, "So there you are and I've found you again. I look at you and I know what you are to me. The fragrance of the earth, after a rain in summer, with the pebbles crunching under our feet. An evening in spring that dies slowly, with the shadows gradually robbing the sky of its light. A garden at night on which the fallen chestnut blossoms form a glowing carpet of white. The soft splashing of waves on the shore of a lake, with boats rolling gently while the rowers ship their oars. A winter's night somewhere in eastern Europe, when one goes home through deep, firm snow, full of the majestic sound of a marvelously played symphony."

She opened her eyes and smiled, and because she was a woman she asked, "That's all Europe. Am I only a kind of homecoming to you?"

He smiled too. "Only?" he asked. "And what if that were true? Do you know what that means? A woman who speaks your language? I don't mean German or English or Greek or Hindustani. But a woman who understands you in half-completed sentences. You mention the name of a city, and she knows the smell of its harbor when the fishermen are unloading the day's catch. You speak of a museum, and she knows where the Breughels hang, in a dim hall with red plush sofas. You mention a favorite dish, and the next day, there it is on the table, and it tastes exactly the way you remember it from when you were a boy at home. When you get angry and say cruel words to her, she smiles because she knows that somebody hurt you when you were a child. You make a joke, and it reminds her of another. You quote a few lines of poetry, and she finishes the verse. She may like your friends and she may not, but she understands that you have to see them because together you once put a torpedo under a professor's chair. She doesn't take fright when you do something unusual; she waits when you go away; she asks no questions; and she never takes you quite seriously. And she doesn't think you have to be a man all the time, because she knows you were once a boy."

A cooler breath of air came through the window. She pulled the covers over his back.

"You'll catch cold," she said.

"I'm warm," he said.

"That's just it, darling," she replied.

He continued, "Yes, you are my homecoming, but you are more than that. You are the woman I dreamed about all my life, but I woke up and knew she never existed. But here you are. You are the sun that comes up, shines, goes down, and comes again. It is not always there, but one knows that next morning it will appear again. You are the young day, and midday, and the evening: eternal change within the same scope. You are the four seasons of the year: in your autumn there is already the hint of spring. You are like a distant harbor that cannot be seen from the open sea, but the mariners know it is there. And when the tattered sails are furled at last, people one knows are standing on the pier, and there is welcoming warmth in the waterfront inn, and the bed is made just as it was on the day of departure. In your eyes there is struggle and victory and renewed struggle, and the sorrow of days that have been lived, but there is no weariness and no defeat and no despondency. In your eyes there is the lovely pride of understanding, a smiling compassion, and firmness without bitterness. The terror of the days just past is in your eyes, but they have remained unclouded, whatever you looked upon. Your feet are torn and cut by the thorny path you walked along, but they have kept their delicate womanly shape. You have remained yourself, and you remain my only law: a joyous duty and a deep security, a going forward without dismay, and victory and defeat that alter nothing."

He had spoken quietly, almost reverently. Her hands were stroking his hair.

"You're dreaming aloud," she said. "I don't know if the woman you're dreaming of is me. But I'm lucky to be the one that hears you dreaming."

"I love your hands in my hair," he said.

"I love your hands on my hips," she said. "Here, darling! Hold me here!"

Now his mouth moved slowly over her body, and his hands released her hips only to make way for his lips.

"You," he said. "You smell like . . . you."

"No," she said. "Better than that. Now I smell like you."

"No," he said, "you smell like hay and like moss. You are as fragrant as a forest."

"I'll tell you something awful," she said. "I love the smell of you when you're very warm. Your odor comes directly from you when you sweat, unchanged from outside."

Their bodies came convulsively together again. Her softness engulfed his hardness, like a wave flowing around a rock.

"Now," she said. "Now I am whole again."

He said only, "Maria!" Over and over again, "Maria! Maria! Maria!"

Their breathing—deep, quickening, and anticipatory—mingled.

"Do you feel me?" he asked.

"No—us."

Their lost absorption in the rhythm of their bodies had a curious quality of alertness. It was a kind of solemn fear lest one hasten ahead of the rhythm of the other.

"I can see you in the dark," he said. "I can see your teeth."

He saw that she smiled.

"Are you happy?" he asked.

"Are you happy?" she asked.

He repeated, "Maria!"

She whispered so softly that he could not hear, "You're mine!"

He remained motionless, his body covering hers.

"I know what you're saying to me," he said.

"I didn't say anything," she said.

"Oh, yes. Much. You are still speaking to me."

He sought her mouth.

20

AFTER the arrest of Argonaut and the closing down of Dr. Leibl's asylum, Peter succeeded in getting a five-day leave, which he spent with Maria. They had to be extremely careful. The non-fraternization law forbidding all social contact between American soldiers and Germans was still in force, and there were especially stern restrictions against members of the Armed Forces living under the same roof with Germans. As an OSS officer, Peter enjoyed certain privileges: he could appear in public places with Germans, converse with them and visit their homes, but like any other soldier he was not permitted to live in a house occupied by a German.

Maria had bought the house when Helga was sent to Bavaria by the *Arbeitsdienst* to work in the fields. Maria had sold the last valuable pieces of her jewelry and purchased the house with its few acres of farmland, which provided enough to support her and to supplement the scanty rations Helga received from the farmers for whom she worked. Maria had become a farm woman during the time she lived in Bavaria. Although she had lived in large cities since her sixteenth year, she quickly adjusted herself to rural life. She had spent her girlhood on a farm. Her parents were Frisian farmers of sound, ancient stock.

She had been barely sixteen when she met the architect Gerd Hoffmann at a ball in Leipzig, and she married him the following year. Encouraged by a Berlin stage director at the Municipal Theater which Hoffmann had designed, Maria went on the stage. But the theater was not in her blood. Several years passed before she admitted that she was devoting her life to a chimera, and meanwhile her marriage, too, turned out to be a failure. Hoffmann, maniacally jealous, was too vain and ambitious to keep her from the theater, but at the same time was neither strong nor affirmative enough to hold her interest and affection in the face of the theater's various enticements. Shortly after her divorce—about the time Peter met her—she said farewell to the stage.

The freedom she had always longed for no longer meant anything to her. When Peter left Germany, she devoted herself wholly to her daughter. Peter was not only the first man she had genuinely loved; he was also the first to make clear to her that Germany was embarking on a dangerous and disastrous course, and that Germans of good will must prepare, one way or another, to survive through the night that was descending on the country. She loved Germany, but she did not love blindly. Twelve years of her life passed in waiting, and she was not always sure exactly what it was for which she waited. But she had inherited from her forebears the deep, calm patience that distinguishes the peasants of Frisia.

As Helga grew up, Maria spent most of her time shielding the girl from the incessant Nazi agitation that was rampant everywhere; she invented countless devices and stratagems to keep her daughter out of the League of German Girls, regimented gymnastic drills, and political functions of all kinds. Solicited for one or two persons near to her filled Maria's whole life; she stood apart, with an alien's shyness, from mankind as a whole and even from the society around her. She was almost always alone, but she was never lonely because no task seemed too trivial to her and no person too lowly. So it was that she was loved everywhere. People who hated misfortune in others because they feared that they would have to help, and people who hated good fortune in others because they envied it, flocked to her. She seemed never to be in need of help, nor did she disturb the conscience of others through an excess of generosity in the help that she gave.

She had quickly won the hearts of the farm folk in Oberndorf, the village where she was living. At first the villagers regarded with native suspicion and distrust the fine lady from the city, of whom it was said that she had actually been in the theater. A single incident altered the attitude of the whole community.

It happened one day that a neighbor's horse fell into a manure pit. The farmer was not at home, the son was away in the Army, and the farm wife was alone. Maria heard her cries and hurried over to see what was wrong. She rolled her sleeves up over her strong, brown arms and set about helping the woman get the horse out of the pit. She took off her sandals, stepped without hesitation deep into the manure, and asked the farm wife to fetch a stout rope. Ignoring the thrashing hoofs, she tied it around the horse. For an hour she worked silently, pulling, shoving, and pushing until the horse was rescued.

The "fine lady from the theater" became a legend in the village.

Then came the German collapse. Almost all of Germany was in Allied hands, with only the Berchtesgaden area holding out. The Americans were surging forward to the southeast from Munich, and the French were advancing from occupied Austria. Oberndorf could be reached from the highway only by crossing a bridge that spanned a torrential stream. The Wehrmacht had fled, and the defense of the town was left in the hands of the most prosperous local farmer, a man named Kurt Holzinger, who was a party functionary—the *Bauernführer*—and an ardent Nazi. The farmers obeyed him unquestioningly when he gave directions for mining the bridge with dynamite and digging trenches on the village side of the stream. At the proper moment the bridge was to be blown up.

On the afternoon of May 4 the men and women of Oberndorf were summoned to go down to the bridge and hold themselves ready to defend the village. They were given weapons at the schoolhouse and marched in closed ranks to the bridge.

It was a sorry procession. Most of the farmers and their women were old, almost all over sixty. The weapons they had been given were as old as they, mostly rusted and unusable. One or two carried a *Panzerfaust*, the clumsy German version of the bazooka, whose operation was so precarious that even experienced soldiers often set it off too early and, instead of blowing up enemy tanks, blew themselves to pieces. To make matters worse, the bridge was the only connection between the village and the outside world. Destroying it meant cutting the town off from contact and supplies from the city, and isolating the inhabitants from relatives and friends. For Maria it meant separation from Helga, who was working in a neighboring village.

Maria marched with the other farm folk. She carried a shovel and spade for the trench-digging. She had refused a weapon at the schoolhouse, but tucked in her belt was her own Luger, left behind by a deserter whom she had helped make good his escape to Austria.

The group reached the bridge. The May afternoon was unseasonably hot. The warm air shimmered, and the landscape looked as if it lay under a wavering sheen of water. Maria's throat and ears burned; she did not know for sure whether the heat came from without or within. The cows lay in the fields as if they had long since surrendered and made peace.

Holzinger brought the marchers to a halt not far from the bridge. He struck an attitude before them. He was a man of no more than forty, dark-haired, small, and powerful.

"We are going to defend the village against the Americans," he said. "That is the command of the Führer. Reinforcements are on the way. At any moment our secret weapon may be turned against the enemy and change the whole course of the war. Our mission is to defend Oberndorf to the last man and the last woman." He broke off, and there was a pause. "The bridge will have to be blown up. The dynamite is in place. I need three volunteers to light the fuses. Who will volunteer?"

No one moved. His dark, furrowed face reddened. "Who will volunteer?" he asked again, bearing down ominously on the word "volunteer."

No voice was raised; no hand was lifted.

"How long do I have to wait?" the Bauernführer shouted furiously. "Or do I have to yank three of you cowards out of the ranks by the neck?"

Maria was standing in the second row. She raised her hand.

"Ah! Frau Hoffmann!" he said. "Who else?"

Maria stepped forward. "I am not volunteering," she said.

"What!" he said, astonished.

"This is all foolishness," Maria said. "Foolishness and suicide. We can't defend the village. And we don't want to defend it. We're fed up with dying for the Nazi party."

She expected support from the crowd. She knew the sentiments of the farmers. But no one moved or spoke. Most of them dropped their eyes. In their blood was no rebellion.

"This traitorous sow will be shot!" Holzinger yelled. His anger reached the point of frenzy, and he took a step toward Maria.

She looked him calmly in the face. "We're not afraid any longer," she said, still as if speaking for the whole group. "We don't want to die for no reason. We are glad that the village is still standing. We don't want it burned to the ground like the German villages that resisted."

"Shut up, sow!" Holzinger bellowed. Then, as if desperately clinging to his own order, "The bridge will be blown!"

Now he stood directly before her. But he did not lay hands on her. She had drawn the Luger from her waist and leveled it at him.

"Raise your hands," she ordered. When he did not react at once, she said, "Raise your hands or I'll shoot." Her finger was on the trigger, and the safety catch was off.

Her blond hair fluttered in a sudden breeze. Veins stood out in her long, lovely throat. No one could doubt that she intended to shoot if necessary. The villagers behind her remained mute and motionless.

"Don't just stand there," she said over her shoulder to the nearest farmers, without taking her eyes off Holzinger. "Cut the fuses. The idiots used ten times too much dynamite. If the bridge goes up, half the village will go with it."

That worked. There was movement in the stupidly silent mob. The men looked uneasily toward the bridge. Tied along the railings and under the bridge were large gray clumps of dynamite. Four or five men stepped forward and seized Holzinger. Two others ran to the bridge to detach the fuses. The women gathered around Maria.

She thrust the pistol back in her waist. She felt tired, almost old. She had the feeling that the trembling of her bare knees was visible to everybody. Over the babble of voices and the thumping of her heart she could hear the soothing rush of the stream below.

The last bombs fell that night, but they sounded far away.

Next morning the first French tanks rumbled over the bridge.

>> **21** <<

PETER and Maria saw no one during the first three days of his leave. Helga was with her grandmother in Munich. Peter had sent Thompson away, and they were alone in the house.

It was a simple farmhouse of the kind that dots Bavaria by the thousands, with a huge tile stove, encircled by a bench, in the wide airy room on the first floor, and peasant furniture of light maple which retained the pleasant smell of wood. The windows were small, but there were six of them. The kitchen was unusually roomy, and a nook with a desk and two chairs served as a study.

Maria's room with its high old-fashioned bed was on the second floor. There was another bedroom adjacent, but it was unused, save as storage space. It looked more like an attic than a bedroom. All around the second story ran an old wooden balcony, whose timbers here and there were touched with decay. A little room under the roof, with rustic furniture painted a bright blue, served as Helga's bedroom when she was at home.

The farmhouse had taken on some of the charm of Maria's personality. Most of her possessions had been lost in the air raids, and far too little remained to furnish a house as she would have liked. But such objects as she had contrived to save were distributed around the house with such a sure instinct for decoration and harmony that every room acquired something of her individuality. She had brought along all the silver she could carry from Trier, and the breakfast table set in country style took on an incongruously charming appearance with the worn but exquisite pieces arranged on a gay tablecloth. In a corner of her bedroom Maria had installed a "boudoir"—a low dressing table and a little bench covered with flowered light-blue chintz. Above the table was an oval mirror, and on it were innumerable perfume bottles, most of them empty. Instead of seeming out of place in its old-fashioned rural surroundings, the bright feminine corner was like a flower pinned on a severely cut suit.

It was a mystery to Peter how Maria was able to run the house alone without letting him see any signs of her housekeeping. By the time he awoke in the morning, she had already been up and about for two hours, visited the stable, given instructions to the two girls who worked in the fields, and was back in the house to join him at breakfast. The table was set on the balcony, the GI coffee supplied by Peter smelled fresh and inviting, the morning's milk ran heavy and yellowish, and the thick honey still tasted of the comb. Flowers picked by Maria on her way through the fields were on the table, which was covered with her best yellow damask. She herself wore a dirndl; she owned only two, but with a bandanna, a different neckerchief, and a colored sash she gave her costumes the effect of endless variation.

During the day Maria sometimes disappeared for an hour or two while Peter leafed through old books he found in the little study. Most of them had once belonged to him; on the flyleaves were the fond dedications, often in verse, which he had written when he gave her the books. Sometimes he would find her busy in the kitchen, but he was never able to cross the threshold. He was always gently but firmly ushered out—on the stove some culinary surprise was in preparation. Their meals were always simple. Peter's friends would have regarded them as meager fare. Maria could offer only what came from her farm: vegetables and salads from the garden, and cream and cheese from the cows, with an occasional bit of poultry. But she prepared everything with skill and affection, and when on the third day she managed to trade a pack of Peter's cigarettes for some meat, Peter swore that never in his life had he eaten a more delicious meal.

They spent their days in the house, in the stable, and in the fields, which began immediately behind the house and ended at a stand of dark green fir not far away. They went for long rambling walks in the evening, along the brook that ran past Maria's house and under the poplars, whose whispering was in soft competition to the murmuring of the water. They sat under the trees with their feet in the stream and became aware, with a feeling of silent content in which there was a small admixture of uneasiness, how little it takes to be happy, and how hard it is to attain that little. After a time they would stand up, almost invariably at the same moment, and go home as if they had always gone home together at the end of the day.

On the third evening Peter said, "I've been doing a lot of thinking since I've been here. I've been planning things."

She interrupted him. "Let's not make plans."

"Why not?"

"Plans are binding. I don't want anything to tie you down. Men don't like planning ahead. I think they make plans only because of the women they love. But you don't have to plan anything on my account. I've gotten used to living without planning." She spoke without bitterness, almost gaily. "Women are silly," she added. "I've often thought about it. To a woman life is like a city in which every street leads somewhere. Really, though, life is just a series of blind alleys. Most of the streets don't lead anywhere at all.

You keep asking yourself, what will happen if I do this or that Usually nothing happens. You wind up in a blind alley, turn around, and begin all over again."

He did not contradict her. He merely said, "You know that doesn't apply to us. We're not in a blind alley."

She did not look at him, but he felt the gratitude in her eyes.

On the morning of the fourth day Maria had to go to the village She wanted to go alone and promised to return soon, but he shook his head. He insisted on going with her.

She was silent as they went down the hill on which the house stood, about a mile from the town.

"Are you upset because I came along?" he asked.

"Oh, no," she answered, a little embarrassed. "Only, I didn't tell you that I do all sorts of things in town. They're not very important, and you'll probably think it's all very silly."

They entered the village and Maria halted before a store. It had been a tailor shop, but now the show window was full of a wild assortment of unrelated objects—kiddie-cars and watering cans clothing and buggy whips, diapers and lampshades.

Maria went in ahead of Peter. "This is a swap-store," she explained. "These days you can't buy anything for money. The black market is flourishing, and people go around trying to cheat each other. So some of us got together and set up this swap system Look"—she pointed to little slips of paper attached to the various objects—"everything is assigned a definite value, and can be traded for anything else of the same value. You can get practically any thing you want here, and nobody is cheated. If you happen to own an old umbrella, Captain Olden, maybe I can get you a nice pork chop for it."

A girl of about seventeen was behind the counter. She greeted Maria with a respect that indicated clearly that Maria was a person of consequence in the management of the swap-store. Maria went behind the counter and leafed through a ledger.

"Hasn't Sepp Piffinger been in yet?" she asked.

"No," said the girl. "And he wasn't in yesterday either. We're lacking twenty liters of milk."

"Has he sent any word?"

"No, but I know he's selling the milk on the black market," the girl said, lowering her voice.

"I'll talk to him," Maria said.

When they had left, Peter asked, "And just what are you going to say to this Sepp Piffinger?"

"I'm going to tell him that the children need the milk."

Peter smiled skeptically. "That will no doubt touch him deeply."

"Maybe it will," said Maria seriously. "You wouldn't believe how often people behave badly just because they haven't thought of the consequences."

Peter wasn't convinced. "And what if he still doesn't deliver the milk?"

"That's simple. We've got a little supply of gasoline that the Americans gave us for the fire engine and ambulance. I've compiled a list at the village hall of all the people who won't co-operate in our community projects. They're barred from the benefits of the community. If fire breaks out in the home of a black marketeer, for instance, he has no claim on the service of the fire department. Sepp Piffinger's wife is expecting a baby. Any minute she may have to be rushed to Bad Reichenhall."

"And you'd refuse her the use of the ambulance?"

"Certainly."

"Why, that's barbaric!"

"It's barbaric to take milk away from children and sell it on the black market too." There were furrows on Maria's high forehead as she said it.

As they turned off the main street on their way back to Maria's house, Peter noticed that they were not taking the same road over which they had come.

"You'll have to bear with me a little longer, darling," Maria said. "I have to make one more short visit."

They entered a neat little farmhouse, surrounded by a flower garden, at the foot of the hill. Peter did not immediately see the old woman hunched over a sewing machine in a corner of the living-room. The room had a faint but unmistakable barracks smell and the peculiar dampness that eats its way into soldiers' uniforms. On the floor, on the chairs, on the table, everywhere, were big bundles of Wehrmacht clothing.

The old woman, her face pleated with folds and wrinkles, came shuffling toward them between the mounds of uniforms.

"This is Mother Fütterer," Maria said, introducing her to Peter.

"These uniforms were left behind at a quartermaster's depot when the soldiers fled. Luckily we were able to take them away before plunderers could get at them. It's probably not legal—Wehrmacht material is supposed to be given up to the authorities. But Mother Fütterer is making civilian clothes out of them for people who'll need them this winter. Returning soldiers have nothing to wear, and nobody's been able to buy anything for years."

The old seamstress was hard of hearing and understood nothing of what Maria was saying. She imagined she was confirming Maria's story by saying, "It was so lucky that Frau Hoffmann thought of rescuing those uniforms! Only we haven't enough for everybody. People keep coming all day from Bad Reichenhall and Berchtesgaden, asking for clothing."

Maria shouted into her ear, "Oberndorf comes first. After that we may have about a hundred and twenty uniforms left over. We can give those to Berchtesgaden and Bad Reichenhall. But don't give any away yourself, Mother. We'll let the mayor distribute them. Understand?"

The old woman nodded. Her head kept wobbling up and down as if she could never stop it again. She insisted on accompanying her guests to the garden. Outside, the cooling shadows of evening were falling along the road that led up the hill.

≫ 22 ≪

MARIA and Peter walked silently side by side.

"I didn't used to be a busybody, darling," Maria said suddenly. "But everybody's got to help now."

"I think you're wonderful," he said.

"No, it's not wonderful at all," she replied. "I don't even know whether I'd have gotten into all this if I had been sure you'd come back."

"I thought you knew I'd come."

"For twelve years I was sure. But not after Trier."

"Why?"

"I saw your wife's picture."

Peter made no reply. But as she spoke he realized again how impossible it was ever to break away from the life one has built for oneself—from the laws that govern human relationships, from the people to whom one has attached oneself, from a house where one has lived, from the hate that survives love, and from the love of two people which grows together but dies separately.

"But I did come back," he said finally. It sounded a little as if he were confirming the fact to himself. "And just now, as we went through the town," he continued, "it seemed as if I had never been away."

Her face was grave, and he loved that gravity which made her seem much older.

"There was another reason why I didn't want you to come along," she said. "All this is over and done with for you, Peter. It has to be."

"How so?"

"Because Germany is just a heap of ruins. All Europe is."

"Perhaps. But houses can be built again."

"Not Europe's houses."

"Why not?"

"Their only reason for being was that they were old."

"Just the same," he replied, "even the ruins mean something to me."

She shook her head. "Too much has been destroyed. Not only houses. More. More important things. What you don't understand is what has been destroyed inside us. We're tired, Peter. A while ago you spoke of the lure of pioneering. The thrill of making a completely new start. But the pioneers you told me about had no memories of the land they were pioneering. I think nothing could be more dangerous to pioneers than memory."

"Maria, I've watched you closely these past few days. In spite of everything, you are still whole and sound and healthy to the core."

"No," she said. "It's just that I do what I have to do. I belong here."

He took her arm. "Why can't I help you?" he asked. "Even missionaries don't always go into the wilderness alone. Just think of what a wonderful adventure it would be. We two together. We could do more than just help. I don't believe in mere help. People often don't want to be helped anyway. We could build things up again. In America the pioneers began alone, with nothing, in little communities. They built the greatest nation on earth."

"Germany will never be great again."

"I don't mean nationalistic greatness. I mean the little things that make America magnificent. The white houses along the roads, where ordinary workers live in comfort their grandfathers never dreamed of. The drugstores where anybody can get a good cup of coffee for five or ten cents, and where a bank president sits down next to a taxi driver and a congressman next to a farmer. I mean the good nature with which the people try to make life easier for one another, not harder. The high spirits with which Americans go about correcting their blunders. It's a country where people come as close as humanly possible to achieving an equality that actually doesn't exist—not because of·ordinances but because differences between people simply don't mean much to them. Where there may be intolerance and senseless bigotry and narrowness, as there is everywhere else, but where the law is founded on the idea that these things are evil and cannot be allowed to prevail. Where the people themselves erect barriers against their own evil inclinations. They're the only people in the world, Maria, who always talk like materialists and invariably act like idealists."

She looked up at him. "You love America," she said. "Why is it you don't want to forget Europe?"

"I can't forget Europe," he answered. He hesitated. "Shall I tell you a story?"

"Yes."

"There's a little town in Italy called Battipaglia. That is, it was called Battipaglia while it still existed. It lay on a crossroads, somewhere between Salerno and Paestum. I was ordered to parachute down near this little town. It was a strange way to return to Europe. Formerly, when emigrants came back to visit, they usually landed at Hamburg. I had a parachute strapped around my body, and somebody gave me a push into space. But it turned out that it makes no difference whether you arrive at a harbor on board a Hapag liner, or jump directly out of the sky into an obscure Italian hamlet."

"No difference?"

"No. It's all Europe." He walked next to her, but he seemed to be far away, somewhere between Salerno and Paestum, in a burning village on the west coast of southern Italy.

"I had luck," he began again. "I came down close to an isolated farm, a mile or two east of Battipaglia. It was the beginning of September, but the night was like summer. I lay there in the high grass, trying to catch my breath. The crickets chirped. The grass smelled warm and damp. From somewhere came the odor of acacia. It came in gusts, with the soft wind that rippled the grass around me. With the wind there came also the strains of a song from the farmhouse. A Neapolitan girl was singing a song I have loved since childhood. I recognized it at once, like a greeting: 'Cante pe'me.' The smell of the acacia and the melody of the song seemed to intertwine and—" he interrupted himself—"but that isn't what I was going to tell you about."

"Go on," she said.

"I suddenly stopped behaving like an American soldier. I had parachuted into enemy territory. The Germans were still in Battipaglia. I was tangled in the harness of my parachute and had lost my pistol, which must have fallen somewhere in the grass not far away. But instead of worrying about getting out of my parachute and finding my gun, I lay listening to the crickets and the song. I breathed in the smell of the earth. I felt no fear—only exultation. I was home."

She wanted to ask a question, but just then a command car roared past at a terrific speed. "Sounds like Dirty Thompson," Peter said. The brakes screeched, the car came to a stop and backed to where they were. Thompson jumped out of the car and approached them.

"What's up, Thompson?"

"Nothin' good, Captain. Sorry to break in on your leave, but Colonel Whimsley sent me. You got to report to him right away. He's waitin' for you in Munich."

23

THE prisoner Teitinger had confessed killing the prisoner Gerecke in the camp latrine. It was a half success for Stroud, who gathered the evidence and wrung the confession from Teitinger, but could not bring the man to reveal the name of a single one of his fellow conspirators, and it was obvious that he lied about the motive. He maintained that Gerecke, who was in charge of the distribution of straw for mattresses in the barracks, had favored his personal friends and ignored the needs of the other prisoners. When Teitinger accused him of this, he said, a bitter dispute arose, and Teitinger determined to do away with him.

The story was entirely implausible. Gerecke was known for his scrupulous fairness in the distribution of bedding straw, and a premeditated murder for so trivial a cause was hardly credible. Teitinger, in addition, gave no explanation as to how he came into possession of the murder weapon. Langhoff, whom Stroud consulted, designated Gerecke as a member of the camp's "resistance movement"—a term he insisted on using despite Stroud's irritated protest. On the other hand, Langhoff professed that he had neither suspected nor known Teitinger.

Meager as these first results of Stroud's investigation were, they nevertheless represented a step forward. The prompt arrest and conviction of a member of the conspiracy—and Stroud no longer doubted that a conspiracy within the camp was involved—would have the effect of preventing further acts of violence. Teitinger's confession had also buttressed Stroud's shaky position and would, he thought, give him the opportunity of carrying on his experiment and ultimately clearing up the other murders.

Stroud received confirmation to this effect when he notified the General of the confession over the telephone.

"I'm sorry I had to bear down the way I did," General Lowell said, "but I had my reasons."

"I've got a request of my own now," said Stroud. "I'd like to hold Teitinger here for a few more days. He's perfectly safe in solitary, under heavy guard. I'd like to examine him further. In addition, I want to try out an idea of mine."

"What kind of an idea?"

"I'd like to stage a trial. Judges, defense counsel, prosecuting attorney—all prisoners of the camp. The verdict won't be binding, of course. We'll call it a recommendation to the American military court. I think it would enable us to find out a great deal about what's going on among the prisoners. The defense and prosecution will try to pile up all the evidence possible. And the verdict will be quite indicative of whether we're making any progress with them. Germans will be able to do that better than any American board of inquiry."

There was a short silence on the telephone.

"Do you think you can find enough prisoners qualified to take part in a trial and at the same time willing to go through with your stunt?" the General asked.

"I'm sure of it."

General Lowell did not give his decision at once. He apparently wanted to confer with higher authority, but Stroud was well enough acquainted with him to know that he favored the idea. The next day the General gave his permission.

It was on this day, after a week of grueling work, that Stroud decided to visit Wanda and take her for a ride in the country.

Though he had always somewhat resisted his thoughts of her, they had never completely left him. Her picture kept coming to him as a kind of counterpoint to whatever he was doing. In the middle of examining a prisoner, while reading a new report on the Teitinger case, while jotting down notes and conclusions, the thought of Wanda presented itself without interrupting or even disturbing his train of thought.

Until his car was actually taking him to the DP camp, Stroud had avoided inquiring into his reasons for wanting to see her again. Then suddenly and clearly he knew that his feelings for her were not entirely fatherly. The realization that he was being attracted by the woman in her came to him with a shock whose impact made him judge himself unfairly. So I'm just out for a cheap adventure, he said to himself. This simplification appeared to him to be the whole explanation of his fondness for Wanda.

Stroud had been married for twenty-eight years, and he could count the affairs in his life on the fingers of one hand. He was fifteen when he first knew Emily Rogers. She was two years younger, the only child of a prominent Spokane banker. It was taken for granted from the first that John and Emily were meant for each other. At high school they went to dances and parties together, were the first to call up and congratulate each other on birthdays, and at tennis, to which they were both devoted, they formed an inseparable team in mixed doubles. Stroud spent his first pocket money to buy Emily ice cream. When Emily, a little plump but wholesomely lovely—she had the prettiest blond hair in Spokane, everyone said—began to have dates with other boys, John was wretchedly jealous.

He developed a loyalty to Emily that gave him an uneasy conscience for the rest of his life. When he went away to Leland Stanford to study law, his companions introduced him to other girls, but he was indifferent and often rude. The first time he kissed another girl he felt that he had to write Emily about it. He could not, however, bring himself to confess to her when the widow of a professor seduced him; he felt not only that he had soiled himself, but that he had lost forever the right to seek Emily's hand. Later when she went east to attend Vassar he saw her less often and had a number of amorous interludes with co-eds, but each time he was oppressed by the feeling that he was being unfaithful to Emily.

When he returned to Spokane after taking his degree, Emily seemed more desirable than ever. With a stern and continuing effort of will, he subdued his body during his two-year courtship of her, but when, as the day approached, his father suggested postponing the wedding for a few months more, he objected furiously: the wedding must take place on the date set and not a day later.

His marriage to Emily was a fortunate one. After a two-month wedding trip to the Orient, they returned to Spokane as happy and as well-adjusted to each other as convention required. During these two months they had mutually satisfied their erotic curiosity about each other, and from then on their relationship assumed a moderation and restraint which made their honeymoon seem a kind of a wild fever to which neither of them would succumb again.

Emily Stroud knew how to create an atmosphere of comfort and stability in their friendly house on the outskirts of the city. She was prominent in numerous social affairs and club activities, but she managed to get along without household help before the birth of their children, and with only one all-purpose maid thereafter. She found ways of persuading Stroud that he was fond of helping around the house. Cutting the grass, wiping the dishes, painting the picket fence, and making the salad for special guests became routine, but at first these domestic activities had been invested with a definite charm for him.

Emily had no interest in his law practice and he soon gave up inviting her to the courtroom to hear him try cases, but she did have a gift for attracting to their house guests who could be helpful to him, and she was shrewd enough to cultivate promising relationships which he himself neglected. At first it worried him that he could not discuss the problems of his practice with her and that she manifestly had no interest in anything which did not directly concern her home and social circle. Later, however, he came to value the relief of leaving behind the pressures of his office at the end of the day, and submerging himself in Emily's world—picnics, golf, the children, evenings of bridge with neighbors, good music, and cocktail parties. Thursday nights he met with friends from the National Guard in the Davenport, and Tuesdays she went to the Spokane Hotel for meetings of the Daughters of the American Revolution.

World War II cast a disturbing shadow on the marriage of the Strouds. When the war in Europe broke out, Emily began to occupy herself with political opinion and activity. She immediately took a firm position on the European war and set about doing what she could to back up her opinion with action. Whether prompted by solicitude for the fate of her son or motivated by the tradition in which she had been raised, she clearly foresaw the possibility of American participation in the war and opposed it unequivocally. She agitated among her fellow members of the Daughters of the American Revolution to send letters of protest to their representatives and senators against the "Roosevelt conspiracy"; she bought a framed picture of Lindbergh and set it on a drawing-room table; and one morning when Stroud, as usual, went to the front door for the morning paper, he found, in addition to the *Spokane Spokesman-Review* which he had been reading for years, a copy of the mail edition of the *Chicago Tribune*.

That John himself would go off to war again never for a moment occurred to Emily. She regarded his activity in the National Guard merely as a kind of male pastime, and his enthusiasm for Roosevelt she took to be an unavoidable outgrowth of his professional dealings with vulgar people. Despite their model marriage, she was made suddenly aware that she understood him as little as he did her. In endless arguments, and with a stubbornness of which she would not have thought him capable, he insisted that the war against barbarism and intolerance, against Prussian militarism and the abuse of human dignity, was the concern of America as a whole and his own personal concern as well.

Not until he sat in his car speeding through the streets of Munich toward the DP camp did it occur to Stroud to wonder whether the fight against Hitler was his only reason for leaving Spokane.

The car turned a corner. The Major looked down at the cardboard box in which he had packed his PX rations to bring to Wanda: the chocolate he had promised her, cigarettes, a bar of soap, a can of tooth powder, a bottle of spot remover, hand lotion, and a tooth brush.

He felt guilty. He was out for an affair, he was running after a girl younger than his own daughter, and he was using the same cheap enticements—candy, cigarettes, tooth powder—that the GI's used in their sordid fraternizations. He began to detest the cardboard box on the seat beside him. He decided to deliver it at the gate of the camp and drive off without even seeing her.

The American soldier posted at the gateway of the camp was an amiable redhead with multitudinous freckles. The Major had the acutely unpleasant feeling that there was a knowing impudence about the boy's grin when Stroud asked him to deliver the box to Wanda Komarnicki. The grin made the freckles merge and run together.

"Sorry, sir," he said. "We're not allowed to accept packages or letters. Maybe you can get permission inside to hand it over personally."

Stroud was about to drive off when it occurred to him that, after all, he had promised her chocolate. Just because I'm getting dirty ideas is no reason to break my promise, he thought. I can give her the box and then leave.

Wanda was summoned to the office. He stood and waited with the box in his hand, like a high-school boy about to present his first bouquet. When she entered and extended her hand, he shifted the box hurriedly from his right hand to his left, and took her hand, then forgot to give her the box. A young lieutenant was sitting behind the desk observing them with unabashed interest. It's impossible to say anything at all to her with that nincompoop sitting here, the Major thought. He asked, "Would you like to go for a drive?"

Permission was granted, and Wanda ran to get her beret. He waited for her in the great dusty courtyard. He was still holding the box under his arm.

They drove out of Munich in the direction of the Starnberger See.

"What have you been doing since I saw you?" he asked.

"Nothing. Waiting for you to come and call on me."

The answer surprised him so that he could not immediately think of a reply.

She asked, "And what have you been doing, Major?"

"I've had a busy week. A lot of work."

"And a lot of worry too," she added simply.

"How do you know?"

"I can tell."

"You're right, Wanda," he said. "I've had a hard week." He felt an urge to tell her all about it. Before he knew it, he was in the midst of the story of the poisonings, the stabbing, the investigation. There had been no specific order forbidding mention of these events, but he knew that they were by no means the business of a Polish DP. Nevertheless, he concealed very little except the visit of General Lowell to the camp.

She listened attentively, her eyes open wide, without interruption. When he finished, she said, "You seem upset by it all. Did you expect anything else from the Germans?"

"Frankly, yes."

"You can't seem to get over the idea that Germans are no different from anyone else."

"I don't want to get over the idea. Look, Wanda. There aren't any godforsaken nations or races. But not all nations can live under the same conditions. They require varying systems of government, different constitutions, different kinds of regimes. I'm not trying to find out whether Germans are human. That's an inhuman question. I'm trying to find out under what conditions they can live peacefully with one another and with their neighbors."

"But," Wanda asked, "if people are really pretty much the same, why do they need different forms of government?"

Stroud was off on a theme that interested him deeply, and to which he had lately given much thought. He welcomed Wanda's questions, and he answered readily. "It works this way: the majority of people in any country are, on the whole, good people. They are the so-called 'little people' who don't want to kill anybody, don't want to rob anybody, but just want to be left alone to live peaceful lives and enjoy what little happiness comes their way. But almost every country is dominated by a minority, and that minority has power and it has money, and those two things invariably corrupt. The stronger this group tends to be in any country, the more need there is for statutes to hold them in bounds. Good constitutions are the shields that protect the people from their rulers. Our public officials in America are no better and no worse than anywhere else. Only we've developed a better system for keeping tabs on them and for getting rid of them from time to time when they get out of hand."

"If all that's true, I don't see anything so terrible about what happened in your camp."

"But it is terrible. It's frightening to see how easily the minority can get the upper hand. Even in a community like a prison camp where one of the corrupting factors is absent—money."

She thought it over. "Still, I don't agree with you," she said. "I know why the minority is successful."

"Why?"

"Because it appeals to the evil in people. And the Germans have fewer scruples than other nations about coming out openly on the side of evil."

He hesitated. "You almost convince me, Wanda, but not so much by what you say as by the fact that you're saying it at all."

"What do you mean?"

"To me the worst indictment of the Germans is that a twenty-one-year-old girl can talk that way about them."

"I'm almost twenty-two."

He laughed. "All right. Twenty-two."

The car was nearing the lake. The September afternoon was hot, and the fields were yellow and dry. The cows lay torpidly in the meadows, sunbathing. Yawning dogs stretched themselves in front of the little farmhouses, and the driver of a rattling cart was dozing with the reins in his hands. Little white clouds drifted through the tranquil blue of the sky like chubby Rubens angels. The lake lay before them. It was as blue as the sky, and there was not a breath of wind to raise a ripple. The water lapped lazily against the shore, and the shrubbery was bright green in the glare of the sun.

"Wouldn't it be wonderful to go swimming?" said Wanda.

"Yes," he said. "It's hot."

"Let's stop somewhere and swim for half an hour."

"Have you got a suit?"

"Of course not. Where would I get a swimming suit?"

He looked at her with such surprise that she laughed outright.

"What do I need a suit for?" she asked.

Stroud felt awkward and uncomfortable. He could not tell why he felt so uneasy. Was he afraid of a scandal, or of looking ridiculous, or of what the driver would say, or was he simply afraid of himself? He did not know how to reply to her suggestion. He only knew that he would agree to it.

He told the driver to stop at a little out-of-the-way summer restaurant. The only living person in sight anywhere was the red-cheeked proprietress, wearing a dirndl, who stood in the garden picking flowers. The water had the smell of overripe apples.

"If you want to stop off here and have a bite, Corporal," Stroud said to the driver, "Lieutenant Komarnicki and I are going for a little walk." He felt that it sounded clumsy and that he had involuntarily overemphasized the word "lieutenant."

"Okay, Major," said the driver, with the air of a man who understands these things.

They took a little path that wandered off from the restaurant along the edge of the lake. Wanda took his arm. After a few steps he freed himself. "I'll be right back," he said.

He hurried to the car and picked up his musette bag, which was always packed and ready.

"What's in it?" she asked when he returned with the bag slung over his shoulder.

"Nothing much," he said. "A couple of towels."

The path was so narrow that they had difficulty walking side by side. But she seemed to want to be next to him. She would not allow him to go through the shrubbery at the side but made room for him on the path, while she herself went through brambles and brushwood. She let go his arm only long enough to take off her shoes. She wore no stockings and went barefoot, lightly and surely, as if stones and roots and thorns could have no effect on her shapely little feet. He recalled that in his boyhood dreams he had often found himself suddenly naked in the midst of solemn, fully clothed people. The same painful feeling of being out of place came to him now as he walked along in his uniform, the musette bag hanging from his shoulder, next to the barefooted girl.

With her left hand, in which she carried her shoes, she parted the bushes, and he followed her almost without a will of his own. She seemed as sure of herself as if she had been along the path a thousand times before. She laughed and chattered continually, and he had no opportunity to say anything.

They left the path and were in the midst of man-high bushes. There was no sound, only the subdued, monotonous lapping of the water on the shore.

"Now for the water!" she said. She let go of his arm and disappeared almost instantly. He heard the branches rustling, and then it was still.

Stroud stood among the bushes, more and more undecided what to do. He hoped somebody would come along and startle her out of her hiding place before matters went any further. Nobody came. Finally he began to undress, pulling off his garments one by one, slowly, as if to gain time, until he stood in his underpants. He noticed for the first time that his underpants, bought in the PX, were several sizes too large. They drooped almost to his knees and were much too loose around the waist. Why in God's name can't they ever have the right size? he thought. Then he stood naked.

"Where are you?" he heard her call.

There was a great splash. Thank goodness, he thought, she's in the water. "How's it feel?" he shouted. He wanted to be sure that she was already swimming.

"Wonderful!" she said. "Don't be scared."

He had taken two towels from the musette bag. With sudden decision he quickly knotted them together and bound them around his loins. Then he made his way through the bushes to the edge of the water.

She had swum far out. He saw only her head and two slender brown shoulders that bobbed up from time to time. He ran quickly into the water.

"Isn't it glorious?" she called.

"Wonderful!" he called back. He felt grateful and much relieved. He hoped that she would stay some distance away, but she came swimming toward him.

"Can you do the crawl?" she asked, demonstrating it herself with long, sure strokes.

She swam up to him. Until now he had seen her only in the badly tailored, shabby uniform, and had known subconsciously that in this dress she was not entirely herself. Now, with her jet-black hair let down, her little wet nose and red mouth, and her taut creole-brown skin, she seemed all at once whole and healthy and young—young, without being a poor little girl.

"The Major seems to be somewhat water shy," she said mockingly and began splashing him with one hand.

He accepted the challenge and, half swimming and half treading water, he splashed back. Soon, panting, shouting, and laughing, they were engaged in a vigorous water fray. After a while she stopped suddenly and cried, "Let's swim to shore! See who gets there first. Here we go!"

His heart began thumping. He knew that it was not only from exertion. He let her win. She reached the shore several lengths ahead of him. She stepped out of the water. He closed his eyes and rubbed them as if to get the water out; he hoped that meanwhile she would vanish into the bushes. When he opened his eyes again, she was standing naked on the shore.

"How about those towels?" she asked.

She stood in the light of the sinking sun, which wrapped her body in a kind of pure, glowing violet. She was thin, but she seemed less thin than with her clothes on. She had firm little breasts, and her hips were so narrow that it almost seemed as if they could be encircled with two hands.

Stroud took in her whole body with a glance, and as he did so the agitation of the past few hours left him. Was it her completely innocent shamelessness, or was it only that the dripping wetness of her body in the twilight gave her again that moving quality of childishness and of needing help? The warmth for her that now surged up in him frightened him no longer.

"Where are the towels?" she asked in the most matter-of-fact voice in the world, shaking the water from her hair.

He looked down guiltily at his own body with the towels wrapped around his waist.

She took in the situation and laughed aloud. It seemed to him as if he were hearing her laugh for the first time, as if her laughter, too, were unclothed—naked and young and free.

"Egoist!" she said and disappeared with one bound into the bushes.

He went back to his clothes, dried himself as well as he could, and got dressed.

Suddenly he heard her voice. "What are you singing, Major?"

"I don't know," he called back, startled. "Didn't even know I was singing."

And he really hadn't known.

PART III

PART II.

24

COLONEL WHIMSLEY looked like an undernourished grey-
hound. He came from Tennessee and spoke with a trace of
the melodious drawl of the well-bred Southerner.

He arose as Peter entered. "Hello," he said. "I've got some urgent
business to talk over with you, Olden." Usually he called Peter by
his given name.

Peter waited.

"Sit down," said the Colonel. He lit a cigarette. His fingers were
so fleshless that they seemed hardly thicker than the cigarette.
"We've a mission for you. An important mission."

Peter breathed an inaudible sigh of relief. The Colonel continued, "Before I take up that subject, however, I'm afraid I must
touch on more personal matters."

"Yes, Colonel?"

"You've probably wondered, Olden, why we haven't promoted
you to major."

"I've been a captain only fourteen months, sir. Lots of men wait
longer than that for promotion."

"That's true. But you know how we value your services. Only recently you distinguished yourself again in recovering the Hitler
documents. Personally, I regard you as my best officer. There is
now an open spot on the T/O."

For a moment the Colonel fell silent and drew on his cigarette,
as if he were deeply absorbed in getting the smoke into his lungs.
Then he asked suddenly in the manner of a cross-examining prosecuting attorney, "Olden, do you imagine that the OSS knows nothing about your German sweetheart?"

"I have full confidence in the efficiency of our organization, sir,"
said Peter.

"So you don't deny it?"

"No, sir."

The Colonel, surprised by the unmistakable defiance behind
Peter's respectful answers, changed his tactics. "Your private life
doesn't concern me," he said. "But you're an officer of the OSS. If

officers in other branches set their men a bad example, that is their business. But the work we do is specialized. As you well know, it is usually secret or even top secret. You yourself have been entrusted with some of our most confidential missions. The General trusts you completely, and so do I. But your position as an OSS officer is absolutely irreconcilable with a love affair with a German woman."

"I've known this woman for fourteen years, Colonel."

"And you therefore trust her implicitly?"

Peter suppressed a smile. Never underestimate the person you are examining—he had learned that at the OSS training school. Hadn't Colonel Whimsley ever attended that school? Did Whimsley actually believe that he would fall into so obvious a trap as that? Peter replied, "I have full confidence in her as a woman. Professional matters or military questions I discuss with no one, man or woman, German or otherwise."

A sarcastic smile wrinkled the Colonel's lean face, which looked like vellum on which a child had scrawled lines at random. "Do you always know what you say in your sleep?" he asked.

"I don't talk in my sleep, sir."

The Colonel dropped his cigarette petulantly into a tiny pot of water on his desk.

"Have you inquired carefully into Frau Hoffmann's past?"

"I know all about it, sir."

"Including what she did in the war?"

"Yes, sir. I know she served as a Red Cross nurse in France and Poland."

"And that doesn't bother you any?"

Peter took out a cigarette and lit it. "Colonel, I'll be perfectly frank with you," he said slowly, weighing his words. "I'm no raw kid falling in love with his first European girl. I've known this woman and loved her for fourteen years. That's no light matter. Meanwhile I married another woman—that's my affair, and I'll have to settle it by myself. But about this woman I know all there is to know. I know more about her than any OSS investigation could discover, because I know her better than she knows herself. This woman cannot, and never will, harm me. She can only help me. However, I understand your position too. The Army has its own laws, and I don't claim any special privilege for myself. I have one hundred and forty-five points. I can get out of the Army any time. I am fully aware of the consequences of what I am doing. I'm ready to go back to America."

The frigid impersonal look on the Colonel's face had undergone a change. In his hard gray eyes there was something like emotion. "Peter, I've known you for three years now. I've always been fond of you," he said, "and not only because you never hesitated to take on the damnedest jobs. Usually I'm suspicious of men who have no fear. They're after decorations, or they're trying to commit suicide, or they want to show some woman that she means nothing to them. But with you the motive was fairly obvious. You had a little score to settle with the Nazis. Now along comes a woman and you want to take off your uniform. Have you settled your score in full?"

"No," said Peter. "I'd be lying if I said so. The most important work here is still to be done. But—"

"But what?"

Peter's voice sounded warm and personal. "Colonel," he said, "to fight for your convictions, to work hard and do a good job—that's all-important. But the most important thing of all is the bathroom mirror."

"What is that supposed to mean?"

"A man has to be able to look at his face in the morning without wanting to spit at it. If I gave up this woman on account of some rules and regulations or other that don't apply to her, I wouldn't be able to shave myself. And I hate to go around bearded."

"Is that your final word, Peter?"

"Yes, sir."

The Colonel picked a cigarette holder up from his desk and began cleaning it meticulously. He seemed to be pondering. There was silence in the room. From time to time the rumble of a passing truck reached them from the street.

Finally the Colonel said, "I'll make a report to the General tomorrow. I don't feel authorized to pass on your case myself. Naturally, I'll make my own recommendations."

"Yes, sir."

Peter was about to get up, but the Colonel kept him seated with a wave of the hand. "About that mission, Peter," he said. "It may be the last assignment I give you. That depends on what the General decides. But I'm assuming the responsibility of giving you this one. I expect you to execute it with your usual efficiency."

"Naturally, sir."

"Good." The Colonel involuntarily lowered his voice a little. "As you know, a dangerous Hitler myth is growing along with lack of definite proof that Hitler is dead. Because of this it has become practically as important to establish the fact of his death, if he is dead, as to track him down if he is alive."

Peter nodded. "The Germans are primitive mystics; when they call someone immortal, they mean it literally. They've doubted the death of their leaders from Barbarossa to Hitler."

"There are two men whose testimony would be invaluable," Whimsley continued. "One is Martin Bormann, the chief of the Chancellery, who was with Hitler in the air-raid shelter until the very last. He has vanished without a trace. We have a good reason to believe that he got through to Spain. The report of a reliable agent in Biarritz indicates that Bormann got across the Pyrenees into Spain the same way many of Hitler's victims did. We've arrested a Catalan mountain guide who smuggled a man resembling Bormann into Spain by way of Le Perthus, but the trail vanishes at Barcelona. From there he could easily get to Argentina."

"To Hitler?"

"Possibly. The other is a man who belonged to Hitler's body-guard and who also stayed in the shelter with him until the last moment. He can tell us either the circumstances of his death or the manner of his flight."

The Colonel turned on his desk lamp. He spoke more quietly than ever. "The man is a Storm Trooper. A fanatical Nazi. His name is Michael Meister. He is a waiter by trade." The Colonel stood up and crossed the half-lit room to a safe in the corner. As he adjusted the dial and opened the door, he continued, "He calls himself Michael Werner now, and he's working as a waiter in the Femina Casino, a Berlin night club."

"Do we have a picture of him?" Peter asked.

"Luckily we have." The Colonel had taken a thin folder containing a few papers and four or five snapshots out of the safe and laid it on the desk. "Not very much to go on," he said. "The rest is up to you."

Peter nodded.

"Read these reports tonight and study the pictures," Colonel Whimsley said. "Leave early tomorrow. I just want to add that you'll have to approach this man with the utmost care. We can't just rush in and arrest him. That way he'll never talk. Your problem is to find him, get to know him, devise ways of drawing him out, and finally learn the truth from him. But this Meister, alias Werner, is described as a very disagreeable character. He has a couple of hundred deaths chalked up against him. I'd hate to see your name added to the list."

"Don't worry, Colonel," Peter said, smiling and standing up. "I know these concentration camp heroes."

The Colonel held out his hand. "Good luck," he said.

The men stood for a moment opposite each other, as if they still had something on their minds that needed to be said. But neither spoke.

No further reference was made to Maria. Peter turned and left the room.

⇛ 25 ⇚

PETER and Stroud had succeeded in getting the same sleeping compartment on the Munich–Berlin express. General Lowell, now stationed in Berlin, wanted to confer with Stroud on the murder investigation and the future of the camp, so Stroud arranged to make the trip with Peter.

The train left Munich at two in the afternoon, and they had the rest of the day and all night to be together and talk. Stroud had brought along a bottle of bourbon, Peter had a supply of cognac, and they settled themselves comfortably in the compartment.

"I haven't seen you for more than two minutes at a time in a dog's age," said Stroud, pouring himself a glass of whisky. "It's about time we had a chance to lean back and have a good chat."

"It certainly is," Peter agreed, "especially since I probably won't be in Germany long. I'm in a jam again, as usual."

"Maria?"

"That's right. Maria."

"What are you going to do if they send you home?"

"Oh, I'll get back somehow. As long as ships keep sailing and planes keep flying, I'm bound to find a way. And there's always swimming."

"What are you going to tell Patricia?"

"Everything."

"How will she take it, do you think?"

"I don't imagine it will exactly shatter her. She never really loved me."

Stroud smiled. "You could be wrong about that, you know."

"What makes you think so?"

"Well, for one thing, you haven't any proof that she doesn't. You just read all sorts of hidden meanings into things—meanings that may not be there at all. Like that business with the parcels."

"What parcels?"

"You told me that since you've been overseas Patricia has sent you dozens of parcels full of choice tidbits—canned asparagus tips, caviar, and God knows what all. But you were sore because the packages all came from a firm that specializes in that kind of thing. 'Parcels for the Forces,' or whatever it was. You were all worked up about it."

"Yes, I was," said Peter. "I said I preferred to get parcels that were badly packed, had all sorts of junk in them, and fell apart on the way, just so they were parcels she put together herself. With a sigh and a tear, maybe, and some trace of her hands among the salami and liverwurst. For all I care, the salami and liverwurst could fall out on the way, as long as the sigh and the tear arrived."

Stroud lit a cigar and began taking off his shoes. He was obviously amused. "I keep saying that you're a cynical idealist, or vice versa. I once had a friend who was as cynical as you but not so idealistic. He used to say, 'Marriage is an institution for the mutual bearing of troubles that one wouldn't have if one stayed single.' I don't agree with that definition. But just the same, marriage is an institution like any other and can't be built on emotion alone. American women can cry over their men who are away, but they don't necessarily send their tears overseas after them. They think there's a risk of losing their men if they show their emotion too openly. American women want to be won. That's their role, and they don't feel at home in any other."

"Every woman wants to be won. That's not an exclusive American trait, you know."

"Yes, but the American woman wants to be won over and over. She shies away from anything that gives her man the feeling that he's absolutely sure of her."

"Exactly. And that leads to a completely twisted concept of love. Don't you see, John, that it's exactly that attitude which leads to the crudeness and churlishness of American men of which their women are always complaining? Women everywhere want to be dominated, but the American woman wants to remain eternally coy. Her ideal is to be a bride forever."

"A charming idea, I'd say."

"An idiotic, inhuman idea! Being a bride may be charming, but it's only a transition. The bride matures into the wife, the romance into marriage. A perpetual honeymoon couldn't help ending in a nervous breakdown on both sides. European women prefer long engagements. American women want to marry early, because for them there's hardly any difference between engagement and marriage anyway."

Stroud looked out of the window. He knew that there was no such thing as a wholly impersonal conversation, and that Peter, for all his sweeping generalities, was at bottom talking about his own personal problem. Stroud resisted the temptation to inject personalities into their talk and remained silent.

"An eternal courtship," Peter continued after a moment, "is sure to end in frustration—the gnawing feeling of most American men that they can't dominate or satisfy their women. The time comes when the wooer drops his chivalry and pretty words and says to hell with the whole thing. That's what has happened to American men."

Stroud thought it over. "You make it sound like a vicious circle, and something so peculiarly American, as though we were unique in failure. Neither American men nor American women seem to be much good at love and marriage, the way you put it."

Peter tilted the cognac bottle and took a long drink. "Yes," he said, "but I think it's mainly the fault of the women. All over the world it's the women who set the tone in emotional relations. In America women seem to be afraid they wouldn't be able to hold their men in a relationship based solely on affection and respect.

They want conflict, a state of uncertainty, out of which they expect to make a profit."

"Oh, come now," Stroud remonstrated. "That's a little thick."

"Not at all," Peter said warmly. "It works like this: the main thing American women want to do with their men is give them an uneasy conscience. That's a very smart maneuver—from their point of view. There's nothing more useful for a woman than a man whose conscience is bothering him. America is the only country in the world where jewelers can palm off diamond wedding rings on husbands. Everywhere else the wedding ring is a simple gold band. The symbol of the bond that lasts a lifetime. In America the husband starts paying right at the start: the more diamonds, the greater the love. And he has to keep on paying, because he keeps on wanting something that is never given him willingly, to say nothing of joyfully. American women—not all of them of course, there are exceptions—have succeeded in convincing their men that for them physical love is a sacrifice, a concession. And it goes without saying that such a concession has to be paid for. Even married women have to be bribed into making the concession—with gifts or with slavery. That explains the American woman's subconscious fear of enjoying happiness in bed. Enjoying it would mean that she couldn't make a profit out of it. After all, she could hardly demand payment for something she enjoyed herself."

"That seems to dispose of that," Stroud said. "But why do you keep ascribing motives to our women that you can't really prove? You're distorting the picture. You don't even mention the Puritan tradition, which is still very much alive in the United States. It helps explain the inhibitions that prevent so many American women from giving themselves completely. You may call those inhibitions hypocritical. For all I care, you can call Puritanism hypocritical from beginning to end. But you've got to take it into account."

"Well," said Peter dryly, "when it comes to that, I'll take my Puritanism straight. If American girls never went to bed with their boy friends—or never went auto riding with them in summer, which is apt to come to the same thing—you'd be right. But it isn't that they withhold themselves. What they withhold is the enjoyment of the act. They're not ashamed of doing it. They're ashamed of enjoying it. That kind of Puritanism is a little too complicated for me."

Stroud did not answer. How bitter he is! he thought. But is it all bitterness, or is it guilt? Is he ranting against Patricia because he has deceived her? Never, since they had first met in Paris, had Peter seemed so foreign, so much like an outsider. Of course, Stroud tried to tell himself, he's an American citizen. He gave all he had to become an American citizen, and he deserves to be one. But the fact remains: he's a foreigner. Where does this stranger get the effrontery to pass judgment on our women just because he hasn't been able to find happiness with one of them? Or because he's found a foreign woman he thinks he can be happy with?

It was not easy for Stroud to suppress his irritation, but he spoke quietly. "I think it's a good thing for our women to do all they can to protect their freedom. Women's rights in our country aren't the result of long growth and evolution, you know. They were won almost overnight. It was not until 1920, for instance, that American women could vote in national elections."

"That's too bad," said Peter sarcastically. "If American women had won the right to vote under Jefferson, instead of Wilson, maybe by this time they wouldn't be so desperately jealous of their privileges."

Stroud offered his bottle to Peter. "Have a touch of bourbon?"

"No, thanks. I'll stick to my cognac."

Stroud took a drink.

"Peter," he said, "you keep talking about women finding their happiness in men. As a matter of fact, though, millions of women can't find a man they can be happy with. What are they supposed to do—jump off the Empire State Building?"

"I think that relatively such women aren't very numerous. That is, if they are willing to behave like women, and not like liberated imitations of women. But in America, where the majority rules in all public questions, it's the minority that has its way when it comes to love."

"That I don't get at all."

Peter spoke in a half-joking, half-serious way, but Stroud knew that again he was attempting to disguise the earnestness of what he was saying with cynicism.

"There is in America," he said, "a great and successful conspiracy of unhappy women—that is, women who aren't able to make a success of their love life. Naturally they don't want to be put in a class apart. So they have decided to lure happy women into a trap. They have drawn up a set of rules and regulations designed to convert women who might otherwise be happy into members of the great Sorority of the Unhappy and Disappointed. In other words, the object is to make women who have found a man just as unhappy as those who haven't. It's the same thing as with cosmetics. Originally only women with bad complexions used cosmetics. They started a universal vogue, and now it's impossible to tell who has a bad complexion and who hasn't. Unhappy American women spread their unhappiness among the others, until you can't tell the one from the other."

Stroud laughed. "Peter, you're exaggerating again. In America the divorce rate is high, and that gives many Europeans the idea that all American marriages are failures. Ridiculous of course. A thing you overlook is that the triangle of husband-wife-mistress is much less frequent in America than in Europe. Where we have divorces, Europe has the triangle, which is just a form of dishonesty and deceit. I don't see much to choose between them."

"Oh, come now," said Peter. "You're trying to tell me that if married Americans fall in love with somebody else they always go honorably to the divorce court rather than deceive their marriage partners. What actually happens is that the deception comes first, and then the divorce legalizes the deception. Anyway, a great many divorces have nothing to do with falling in love with somebody else. Usually the wife simply finds the marriage bonds uncomfortable. She wants her freedom, as she calls it. That's the bait that the emotional failures hold out to the others—freedom. The failures can hardly attack marriage itself, so they do their best to turn it into something like the mating of black widow spiders. The male black widow, you know, dies after mating. The average American male has fulfilled his function when he marries."

"Peter, that's silly!"

"It's not as ridiculous as you seem to think. Do you happen to know that there are more widows in America than in any other country? Every year there are four hundred thousand new ones. Altogether there are seven million of them."

"Good God," said Stroud, "spare me the statistics!"

"All right. But American men work themselves into an early grave, or drink themselves to death, or both. The women contribute to it by demanding that their men buy them everything that's advertised on the radio; they feed their men salads because that's what they eat to keep their figures; they encourage their men to play golf when they are too old for it, and generally to act younger than their years, because having a young husband makes the wife seem younger too. It usually ends up with the wife retaining her youth, and the husband succumbing to coronary thrombosis."

Outside the window the fields were fading in the evening sun. As the train rushed by, they seemed to be revolving slowly, as if mounted on giant turntables. Smoke was curling from the chimneys of the farmhouses; hay wagons stood waiting at the crossing barriers; the children of the railway watchmen waved at the train as it roared past. The whole landscape was serene and undisturbed, with no hint anywhere that a year before bombs had been falling, low-level fighters sweeping the skies, and men digging trenches to meet an oncoming enemy. But a little later, as the train approached Stuttgart, the ruins were outlined against the sky, with their charred walls and dead streets and heaped-up rubble.

"We might as well enjoy this trip while we can," said Stroud, who had been looking out of the window. "It's pretty nice sitting here in a comfortable sleeper, smoking and drinking and talking about American women. But Berlin will probably be a different story."

Peter nodded. "You're right, John," he said. "I don't know what Berlin will be like, but I doubt whether it's going to be pleasant."

⇨ 26 ⇦

THEY made their way with difficulty through the outer room of the crowded night club. The air was heavy and foul. Smoke hung like fat white balloons in the long room, which was profusely decorated with chipped and peeling gilt. In many places the gilt stucco-work had crumbled from the walls, and the management, unable to make repairs, had fastened red plush over the bare plaster. The odds and ends of plush hung limply from the walls like red underwear on a clothesline. The customers were so densely packed that couples who stood up to dance pushed the tables into one another's stomachs.

Inching sideways through the jam of tables and chairs, Peter and John came into the night club proper, a larger room with a bar to the left of the dance floor and a series of booths to the right. The orchestra was installed near the bar. Here the walls were too extensive to be camouflaged with plush. The cracks and peeling often ran from the molding to the floor. Through a hole in the ceiling over the bar, dust and dirt sifted down like fine rain. A champagne bucket was placed on the bar to catch the downpour, and had to be emptied from time to time. The booths were lined with the inescapable red plush; it had the worn and shabby look of long-used circus trappings. The orchestra played without interruption, as if trying to drown out some competing noise. It was an opportunistic orchestra that proclaimed its political reliability by blaring out fifteen-year-old American jazz numbers. The musicians, dressed in manifestly rented or borrowed tuxedoes, swayed and bounced to their own rhythm in awkward imitation of an American Negro jazz band.

Peter and Stroud finally found a place to sit. A Russian soldier, flanked by two German whores, was already in possession of the table. One girl had her hand on his left thigh, the other on his right. On the soldier's dirty-gray blouse were pinned five or six decorations, including the Stalingrad medal. He was blearily drunk and mumbled incoherent sentences in Russian, to which the girls paid no attention. They talked dully to each other about ration cards and the impossibility of finding adequate living quarters. From time to time they smiled fondly as if they were speaking to him sentimentally. One of the girls, a brunette with a repulsive eruption on her chin, now and then slipped her hand caressingly inside the soldier's blouse without interrupting her remarks on rations and housing.

Peter and Stroud sat with their backs to the dance floor and had to twist around to watch the dancers. The conquerors were disporting themselves with the conquered. A husky, wavy-haired American pilot danced cheek to cheek with a German girl who looked like a caricature of a German girl. A reeling British sergeant was insisting, despite her protests, on dancing with a waitress who wore a red and gold uniform, like a circus usher's. A French captain, with many a whirl and dip, was teaching a new dance step to a bedraggled beauty a head taller than he, an operation that endangered everyone else on the floor.

Most of the male dancers, however, were Russians. Majors with gold epaulettes, privates in greasy blouses, sergeants in jackboots, officers in dress uniforms, all hung with medals, pressed German girls tightly in their arms as if everything had been forgotten—the Ukraine and Stalingrad, the siege of Leningrad, and the dead of Smolensk. Peter and Stroud ordered red wine, the only drink available to those who did not bring liquor of their own.

Peter lit a cigarette and offered the pack to the two girls. The brunette began to smoke greedily, but the other slipped the cigarette into her large black handbag. The Russian was too drunk to bother about the intrusion.

"Well," said Peter to the brunette, "how do you like it here?"

"It's nice to have music again."

"Do you come here often?"

"As often as I can."

"Always with Russians?"

"No. Whoever comes along." Her answer was cold and business-like.

Peter turned to the girl who had put the cigarette in her bag. She was so wan and scrawny that she reminded him of those sun-starved plants that grow in tenement windowboxes. "How about you?" he asked. "Do you come here much?"

"This is my first time."

The brunette explained, "She just got out of a concentration camp. Half-Jew. They killed her father."

To keep the conversation going, Peter asked, "What sector do you girls live in?"

"The Russian—unfortunately," the brunette answered.

"Why 'unfortunately'?" Peter asked.

"I was assaulted fourteen times in one night. Ilse here was raped the day before yesterday. Three hours after she got out of the concentration camp."

Stroud had been listening in silence. He had come along only to help Peter in case some unforeseen difficulty arose in dealing with Storm Trooper Meister. The whole thing was no concern of his: the fetid night club amid the ruins; Berlin itself, a city unlike the one he had known before the war; the German floozies in their wretched finery; the drunken soldiers and the ear-splitting jazz that sounded like martial music. It had been months since he had felt any homesickness. Now, in the Femina Casino in Berlin, nostalgia came to him in a way that he had never before experienced. It was not a yearning for his wife, his children, his home, nor for Spokane itself. It was simply as if he had befouled himself in the depths of some pit or in the slime of a trench, and needed to bathe quickly and thoroughly. He yearned for America as if his homeland were one huge bathtub.

Then the girl across from him had spoken of being raped fourteen times, and the other girl once, right after she had been liberated from a concentration camp. That was certainly just so much bunk, Stroud thought; she was a whore, after all, and whoever heard of a whore being raped? The other girl's story of the concentration camp was probably a lie too. But he found himself listening with attention as the girls talked, and gradually the urgency of his desire for home and cleanliness seemed less and less important. What did seem tremendously important was that this sort of rottenness stop once and for all—the mutual murdering and plundering, and the victors using the women of the defeated as their natural prey. In the sick, white face of the half-Jewish girl he now discovered features that he seemed to know, and in the empty blue eyes of the drunken soldier he imagined that he saw the same brutish glint that he had detected in the eyes of the SS officer in the prison camp at Bad Reichenhall. In the smoky haze of the Femina the real faces before him blurred into faces his memory conjured up, and for an instant he could not tell which was which.

Meanwhile, all through the conversation, Peter had been surveying the night club. During the past few days he had studied the photographs of Michael Meister with such attention that he felt he could recognize the man even in a good disguise. So far he had seen no one among the waiters who resembled the pictures and descriptions of Hitler's former bodyguard.

"I'm going to the bar," he said to Stroud. "I'll be right back."

Wriggling through the press of dancers, he crossed the floor, bumping into the soft bodies of the women and against the hard ammunition pouches of the men who were dancing with pistols on their hips. Some soldiers, who carried no pistols, had come with rifles that were now leaning against the bar. Now Peter, too, was overcome with an emotion like homesickness, an aching desire for tidiness and lightness of heart, for women who had suffered no disasters and men who carried no weapons.

He ordered another glass of wine at the bar. The bartender was a wizened Italian who immediately began talking English and telling Peter about his fifteen years in Brooklyn. Peter chatted with him while watching the door behind the bar through which the waiters and waitresses passed on their way to and from the kitchen.

The atmosphere had become intolerably stifling. The big window at the right of the bar was boarded up, and not a breath of air was getting through.

"Isn't there some way to get a window open?" Peter asked the barman.

"That one opens."

Peter pushed the window open. He was startled to see that it was still broad daylight in the street. Curfew was at nine o'clock in Berlin; the "night clubs" opened at three in the afternoon and were required to close at eight in the evening. While the men and women inside gave themselves the illusion of night-time revelry, the hot sun of the summer afternoon beat down outside.

Peter remained at the window, breathing in the fresh air. There were ruins, and nothing but ruins, wherever he looked. Nowhere was a whole house still standing. But in the strong sunlight the buildings did not, somehow, look shattered, but rather as if they were in the process of being built, or as if they were half-finished sets on a movie lot. One wall of a many-storied department store across the way was still standing, and the dirty rubble was piled up in its long show window. The tall thick letters that spelled out the name of the store had strangely resisted destruction. They still hung between the third and fourth floor, and there was something almost alive in their drunken appearance. The two upright pillars of an "M" hung from the wall like the legs of a man dangling out into space from a window. A little way down the street was a group of women, with kerchiefs around their heads and buckets in their hands, laboring to clear away the rubble. In the face of the enormousness of the wreckage that lay all around, their infinitesimal beginning was tragically hilarious. Below the window, in front of the Femina building, a long queue had formed of men, women, and Allied soldiers waiting to be admitted to the night club. It was a patient crowd, inured to standing in line for bread, milk, and mess. The soldiers had precedence. They shoved men and women aside, so that many who once had places at the head of the line found themselves farther and farther from the door as time went on. Now and then a soldier grabbed a girl out of the dance-hungry line, and she went obediently off with him. The September afternoon had the unhealthy dampness of a fever patient's bed. Behind Peter the orchestra was playing "Yes, We Have No Bananas."

Then there came to Peter the feeling that he ought to turn around at once. He did not believe in premonitions and he was skeptical of hunches, but years in the OSS had developed and sharpened an inexplicable instinct in him. He had learned to catch the scent of people and of danger like a bloodhound.

At the bar, a tray full of glasses in his hands, stood the man who was probably the last to have seen Adolf Hitler alive.

⇛ 27 ⇚

EARLY next morning Peter was already posted out of sight but within view of the cellar door to which he had trailed Meister the evening before. At about ten Meister emerged and walked off in the direction of Kurfürstendamm. Peter did not follow, but descended into the cellar.

Nothing was left of the house except the cellar, and in it the family of a tailor named Kofler had installed itself. The tailor, his wife, and their three children, whose ages ranged from two to seven, lived in one damp room. A second room, much smaller—apparently a storage compartment in the days when the house had been standing—was rented to Meister, who now called himself

Werner. Opposite the door through which Peter had entered was a stairway that once had led to the hallway of the first floor, but now boards had been nailed over it to form a rough ceiling. A trap door had been cut through them to furnish an additional exit.

Peter was quickly convinced that the Kofler family had no inkling that their boarder was anything but an ordinary waiter who had taken up his trade again after being released from the Wehrmacht. The tailor was an old Social Democrat who had been mistreated by the Nazis and was now terrified by the thought that he might get into trouble with the occupation authorities. He assured Peter sincerely that he would do everything he could to be of help to the American Army.

"I'll take a chance on you," Peter told him. "Say nothing to your lodger about my visit. I'll be back this evening, in civilian clothes. You're to tell this Herr Werner that I'm a cousin of yours who escaped from Silesia. I'm on my way to the American zone, and I'm spending the night here. My name is Peter Kern. Got it?"

Peter spent the afternoon at OSS headquarters. He had previously checked on the political reliability of the tailor and found that his impression of the man's anti-Nazi attitude confirmed his own investigation. He selected garments from the well-stocked OSS wardrobe and dressed himself like a fugitive workman, in tattered dungarees, a worn Wehrmacht coat and run-down shoes.

A curious dread overcame him as, toward seven that evening, he turned off the street into the doorway that led to the cellar. He was no stranger to fear; he had been afraid of every parachute jump he had ever made. But always before he had managed to convert his fear into a purely physical discomfort. He had been able to banish the thought of danger from his mind, and fear remained only in the form of a bodily pain somewhere in the pit of his stomach. Now, as he slowly stomped down the dark stairway, fear assaulted him with the violence of his childhood days: it reached out for him with invisible hands, and he wanted to run as a small child runs until, breathless, it reaches an illuminated room. He stopped and tried to pull himself together. What's wrong with me? he asked himself. Is it because I've found happiness that I no longer want to take risks? Or is it simply that everything was easier during the war? He could not tell.

A smoking kerosene lamp was the only illumination. Two candle stubs, fastened to the table with wax, were not lit. The place smelled of bedding and wine. The three children were playing in a dark corner with a broken hobbyhorse. Frau Kofler was washing dishes over a trough, and the tailor was darning a pair of pants. He sat at the long board table, his spectacles teetering on his bony nose, and blinked shortsightedly at the light of the lamp. Peter sat next to him.

They waited. Peter had already searched Meister's cubbyhole; he had found nothing but a few pieces of clothing and some routine identification papers bearing the name of Werner.

"How did you meet this Werner?" Peter asked, his eyes on the rickety stairs that led from the street to the cellar.

"The owner of the Femina sent him here. He wanted some work done on a jacket. Werner told me he had been bombed out and had to sleep in a different place every night. We needed the money, so we moved the children out of that room and rented it to him."

"Have you noticed anything unusual about his behavior?"

"No. He sleeps late, goes out about ten or eleven, and comes back shortly before curfew. Then he usually sits here and chats with us for a half hour or so. We never talk politics. He doesn't have any visitors, and he pays regularly. He pays in Allied marks that he gets at the Femina. That's a big advantage for us."

Peter looked at his wristwatch, which he was carrying in his coat pocket, since no fugitive would be wearing a wristwatch. It was almost nine, and he began to get impatient.

"Where did you say you used to live?" he asked the tailor to break the silence.

"Here, on the third floor. We were bombed out. We were lucky to get the cellar."

"Well, at least the children get out into the open air during the day, don't they?"

"Oh, yes. They play games among the ruins."

"What kind of games?"

The tailor laid the pants aside for a moment. He looked at Peter over his spectacles. His little red-rimmed eyes were lifeless and looked as if they saw nothing. "They play war," he said. "The biggest and strongest are always the Americans."

"Americans!" said Peter in astonishment. "Do you mean to say that German children make games out of Germany's defeat?"

"Of course. All they love is strength and power."

It was nine o'clock now. Peter thought, is this man playing me for a fool? Has he warned Meister? Just then he heard heavy, unhurried footsteps outside the door.

Meister-Werner was dark and hulking, apparently about thirty years old. Where there was hair on his balding head, it was short and bristly. His head, shoulders, and hands were all squarish, so that he would have looked disturbingly like a robot except that an unusually large, flabby nose and wide, thick ears added a gross flesh-and-blood vulgarity to his appearance. But it was not the baseness of the man's features that alone repelled Peter. At the night club, probably even in the photographs, Peter had detected something in that face that hinted at a familiar malevolence, a taint that recalled someone he had once known but who had slipped from his conscious memory. Now, as the Storm Trooper stood opposite him in the light of the kerosene lamp, Peter's indefinable feeling of revulsion grew stronger.

"Good evening," Meister grunted.

"Good evening," said the Koflers.

Meister looked searchingly at Peter a moment.

"This is my cousin, Peter Kern," the tailor said. "He's just in from Silesia. He's spending the night here."

"Pleased to meet you. My name's Werner," said the waiter. He was obviously far from pleased and he avoided Peter's eyes.

"Sit down, why don't you?" Kofler said. He was playing his role as well as he could.

Meister sat down at the table. "Where you from, Herr Kern?" he asked.

"Breslau."

"Pretty badly smashed up there?"

"Everything smashed."

"Breslau put up a pretty good fight."

"Ja. We were still holding out when the Russians were a good hundred kilometers to the west," Peter said proudly. He added, "Berlin didn't do so badly either. They gave the Russians a fight for it."

Meister muttered something.

"Were you in Berlin during the siege?" Peter asked. It was intended to sound casual and conversational, but Peter felt he hadn't brought it off very well. His own voice sounded odd and false to him. He looked up. Meister seemed to be studying him.

Frau Kofler was trying to put the children to bed. Dirty mattresses without sheets were lying along the wall. The little girl cried, and the two boys protested loudly. The younger of the two boys, who was about five, wanted something to eat. His seven-year-old brother, in the voice of a petulant old man, said, "Ach, Gerhard always wants something to eat."

The tailor turned to his guests apologetically. "You just can't give the kids enough to eat these days."

Peter asked, "Don't you get special rations for young children?"

"Oh, yes," said Kofler. "But they're not nearly enough."

"You can't even get all the rations your card calls for," Meister added.

"God damn it!" said Peter bitterly. "If only we could have held out two months longer! We wouldn't have lost the war then!"

The Storm Trooper looked at him with frank curiosity. "How do you figure that?"

"In two months' time the secret weapon would have been ready," said Peter, lowering his voice. "That's why the Führer wanted to fight on. But he was betrayed."

"Betrayed? By whom?" Meister asked.

"Why, the whole bunch," Peter replied. "Himmler and Göring. The generals. Even the Storm Troops and the SS." Peter waited tensely for Meister's reply. It came after a long silence.

"Maybe," he said.

Peter did not want the subject to die out. "They say in Breslau," he said, "that even on the very last day the Führer issued orders to fight on. But the orders were never relayed to the troops."

Meister turned to the tailor. "If they say that, they know more about it in Breslau than we do," he said with an offensive laugh.

"Well, isn't it so?" Peter asked, as if anxious to get at the truth.

"How should I know?" Meister retorted. Suspicion came back into his wooden face, and something that looked like fear. Where have I seen that face before? Peter wondered again.

The two boys had gone to sleep. Frau Kofler sat at the table with the girl in her arms. In her weariness and emaciation she looked like the child's grandmother.

Peter felt he wasn't getting anywhere. The tailor yawned. Th lamp spluttered feebly. In a few minutes they would all be going to bed. Peter had to risk a more direct approach.

"I keep telling Cousin Anton here," he began, "it's not all lost even yet." He leaned closer to his "cousin" and continued. "In Silesia they say the Führer isn't dead at all. They say the English have got him on an island, like Napoleon. Some day—"

He did not risk looking at Meister. The big silence in the room seemed to have been put together from smaller pieces of silence. Each of them was silent in a different way. Meister was stubbornly and malevolently silent. Frau Kofler was drowsily silent. The tailor was clumsily silent, like someone waiting for something to happen.

The silence was broken in a way that Peter did not expect. It was Meister who spoke. "The Führer is dead," he said.

"How do you know?" said Peter indignantly.

"I saw his corpse," said Meister with deadly quiet.

Peter thought, this is all implausible. It's like a bad movie. Something's wrong here. But he could not tell what it was. "Nobody has seen the Führer's body," he said challengingly.

Meister stood up. He crossed the room to the stairs which led to the trap door. Peter followed him with his eyes. He saw that Meister remained standing at the foot of the stairs. "I carried the corpse out of the shelter myself," said Meister.

Peter could not see his eyes, but he felt that they were full of menace. At that moment the face he had been groping for came to him. It was the face of the strapping half-brother with whom he had fought in the yard of his father's estate. The resemblance was not pronounced, but to Peter it seemed uncannily strong as he sat rigid, waiting for what Meister would say next.

"We burned the body in the courtyard of the Chancellery, so that the Russians could never defile it," Meister said. "But it makes no difference whether the Führer died or not. The Führer will come again!"

The lamp had almost burned out. Peter thought, the man has something else in mind. He's not revealing all this just to do me a favor. Now Peter became acutely conscious that the children were asleep on the floor directly behind him, but he did not know at once why this circumstance seemed so important. Then, as had happened often before when danger was so close that he felt he could reach out and touch it like a physical presence, a cool, de-

tached calm came over him. The tenseness and agitation inside
subsided; his thoughts and reactions sharpened and clarified, like
outlines coming into focus under a microscope. This man is going
to shoot, he thought. The children are in the line of fire. I've got
to move from this spot.

"I think I'll go to bed," he said. He stood up and stretched.
"Where can I lie down?"

He took a few steps, so that he stood with his back to the wall
where there was no one behind him.

At that instant he heard the voice of the Storm Trooper, harsh
and peremptory, "Hands up, all of you! *Hände hoch!*"

Frau Kofler screamed and pressed the child to her. Meister was
standing on the first step, his revolver pointed into the room. A
fraction of an instant passed. Peter looked swiftly around in the
narrow, crowded room. It was hopeless. He raised his hands.

"You lousy American spy," Meister said. "Do you think I didn't
see you snooping around the Femina? So you want to know if the
Führer is dead? He's dead, all right. But you won't live to tell
about it." Walking backward, he mounted another step. "Do you
think I fell for that silly line of yours?" he said.

"You're crazy," Peter replied calmly. He was playing for time.
He tried to calculate quickly what would happen in the next few
moments, so that he could anticipate Meister's move with one of
his own. The room was narrow, but long. With Meister standing
on the stairs, Kofler and his wife were too far removed from Peter
for the pistol to cover all three at once. The question in Peter's
mind was whether Meister trusted his host sufficiently to permit
him to keep standing out of the pistol's line of fire. If not, Meister
would have to bunch all three together in a single group.

"Kofler, you bastard, go stand next to the American," Meister
ordered.

This was what Peter had been waiting for. Meister's gun had
veered for the shade of a second from Peter to Kofler. Peter ducked
and catapulted himself forward. His lunge carried him to the table,
and with a sweep of his left hand he grasped the lamp and pro-
pelled it at Meister, all in one motion. At the same time his right
hand went inside his coat to his shoulder holster and drew his
automatic. The room was in total darkness.

He did not want to shoot. A dead witness was no good to the

OSS. But he had no choice. Meister fired blindly into the darkness. The lamp had apparently missed him. Peter crouched behind the table. Meister shot again. The children, Peter thought. He rested his automatic on the edge of the table and fired in the direction of the stairs. He heard a scream of insane fright. It was Frau Kofler. He shot again. His hand squeezed the trigger three or four times. The reverberations of his last shot died away and the cellar lapsed into silence. It was so still that it seemed as if the sound had broken to pieces and fallen to the floor like splinters of glass. The silence was stifling. It lasted only a second. Then he heard the wailing of the woman and the crying of the terrified children.

Peter lit a match under the table. As he cautiously raised himself from his crouch, he saw Meister stretched out on the stairs, his head toward the bottom. A rivulet of blood was seeping out from under his body. Peter saw that he was alive; he was trying feebly to raise his head.

Not until Peter had risen fully did he become aware that he was wounded himself. At first he felt nothing but a wet warmth over his left breast, just under the collarbone. Then his whole chest began to pain, while the warmth seemed to spread all over his body. The pain was not intense, but rather a peculiar, steady pounding, as if someone were trying to hammer a nail into his chest.

"Light the candles," he said to Kofler, who was bent over his moaning wife.

In the light of the candle stubs Peter saw that his clothing was drenched with blood. "Go out and get help right away," he ordered. "Stop the first American jeep or soldier you see. Tell them to rush an ambulance here. Tell them to take care of Werner first. It's important."

Kofler was on his way as Peter repeated, "Remember, Werner first . . ." He did not know whether Kofler heard him; he could barely hear his own voice. He could no longer remember why it was important to take care of Meister-Werner first. He wanted to say something else, but it was as if his voice came from his brain to his mouth through a thin glass pipe, and the pipe suddenly broke.

Then the flickering light of the little candles was blotted out, and he pitched forward into the blackness.

WHEN Stroud entered the recreation hall, usually the scene of amateur theatricals, movies, and concerts, he hardly recognized the place. The enthusiasm and thoroughness with which it had been converted into a courtroom seemed to indicate that the prisoners were taking the proceedings seriously and that his idea for an experimental trial was a happy one.

On the stage stood a long table covered with green cloth, and upon it in neat array were bound records, books, papers, and pencils. Before the place reserved for the president of the court was a crucifix. A jury box had been dispensed with on account of lack of materials, but chairs for the jurors were arranged to the right and left of the president's chair.

In front of the stage, to the left, was the dock, and next to it a table and chair for the defense counsel. To the right, where the jury box would normally have been in a German court, was the witness stand. The first row of seats in the auditorium was reserved for Stroud and his officers; no other American soldiers were in the audience. The second row was occupied by stenographers and reporters for the camp newspaper. All the other seats were taken by prisoners, who were admitted to the hall without any restrictions except those imposed by space. Only the two Military Police who stood on either side of the dock indicated that the proceedings were taking place in an American prisoner-of-war camp.

The defendant Emil Teitinger was already seated in the prisoner's box when Stroud entered. He looked even thinner than before, and his long, scrawny neck emerging from his oversized collar gave him something of the look of a starved vulture in a cage. His counsel was busy with papers and transcripts at the table near by. Teitinger had chosen his defender himself. He was Dr. Josef Stülpnagel, a trial lawyer by profession, who had been a top sergeant in the Wehrmacht. He was a small, rotund man with flaming red hair, gold-rimmed glasses, and nervous, jerky movements; in his untidy uniform he looked more like a lawyer playing at being a soldier than a soldier playing at being a lawyer.

When the president of the court, followed by the jurymen, entered and took their places, everyone in the auditorium arose.

Stroud had insisted, over the protests of his staff, that the American officers also show their respect for the court by arising. He himself was the first to do so.

The president and the prosecutor, who sat at the extreme right end of the long green table, were the only two officials in the court whom Stroud had selected and installed himself. Dr. Hermann Kresse, the president, had not only been a county judge in a small Hessian city, but had also won a position of unquestioned authority in the camp. He was more than fifty years old and had been drafted into the Wehrmacht only in the last desperate call-up. His snow-white hair and finely modeled ascetic head gave him an austere dignity, modified only by the warmth of his steady gray eyes. For some time Stroud had noticed that in disputes among the prisoners Dr. Kresse's judgment was frequently appealed to and invariably accepted. Since he had never been a member of the party, he seemed ideally suited in every way for the role of president of the court.

The prosecutor was not a lawyer by profession. Political consid-erations had to be taken into account in choosing him. Stroud consulted at length with Langhoff and with his own barracks ser-geants before settling on Hans Honegger, a young anti-Nazi of thirty who had been a newspaper linotyper in civilian life. A blond, blue-eyed giant, he had been a particular source of aggravation to the National Socialists, since physically he corresponded precisely to their own text-book descriptions of the Nordic ideal. During his years of uncertain employment he had devoted himself chiefly to study, in the hope of trying his luck as a journalist after the war. Stroud hoped that Honegger's lack of legal training—which put him at a distinct disadvantage as opposed to the experienced defense counsel—would be compensated for by his intelligence, fluency, and unusually winning personality.

The most important men in Stroud's great experiment were un-known to him: the twelve "good men and true" who were to pronounce the verdict in the murder of Private Gerecke. They had been chosen by public lot from a list of more than a thousand vol-unteers—a gratifyingly large number, in Stroud's opinion. Now they meant nothing more to him than twelve names.

While Teitinger's civilian status was being recorded and the indictment read, the Major attempted to read the faces of the twelve jurors. It was far more difficult than he expected. At home an experienced trial lawyer could read everything he wanted to know from the faces of the talesmen. He sometimes made mistakes, of course, because in America as elsewhere there are faces that conceal more than they reveal, but Stroud had almost always been able to probe behind the face into the personality of the prospective juror. Here even the faces seemed to speak a foreign language.

The morning was consumed in formalities and in establishing the undisputed facts of the crime. Shortly after the noon recess the court visited the barracks in which Teitinger and his victim had lived. The latrine and trash can where the dagger was found were also inspected. At two o'clock the examination of the accused began.

The recreation hall was packed. The prisoners sat squeezed shoulder to shoulder on the long benches. Looking them over, Stroud wondered whether the strong cordon of MP's he had posted around the building as a precaution against possible incidents was necessary at all. He was still capable of astonishment at the flawless discipline of these men who automatically obeyed every order and direction given them. No incident was going to occur.

The defendant took his place opposite the green table, in front of the president, and the examination began.

President: Defendant Teitinger, you have admitted that you killed your fellow prisoner, Private Helmuth Gerecke, with a dagger in Latrine B on September 9, 1945, at about 1:15 A.M. Do you stand by this confession?

Defendant: Yes, sir.

President: In the course of the preliminary hearing, doubt was raised as to the credibility of your motive. You will concede that a murder or homicide resulting from so trivial a dispute as that which is related in your confession is unusual, to say the least. Did you have additional grounds for holding a grudge against Gerecke?

Defendant: No, sir.

President: Was there some circumstance about the alleged unjust distribution of straw that especially aroused your anger?

Defendant: Yes, sir.

President: Please explain to the jury.

Defendant: Gerecke regularly discriminated in favor of his friends. The instance which started the quarrel was not the first one. Gerecke had been doing the same thing for weeks.

President: Had you previously remonstrated with him on this account?

Defendant: Yes, sir.

Prosecutor: Mr. President, if I may—

President: Mr. Prosecutor.

Prosecutor: I respectfully request the court to note that in the preliminary examination the defendant stated that he had just met Gerecke the day before the murder. [Stir in the courtroom.]

President: Defendant, tell the court how you came into possession of this weapon [indicating dagger on table].

Defendant: I decline to answer. [Stir in the court.]

President: Tell us what happened in the latrine.

Defendant: When I got to the latrine, Gerecke was already there. He spoke angrily to me because of the way I'd acted that morning. I repeated my charge that he played favorites. I told him this was not a comradely thing to do. One word led to another. Finally Gerecke threatened to report me to the camp authorities. We started to fight. I lost my head and stabbed him.

President: A question, Mr. Prosecutor?

Prosecutor: Yes, sir. Will the defendant tell us what Gerecke accused him of? He has testified that Gerecke threatened to denounce him to the camp authorities. What did Gerecke know that was to the disadvantage of the Defendant Teitinger?

Defendant: When I was first brought to the camp and interrogated, I concealed the fact that I was a party member. Gerecke knew and threatened to tell the camp authorities about it.

Following the examination of Teitinger, the calling of witnesses was begun. Two witnesses testified for the defense that they heard the dispute between Teitinger and Gerecke, and the American guard—examined by an American officer—described how he caught Teitinger trying to sneak back into his barracks on the night of the murder. Several further witnesses supported the contention of the prosecution that Teitinger must have heard Gerecke leave his bed and go to the latrine.

The second day was to be devoted to cross-examination by defense and prosecution, as well as to summations. It was likely that a verdict would be reached that evening.

As the second session opened, Stroud felt an increased tension in the courtroom. There was a vague but unmistakable restlessness in the air. Nearly thirty years of law practice had developed in Stroud an almost infallible sixth sense for gauging the moods of courtroom crowds. He trusted this instinct so implicitly that the opening words of the session had hardly been spoken when he went outside to inspect the guards around the building. He was no longer certain that an incident of some kind was out of the question. He returned to his seat satisfied that all necessary precautions had been taken. The prosecutor had begun his questioning of Teitinger.

Prosecutor: Defendant Teitinger, you testified that you first concealed your membership in the National Socialist party. Why did you do that?

Defendant: I was afraid that party members would be treated less well here than others.

Prosecutor: Defendant Teitinger, were you aware of the political attitude of your victim, Gerecke?

Defendant, hesitates: No.

Prosecutor, emphasizing every word, after a deliberately calculated pause: Isn't it true that you remarked to Technical Sergeant Ulrich that Gerecke was a traitor? [Sensation in the court.]

Defendant: I don't remember.

Prosecutor: I'll try to refresh your memory. Isn't it true that on September 7, two days before the stabbing, you said to Corporal Wilhelmsberg, "Gerecke has betrayed the Führer"? You added, "And he'll pay for it too."

Defendant, with an appealing look toward his lawyer: I don't remember.

Prosecutor: Isn't it true that in your quarrel with Gerecke you made a reference to "a dirty bunch of traitors"?

Defendant, rattled: I don't remember.

Prosecutor: Isn't it true that you discussed the three poisonings in the camp with Private First Class Brink?

Defendant: It's possible. Everybody talked about them.

Prosecutor: Isn't it true that you stated, "That's what they get for licking American boots. It served them right."

Defendant, hesitates, and turns to the president: I request permission to confer with my lawyer. [Commotion in the court-room.]

President: Has the prosecution any objections?

Prosecutor: No, sir. But I would first like to inform the court that when the examination is resumed, I intend to ask permission to call the prisoners Ulrich, Wilhelmsberg, and Brink to the stand.

President: Your request is taken under advisement. Meanwhile this court is recessed for fifteen minutes.

Outside, the prisoners attending the trial gathered in groups and discussed the new turn the examination had taken. Other prisoners, who had not been able to obtain seats, joined them to hear what had happened. The defendant and his lawyer stood together, apart from the others. The lawyer was talking excitedly to his "client." His round face was now almost as red as his hair; it was hard to tell where his forehead ended and his hair began. Members of the court sat on the whitewashed stones around the recreation hall, while the president paced up and down fending off the curious who attempted to approach the jurors. Hans Honegger, the prosecutor, was the only one who had not left the hall. For Stroud, standing in the doorway with his officers, the proceedings had taken on a more blatantly theatrical aspect than ever. He was no longer satisfied with his experiment. The whole thing now gave him the feeling of being the manager of some shoddy road company, whose rehearsals had been interrupted for a few minutes. The actors had left the stage for a hurried smoke in the sun outside the theater. A disturbing aura of unreality and make-believe hung over everything.

As soon as the court reconvened, the defense lawyer requested the floor. He asked the president to permit the defendant to make a declaration.

President: The defendant may speak.

Defendant, quietly at first, but with increasing firmness: I would like to make a statement to the court. I stabbed Helmuth Gerecke to death because he was a traitor to the Fatherland. [Commotion in the court; murmuring and half-suppressed calls.] We prisoners in this camp are nothing but guinea pigs. The Americans want to prove that we are a band of traitors and weaklings, devoid of loyalty to our own country. They want to shame us before the whole world and prevent forever the restoration of Germany's honor. Not content with our defeat, they want to destroy our pride in being Germans and National Socialists.

Teitinger paused briefly. The president looked at Stroud for some indication as to what he ought to do. The impact of the risk Stroud had taken in staging the trial now came home to him in full force. He became suddenly aware that freedom could be exactly as dangerous an instrument as tyranny, and that everything depended on whose hand wielded the instrument. At the same time he realized that both freedom and tyranny were affirmations which, once made, had to be adhered to. There was no way back.

He nodded almost imperceptibly to the president as a sign that he was to allow Teitinger to continue. Teitinger resumed:

Defendant: Gerecke was a traitor. He licked the boots of the Americans. He informed on comrades who remained loyal to their Führer. He toadied to the guards and gained personal advantage by doing so. He did everything he could to prolong our stay in this camp because here he felt secure.

President, interrupting: The court takes cognizance of your confession, Defendant. You are admitting the premeditated murder of Private Helmuth Gerecke for reasons of political opposition.

Defendant, loudly: Not because of political opposition. Gerecke was a traitor.

President: When was it that you decided to kill Gerecke?

Defendant: I don't remember.

President: Did anyone give you orders to kill Gerecke?

Defendant: No, sir. Gerecke was a traitor. I know the Americans will hang me. [With burning eyes.] But from this court of German men I demand understanding and support for my deed, which was nothing but the justifiable execution of a traitor. Nobody knew my intentions in advance. But because I was among the first to lift up again the fallen banner, my name will go down in the history of our Fatherland. Men everywhere will follow my example. Down with traitors! *Heil Hitler!*

There was complete quiet in the hall. Stroud sat forward tensely, trying to fathom the meaning of the strange silence. Did it indicate fear of punishment, or had Teitinger's speech fallen on unresponsive ears? Only one thing was certain: the play-acting had become reality, the farce had become deadly earnest.

Teitinger made no further statement. Hans Honegger delivered a summation that Stroud himself could not have bettered. He stressed the moral significance of the verdict which was about to be reached. The trial, he said, had become more than a mere process for passing judgment on a murderer—much more was now at stake: it was up to the jury to prove that German men no longer wished to be identified with National Socialism and its methods. It might be true, as the defendant stated, that this camp was an experimental institution. But what the Americans were seeking was not the humiliation of the Germans. On the contrary, the Americans were offering prisoners an opportunity to demonstrate that Germans were worthy of being accepted into the family of nations on an equal footing with their neighbors. "This court," Honegger concluded, "has only limited powers of judgment and recommendation. It can propose that the accused be cleared. It can convict him and recommend mercy, or it can convict him and suggest the death penalty. But the fate of the defendant Teitinger is no longer the major issue. With your verdict, gentlemen, you pass judgment on yourselves. With your verdict you sit in judgment on the whole German people."

Stroud studied the faces of the jurors as Honegger spoke. Again he was baffled, unable to read any reaction in them.

The counsel for the defense arose and began his plea. Dr. Stülpnagel's summation was cautious and skillful. He did not attempt to vilify the victim. He attacked the National Socialist regime under which the defendant had grown to manhood. The regime, he argued, had made moral slaves out of the German people. It had inoculated Germans, who were inclined to discipline—yes, to blind obedience—with a completely fallacious concept of duty. The defendant, as a prisoner, simply could not bring himself to accept a sudden "transvaluation of values," as Nietzsche had phrased it. Teitinger had continued to act the part of a soldier. "Consider, gentlemen of the jury," Dr. Stülpnagel concluded, "consider how you yourselves would have judged this case one short year ago. I agree with the prosecutor that your verdict will include a judgment on yourselves as Germans. If you condemn this man, you thereby declare yourselves to be adherents of that policy of 'no mercy for the Germans' which would make a new life impossible for millions of Teitingers. To ask the death penalty for this man means proclaiming to America and the world at large that we Germans ourselves advocate, not a national rebirth and a new Germany, but revenge, revenge, revenge! The choice is up to you."

The jury withdrew to deliberate. No one in the courtroom moved. Outside, it had begun to rain. It was still early afternoon, but Stroud had to order the lights turned on. The heavy raindrops beat with such force on the flimsy walls and loose windowpanes that voices had to be raised to be heard by neighbors. The atmosphere of the hall was fidgety and uncomfortable, like that of a schoolroom toward the closing hour, when everyone is impatient to go home but knows that first an examination must be taken.

The deliberations lasted two full hours; the dinner hour had to be postponed. Finally the president of the court and the jurymen filed back into the hall and took their seats. Once again Stroud searched for some clue in the faces of the jurors. Then the president began to speak. He talked so quietly that only the first few rows could hear him: "The jurors of the first German prisoner-of-war court, after two hours of deliberation, have reached a verdict in the case of Corporal Emil Teitinger, accused of murdering his fellow prisoner, Helmuth Gerecke. In secret balloting, by seven votes to five, the jury finds for acquittal."

Stroud stood up. He walked past the silent rows of prisoners to the exit. The president was still speaking, explaining the grounds on which the verdict had been reached. Stroud did not want to hear them. He went bareheaded through the warm rain. Water trickled down the back of his neck. He did not notice. The sky over Munich was stabbed with lightning from the storm as it rolled away.

In his office Stroud sat down and addressed a letter to General Lowell. He wrote: "The undersigned, Major John T. Stroud, 0-306893, respectfully requests that he be relieved of his present duties, and sent to the United States."

29

"A VISITOR to see you, Major Olden," the nurse said and withdrew.

Peter had time to wonder whether he had heard correctly. If she really meant "Major" Olden, that was certainly good news—beyond the mere fact of promotion. If the OSS had actually put him up for advancement, they must have regarded his mission to Berlin as successful. And that would mean that Meister had not died and taken his secret with him after all. Everything comes down finally to a matter of trifles, Peter thought. Often only a few inches. A few inches one way or the other and the last witness to Hitler's death would have gotten a free passport to hell before he was due. One or two inches lower in my chest, and I'd be stretched out in a coffin, six feet under. He looked around the pleasantly cool white hospital room. Much better than a coffin, he decided.

He watched the door eagerly, and was a little disappointed when it opened and Colonel Whimsley entered.

"Hello there, Major Olden," said the Colonel, grinning. "How do you feel?"

"So it's true. Many thanks, Colonel."

"Don't mention it, my boy." Although the Colonel was only a few years older than Peter, he was fond of using a fatherly tone toward him from time to time. "It was about time you got your pair of those little oak leaves. How are things?"

"Fine. I think they're taking the bandage off tomorrow. Major Wynder figures I can leave the hospital next week sometime."

"Glad to hear it."

"Colonel, what about our friend Meister?"

"He survived too. I don't think we'll promote him to major though. Could you dictate a report on the affair tomorrow?"

"I can do it today."

"Tomorrow will be time enough. I'll send you a clerk."

Peter's face clouded. "How about the others in the cellar?" he asked. "The children?"

"They came through with nothing worse than a bad scare. Kofler is all right too. But the woman is dead. She got it in the head."

"Damn," said Peter. "Always the innocent bystander. Maybe I could have done something for her if I hadn't passed out. A stupid thing to do, passing out."

"You bled like a stuck pig," said the Colonel. "If the ambulance had come fifteen minutes later, you'd be dictating your Meister report to the angels."

"How long was I in the hospital in Berlin?"

"Three days."

"I'm much obliged to you for having me flown here to Munich, Colonel. I don't know a soul in Berlin."

Colonel Whimsley turned a cigarette between his fingers without lighting it. "You can be sure we didn't bring you here just to make you happy. We don't want any more OSS officers in Berlin than necessary right now. Not if the Russians know it, at any rate. And we want you around when Meister begins to talk."

The Colonel stood up. "Are you allowed to smoke, Peter?"

"After tomorrow. But I think I'll try it today."

The Colonel gave him a cigarette and lit his own. They smoked silently. The Colonel walked up and down the little room and Peter sat up in bed.

Colonel Whimsley broke the silence. "Did you hear that they relaxed the non-fraternization law day before yesterday?"

"Yes," Peter said. "She's coming to see me today."

"I've talked to the General," the Colonel continued. "You need a rest. As soon as you can travel, you're to go to the States for twenty-one days."

"So you're giving me a chance to forget?"

"No," said the Colonel with one of his derisive smiles. "You're not exactly a royal prince that gets sent off on a world tour when he commits some indiscretion. The General wants to hear your report on both Argonaut and Meister. And you're supposed to answer a lot of questions for some Senate committee too."

"And that's all, Colonel?"

"The General also wants to give you an opportunity to get things straightened out in your own mind. Everything looks different from over there." Again the Colonel assumed his fatherly tone, this time seriously. "Believe me, Peter. Everything looks different from over there."

30

NOT until they were on the way to the hospital did Stroud begin to talk of Maria.

He had called for Wanda at the DP camp, and they were walking to the hospital, which was only about twenty minutes away. Stroud had told her of the episode in Paris, of Peter's extraordinary career in the Army, and he had often elaborated to her on his conversations with Peter. He had also mentioned Maria from time to time, but Wanda always changed the subject when her name was mentioned.

Now Wanda broke into Stroud's random remarks. "Are we going to meet that woman at the hospital?"

"Maria? Yes," Stroud replied. "In fact we have to pick her up at a café near the hospital and take her in. Germans aren't allowed in unless accompanied by an American officer." He added apologetically, "I promised Peter."

She involuntarily tossed her head. "Then I'd better not go along."

"Why not?"

"So far I've avoided shaking hands with a German—man or woman."

"I know Maria," Stroud answered warmly. "Not only from what Peter's told me about her. I brought her the news when he was wounded. She's not the usual type of German."

"Are you in love with her too?"

He looked at her in surprise. "Of course not," he said. "I couldn't possibly be in love with her. I'm much too fond of you."

He was certain that he hadn't wanted to say that, and he wasn't even sure he wished to admit it to himself. All his life, even as a young man, he had made it a rule to consider carefully before he spoke. Now he was dismayed: he had spoken without thinking.

It somehow reassured him that she seemed as astonished as he. She could not reply. They walked along in silence.

Maria was waiting for them in the café around the corner from the hospital. Stroud introduced the women to each other. They said "How do you do?" in English, and did not extend their hands. Stroud had trouble hiding his embarrassment.

On the way to the hospital Maria asked, "How is Peter?"

"Fine," Stroud answered. "He ought to leave the hospital Thursday or Friday."

"Do you think he'll be able to come out to our house to rest a little?"

"Maybe. But I hear they want to send him to America for a few weeks. To recuperate." What's the matter with me? he thought. I didn't want to say that either. It's Peter's business to tell her. He added hurriedly, "That's not certain though. I just heard some talk."

He avoided looking at her and stared ahead down the street. He felt that he had actually heard her heart stop for an instant when he said "to America." But then she said calmly, "That would do him a lot of good."

They went through the corridors of the half-ruined hospital. It smelled of disinfectant, like a hospital, and of dust and plaster, like a bombed building. Nurses in trim uniforms went in and out of jagged holes that had once been doorways.

Then they were in Peter's room.

Maria entered first, and Peter reached out both hands to her. Only after he had kissed her hands did he notice the others.

There were only two chairs in the room. The two women sat on them, while Stroud found place on the edge of the bed.

"First of all, congratulations!" he said. "I hope nobody's brought you your oak leaves yet."

"Thanks, John. No, nobody did."

Stroud took the little gold insignia out of his pocket and attached them to the collar of Peter's pajamas. His visitors gave the new major a round of applause.

Then there was silence in the room. There was much of which they did not want to speak. Peter did not want to talk about his injury; nor Maria of his leave; nor Stroud of Wanda; and Wanda had no inclination to open a conversation in which a German woman would take part.

Finally Maria said, "How was Berlin?"

"Hardly recognizable."

"Were you in Kronprinzenallee?"

"Of course. I wanted to see what was left of the house you used to live in. There's hardly anything standing."

"I know. It was bad enough when we were bombed out. It's probably worse now."

"How's Helga?"

"Very well, thanks. She's at home."

The conversation lagged again. This time it was Stroud who took it up. He asked, "Does your wound still hurt, Peter?"

"Not at all. I don't know why they keep me here." To change the subject, he turned to Wanda. "Are things any better at the camp? John is forever complaining about how you are treated there."

"It gets worse every day."

"There's a Polish DP camp in our village now," Maria interjected. "They complain about conditions there too."

Something prompted Peter to ask, "Have you spoken to any of them?"

"Oh, yes. Many of them come up to the house for a couple of eggs or a glass of milk."

Wanda cut in, "So it's come to that. Poles going to Germans for charity. That's just another result of shutting us up in DP camps. And that's what we call victory!"

The men wondered what they ought to say. But Maria went right ahead, "No, Miss Komarnicki. The Poles are too proud to ask for anything. They break into houses and take what they need. Or they just come and sit and talk. Charity doesn't enter into it. They have a right to get back at least part of what we took from them."

Both men looked at Wanda.

She did not answer for a moment. Then she said, "Do you know what the Germans took from us?"

"I don't know all of it," Maria replied. "I was a Red Cross nurse in Poland. I saw the plundering and the killing and burning. But I know that isn't all there is to it. I said to Peter the other day that ruins are nothing. You have to understand what has been destroyed inside people. I can try to imagine what has been destroyed inside the Polish people. But I can't really know."

Stroud and Peter felt it was up to them to change the subject. They felt like locomotive engineers who discover that their train is rushing down the wrong track, but before either of them could do anything about it, Wanda asked, "Were you in Warsaw?"

"No," Maria replied. "I was sent to France in time."

"What do you mean—'in time'?"

"Before the atrocities began in Warsaw." Then Maria asked matter-of-factly, "Were you in Warsaw?"

"Yes."

"Do you happen to know Captain Twardowsky?"

"No. Who is he?"

The two women appeared to be conversing alone, as if the men were not in the room.

"In the camp at Oberndorf," Maria explained, "there is a Captain Twardowsky. He was among the defenders of Warsaw. The other night he talked for hours, telling us about it." She turned to Peter. "I practically forced the poor fellow into it," she said. "I wanted Helga to hear. Most of it wasn't new to me. But it is important for the child to know these things. From someone who was there."

Peter knew that there was no stopping the locomotive now. "Miss Komarnicki was in the heaviest fighting," he said. "The fighting in the sewers."

Wanda smiled. It was the same what-do-you-know-about-it smile that had more than once offended Stroud. She said, "There wasn't any fighting in the sewers."

"No?" said Peter, taken aback.

"No. The sewer was the only connection between the old town and the new. All the other connections were cut off. I was a communications officer." She broke off abruptly. "That's all," she said.

"Captain Twardowsky told us about that too," Maria broke in again. "The communications officers had to crawl through the sewer on all fours. Through human excrement. He said the sewer was so narrow in most places that the defenders had to crawl one behind the other. Many collapsed on account of the stench. They fell face forward into the filth. The others crawled over them and kept going."

The buzzing of flies could be heard in the silence of the little white room. The two men, whose sympathies should have been opposed because the women they cherished were waging war against each other, actually felt closer together than ever before—and each knew how the other felt. It was painful to both of them that Maria had appropriated Wanda's story and told it herself. They were the more astonished, then, to hear Wanda say merely, "That's just how it was."

Silence threatened again. Peter said hurriedly to Stroud, "Colonel Whimsley was here. He left just before you came."

"So I guess you know what they have in mind?"

"Yes," said Peter, half turning to Maria. "They want to send me home for a few weeks."

He could have said, "They want to send me home," but he added the words "for a few weeks" to lessen the shock for her.

"The Major told me," Maria said. "You need a rest."

"Maybe," Peter answered. "But that's not why they're sending me."

"It's on account of me then," Maria said. It was half a question and half an assertion.

"Just the same," said Peter, "I'll come back."

He waited for Stroud or Maria to say something, but it was Wanda who spoke. "Of course you'll come back, Major."

Peter smiled. "What makes you so sure, Wanda?"

Wanda was grave. "Because you have something to do here," she said. "One day I too will go back—to Poland. One must go where one has something to do." She turned to Maria. "You're going back to Berlin, aren't you?" Even now it was impossible to tell whether she meant to be friendly or aggressive.

"It happens I'm not from Berlin, Miss Komarnicki," Maria replied. "But you're quite right. If I belonged there, I would go."

"I thought you were bombed out in Berlin."

"I only lived there for a while."

"Were you there during the siege?"

What are these women up to? the men wondered. Is Wanda going to tell Maria's story now? But she said only, "I'm glad I was a soldier during the worst days of Warsaw. In war, soldiers have it easiest of all. Did you save anything from your house?"

"A few trifles. Not much. When we came out of the cellar everything was already in flames." She smiled. "But Helga and I were alive."

"What did you do then?"

"Nothing special. It's not worth talking about."

"Why not?"

Maria answered without rancor, "The defeated have no story, Miss Komarnicki."

The two women seemed to be alone again in the room. Do they hate each other? Peter asked himself. Are they fond of each other? Stroud wondered. Both men felt that something, whether love or hate, formed a tie between these two women—an abstruse bond, a profound and mutual understanding, an emanation in which the two men could not share.

Stroud looked at his watch. "We have to go," he said.

They stood up.

Stroud leaned over and spoke quietly to Peter. "I can't come tomorrow. But one of my lieutenants will bring Maria."

"Thanks," said Peter, pressing his friend's hand.

Stroud and the women walked silently through the battered corridors. Maria stopped at the exit.

"Many thanks, Major, for bringing me," she said, and added, "Don't you think Peter looks awfully pale?"

"He lost a lot of blood. But he'll recover quickly now."

"Well, thanks again."

She wanted to leave with a hurried good-by.

"*Auf Wiedersehen!*" Wanda said. And with a smile she gave Maria her hand.

➤➤ 31 ◄◄

PETER's last week-end in Europe passed tranquilly. Saturday he went to Oberndorf, and Stroud and Wanda arrived the following evening. Peter was to leave for America on Wednesday, after a brief stay in Munich.

General Lowell had rejected Stroud's request to be sent home. At this time American policy toward the German people supported the theory of "collective guilt," and Stroud learned to his astonishment that the verdict of the prisoner court was welcomed by Military Government as a clear-cut demonstration that the official attitude was correct. Stroud, expecting bitter reproaches from the

General, received instead congratulations on the outcome of the trial. Pondering the reasons for this totally unexpected turn of events, Stroud concluded that the answer lay in the truth of a remark which Wanda had recently made that experiments are usually undertaken to substantiate opinions already held. The camp was to be disbanded in three or four months, and the General assured Stroud that he was needed at his post until then. "Your disappointment," the General declared, "is the disappointment of a starry-eyed idealist. We're after facts."

Sunday evening the four of them sat a long time on the balcony of Maria's house. Wanda had, for the first time, managed to obtain a twenty-four-hour leave from the DP camp. It was not Stroud's plan to stay overnight in Oberndorf, but Wanda's delight at spending a whole night away from the camp was so childishly excessive that he did not have the heart to propose taking her back to Munich before her leave was up. Maria had arranged for rooms at the village inn, and now they were on their way to the inn.

For a time they walked silently through the moonless night. She was holding his arm. "John," she said, "you can't imagine what this night means to me."

Of late he was inclined to be alarmed at almost everything she said. This, too, alarmed him. But she continued, "Think of it! White bed linen. A room without twenty other people in it. A featherbed. No noisy roommates. And no awful odors."

Once more, as had often happened recently, he was ashamed of his own thoughts. So he said gently, "And maybe tomorrow morning I'll even bring your breakfast in to you."

"Breakfast in bed! That would be too good to be true."

It was cool. Fall was in the air. A wind whistled softly through the trees, like the sound of a far-off locomotive, as if warning of the coming winter. Through his uniform Stroud could feel the warmth of the girl pressing against his side.

They were the only guests at the little inn. It was in the center of the town, a small, two-story building whose entrance led directly into the taproom. There were four or five rooms on the second floor, toward the back, and their windows looked out on an orchard. There was a musty, old-fashioned smell throughout the house.

A corpulent Bavarian woman showed them to their rooms, which were next to each other. She brought them towels and apologized for the lack of running water. "If you need hot water in the morning," she said, "just call out the window. There's always somebody in the yard."

As they stood in the darkened corridor, Stroud asked Wanda, "Which room do you prefer?"

"They're both lovely," she said, entering one of the rooms. She laid a little bundle she had been carrying down on the table.

"So you pick this one," said Stroud, smiling.

It was a wide room, furnished in the hideous style prevalent at the turn of the century. Everything was of plush—the sofa, an easy chair, the drapes, and the table cover, which was decorated with tulips embroidered out of wool. The bed was of dark wood, big and high. But the wash basin was spotlessly clean, and the bed linen gleamed.

Wanda opened the window. "The first thing in the morning the sun will come in and shine right on my face," she said.

Stroud remained in the doorway.

Still standing at the window, she turned around and looked at him. "Come and say good night to me when I'm in bed," she said. When she saw that this disconcerted him, she added, "Today I want to enjoy everything. It's been years since anybody said a real good night to me."

He went to his room, but did not undress. He paced up and down with great, restless steps. He tried to settle his thoughts, but could not bring them in order. He wanted to think of his wife and children, but their images eluded him. He sought to concentrate on the camp and what he would do there in the coming months. It all seemed remote and nebulous. Through the wall he could hear her every movement. He could hear her pouring water into the basin and the sounds she made as she washed herself. For a moment he stood still and listened; then he moved quickly away to the far side of the room. He lit a cigarette and pulled the smoke deep into his lungs. He looked at his watch. Hardly ten minutes had passed since he had left her. A few moments later he heard a tapping on the wall. He thought it was an accidental noise and continued pacing. The tapping was repeated. She called to him.

She was sitting up in bed when he entered. She wore a white nightgown with lacework on the breast. For an instant he almost did not recognize her. She looked beautiful and womanly, and much more mature than she had in the water or in her made-over uniform.

"Don't look at me," she laughed. "Maria loaned me this nightgown. I'm lost in it."

The nightgown was indeed much too big for her. It vexed him that her appearance again moved him in the same curious way as when he had first seen her sitting in his office with the toy red handbag in her lap. She's a woman, he told himself. Only a woman. Just because everything seems too big or too small for her is no reason to get sentimental.

"Bring a chair," she said, "and sit down next to me."

He pulled an armchair over to the bed and sat down.

"Let's have a cigarette," she said.

They smoked in silence. Outside, the wind had died down. Only the pleasantly cool breath of the night came through the window.

"Major Stroud," she said with simulated gravity, "I would like to ask you a personal question."

His eyebrows went up. He was on the defensive again.

"Major Stroud," she continued, in the tone of a commanding general, "tell me—were you ever afraid at the front?"

"Sometimes," he said, surprised. "Everybody gets scared once in a while."

She would not be put off. "But on the whole you are not an especially timid man?"

"Not especially."

"Good," she said, looking at him steadily. "Then why are you afraid of me?"

He thought a joke would be the best defense. "Why," he answered, "you're far more dangerous than the German Army."

She did not react to the gibe but looked at him with great, serious eyes. She asked, "Do you think I'm trying to get something out of you?"

"No," he said quickly. "I know that's not the case."

"Do you think I would cause you trouble?"

"No."

"Do you think I'm too young?"

"Among other things."

"What other things?"

He bent his head, looking down thoughtfully at his folded hands. "I'm terribly fond of you, Wanda," he said. "And you know it. But I have a wife and two children. My daughter is two years older than you."

"You've told me that at every opportunity. I'm beginning to know your family better than you do." It sounded a little caustic.

"Wanda," he said. "I'm fifty-three years old. I don't say that to bring up the differences in our ages again, but for this reason: at that age a man doesn't change any more. All my life I've been what we call a solid citizen. Having affairs is just not my way."

"What do you call an 'affair'?"

He considered. "Something fleeting, superficial, forgotten the next day. In two or three months I'll be leaving Germany. I have never done anything that I knew I would want to forget in two or three months."

She looked straight ahead. Her hands played on the covers. "I always knew that one day you would leave, John," she said, "but I never thought of forgetting you."

"What did you think, then?" he asked. It sounded cruder than he intended.

"You're right," she said calmly, "about an affair being something that one forgets the next day. Just the same, it isn't brevity that makes an affair, or hopelessness. Love can be brief and hopeless too. But you never want to forget it."

He stood up. It now seemed unbearably hot in the room. He went to the window.

She asked, "Do you think I want an affair?"

He did not know why, but he had to wound her. "Perhaps."

She spoke without anger. "Why?"

"I don't know. I don't know anything about you, really. And I don't want to know."

She let a second or two pass in silence. Then she said, "You say you're very fond of me, John. But I love you."

He stood motionless at the window. She's just playing with me, he tried to tell himself. She's just a little tramp, after all. At the lake she was playing with me too. Using all the cheap little tricks of a woman. But while he thought these things, it was as if somebody else, not he, was using his brain to think them. In his veins the blood was pounding, and the veins and blood were all his own.

Almost inaudibly he said, "I love you too, Wanda." He was standing with his back to her and could not see her. In his mind was not the woman lying there in bed, wearing a nightgown that was too big for her over a body with which he was acquainted but which he did not know. This girl was not the one he dreamed of almost nightly, the one who stepped out of the lake with wet hair, and big drops rolling down her face, over her chin, her neck, and onto her little breasts. The girl he now saw was the one for whom a German soldier had reached out ruthlessly, with a cruel and greedy grip. He even imagined he knew the lustful face of the soldier: it was the pockmarked officer of the SS camp. Then an overwhelming surge of warmth for her washed away his visions and his thoughts. This girl, he suddenly felt, had a greater right to happiness, to cleanliness, and to love, than he had to cling to his smug consciousness of being a solid citizen. He was ashamed of himself for using the word "affair"—a word out of a world she could not understand. He walked away from the window and stood next to the bed. He took her hand.

She kept her hand in his, without saying anything, without looking up. Forget? he thought. Am I afraid I will forget, or that I won't ever be able to forget? But it doesn't matter about me, about forgetting. What matters is that she must forget, not me, but the SS, and the sewer, and the camp, and the weeks of marching, and the strange hands. But these thoughts too seemed distant, off somewhere on the edge of his mind. Here, close to him, were her little hands, and the shape of her shoulders, and the back of her neck with its tiny, fleecy hairs, softer than any down. He bent over and kissed the back of her neck.

She let it happen, silently, without moving, almost devoutly.

Then he felt her arms around his neck.

⋙ 32 ⋘

PETER had received his travel orders. He said good-by to Colonel Whimsley and other friends at the Munich OSS headquarters and had a farewell drink with John Stroud. Now he and Maria wer ewalking along the Ludwigstrasse toward the Victory Arch.

Together almost without interruption during the past three days, they had seldom made any reference to his departure. Sometimes, though, a silence would come between them that might last as long as an hour; but so great was the harmony of this silence that at the end of it they were able to carry on in speech what they had been thinking in the interval.

It had happened so often that now he was not surprised when Maria, without any reference to what had gone before, said, "No, Peter. I'm not afraid of Patricia any more." She emphasized the word "Patricia."

"What are you afraid of then?"

"Confusion. Confusion in your mind."

"But I'm not a bit confused. I know what I want."

"That's what you think now, darling. You think you've put America behind you. But you'll discover it all over again: the un-damaged houses; the streets that aren't dead and burned-out; people who aren't constantly fighting and wrangling with each other, because they know they'll have enough to eat tomorrow; the show windows full of everything anyone could want, and the women in new hats—"

"But where does the confusion come in?"

"You'll fall in love with it all, Peter. But you love me too. On the one side there'll be the houses and the lights, the comfort and the laughter. On the other side there will be me. I can compete with another woman. But not with a whole country."

They passed the Victory Arch. A bomb had exploded near by without damaging it, but the lion had been knocked off. It lay in the street, its majestic head nestled against the paving stones. It was chipped and its tail was broken off; it looked like a great mangy dog.

"I don't know," said Peter. "I think I'll feel nostalgia for the ruins."

"You can't feel nostalgia for ruins, Peter."

"You can, when the ruins are where you belong. You've always been where you belonged, Maria. You've never been away. So maybe you can't understand how it is. I don't love the poverty of Europe. But it's my poverty too. The wealth of America has nothing to do with me. I learned a number of things about my self in that cellar in Berlin where I took Meister. Take the fact that I knew instantly that I could trust the tailor. And as soon as I knew that, I wanted to help him. In America it takes me weeks to get acquainted with anybody. And nobody needs my help there. One feels drawn to people whom one needs. But there's an even stronger pull in being needed."

They came to the ruins of the Pinakothek.

"Those are things I've learned since I came back." He indicated the ruins of the museum, only one wall of which was still standing. "There," he said, "in the right wing were the Dutch masters. Rembrandt's 'Holy Family' and Ruysdael's wonderful landscape with the waterfall, and Hondecoeter's 'Chicken Yard' that made such an impression on me as a child. I don't know whether those pictures exist any more. But I know they were once there. To me that means more than whether they've survived."

"Just the same," Maria replied, "I don't quite understand you. Often you yourself don't seem to realize what a hold America has on you, how much the country has gotten into your blood."

"That's true," he said. "I love America. When I sail into New York harbor and see the Statue of Liberty, I think, the symbol of freedom! But an American doesn't have to think anything when he sees it. His heart simply begins to pound. When he travels through America he feels a pride in his very bones: how vast and boundless his country is! I admire its bigness, but for me it's too big. In America there are purple mountains, and lakes strung out like pearls, and moonlit nights in the great desert, and mysterious forests extending mile after mile. In Europe all that is squeezed together in a little space, side by side. They have strawberries in the middle of winter in America, but I like strawberries once a year, in August. They have gorgeous red roses over there, but here the roses still smell of the garden where they grew."

"I'm not sure," she said slowly, "whether I should be happy about the way you feel, or not. But I know I must tell you something before you go."

"What?"

"Don't be afraid of feeling differently tomorrow, darling. Let America work on you. Let it stream over you—the country and the people. Feel that you have no obligations, no ties—"

"What would you do if I didn't come back?" he interrupted.

The question was out. It loomed between them like a high, hazardous barrier before a horseman. What answer was he waiting for? Was there any satisfactory answer? She replied quietly, "I'd live on, darling."

They fell silent again.

Maria spoke first. "Have you noticed how silent we've been lately?" she asked.

He laughed shortly. "We don't have to talk any more."

"No," she said. "And we don't have to make promises to each other, the way people who part usually do."

"That's right," he said. "We know everything without promises."

"Even so, I'd like to tell you something."

"What is it?"

"You've had a lot to worry you in these months since we found each other. Don't think I wasn't aware of it. The non-fraternization law. I know they held it against you. You never said anything, but I felt the way you winced when Thompson came to get you that time. Peter, I don't want your life to be clouded. I want you to be happy."

"Nonsense," he said. "I'm happy."

"A lot will have to change before you're really happy, Peter." She continued, "I want to do everything I can."

They turned off the sidewalk and walked through the ruins. They stepped over scattered building stones, twisted remnants of an iron gate, rusted girders, crumpled stucco-work. Maria halted suddenly. "Look!" she said.

He stopped.

She bent over as if to pick up something, but straightened up again, empty-handed. Now he saw it too. A tiny tree was growing out of the rubble. It was a forlorn little growth, more like a shrub than a tree. But there were little green leaves on the branches. The tree had thrust its way out of the black, loamy earth between two stones. Near the tree grew three or four wild flowers. Maria bent over to pick them, but changed her mind.

"What kind of flowers are those yellow ones?" Peter asked, to say something.

"Goldenrod," she said. "I must remember this place. It's so dry now. The little tree needs water."

When they looked around they were surprised to find that they were not alone. Two workmen were sitting on the ruins, eating a meager lunch they had brought along wrapped in newspapers. Others were clambering over the ruins like tourists in the Roman forum. Several American soldiers came by. They took a long look at the American major standing amid the debris with a German woman, admiring a miserable little shrub. They did not salute.

"Come," said Maria.

And as they, too, clambered together over the ruins, a deep, gratifying sense of peace came to them. It was like the coming of summer rain after a hot day, like the awakening of a mother after childbirth, like the first blossoms after snow. It was an exultant certainty and a serene content. It was the overcoming of a fear they had never admitted: the assurance that two people together can be stronger than space and time.

⇶ *33* ⇶

Peter and Thompson had driven from Munich to Frankfurt, spent the night there, and reached Paris the next evening. They had only the forenoon to spend in Paris. That evening Peter was due at Camp Homerun at Le Havre, from where his ship would sail for the United States.

They sat at a sidewalk table in front of the Café Colysée on the Champs Elysées, drinking an *apéritif*. It was a beautifully bright autumn morning. The air had that sparkling clarity which only Paris knows. One could drink it instead of breathing it. It was half air, half wine.

The avenue was so thronged with people and traffic that it seemed all Paris was streaming past their table. Men and women promenaded, stood in groups before shop windows, crowded the terraces of the cafés. They seemed to be wholly at ease, without care or anxiety. American soldiers lined up before Guerlain's perfume shop near by, forming what looked like a chow line. The women were as lovely as Peter remembered them, but now their summer dresses were replaced by fall suits. Nobody spoke of the Germans any more. The barricades that had blocked the streets thirteen months ago seemed to be only a historical memory, like the Empress Eugénie or the Battle of the Marne.

"Paris sure has changed," Thompson said. "I liked it better a year ago."

"Why?"

"They were glad to have us then."

"People can't go on rejoicing forever, Thompson."

"Hell, no. But they at least ought to remember once in a while that we drove the Krauts out."

"No one wants to be reminded that he needed help once. That's what they call pride."

"It's what I call ingratitude."

"Often the same thing, Thompson."

"And the prices are too goddam high." Thompson continued the inventory of his grievances against Paris. "For Americans everything's just twice as high. They take us for tourists."

"Well, that's what happens to liberators when they stay too long. They become tourists."

Thompson shrugged. "Like I say, it was better a year ago. I can understand why the guys prefer German girls."

"What's the difference?" Peter smiled. "The German girls are out for what they can get too, aren't they? PX rations and coffee and so on."

"Could be," said Thompson, "but they ain't so open about it. At least they give a guy an illusion. You know, Major, the way I figure it, that's about all you can ask from a dame. Just so she gives you an illusion."

Peter thought, he's cynical. It isn't like Dirty Thompson to be cynical. That letter from his wife is what did it. Maybe I should have talked some more to him about that. "Thompson," Peter said, "have you heard any more from your wife?"

"Yeah, I did. I wrote her. She answered."

"And?"

"And nothin'. She's stickin' to it. She wants a divorce." He pondered for a moment. "Major, I'd like to ask you a favor."

"Certainly."

"When you get to the States—could you maybe talk to Doris?"

"Be glad to. Do you think she'd come to New York to see me?"

"Maybe. She's got an aunt in New York."

"Good. Let's have it. What shall I say to her?"

Thompson looked straight ahead. "I dunno," he said.

"Oh, come. There must be something you want me to say to her."

Thompson avoided Peter's eyes, and his face was set in a studied expressionlessness. "Just tell her I still love her."

"Will that make much of an impression on her, do you think?"

"Damned if I know, Major. But I can't think of anything better." He shrugged again. "What else can you tell a woman when you want her to come back?"

Peter did not reply to the question. He asked, "Why don't you go home yourself? You've got plenty of points."

"I don't dare, Major."

Peter looked at him. There sat Dirty Thompson in front of the Café Colysée on the Champs Elysées—a giant of a man with a huge head and Wallace Beery lips, an American soldier with boots bigger than life and a bullneck dirtier than ever, who had fought his way through North Africa, Italy, and Normandy, who could drive at night as if the sun were out, who wasn't afraid of death or the devil, of Germans or top sergeants—there he sat, afraid to go home.

"What are you afraid of, Thompson?" Peter asked.

"If I saw her with that guy, I'd kill her. Her or him. Or both of 'em."

"That's what you said in Frankfurt. But that was months ago. I thought that perhaps you might feel differently about it by now."

Thompson looked at him in surprise. "A thing like that, Major," he said, "it don't get better. It gets worse."

"Not always."

"Well, first you're so goddam sore, you go kind of nuts, see? You want to smash things up or go out and get good and plastered. All you can think of is, she's goin' to leave me. She's got another guy. It keeps poundin' away inside you. All that ain't so bad, though, because you're still all taken up feelin' sorry for yourself. It seems too awful to be real, if you know what I mean. You just can't understand it. But then the little things begin plaguin' you, and you can understand them, all right. It don't hurt so much no more, but you start rememberin'. You remember the first time you met her and how you felt, this is it, this is the goods, this is goin' to be for keeps. And you remember the first time, on a Sunday, that you cooked breakfast for her. And how you'd have to buy her the paper with Dick Tracy Saturday nights, comin' out of the movies. She always put on the same act when she got home. She wouldn't come to bed till she read Dick Tracy and the other comics. She'd keep you waitin', layin' there, waitin' for her to slip in beside you. And then, goddam it, you think, she ain't changed her ways any now, either. She'll be doin' the same things, only you ain't there. Somebody else'll be buyin' her the Dick Tracy paper on Saturday nights, and he'll be layin' there in bed waitin' for her to finish readin' and get in beside him. Or maybe he won't have to wait. Maybe he won't buy her no paper and cook breakfast for her —and that's a hell of a sight worse. And then you think to yourself, you loused it all up, you dope. Maybe that's what she needed— somebody that didn't give in to her, but made her bring you breakfast in bed. And then you don't know what in hell to make of the whole thing from start to finish."

Peter let him talk. He wanted Thompson to relieve his mind, get as much off his chest as possible.

"How about another Vermouth, Thompson?"

"No, thanks, Major," he said. "I don't hardly drink no more."

"I've noticed it."

"No sense to it," Thompson continued. "I figure it this way—if you're happy you don't have to drink. If you're a little unhappy, why, you drink. If you're real unhappy, drinkin' don't do no good anyway. For a while it kind of clouds things over, but afterward it's worse than ever. Everything gets clearer. And that's bad."

Peter waited to see if Thompson had talked himself out. After a while he said, "Didn't the girls help you forget?"

"Naw," said Thompson. "It's like with liquor. At first they help some. But then it gets worse again. For a while you think you're gettin' back at her, and crap like that. You kid yourself along. But then you begin makin' comparisons. And you're worse off than ever."

Peter sighed a little. "Okay," he said. "I promise I'll talk to her. If she won't come to New York, I'll fly out to Chicago. You'll have to give me her address."

He took out his notebook and handed it to Thompson, who wrote the address in large sprawling letters.

"Funny," he said, "writin' it down that way—Mrs. Ralph D. Thompson."

"What's the 'D' for?"

"David. After my grandfather. My mom's father."

Peter put the notebook back in his pocket.

"In five weeks, six at the most, I'll be back here," he said. "I want you to promise me something, Thompson."

"What?"

"I'll tell you honestly what I've seen and heard, and whether I think it's hopeless, or whether I think you still have a chance. But if I tell you there's no hope, you'll have to pull yourself together and forget it. You're only thirty, Thompson. Life isn't over at thirty. Doris or no Doris. How about it?"

He put out his hand. Thompson put his big, dirty paw into Peter's firm, well-formed hand.

"Okay, Major," he said.

Peter paid, and they left the café. They had gone only a few steps down the Champs Elysées toward Peter's hotel when Thompson stopped.

"Major, do you think Doris would like a bottle of perfume?" he asked.

"Probably. They usually do."

"Would you take it along?"

"Sure."

"Good deal," said Thompson. For the first time a satisfied grin came over his face.

He took his place as last man in the line of GI's waiting in front of Guerlain's.

❧ 34 ❧

CAMP HOMERUN was not a camp but a fortress. Built long before 1918, it had figured prominently in both world wars. In the second, a desperate band of German soldiers and sailors had been able to hold the fortress and harbor of Le Havre long after American armor was rolling east from Paris. When it was finally taken and the harbor had been restored by the miracle workers whom Americans prosaically call "Army engineers," the fortress had been converted into a camp for homeward-bound soldiers. It was here that returning warriors idled for days and weeks, waiting for a ship to carry them to the States.

During the three days that Peter waited for his ship he had ample opportunity to converse with officers, soldiers, nurses, and Wacs. What he missed almost at once was the feverish excitement that had marked such groups about to go home on leave during the war. There was still, of course, a great deal of talk about the joys that awaited everyone in the States, and "Any old tub headed in the right direction is okay with me" was a standing remark. But in almost every soldier he talked to, Peter detected a concealed pang at leaving Europe and an even more deeply hidden fear of what was waiting on the other side. These soldiers, most of whom had stood up to death a dozen times, were afraid of peace in their own country. It struck Peter that what disturbed most of them was not so much the competitive struggle for jobs and daily bread, but the feeling that the war had disorganized their personal lives so chaotically that they saw no way of getting back to normal again. Few spoke of divorce, but fewer still spoke of their wives. The soldiers at Camp Homerun seemed determined to make the most of what they regarded as "freedom" while there was still time. As Peter walked through the camp area in the evening, enjoying the fresh air before going to bed, he had to pick his way carefully, for in every bush and hollow were soldiers and girls covered with army blankets, most with an empty bottle near by, and all intoxicated not only by alcohol, but also by the sea air, and hasty, last-minute love whose deeper causes they did not understand.

It had been different during the war. Then the men came directly from the filth, mud, and rain of battlefields. To them Europe meant nothing but death. America was life. They spoke in short, matter-of-fact sentences of what they had been through—of the hellish barrages of German 88's, of gliding back to their own lines with an engine shot away. But mostly they spoke of home, as if nothing else really mattered—of the first steak, the first glass of milk, the lights on Broadway, real Scotch with plenty of ice, and white sheets on a Pullman berth. They talked of the women who were waiting for them. All had photographs of wives or sweethearts, pictures which were often the only possessions they had been able to save. Usually the photographs were in color and the wives and sweethearts looked remarkably alike with their pink faces and pink dresses and pink smiles. The soldiers then spoke as little of the faithfulness of their women as they did now of unfaithfulness; but then it was taken for granted that everything was in order at home, while now it was almost as readily assumed that something was amiss. The talk in Italy had been of girls in Ohio and Nebraska and Texas; now it was of girls in Paris or Brussels or Berlin. Behind the talk Peter sensed a defensive bitterness, an attempt to escape ridicule, a braggadocio that stemmed from uncertainty. It was the usual maneuver of betrayal, an attempt to prove that he was the betrayer, not the betrayed.

One afternoon Peter sat down on the turf that bordered the rampart to read for a few hours in the mild fall sun. He did not notice at first that an Army nurse had settled herself near by. When he looked up, he saw that she was blond and attractive. Her blondness was somewhat faded and her features a little washed-out, but she had something of that college-girl charm which American women often retain long after their college days are over. On the collar of her OD shirt she wore the silver bar of a first lieutenant.

"Hello, Major," she said.

"Hello, Lieutenant."

He did not feel like getting involved in a conversation, but did not want to be impolite. "How long have you been waiting?" he asked. It was the usual question.

"A week," she said.

"Do you know what ship you're taking yet?"

"No," she said irritably, drawing up her knees in their GI pants. "We were supposed to get on a boat yesterday, but at the last minute they called the whole thing off."

"That was tough. What happened?"

"Didn't you hear?" she asked. "The whole camp's talking about it. Three hundred war brides showed up. Mostly French. They're on their way to the States. They've got priority. Even a general had to give up his place on the ship."

"Hmmm," said Peter, to signify an interest he did not feel. He did not know what he was expected to say, and the conversation lagged.

"The brides are traveling two in a cabin," the nurse resumed. "We have to travel eighteen in a cabin. I don't know why we're letting these women into the States anyway."

"Well, after all, they married Americans."

"What of it? Why don't the guys who married them stay in Europe? American girls weren't good enough for them, and they seem to like it here." The girl's agreeable little mouth was distorted by a twitch of disdain.

Peter smiled. "You can't expect the boys to stay here just because they happened to fall in love with European girls." He wanted to return to his book without offending the girl. He added pleasantly, "There just weren't enough pretty American girls in Europe, that's all."

"You know that isn't true, Major." The nurse was determined to pursue the subject. "Anyone who wanted to could find an American girl over here. These foreign girls just used every trick they could think of to grab off an American husband. After all, there's plenty to eat in the States. Cigarettes in every drugstore and a car in every garage."

"You're being a little unfair, aren't you?"

The nurse looked at him. Her blue eyes flashed. "Oh, I don't know," she answered. "You ought to know better than I do. But these European women must have something that we don't, the way they get our boys."

"Maybe I do know," said Peter, amused. "But I'd like to hear your idea."

"I'm not a man," said the nurse. "Maybe it's just that they're better in bed."

"It's hardly that simple."

"I thought there must be more to it myself," she said. "Maybe it's because they make more of a fuss about their men."

"I think you've got something there."

"They take their men so damned seriously over here. When they fall for a man, right away the whole world revolves around him and nothing else matters. And another thing—though it may sound silly. You know, sometimes I think European women attract our men so much because they're always taking cigarettes and things from them."

"That's a new one on me, Lieutenant," said Peter. "I don't get it."

Pleased that she had finally said something that stimulated his interest, the nurse continued. "American girls don't need anything from their men. I'd feel silly if I had to depend on a man for every little thing. But these European women are always playing poor helpless little lambs, and the men love it. The way our MP's broke their necks helping those French women getting on board you'd think the poor little creatures were made out of glass and marked 'fragile, handle with care.' Tender MP's of all things! I never saw anything like it."

They looked out over the harbor in which three or four ships lay at anchor. The water was deep blue and calm. There was a white hospital ship that looked like a luxury liner.

"Maybe one of them is for you," said Peter, getting up. "See you at supper, Lieutenant. So long."

"So long, Major," the nurse said, disappointed at his departure.

He walked along the rampart. Rusty, half-dismantled cannon stood on the gun emplacements, their barrels pointed out over the harbor. A year ago they were still in action, now they looked like museum pieces. Peter thought, it's some comfort anyway that guns age so quickly. Turning around, Peter saw the hills behind Le Havre, bright in their fall finery. Beyond the hills lay the country and the highways that led to Paris, Frankfurt, and Munich.

Peter shivered. He felt feverish, and there was a throb from his wound. Up to now, he realized suddenly, everything had been much too simple. Back there with Maria nothing seemed difficult or complicated: he would speak frankly with Patricia, she would admit that she had never really loved him, and they would part on the best of terms. It was easy, back there, to accuse Patricia of being cold and without feeling, of writing letters devoid of understanding and warmth, of giving gay parties at home while he was over here risking his neck. But now she would be able to answer. And what, after all, could she actually be accused of? Whatever he could say, she would not only answer; she would have questions of her own to ask. And one had to put some questions to oneself: how had it all come about, and where did one get the right to break off a marriage?

He turned again toward the sea. Over there was America. And as he looked out across the calm expanse of ocean he remembered all that he had sought to forget during the past half year: over there were friends, people who were near to him, and thirteen years that could not simply be wiped away like chalk from a blackboard. Across the ocean, as beyond the hills, were memories—the years of uncertainty and struggle, of rebuff and advancement, disappointment and success. The little things, as Dirty Thompson had said. He remembered the first meetings with Patricia in the Hotel St. Regis, the wedding trip to Mexico, their first harmonious vacation at Cape Cod, the quiet evenings in their home when everything had seemed settled and decided for life. There was Fifth Avenue at six in the evening when the shops were closing. Grand Central Station as he got off the train on leave from training camp. The little flower shop at the corner of Sixth Avenue. . . . For the first time he became conscious also of the double-dealing game he was playing: he planned to return to Germany as an American major, but his intention was to remain there permanently.

Peter descended the steps from the wall to the barracks area. Before the bulletin board on the administration building was a crowd of officers, nurses, and Red Cross girls, looking for their names. He found his own at once. His ship was leaving tomorrow.

PART IV

A FINE rain drizzled down as the U.S.S. *General Brooks* approached New York. The soldiers were jammed on the decks, determined to enjoy every moment of the ship's passage through the harbor. Most of them had looted German field glasses with which they hoped to be the first to discern the outlines of the Statue of Liberty through the fog.

Sirens howled a greeting to the ship as it made its way between the green and blue buoys of the channel. Squawking sea gulls swarmed around the ship. On the left were the oddly assorted buildings of Staten Island, and on the right the bare-looking houses of Brooklyn's outskirts.

Then came the first of the little ships that were to escort the *General Brooks* through the harbor. They carried huge signs, already a little faded, with inscriptions: "Welcome Home!" and "Well Done!" and "Boys, We Salute You!" For Peter there was something offensively stereotyped and insincere about them, like the printing on the checks in cheap restaurants: "Thank you! Call again!"

The uproar of welcome increased minute by minute. A yacht took up position next to the troopship. On board was a band in uniform, but it did not play patriotic anthems or soldiers' songs. It played hot jazz. The soldiers on the *General Brooks* hummed, snapped their fingers, and bobbed up and down in rhythm with the jazz as violently as they were able on the crowded deck. The homecoming of the liberators! Peter thought.

Mothers, wives, fathers, sisters, and sweethearts had managed to board small harbor craft to greet the troopship. A fat woman in a black dress—obviously an Italian mother from Mulberry Street—stood on the deck of a motorboat holding up a tremendous placard which said "Hello, Al Morello!" On the ship a wild search began at once, and before long Pfc. Morello was found and shoved with yowls and cheers to the railing where he could wave to his mother. She spotted him and began a heavy-footed caper of joy that was half Indian dance and half jitterbug to the measures of the band.

Peter did his best to feel moved. But he felt only like an outsider, somehow wounded in his dignity. The picture of his father in the Braunschweig jail appeared before him. He went down to his cabin and began stuffing shirts into his Val-pack.

He was able to leave the ship almost as soon as it was moored. For most of the passengers there would be slow, lengthy formalities, since almost all on board were returning home to stay. Those who were merely on furlough were passed through immediately and permitted to go their way.

It had stopped raining, but the sky over New York was leaden and a chilling wind swept the streets. Peter, bag in hand, turned up the collar of his trench coat and hailed a taxi. He had not informed Patricia of his arrival, and now he felt a certain misgiving about going home unannounced. He told the driver to stop at the Plaza.

There was something dreamlike about his walk through the lobby of the hotel to the telephone booth. The coin was already in the slot when he realized that he had forgotten his own telephone number. He was about to reach for a phone book when he recalled that Patricia had insisted on having an unlisted number. Oddly, he had no difficulty remembering the number of his publisher, Vernon O'Brian. Vernon answered the phone.

"Hello, Vernon," Peter said.

"Peter!" said Vernon. "It's great to hear your voice again. How long've you been back?"

"I'll tell you all about that later. The reason I called is, can you tell me my telephone number?"

Vernon laughed. "Of course. Plaza eight—seven, five, four, one."

Peter thought there was a note of amazement in his voice. "Thanks. I'll call you back later."

"Fine. And welcome home, old man!"

Peter thought, all I need now is for him to say "well done." He hung up.

He dialed his number. He did it slowly, with more care than was necessary. Three o'clock, he thought. She's probably not at home. A woman's voice he did not recognize answered, "Mrs. Olden's residence."

"Is Mrs. Olden at home?"

"No, sir. Who is calling?"

"Mr. Olden."

"How's that, please?"

There was no harm in the question, but Peter was exasperated that his voice was unknown in his own home. "Mr. Olden," he said distinctly. "Should I spell it out for you?"

"Oh!" The woman's voice was frightened. "Is this Major Olden?" At least, then, Patricia had spoken of his promotion. "Yes."

"I'm sorry, sir."

"Is Stephen there?" Stephen was the old butler.

"No, sir. Stephen is no longer with us."

"When will Mrs. Olden be back?"

"Madame is out of town, sir. But Mr. Vanderwoort is here. Shall I call him to the phone?"

"No, thanks. I'll be home shortly." He left the phone booth. The word "home" that he had just spoken rang falsely in his ear. He was fully aware that he was not going home. He was not pleased with the prospect of having to see Mr. Vanderwoort right away. Uncle Newell, as the family called him, was Mrs. Draper's brother, Patricia's uncle. He was some sixty years old and a bachelor. Uncle Newell referred to himself as a banker, although as long as anyone could remember his sole activity had consisted in managing the Draper estate. He and Barbara Draper were the only children of the late Newell Vanderwoort, a man who had taken inordinate pride in the fact that his family had come over on the *Mayflower*—or at least on one of the apparently innumerable ships that followed immediately—and in the knowledge that a byway in old New York was called Vanderwoort Street; since the early days of an authentically distinguished Vanderwoort no member of the dynasty had ever sullied himself with work.

When the beautiful Barbara had announced her intention of marrying the young and little-known business executive Charles Draper, her brother did everything in his power to oppose the match. He had two compelling reasons: first, though he would not admit it to himself, he was in love with his sister, and he hounded all her suitors with a furious hatred; secondly, he objected because Charles Draper's family had come to America barely fifty years before on a ship after which no hotels or laundries had been named. When Barbara's marriage turned out to be completely happy and Charles Draper became a spectacular success in the business world, Uncle Newell suffered a double defeat to which he was never able to reconcile himself.

While Charles Draper lived, Uncle Newell played an exceedingly minor role in the family's scheme of things. Draper did not even give him the satisfaction of forbidding him the house. On the other hand, he stubbornly refused Uncle Newell's invitations to dine at the Harvard Club because, he said, it would be impossible for him to eat in a place "where the waiters are more aristocratic than I am." And since Charles Draper had a streak of sarcastic humor, he finally offered Uncle Newell a chair on the board of directors of the Draper enterprises. Uncle Newell wrestled with his soul for two days and then accepted, explaining to Barbara that he felt it his duty to "look after the best interests" of her and her children.

When Charles Draper died, Uncle Newell began to stretch his protecting hand over his sister and her children. Barbara Draper was a far too emphatic personality to allow herself to be decisively influenced in business or personal matters by "the old fool," as she half fondly and half jeeringly called him. However, she was aware of the advantage of having a representative of her own on the Draper board of directors, which was composed mainly of aggressive, self-made men who had idolized Charles but who had little use for his family. In addition, she had a phobia about details—taxes, bank balances, insurance policies, and servants' salaries. With brotherly solicitude, and for a very considerable salary, Uncle Newell assumed all these duties and became something of a social secretary and escort as well. Actually, however, he acquired more and more personal influence because he alone had accurate knowledge of the family finances and knew what could be done with available funds and what it would be "wiser" not to do. Thus Patricia, whom Uncle Newell went out of his way to cultivate, came to regard her lean, fastidiously groomed uncle as the real power in the Draper enterprises and the man responsible for accumulating the family's wealth. The memory of her father was gradually blotted out. He had been, after all, merely a man of lowly origin who by one means or another laid the groundwork for restoring to the lordly Vanderwoorts the glory that was due them.

Uncle Newell came to meet Peter as he stepped into the hall.

"What a surprise, my boy! Welcome!" His right hand grasped Peter's, while his left clapped him on the shoulder. "Patricia will be wretched at not being here," he went on in a fatherly tone. "Why didn't you cable, my boy?"

"I didn't know just when I'd get here. Where is Patricia?"

"Up at Ossining—in Sing Sing prison, to be exact." Uncle Newell laughed at Peter's astonishment. "Oh, you know, this business with the children of criminals. She's visiting the fathers of some of her little charges."

They went into the drawing-room. "What happened to Stephen?" Peter asked. He had given his bag to a servant he did not know.

"Stephen is gone," Uncle Newell replied, sitting down. He did not explain further.

Peter paced back and forth. Nothing had changed in the drawing-room. The Louis XVI clock he had bought for Patricia on their wedding trip was still on the mantelpiece. Above the chaise longue hung the David portrait that was too big for its setting; it had come from one of Barbara Draper's larger houses. On the piano were a dozen family photographs in silver or lucite frames, all displaying bright, self-assured faces. His own portrait was in the first row. His face looked as strange to him as those of the other members of the family.

"Have a seat," said Uncle Newell.

Peter remained standing. That's going a little far when Uncle Newell offers me a chair in my own house, he thought. But then he sat down without saying anything.

"You're probably surprised to find me here," Uncle Newell began. "But they're painting my apartment. It was high time the old place was spruced up a bit. I'd never have done anything about it, of course, but Barbara and Patricia insisted. So I moved in here for a few days. Naturally, I'll leave right away. There's always room at the club."

Peter listened absently. "Why?" he asked. "There's plenty of room in the house."

"No," Uncle Newell insisted. "Since Patricia gave up the guest room—"

"Gave up the guest room? I hadn't heard about that."

Uncle Newell cocked his head appreciatively. "Wait till you see what Patricia's done with that room!" It was a cue, and he waited for a sign of interest. All male members of the family were duty-bound to express admiration for everything that Patricia and Barbara might do. Uncle Newell decided to overlook Peter's lapse.

"Patricia has taken so many children under her wing," he explained, "that she can't keep track of them all. The crime situation gets worse all the time, you know. And mothers and guardians keep writing Patricia for help and advice. It's incredible how much confidence they have in her. They appreciate her answers more than gifts or money. So she has turned the guest room into an efficient office with a full-time secretary. Patricia answers all the letters personally and keeps a full record of all the cases on index cards filed under the children's names—parents' names, of course, and addresses, nature of parents' crimes, motives, environment, sentence, location of prison, visits to prison and home, I.Q. of child, letters, donations, and all that sort of thing. Patricia is a wonderful organizer."

Peter smiled politely.

Uncle Newell shook his head in admiration. "It's remarkable the way a thing like this gets around," he said. "You know how Patricia dislikes publicity. But these things simply can't be kept quiet. The newspapers won't let her alone. They're forever printing stories about her and her work. Patricia's secretary has filled six scrapbooks with clippings."

"Very interesting," said Peter. "I haven't had a chance to wash up. If you'll pardon me."

In his room he was finally alone. He turned on a lamp, sat down in an easy chair, and lit a cigarette. He could find no changes in the room, except for Uncle Newell's pajamas laid out on the bed. On the radio lay a volume of Heine's poems which he had been reading the last time he was home. Except for the muffled tapping of a typewriter in the guest room across the hall, everything was quiet, too quiet. He was overcome by a longing the intensity of which almost frightened him—a longing for Maria, for the little Bavarian farmhouse, for the village, and for the ruins of Munich. He had the uneasy feeling that he was in a trap. Barbara Draper was a woman of wide influence; in her house generals came and went. Perhaps tomorrow he would get orders to remain in Washington. Or he would be given his discharge papers; he had plenty of points if they wanted to demobilize him. At the same time, he realized that until now he had continued to underestimate the difficulties he faced. During the nine-day voyage he had prepared himself for his conversation with Patricia. But he had not reckoned on the house. He had not considered the fact that it was impossible for him to live here so much as a single day. He crushed his cigarette into a tray, stood up, and left the room.

On the stairs he encountered the new valet.

"Shall I unpack your things, Major?"

"No, thanks."

He felt an urgent need for a familiar face. He was sure that the maid and the cook were also new, otherwise Yvonne and Helen would certainly have greeted him before this. He did not go into the kitchen, for he had had enough of new faces that seemed to ask who he was, why he had come, and whether Mrs. Olden would approve of his visit. He reached the point where it was almost pleasant to find Uncle Newell waiting for him in the drawing-room.

Uncle Newell put aside his newspaper and tucked his glasses into their case.

Peter sat down and asked, "When will Patricia be back, Uncle Newell?"

"Let's see—today is Wednesday. She didn't plan to be back until Monday. She's staying with the Walter Clarks, on the Hudson. From there she goes to the jail every morning. It's near by. We could easily reach her by phone. I'm sure she'll come right back when she hears you're home."

"I'll call her," said Peter. "But there's no point in her coming home before the week-end. I have to go to Washington tomorrow anyway. I've got to report to the General, and Friday I'm due to appear before a Senate committee." He spoke rapidly and urgently, as if trying to convince Uncle Newell.

"But this time you're home to stay, aren't you?" Uncle Newell asked.

"No. Only three weeks. Maybe not that long."

"That's too bad," Uncle Newell said. "Patricia will be sorry to hear it." It had the same patronizing ring as when he offered Peter a chair. "Have you people got a lot of work to do over there?"

Peter passed over the question. "At any rate," he said, "don't put yourself out for me, Uncle Newell. I can easily spend the night at the Plaza."

"Out of the question, my boy," Uncle Newell protested. "I'm certainly not going to take the returning hero's bed away from him."

"The returning hero," Peter tried to joke, "probably couldn't get a wink of sleep in his own bed. If I were staying here, it would be different, but it's only for one night. It would be silly to chase you out for that. As to that, I could sleep in Patricia's room. But I think I shan't disturb it for one night. You stay as you are and I'll go to the hotel."

He was afraid Uncle Newell would refuse. But Uncle Newell always accepted, as Charles Draper had long ago discovered.

"If you really think—" he said. "By Saturday I'll be back in my own apartment." Then, jovially, "How about a real homemade Old-Fashioned?"

"Thanks. I'm going right away. I'll call Patricia from the hotel."

As soon as he was given a room at the Plaza, Peter called the Walter Clark residence. Patricia was summoned to the phone at once.

"Peter!" she said. "Where are you speaking from?"

"New York," he said.

"Are you home?"

"No. At the Plaza. I didn't want to inconvenience Uncle Newell."

"Why didn't you let me know?"

"It all happened too suddenly."

"How long are you staying?"

It doesn't even occur to her that I might be staying home for good, Peter thought. "Three weeks," he said. "But I have to go to Washington first thing tomorrow."

"Then when will I see you?"

"I'll probably be able to get back Friday."

There was a little silence at the other end of the line. "How awkward," Patricia said. "There's something I should do here Saturday. A conference, you know. At the prison. The warden thinks it's important that I attend."

Peter felt himself go rigid. He stifled the impulse to remind his wife that it was only thirty miles from the Grand Central Station in New York to Ossining, and that even the slow trains made the trip in less than an hour. Hundreds of people commuted every day. He said, "Well, in that case, I'll see you Monday."

"Oh, no," she protested. "We can't wait that long. Hold on a moment."

She talked to someone in the room. He could not understand what she was saying. Then she spoke into the phone again. "The Clarks would be delighted to have you here for the week-end. Could you make it Friday night?"

At first he wanted to use some pretense for saying no, but he dismissed the idea immediately. He realized that it would be better to talk to Patricia outside their home. "Yes," he answered, "I think I can make it Friday."

"What a surprise you're here!" said Patricia. "How are you feeling? Have you fully recovered?"

He was on the defensive at once, as if her solicitude spelled danger. "Oh, I never felt better. How about you? Everything all right?"

"I'm rather tired, Peter. It's been a little too much lately. This crime wave, you know. And all the criminals seem to have swarms of children. And now the newspapers have gotten hold of what I'm doing, unfortunately. Now they want me to lecture in Washington, Springfield, Buffalo, and Cincinnati. You know how I hate speaking in public. But people tell me it's important for my work, so I have to do it."

Peter did not know what to say. Two feelings contended within him, one old, one new. The Peter who had loved Patricia was not entirely dead, and this Peter was hurt by every word she said. The children of criminals, the crime wave, lectures in Cincinnati—what were they to him, or to her? Why didn't she drop it all—the conference, everything—and rush back with her arms open to receive the man who had come back to her? Why did she babble on about things of utterly no interest to him, instead of asking a thousand questions, about his work, his plans, and what they would do in the days they were going to spend together? But then there was the new Peter, and he took delight in everything that saddened his other self. Every word she spoke was testimony that he was right, confirming him in his decision, soothing his conscience.

"You poor child!" he said, not sure how much irony and how much sincerity there was in his words.

Patricia noticed nothing.

⇶ 36 ⇷

PROBABLY for the first time in his life, he was afraid to be alone. He called Vernon O'Brian, and one or two other friends, but found no one home. Freshly shaved and clothed, he went out to dinner alone. At a Broadway restaurant he ate a leisurely meal, ordered with great care and much deliberation. He experienced again what he had often felt on returning from the front—that it was possible to get drunk without alcohol. One can get drunk on food, lights, and people.

After dinner he walked slowly down Broadway, a street for which he had no affection. The neon lights were too big and blatant, the crowds too dense, the shops too monotonous and undistinguished. Over the whole street, he always felt, was a distinctive atmosphere of homelessness. One had the feeling that the cinemas stayed open all night only because people would otherwise have no place to go. It was impossible to imagine that the men and women who hurried by, bumping into each other, crowding and elbowing, could have homes in which they were accustomed to sit back, relax, and sleep.

Now, for the first time, he felt a kinship to Broadway. I've probably never mingled enough with people, he thought. Ever since his childhood he had felt a compulsion to do something for others, but he had never had much in common with others. He himself was surprised that, after calling New York his home for eight years, he now felt so little regret at being without a home here. But Broadway opened its arms to him.

Peter turned into a restaurant in the center of which was a huge bar. He sat down on the only free stool and ordered a glass of cognac. Sipping his drink, he was staring absently into the oversized mirror on the wall opposite when a voice at his shoulder startled him.

"Say, Major," it said, "you must have gotten around plenty." A young soldier was looking at his left breast: at the Silver Star, the Bronze Star with two oak leaf clusters, the French Croix de Guerre, the Luxembourg Couronne de Chêne, the Order of the British Empire, the ETO ribbon with one silver and four bronze battle stars.

"I got around a little," Peter said, smiling. Then he saw the ribbons on the soldier's chest. "You didn't fight the war on Broadway either."

The soldier waved his hand in dismissal. "That's all over, to hell with it," he said. "Where were you at, Major?"

"Africa, Italy, France, Germany."

"With an airborne division?"

"Only for a while. Where were you?"

"Normandy, Belgium, Germany. The goddam infantry. We were the first ones at Remagen. I just got back two weeks ago. I was in Berlin the last two months. Were you in Berlin?"

"No. Just a leave. You're out for good, though, aren't you?"

The soldier grinned. "Get a load of that ruptured duck," he said. "I'm only wearing the uniform because I can't get any civilian clothes. And no white shirts, of course."

The man on Peter's left, who had evidently been listening, joined the conversation. He wore a shabby blue suit and had a lined and leathery face, which seemed to make him older than he actually was. Although he was almost as tall as Peter, he somehow suggested a prematurely aged dwarf. On the bar before him was a double whisky, straight, and in his eyes were many double whiskies, straight, that were no longer on the bar.

"I know a place where you can get plenty of white shirts. If you want to pay the price," he said. He also was wearing the discharge button.

"Were you in the Army?" Peter asked.

"No. The Navy. I've been out four months already."

"In the Atlantic?"

"Pacific. Guadalcanal, Bougainville, Okinawa, and so on."

"Glad to be back?" said Peter, to make talk.

The ex-sailor looked at him blearily. "I wish I was still at Guadalcanal," he said. "At least there's no women out there."

The soldier laughed. "What you got against women?"

The sailor paid no attention. He talked to Peter. "The trouble with me is, I'm dead. When you're dead, you shouldn't come home."

Too many straight whiskies, Peter thought. "You don't look dead to me," he said politely.

"That's what you think! That's what I thought too. But when I got home I found out different. I found out I was dead. I saw it black on white. Letter from the Navy Department to my wife. 'The Navy Department regrets to announce—' and so on. The Navy Department ought to know." He shrugged.

The soldier noticed that Peter's glass was empty.

"Another cognac, Major?" he asked. "This one's on me."

"Okay," said Peter after a moment's hesitation. Suddenly he thought again of Maria and the village. If I can only make them understand this, he thought. It's easy enough to build Main Streets and drugstores and city halls. But that isn't what counts. What counts is that here it's perfectly natural for the little corporal to offer the major a cognac. And for the major to accept, and then buy the corporal a whisky. That's what they will have to come to understand. He felt an affection for the corporal.

The soldier, more inquisitive than Peter, turned to the man in blue. "So the Navy reported you dead?"

"That's right. They informed my next of kin. My wife. She must have done a lot of mourning, the poor girl. At least a month. In six weeks she was married again." He addressed Peter, "You understand, Major. The things people won't do in the throes of sorrow!"

"That's a bad break," said Peter sympathetically.

The sailor emptied his glass. "Now she's got two husbands. And I've got no wife."

"That's impossible," said Peter. "The second marriage is void."

The man laughed. "You talk like the Navy Department. The Navy Department says, 'The second marriage is void.'" He repeated himself thickly, "That's what the Navy says. Void. Second marriage void." He flung his hand sideways, as if to indicate that the Navy had thrown the second marriage out of the window. "But the wife says, 'The first marriage is void.' She says she ought to know. She's got it black on white. Dead is dead." He shrugged again. "She's right too. Dead is dead. When you're dead you shouldn't come home."

"Have another drink?" Peter asked.

"Thanks." The man ordered a double rye. He smiled, and the wrinkles seemed to run across his face like telegraph wires seen from a speeding train. "You think I'm drinking like a slob," he said. "But I'm easing off. At first I was stewed all the time. But then I thought, after all, eternal love lasted six weeks. Six weeks for eternal love isn't so bad when you come to think of it."

For a while they drank in silence. Then the corporal said, "How come you're going back, Major? You must have points to burn."

"I've got some work to finish over there. What are you going to do now?"

"I don't know. I'm a radio repairman. But maybe I'll do something else. I'll find something. It's not so bad."

"Oh, sure," said the sailor, breaking in again. "But don't forget to take off that uniform. And don't wear that ruptured duck. Otherwise you'll be a ruptured duck yourself."

"It's not so bad," said the soldier. "I been offered two jobs already."

"No," said the sailor, "it's not so bad. If you've got an apartment, and civilian clothes, a job they held open for you, and a girl who's not sore at you because you're not dead—it's not so bad. It's just a little difficult is all." He looked up from his whisky glass, into which he had been staring. "See that man over there?" he asked Peter. He indicated a thin man with glasses who sat on a stool down the bar, talking to a girl.

"Who is he?" Peter asked.

"He was with me on the *Barnett* at Guadalcanal. He's got wonderful connections at Macy's. He knows a department head there."

"Well?"

"For three weeks he's been sleeping in the furniture department at Macy's. Innerspring mattress, with connecting bathroom. Pink tile. No water, of course, but the illusion is perfect. Just what we dreamed of at Guadalcanal."

Peter looked around. The oval bar, which seemed to glitter with a thousand lights, was occupied almost exclusively by men. Most of them were young, thirty or less, and Peter knew that virtually all of them must have been in the war. Few were in uniform, and not all the others wore the discharge button.

The sailor followed Peter's gaze.

"I don't know any of the others," he said. "But every night I see the same faces here. If you're going to be around long, Major, I can give you some advice. Don't start any conversations with anybody. With people like me, for instance. Otherwise you'll hear the same story so often, you'll want to cut your throat. Nothing but people going around trying to convince you that they're alive, and nobody'll believe it. Their wives won't believe it, and neither will their girl friends, or the landladies, or their former bosses. They're all just as dead as I am, only they don't know it. That's why they sit around here and drink. They're drinking themselves alive. Or that's what they think." He laughed heavily. "Or they wait until they find somebody they can talk to about Saipan, or the Philippines, or Cologne. When they can talk with the others that're dead, they imagine they're not dead themselves. But take it from me, Major, it's an illusion. Like the pink tile bathroom."

He said no more. Peter would have liked to continue the conversation. He was growing fond of the sailor. It was the same feeling of being part of the homeless crowd that had come to him on Broadway. He looked around the bar again. The radio was playing so loudly that he could not hear what was being said. But he felt like a soldier who, believing himself alone in a forest, looks around and finds his whole company behind him.

A few minutes later he paid his check and said good night to his friends.

The soldier shook his hand. Without looking up, the sailor said, "Good luck to you, Major."

It sounded like sarcasm.

⟫ 37 ⟪

STROUD returned from church service with a feeling of satisfaction. At first it had been necessary for German clergymen, Protestant and Catholic, to submit copies of their sermons for approval before mounting the pulpit. Stroud gradually dispensed with this censorship, of which he had never approved. His broadmindedness had borne fruit. This morning the Protestant pastor, the Reverend Karl Gebhardt, had preached on the collective guilt of the German people and had acknowledged the responsibility of every German, and of the Church itself, for what had happened under Hitler. Millions of Germans, he had said, became accomplices in the Nazi crimes through passive acquiescence, and the Church was guilty on the same score. Pastor Gebhardt had managed to say all this without offending his audience; he argued that the very extent of the complicity demanded leniency in dealing with the little ordinary people involved in it. He had startled his listeners by quoting a passage from Hitler's *Mein Kampf*: "When a nation is being led to destruction by its own regime, then revolt on the part of every member of that nation is not only a right, but a duty." Pastor Gebhardt characterized the lack of inner and outward revolt against the inhuman regime that led Germany to destruction as a crime against Germany and the world. It would have to be expiated by the German people. The crowded camp chapel had listened in respectful silence; Stroud thought he detected agreement with the preacher's words.

Master Sergeant Parker, grinning broadly, was waiting for the Major in his office. "I've got a surprise for you, Major," Parker said. "Lieutenant Stroud is here."

"Where is he?" asked Stroud, overjoyed.

"He's out looking the camp over. He'll be back any minute."

Jim! The happy warmth inside Stroud grew as he repeated the boy's name to himself. He had not seen his son for more than a year. Not long after Jim got his wings, he was flying airborne troops to Germany. By that time Stroud had already been in Germany for some time, and though they had repeatedly planned a meeting, it had never taken place. And now Jim was here to visit him.

"How does he look?" asked Stroud eagerly.

"First rate!" said Parker.

Stroud sat down at his desk, but he could not work. His pleasure at Jim's arrival was shadowed by something which he recognized as stemming from a guilty conscience. It had been weeks since he had written to Jim, and days since he had thought of him. He now realized that he had deliberately suppressed thoughts of his son, just as he had avoided thinking of home and Spokane. At the same time he felt an overwhelming gratitude to fate for not punishing him as he deserved. It was true that Jim had not been flying dangerous missions for some time, but anyone who spent hours in the air every day was never entirely out of danger. For weeks Stroud had neglected the duty of a father: holding off danger from his son by thinking about it. It was doubly good that Jim was here.

"Hello, Dad!" said Jim, stepping into the room.

Stroud leaped up and embraced his son. "Jim!"

"Dad, you look wonderful!"

"You too. Sit down! Where did you come from?"

Jim sat down. The folding army chair was too small for him. Chairs had always been too small for him, one way or another. As a child his long legs had dangled down from the high chair as if they belonged to somebody else much older.

"I've come to say so long," Jim said. "I'm going home next week."

"Home! Have you got enough points?"

"Not quite. But now I'm General MacMillian's pilot. C-47. I just brought him to Munich. He's on his way home, and I'm going to fly him. I may have to spend a couple of months in Washington before I'm discharged. We were going to China at first, but they called that off."

"Well, good for you, Jim! I hope you can spend a little time here before you go."

"Afraid not, Dad. I'll have to take off this afternoon. But I thought I'd come out and spend a couple hours with you anyway. Quite a camp you've got yourself here. Must get pretty boring though. When are you going home? You must have enough points to lend me some."

"I'll go home when they close down the camp," Stroud answered. "In two months, say. Three at the most." Something constricted his throat as he said it.

"What do you hear from Mom?" Jim asked.

"I had a letter yesterday," Stroud replied. "She's fine. Busy as usual. You know how she is. Meetings and charity affairs and clubs."

Mom's ceaseless activity was a standing joke between them. Stroud succeeded in laughing.

"I had a letter from Eleanor day before yesterday," Jim went on. "You know the big news, of course?"

"What news?"

"She's going to have a baby. It'll be a boy, she says. She's made her mind up. And if I know Eleanor, it had better be a boy."

Jim continued chatting, but Stroud hardly heard him. Eleanor expects a baby! he repeated to himself. Spokane suddenly seemed so near that he forgot where he was. He felt as if he were sitting in the living-room at home; if he looked up he would see Emily sitting across from him. For the sake of Eleanor, for the sake of the child, for the sake of Spokane, he tried not to think of Wanda. But at the same time he found himself trying to fend off the world that had come into the room with Jim, for it seemed like a betrayal of Wanda. He should have considered the clash of the two worlds sooner, he thought. Soon I'll be a grandfather. On his tongue he tasted a bitterness, as if he had bitten into rotten fruit.

"Why, you're not even listening!" Jim said.

"Of course I am, but it's so unexpected. I hardly know what—they could at least have written me."

"Probably they want to surprise you."

"Probably. Anyway, I'll pretend I don't know until they tell me themselves. By the way, have you had lunch?"

"No. And I could eat a horse." Jim was always hungry enough to eat a horse. "How's the chow in these parts?"

"Not bad. We've got a good German cook. It's amazing what they can do with C rations even."

They went to the mess hall. Usually Stroud ate at the same table with three other officers, but since it was Sunday the officers had eaten early in order to leave the camp as soon as possible. Thus father and son found themselves alone at the white-covered table. German prisoners brought them their food as if waiting on table were also a military function. They almost clicked their heels with every new plate they laid on the table.

"Do you think you'll get a leave to visit home?" Stroud asked, sipping his tomato juice.

"The General's already promised. I may even be able to fly to Spokane. The General's taking a leave too. He's from Idaho."

"That should work out nicely. How is flying these days? Are you still crazy about it?"

"Oh, sure! Naturally, I'd rather be flying a C-46. That's a sweet job, that C-46. The General tried to get one, but most of them were sent to Japan."

Jim began a long technical explanation of why he preferred a C-46 to a C-47. Stroud listened absently. It occurred to him that he would have to ask Jim about his plans for the future. Why is it, Stroud asked himself angrily, that lately I have to force myself to do the normal thing? I should have inquired long ago what Jim intends to do when he takes off his uniform. He asked, "When do you think you'll be able to go back to college?"

"Not this year any more. I want to take a good long rest. Next fall, probably."

"Don't you think we ought to send in an application pretty soon? I hear it's getting harder all the time."

"Oh, it'll work out all right. It usually does. People always exaggerate difficulties." He broke off and stared at his plate as if the chicken leg on it were absorbing his entire attention. Then he said casually, "Don't you think it would be a good idea if I studied a term at the Sorbonne?"

"The Sorbonne? Do you know enough French?"

"No. But I'd like to learn," Jim answered quickly.

The Strouds are no good at lying, Stroud thought. They rarely blush except when they're lying. He saw the red mount in Jim's neck. He pretended he had noticed nothing, but he suspected at once what was afoot. A little while later he asked, "What do you hear from Marjorie?"

Marjorie was the daughter of his law partner, Anthony E. Doughty. She was a year younger than Jim, who from his fourteenth year on had insisted he was going to marry her. Whether he would or not was naturally his own affair. But Stroud had always been excessively fond of the laughing, unspoiled girl who was continually around the house, and whom Emily had often accused him of preferring to his own daughter.

Jim was blushing again. "I haven't heard much from Marjorie lately."

"Did you kids have a fight?"

"No. Not especially."

Jim concentrated on his plate. Stroud observed him with care, and as he did so felt how much he loved the boy, how deep was his concern for everything that affected Jim. Lieutenant James H. Stroud, United States Army Air Forces, had become a little strange to him. But the blushing youngster with his nose in his pudding was the Jim he knew, his Jim. It was obvious that Jim needed him. It was good that Jim needed him.

Stroud cleared his throat. "Have you by any chance fallen in love with some little French girl?"

Jim looked up. "How did you know?"

"It wasn't hard to guess. Up to now your interest in foreign languages has been limited."

Jim laughed, relieved. "Right!" he said. "I'm in love." His tone changed. "But I want to tell you, Dad—this is serious."

"How serious?"

"I'm going to marry her as soon as I'm through school."

"Who is she?"

"A wonderful girl, Dad. I never met a girl like her in all my life. She's got the prettiest blue eyes you ever saw and—"

"I know all that," Stroud interrupted.

"How could you?" said Jim.

"Easy. We Strouds are famous for our good taste. But I still want to know: Who is she? Where did you meet her? How long have you known her?"

"Well, she's twenty, the daughter of a widow. Her father ran a hotel but he died, and her brother used up all the money. I met her in a Red Cross Club. She's a secretary there. About two months ago. And now you know the whole story." With a satisfied air he resumed eating his pudding.

"Two months?" Stroud said. "Isn't that a little brief?"

"Dad, this is something you know right away. And, anyhow, during the two months we were together practically day and night."

"What is that supposed to mean—'day and night'?"

Jim looked directly at his father. He did not blush. He said, "We lived together."

For God's sake! thought Stroud. What's going on here? The changes were coming a little too quickly for him. First there was Lieutenant James H. Stroud, then little Jim gulping his pudding, and now it was Lieutenant Stroud again, who not only lived under the same roof with a French girl, but could say so to his father!

"We have a little apartment in Paris," Jim continued.

"In other words," Stroud said, "she's your mistress." He regretted the word as soon as he said it. He had always been proud

of not being a hypocrite. Only those who have something to conceal themselves pass judgment on others—this had been a guiding
principle with him. But that was just it. He himself had something
to conceal that was a thousand times worse than the relationship
of Lieutenant James H. Stroud with a little Parisian grisette. But
there was more. In his mind he saw the French girl, and she had
the features of Wanda; and Jim and Wanda went hand in hand
through the Tuileries and had themselves photographed under the
Arc de Triomphe, and laughed to each other on a carrousel in
Montmartre. It is quite in order that Jim and Wanda are living
together, Stroud thought. A hateful, monotonous melody beat in
his brain. He tried to light his cigar. His hands were trembling.

He had expected a brusque answer from his son. But Jim merely
laughed. "Oh, Dad, don't use words like that. I've already told you
I intend to marry her."

Stroud slowly began retreating. "But you want to be sure you're
marrying a nice girl—"

"She is a nice girl," Jim retorted. "You've just got old-fashioned
ideas. I've learned a few things about life lately. You can't learn
about life in Spokane, of course."

"And Marjorie?" asked Stroud, now in disorderly retreat.

Jim snapped on his cigarette lighter with a superior gesture.
"Marjorie," he said, "is a charming girl. There's nothing to be said
against Marjorie. Only she's something of a bore."

"You've certainly changed your opinion."

"We all do, now and then," said Jim with the wisdom of a man
who has lived.

They drank their coffee and spoke no more about it. Stroud
showed Jim a part of the camp he had not yet seen: the recreation
hall, the workshops, the library, the chapel, and the schoolrooms.
He took Jim to his own quarters and gave him a bottle of bourbon.
Not until Jim was in his jeep did Stroud ask, "What's her name?"

"Madelon."

"That sounds like a song from World War One."

"The whole girl is like a song," said Jim. He colored.

I always thought that the Strouds blushed only when they were
lying, Stroud reflected. Slowly, his hands clasped behind his back,
he walked back to his quarters.

38

THE Clarks lived in a huge house, east of the Hudson, on a hill that offered a sweeping view of the river.

"My dear boy!" said Walter Clark heartily as he welcomed Peter. "Patricia didn't expect you until later. She's at the prison, as usual. What magnificent work the girl is doing! How seriously she takes it all! I'll have Henry take you there at once."

Over Peter's objections that he did not want to cause any trouble, he was escorted to the waiting limousine by his host.

"Not another word!" said Walter Clark. "Patricia would never forgive me if she had to wait any longer than necessary before seeing you. Three weeks in the United States is little enough time." He smiled pleasantly as Peter got into the car. "Lucky we live near such a popular institution as Sing Sing! Otherwise we'd never get to see you and Patricia."

A short ride through flaming countryside brought Peter to the door of the prison. Even the soft October sun of Indian Summer— it was called "old wives' summer" where Peter came from—did nothing to relieve the cold, naked grimness of the high stone walls.

"What can I do for you, Major?" said the guard at the entrance.

"I'd like to see my wife," Peter answered. He gave a short nervous laugh as he saw the guard's surprise. "No," he tried to joke, "my wife isn't locked up. She's a visiting lady, or whatever they're called here. I've just come back from overseas, and I was told I'd find her here."

"A hell of a place to find your wife," said the guard good-humoredly. "What's your name, Major?"

"Olden, Peter Olden."

A look of mingled respect and sympathy came over the fleshy red face of the guard.

"Are you Mrs. Olden's husband?"

"Yes. I am Mrs. Olden's husband."

"Come right in," said the guard, taking Peter into the little office at the entrance. "We'll take care of you right away." He began paging through the prison telephone book. "We all know Mrs. Olden here. A wonderful lady. You can be proud of her. She spends whole days at a time in the prison. I often wonder why a woman as pretty and rich as she is spends so much time in this godforsaken place. Just wants to be helpful, I guess." He found his number and began to dial. "I can't let you into the prison without a pass, Major. But we'll find Mrs. Olden for you in short order."

It took several calls to various offices before Patricia was reached. The guard handed the receiver to Peter.

"Hello, Patricia. Here I am."

"Hello, darling. I didn't think you'd be here this early."

"I didn't either."

"Would you mind waiting for half an hour, Peter? I'm right in the middle of a talk with the superintendent. I'll make it as short as I can. Or would you rather come up?"

"No. I'll wait."

"All right, darling. I'll be with you soon."

He hung up. "Is it all right to wait here?" he asked the guard.

"Sure thing. Want a paper to read?"

Peter took the newspaper and sat down. The guard resumed his post outside. Peter was adroit at newspaper reading; usually he was able to finish one in a few minutes. This time he took pains to read every line. Almost an hour passed before he saw Patricia emerge from the prison door.

Peter did not move from the window at once. He studied the woman who came toward him across the court, not too hurriedly, not too slowly. She was wearing a simple gray suit and a little hat with a cluster of bright flowers. The convicts stopped working and looked after her as she passed. Peter began observing himself, more than the approaching woman. It's good, he thought, that I can see her before she sees me. But as she came nearer and nearer in the oddly disembodied manner of a figure on a movie screen, he knew that his attempt to eavesdrop on his own emotions was fruitless. Inside him everything was still: a deep, unruffled calm. He went outside and walked toward her.

She kissed him on both cheeks. "I'm sorry, darling," she said. "I just couldn't break away. Have you a car?"

"Yes. Walter gave me his."

"Wonderful. He was going to send it for me anyway."

They thanked the guard, who watched them attentively. He's probably amazed that she kept me waiting so long, Peter speculated, but immediately dismissed the thought as petty vanity.

"I'm sorry I wasn't in New York when you arrived," she said, as they were seated in the car. "These last few weeks have been terribly strenuous. I'm exhausted."

"You're working too hard."

"Probably. But there's so much to be done. Most people think only of one part of my work. It's not enough to visit the children, you know. I have to visit the prisons too, and tell those unfortunate men about their children. It's the only way to maintain family ties. It's really amazing how even the worst criminals seem to have a conscience. When you tell them about their children they're more affected than when you remind them of their crimes."

"Do you do it all alone?" Peter asked, just to say something.

"Oh, no. I've got a number of women interested. Fanny Logan has an organization of her own now. And Mrs. Harrison recently gave a marvelous cocktail party to help us out. More than a hundred and fifty people. Too bad you weren't there. Imagine, Mrs. Allen brought the British Minister. I spent practically the whole afternoon talking to him."

Throughout the trip she spoke of her work, of parties, and again of her work. Peter, only half listening, looked at her in silence. She actually did look tired. She was beautiful; Patricia would always be beautiful. But her thin, delicately carved face seemed even thinner, and there were two lines he had never seen before on either side of her somewhat too narrow lips. Shortly after their marriage Patricia's friends used to please Peter by saying that "for the first time in her life she looks happy." She did not look happy now. Even in her liveliness there was something of the graceless animation of the old maid. It struck him now that though her eyes had the rare and perfect shape of hazel nuts, their blue was not beautiful: in them was too much of the clear gray of impenetrable steel.

Peter had imagined that his talk with Patricia would be less difficult in a strange house, but this hope was abandoned soon after their arrival. The Clarks had tactfully attempted to make the honeymoon of the returning soldier as pleasant as possible. Patricia's luggage and clothing had been moved from her room into the large guest room, which seemed an ideal setting for a renewed wedding night, with its big fireplace, flowered wallpaper, and double bed. Peter's bags were unpacked, and his freshly ironed pajamas were laid out on the bed next to Patricia's nightgown. Sheltering the "young couple" was a thrill that the Walter Clarks were determined to enjoy to the full. Cocktails, expertly mixed by the host himself, preceded an especially elaborate dinner, and at dessert the prize of the Clark cellar, a Lanson 1921, was served.

Howard Clark proposed the first toast to Peter's return and the second to his reunion with Patricia. Peter looked across the table to his wife. She smiled graciously. He smiled too. He felt that no one could fail to notice how artificial his smile was. The muscles of his face hurt, as they always did when he forced a smile.

It was late before Peter and Patricia were able to go upstairs to their room. Patricia disappeared into the bathroom for several minutes, and then emerged in a long, almost transparent silk negligee. She seated herself before the dressing-table mirror and began letting down her hair. Peter was sitting in an easy chair by the fireplace, smoking a cigarette.

Before Patricia could say anything, he began, "Patricia, I must have a talk with you."

"Yes, dear?"

"You've probably noticed," he said, "that in the last few months something happened to our correspondence."

"Yes," she said. "You didn't write quite as often."

"Neither of us wrote as often. But that's not what I mean. The tone of my letters changed. I wrote you what was happening, in a general way." He tried to smile. "But I didn't write any love letters."

"I know," she replied. "You were probably cross with me. You know I can't write love letters."

"It wasn't your fault," he answered. "It was just that I couldn't lie to you, Patricia. I love another woman."

The sentence filled the room. He had imagined a thousand times what it would be like when he spoke it. He had always supposed that, no matter what happened next, the worst would be over, once he was able to get the sentence out. What he had not taken into account was the overpowering silence that followed his words, a silence in which the sentence seemed to multiply itself, to take on a life of its own, to grow and expand until the room seemed too small to hold it.

Patricia put down her comb. Without turning around, she asked, "Since when?"

"That's hard to say. I met her again for the first time in March. But I've known her for fourteen years."

"A German?"

"Yes."

"You never told me about her?"

"No."

Patricia turned around.

"So you have deceived me?" she said.

"Yes," he said.

"And you lied too?"

"No."

"You did. You never told me about it."

"It's useless to write a thing like that in a letter."

"But it isn't useless to lie?"

Since her first question Peter had been trying to suppress a feeling that he knew was unseemly. He was comparing Patricia with Maria. But the Maria whom he used as a criterion in judging his wife had never confronted a situation like this. He imagined what she would do in Patricia's place. He was not sure whether Maria would cry or rage, whether she would forgive or vilify her rival, whether she would understand or hate. But this he did know: she would not sit there calmly and ask pointed questions like a skilled cross-examiner. She would not look at him out of untroubled eyes in which was more scorn than hate, more curiosity than concern for her husband, more contemptuous assurance than anxiety for the future. And Maria would not have been surprised, for she would have long since sensed everything from his letters, from his silence, or from nothing at all. He had come back oppressed by a feeling of guilt. He was a man who had betrayed his wife. But now she was subjecting him to a dressing down, as if he were an obstreperous boy caught misbehaving.

"Well," she asked, "what do you intend to do?"

He stood up and began walking around the room. "Patricia," he said, "it's not just that I have deceived you. If that were all, I could try to make it up to you. If you wanted me to, of course. But I love this woman. I want to marry her."

Now she arose. As she stood, perfectly erect, before the mirror, she seemed to be a head taller than usual.

"At the moment," she said, "you happen to be married to me."

"I know," he said. "I would like you to give me a divorce."

"It's incredible!" she said, not moving.

He said nothing.

"The effrontery of it!" she continued. "The first night you're home you calmly inform me that you're in love with some German woman or other and demand that I give you a divorce. You don't try to excuse your actions. You simply announce them. What have you got against me, Peter?"

He had let her talk without interrupting, although he felt the blood mounting to his head. "It's not a question of holding anything against you, Patricia," he said. "If anyone is to blame, I am."

"And that settles the matter for you," she said. "For me it's by no means settled."

"What more can I say?"

"I've already asked—what have you got against me?"

"And I've already answered—that doesn't enter into it."

"It does. You have never said our marriage was unhappy. But it must have been. There isn't any other explanation. I want to hear what you have to say."

He could not help admiring the cool self-possession that, even now, did not seem to leave her.

"All right," he said. "If you really want to know. But I don't think you'll understand, Patricia. Your question indicates that. You are not aware that our marriage has been unhappy for years. But that's just it."

She toyed with a nail file. "Go on," she said abruptly.

"A while ago you said that you can't write love letters. There are many other things you can't do that would give a man over there the feeling he is not alone. Do you remember the days of the bulge offensive? I was in the middle of it, and you knew it. A few days afterward the papers came from New York. We were still somewhere in the snow, in the Ardennes. I found your name in practically all the papers. You were giving dinners and attending all sorts of parties."

"What was I supposed to do? Cancel all my engagements? After all, you weren't dead. Did you expect me to play widow in advance? Would that have been of any benefit to you?"

"Benefit? No. A man doesn't want his wife to benefit him. Sometimes it's enough for him to know that she is pacing up and down in a room, twisting a handkerchief. And that she's listening to the radio, turning it off, wandering around the house, not knowing what to do."

"I always know what to do."

Again he tried to smile. "Maybe that's what was wrong with our marriage, Patricia."

"I couldn't act like an idiot just to make you happy."

He ignored her answer. He asked, "Do you remember Hagerstown?"

"Yes. After all, I spent two months in that miserable place."

"That's right. I was lucky the training camp was so near the town. Every night I could come and spend the evening with you. I was very happy in Hagerstown. I thought you were happy too. We were alone for the first time in our married life. You were living in that little hotel. We ate in a cafeteria. We had only one room—"

"Did I ever complain?" she interrupted.

"No," he answered. "But months later, when we talked about it, you told me how you hated it."

"I merely said that Hagerstown was unbearable. The food was unfit to eat and the hotel dirty. I had to interrupt my work for two months, just to be with you for an hour in the evening. You could have come to New York every week-end. But instead you shut me off for two months from my work and my friends. That was all I said. All day long I sat around and waited. Why should I have been happy? I never pretended to be a Penelope. I never misled you as to the kind of person I am."

He stopped his pacing for a moment. "No," he said, "you never misled me. You apparently never did the wrong thing. You just never did the right thing."

She threw down the nail file. "Ridiculous!" she said. "All this is just evasion. I know exactly why you hate me. You hate my independence. And the fact that I've always used my own brain. And that I worked, and made a success of it. You're jealous, that's all.

It's not my fault that you haven't written a book for four years and that nobody remembers the last one. Was I supposed to fade out of the picture just because you did?"

Again he avoided answering her directly. "I had nothing against your work, as long as it didn't use you up completely," he said. "But then it became just a crotchety obsession. You began acting like an old maid."

Her laughter interrupted him. It was a laugh that made him wince—a theatrical laugh of the kind taught in acting schools when the stage directions read "Mocking laughter."

"For the first time you're telling the truth," she said. "For the first time. You've simply had enough of me in bed. That's why you're calling me an old maid. Just because I wasn't willing to be your prostitute."

He was suddenly weary. He could almost feel physically the wall between him and the woman who stood opposite him. It was as if he wanted to throw a ball over the wall but was never able to throw it high enough, and it always bounced back. He knew that not she alone was to blame. He could picture her there on the other side of the wall. She, too, was throwing balls. The balls she threw bounced back too. "Look," he said, changing his tone, "this isn't getting us anywhere. Maybe it's too soon. Maybe there's no sense to it anyway. I didn't want to make any accusations against you, Patricia. I'm no hypocrite. The fault is not in our marriage. It lies in the fact that I love another woman and will love her all my life. Our accusations back and forth are just blind alleys. I accept the blame. I regret it. But I can't change it."

"When you married me you also said it was for all your life."

"You're right," he answered. "You will always be right in whatever you say. But that still doesn't change anything."

"It changes a great deal," she said. "Please sit down. It makes me nervous when you keep walking up and down."

He sat down. "What does it change?" he asked.

"In my country," she said, "adultery is a crime. In my country people can be put in jail for adultery. I don't know whether you are aware of that. With us"—she emphasized the "us"—"the law protects women. Over here they can't just be taken and tossed away at will."

He had to force himself not to retort. Something in him said,

Think of Maria! Don't answer! He could feel the blood straining in his temples, but gradually his agitation subsided. The realization that he could hate this woman came to him like a balm.

She crossed the room and lay down on the bed.

"I've got a headache," she said after a pause.

He knew that these four words introduced a new chapter. He sat smoking in the easy chair and waited. After a few minutes she spoke again.

"I'm too tired to talk any more tonight. I have a lot to do tomorrow. If I don't get some sleep I'll die."

"We can talk some more tomorrow," he said, relieved.

At least a quarter of an hour passed. The two alabaster clocks over the fireplace ticked loudly. Once they struck the hour, not together, but one slightly after the other, as if one were politely allowing the other to go first. Suddenly she said, "Don't you want to lie down?"

It was the moment he had feared more than that of making his confession, or the wounding words, or her contemptuous laughter. All through the silent quarter hour he had felt that something was in preparation. He knew that tone of voice. It had been that way before. "Come to me!" And he had come. Then, for a little while, they were on the same side of the wall. Without speaking. Afterward he climbed back to his side and the play began again. Two balls on two sides of a wall.

He stood up and went over to the bed. She lay with her knees drawn up, her arms crossed on her breast. Her shoulders were hunched up, like those of a little girl who is cold. The silk negligee, under which she wore a thin nightgown, only partly concealed her still girlish body.

"I'm cold," she said.

He took a blanket from the foot of the bed and covered her. Then it was quiet again.

Without changing her position, she said, "Maybe it's all just a bad dream."

"Why don't you sleep now?" he asked gently. "We can discuss it some more tomorrow." He took a pillow and a blanket and went to the couch. He felt, rather than saw, that she was watching him.

Suddenly she asked, "Are you afraid of me?"

"No."

He took off his tunic and lay back on the couch. "Shall I turn out the light?" he asked.

"If you like."

Lying on his back, his eyes open, he heard her breathing. Minutes passed. He knew that she was lying there awake.

All at once she laughed again. It was a short, hysterical laugh.

"Why do you laugh?" he asked, sure that she would speak even without his asking.

"It serves me right," she said. "I worked and neglected myself and made a hero out of you."

"I never claimed to be a hero."

"But I talked to everyone about you. My friends took you up as if you were one of us."

He did not answer.

"Why don't you say something?" she asked.

"There's nothing to say to that."

"Haven't you a trace of gratitude?"

"I've told you that I'm sorry for what has happened, Patricia. But what has that got to do with gratitude?" Gratitude? What for? he thought. Why does she want to humiliate me? At the same time he tried to understand that she, too, felt deeply humiliated.

"Do you know what my mother thought of you when I first met you?"

She wanted to continue, but he interrupted. "It would be better for both of us if you didn't say anything now that you will regret tomorrow."

"I resent that superior tone, Peter," she said. "Are you proud of sleeping with a German whore, perhaps?"

I won't answer her any more, he decided. It's futile. To a woman who has been in love herself, one can explain what it means to be in love with a woman. But it is useless to talk about such things to Patricia. He said nothing.

He lay there without sleeping, thinking, until morning. As the uncertain gray of the dawn began to light the room, he could see the woman who lay alone on the bed that had been prepared for a second wedding night.

Patricia was asleep.

39

THE first snow had fallen. A thin covering of white lay over the village; by tomorrow it would be gone. A warm wind rattled the windowpanes, and the trees in the orchard stood naked in the winter landscape. On the mountains lay deeper snow. The Alps that shut in the valley were white, and it seemed that there was no world beyond them. There was only the valley, and the mountains that guarded it.

Stroud and Wanda had remained loyal to the little inn at Oberndorf. They had returned three times since the first evening and had come to look upon the little room with the heavy 1890 furniture as home. When they arrived the proprietress handed them the key to their room without a word; and as soon as they entered Wanda would try to arrange the furniture to look as if she and Stroud had never left. They always brought along a variety of objects they did not need, and which only served the purpose of giving the hotel room the character of a home. Stroud never failed to announce gravely that he had a great deal of reading to do over Sunday and always unpacked four or five books, which Wanda carefully lined up on the commode so that they looked like a miniature library. Sunday evenings the books were packed away again, unread.

Evening came early. It was Saturday, and they had arrived an hour before. The proprietress had prepared a surprise for them by heating the room. Wood was crackling in the big white tile oven. Stroud stood at the window and looked out. It was almost dark, and a streak of light shone out of the taproom below across the white garden. It began to snow again in great soft flakes.

Wanda had taken off her wet stockings and was sitting in a far corner of the room with her bare feet propped against the tile of the oven. She said nothing. This silence, too, was part of their game of playing home—the silence of two people who still have a whole lifetime to talk to each other.

Odd, Stroud thought, aware for the first time how completely the room had come to be home to him. In a twinkling she makes every Saturday night seem as if it would last forever. But she never speaks of the future, as if she has reconciled herself from the very first to the idea that there is no future.

"What are you thinking of?" she said.

"Of you," he answered without turning around.

"Why is it you never talk when you think of me?"

"What makes you think I don't?"

"I can tell instantly by your face when you're thinking of me. When it's clouded, I know you're thinking of me. Sometimes I don't even have to see your face."

"That's not true," he began. He got no further.

"You worry about me, John. You don't understand me."

"I understand you very well."

"No. You can't bring yourself to believe that there's nothing I want from you. I don't want to take you from your family and your home and your work. Naturally, I want you to stay with me as long as you can. But not a day longer."

He was still looking out of the window. "You talk as if I were afraid of you," he replied. "Maybe I was, once. But that's long past." He added almost rudely, "You're right, of course. You usually are. I worry about you. But not because I think you want something from me. You'll have to give me credit for being that much of a judge of human nature. I worry about you because I don't know what will happen to you when I leave Germany."

"What if I had never met you?" she asked.

"That would be different."

"Why?" she replied. "Still, I know what you mean. Most women imagine they would be lost if their men left them. But women like that are ungrateful."

"Ungrateful? They're in love, that's all."

She jumped up and ran barefoot across the room to him. From behind she threw her arms around his neck. "So I don't love you?" she asked laughingly, nuzzling her face into his back.

"Sometimes I wonder," he replied.

"Good," she said. "That's how it should be. As long as you're here, Major Stroud, I want to be on your mind all the time. It's good for you to be a little uncertain about me."

He turned around and took her in his arms.

Later, as they sat before the stove, he asked, "What did you mean about being ungrateful?"

"Oh, you're going back to that. Well, I call women ungrateful when they judge the past only by what comes of it later." She took his hand.

He noticed again, as he had done a hundred times before, how unbelievably small and shapely her hands were; they seemed to be swallowed up in his.

"I'm happy with you, John. Terribly happy. For the first time in my life. Before I met you I was miserable. Not only on account of the camp, and of my family and Poland. But on account of my memories. Every night they came, in the dark when I lay awake, and in dreams when I slept. You blotted all that out, John. Now, when you go away, I will dream of you. I dream of you already, every night. I'm never alone any more. I'm so much richer than on the day when I stood trembling before the American major who looked at me as if I were some kind of strange animal."

He laughed. "I'd hardly say you gave the effect of trembling. In fact, the American major got the distinct impression that you had more than your share of nerve."

They talked of their first meeting. It was a favorite topic with them; once more they recounted the smallest details of it, rehearsing again their earliest mutual emotions which they had sought to conceal from themselves and from each other.

Then, when he had once more lapsed into silence, she said, "I have to explain everything to you as if you were a child." Her eyes were large and grave. "You don't seem to understand. Even before I was able to take care of myself, but now I will be able to get along much easier. It is as if everything that dragged me down is gone."

"Yes, I know," he said. His tone was fatherly. "But I want to get things settled for you. Where do you want to go after I leave? Have you changed your mind about Poland?"

"No," she said decisively.

"How about London? That could probably be arranged. They say that the Polish Army commanded by General Anders in Italy is going to be taken over by the British."

"No," she said again. "I'm really not much of a soldier, John. Women have to do all sorts of things today that aren't the business of women, at all. Sometimes they even have to fight. But they don't have to like it. Anyway, what are the London Poles after? Do they want war? Do they want to keep their guns in their hands until the world is ready for another blood bath, and they can plunge in again? I've had enough of war, John."

"But you don't want to stay in the DP camp," he argued, glad that finally she was not avoiding the question of the future. "America is closed to Poles for the time being. But something could certainly be done to prepare the way."

"I don't want to go to America, John. You'll be in America." She attempted a smile, but for the first time she failed. Her smile went wrong, like a toy train going off its track. She could not wholly hide her bitterness as she added, "America is big. But not big enough for both of us. One journeys into the future, not into the past. When you board your ship, we'll both be part of the past for each other."

"Well, where to, then?"

"I don't know yet. Somewhere where things are being built up again. Where women are needed. You and Peter were talking about the pioneers not long ago. I've been thinking of them ever since. Half the world is in ruins. Maybe men will build it up again. But women will be needed more than ever before." She looked into space. Again she pressed her bare feet against the stove. "Women will be needed to carry meals into the fields, and to men working in the ruins. They'll be needed to care for the children, so the men won't have to worry. And to make homes out of the houses the men have built."

Stroud smiled. "That's hardly General Bor's lieutenant talking," he said. "The womanly woman—it sounds like the theories of my friend Peter."

"I don't know about Peter's theories," said Wanda. "But don't misunderstand me. I'm not conceding anything to you lords of creation. I just believe that a man must have strength—and a woman must give it to him."

Stroud looked at her in silence. Is she really as strong as all that, he wondered, or is it just blind courage? It occurred to him, too, that he had never considered the possibility that he might be the one who was ruined by his love for her. Was he himself so strong, so sure of himself? He thought, almost with envy, of men he had known who were willing to give up everything for a woman—family, career, and the serenity of age. In the tragedy of those men, he saw now, there was a great deal of courage, contempt for convention, and a willingness to defy the world. He knew that he would never be capable of that. Why not have the decency, then, to make an end of it before everything gets worse, for him and for her—just as it had gotten worse with every encounter after the first evening in this little hotel room? Hadn't he promised himself, after his talk with Jim, to explain to Wanda why they would have to part, immediately, as soon as possible, and not wait until he left Germany?

She seemed too occupied with her own thoughts to notice his long silence. With a suddenness that was now familiar to him and that had in it something marvelously youthful and lighthearted, she jumped up and said, "I'm neglecting my duties! You must be starving."

He had brought along rations and a small Coleman stove; immediately on arriving she had converted a corner of the room into a tiny kitchen. He watched her as, still barefoot, she ran across the room and unpacked the "Ten-in-One" carton with little cries of excitement and enthusiasm when she found something she liked. He saw that she could not resist munching a piece of the hard army chocolate while she lit the stove and began preparing the egg powder for cooking. Stroud knew for certain that, once again, he would be unable to summon the courage to talk "reasonably" with her; on the contrary, he soon convinced himself that to destroy the happiness of this girl, however brief, would not be courageous, but cowardly and mean. He arose, crossed the room to the "kitchen," and kissed her on the back of her firm brown neck.

"Major Stroud," she said, "please make up your mind. Do you want to make love or eat?" Then she turned around and kissed him on the mouth. "If you want to eat, you'll have to give up kissing the back of my neck. The back of my neck is very sensitive."

He felt her body against his. And again came the deep enticement, the dizziness in head and stomach, the sweet nausea that silenced sense and reason.

"I don't think I'm hungry," he said. He turned off the little gasoline stove, lifted her up, and carried her to the bed.

The night was all tenderness and wordless harmony.

Soon she slept. He could not sleep. He lay and looked at her. The rising moon brightened the room. The face that he saw in the moonlight was not tranquil. From time to time she spoke a few unconnected sentences in Polish. Once she raised her head, like an animal startled in ambush, as if to shut off the sight of something—a doubly painful gesture since her eyes were already closed in sleep. She has not told me the truth, Stroud thought. Her dreams are still not peaceful.

Then, in the middle of the night, she awoke. She opened her eyes, smiled, and was not surprised to see him looking at her. Without speaking she put her arms around his neck. "How good it is that you are with me," she said.

And later, "John, I want something—something no one can take away from me." Almost inaudibly she whispered, "John, I want a child."

❦ 40 ❦

THERE was in Patricia a kind of strength that permitted her to pass over what was unusual and disturbing and take up her daily routine as if nothing had happened.

If Peter had expected her to resume their interrupted discussion of divorce on the morning after he had broached it, then he did not know the woman to whom he had been married for more than eight years. If she was merely acting, if inside she was not as calm as she outwardly appeared to be, Peter could not help acknowledging that she played her part with complete conviction.

Most women, forced to pretend in the presence of others that nothing was amiss, would have relieved their nerves, gradually or explosively, when left alone with the man responsible for their predicament. Patricia did nothing of the sort. She made no further reference to what had happened. He could not tell whether she wanted to subject him to the unpleasantness of bringing up the subject again, whether she believed that his own nerves would betray him into saying or doing something damaging, or whether she hoped that a pretense of normal routine would bring home to him the senselessness of his passion. On Saturday she went calmly about her usual activities, returned to the house for dinner, and seemed as self-possessed and unruffled as ever. That evening she retired with Peter to their bedroom, obviously not in the least disturbed by the unresolved situation in which she found herself. She spoke to him conversationally of her usual interests—the prisoners and her future engagements—and she inquired as to whether Peter was planning a new novel. Her bedtime toilet consumed as much time and care as before, and she seemed completely unmoved as Peter again prepared his bed on the couch. She said good night to him as if they had not been parted in years, but also as if she had not shared his bed for years either.

Sunday morning she suddenly informed him that they were expected at dinner in her mother's house in Philadelphia that evening.

Peter felt, almost as soon as he entered the mansion on Rittenhouse Square, how foreign were the people in whose society he had spent so many years of his life. He could not otherwise explain his complete inability to read anything in the faces of Barbara Draper and Uncle Newell; he could not even tell whether Patricia had informed her mother by telephone of what had happened. The presence of Uncle Newell suggested a hurriedly summoned family council. Also, as Peter found to his relief, his baggage had been taken to a separate guest room. On the other hand, his room was adjacent to Patricia's, and week-end visits by Uncle Newell were by no means unusual.

Barbara Draper was dressed for the evening when they arrived. She was still a woman of extraordinary beauty, though her loveliness was of a quite different kind from that of her daughter. It was impossible to imagine this woman of sixty, who seemed no more than fifty, as a young woman, to say nothing of a young girl. Her personality was dominated by the assurance that comes from possession. Barbara Draper, with her majestic bearing, her crown of white hair, her flawless white skin, and her imperious gray eyes, instantly communicated to anyone who entered the room the impression that she possessed everything; not only money and power and chattels, but the servants, the brilliance of the lights, the tones of the piano, and the guests themselves. It was as if Barbara Draper wanted to make her visitors constantly aware that nothing was impossible to her—she could heal the sick, bring the Palace of Versailles to Philadelphia, or transform the visitor himself into a hedgehog. Her table was invariably laden with foods that were out of season. But these minor manifestations of her personality were not mere snobbery or even eccentricity—they were unconscious demonstrations that Barbara Draper could at all times make the impossible possible.

Barbara Draper was almost never alone. It was, oddly, her bathroom that most strikingly revealed her obsession for company. The size of the room was such that a whole family could have lived in it without crowding. The fixtures and toilet articles were of gold, the bathtub and the rest of the room of black marble. But it was not principally the unrestrained luxury that was significant of Barbara Draper's character. The bathroom was hung with dozens of photographs; along with portraits of Charles Draper were family groups of all sizes and pictures of Draper houses in New Hampshire, Sun Valley, California, Long Island, and Florida. The furnishings of the room included a little writing table of black marble with a gold telephone. Barbara Draper remained in contact with the world even in her bathroom. She dictated to her secretary, made telephone calls, or communed with the photographs of her family.

As lacking in taste as all this was, bad taste alone did not explain it. Those who did not know Barbara Draper would have to assume that the mistress of a house where a clumsy modern portrait of Uncle Newell hung next to an Infanta by Velasquez, where even lunch was served on heavy gold plates, and where cheapjack objects were found side by side with works of art, was a woman of little culture and no refinement. But it was only one aspect of Barbara Draper's character that she could, without thinking twice, add a Venetian brooch worth fifty cents to her collection of seventeenth-century French jewelry—anyone who objected to such a lack of discrimination could simply get himself invited elsewhere. In Barbara Draper's lack of taste there was an element of challenge, and even of humor. It was, further, hardly possible to brand as tasteless a woman who displayed such superlative taste in her dress, her personal grooming, and in everything that pertained to her own person.

The big drawing-room was already occupied by a gathering which, besides Barbara Draper and Uncle Newell, included a former French ambassador, a general from Washington, the widow of a department store magnate named Nolan, the president of a New

York bank and his wife, and the daughter of a governor and her fiancé. Watson, the Drapers' English butler, who in every way resembled an English butler, was serving cocktails. As soon as they had changed, Patricia and Peter joined the party.

At dinner Peter sat between Mrs. Nolan and Mrs. Grant, the wife of the bank president. Mrs. Nolan talked with prodigious rapidity of psychoanalysis, taxes, communism, and of a party in the California home of Barbara Hutton, to whom she invariably referred as "poor little Barbara" without explaining what was so little and so poor about Barbara.

Mrs. Grant, to his right, was a woman of more serious interests. She was concerned about the readjustment of soldiers to civilian life, and Peter soon learned that she headed a committee whose function was to greet soldiers on their return from abroad. Peter's untutored supposition that the committee received homecoming soldiers with coffee, hot dogs, white shirts, and directions for finding rooms turned out to be in error. Mrs. Grant explained that her group conducted a ten-day readjustment course in which ex-soldiers were instructed how to behave in civilized society, with emphasis on how they should conduct themselves with their wives. Such courses, Mrs. Grant firmly believed, would avert most of the postwar marriage tragedies. Peter ventured to suggest that such a course ought to last at least fourteen days, and Mrs. Grant agreed that there was something in what he said. She promised to bring up his proposal at the next meeting of the committee.

The table chat acquired added fascination through the circumstance that Mrs. Nolan and Mrs. Grant alternated in talking to each other over Peter's head in order to keep each other posted on the progress of the conversation, starting every sentence with "I was just saying," which resulted in croaking frogs, psychoanalysis, and the spiritual equilibrium of GI's being mingled in one uninterrupted stream of talk.

Peter had hoped to avoid personal questions at dinner, but his table companions were well bred and did not fail to ask whether he was not delighted at being home. Both Mrs. Grant and Mrs. Nolan then fell to talking about Patricia, who sat opposite. They lowered their voices as they assured Peter that he was a remarkably fortunate man to possess such an enchanting woman for a wife. When they noticed that Patricia was observing them, Mrs. Grant leaned across the table and said, "Don't you dare listen, Patricia. We're saying perfectly dreadful things about you."

The ladies withdrew to the drawing-room after dessert. Uncle Newell took Barbara Draper's place, and the servants passed around coffee and liqueurs. For a moment it was uncertain if the talk would concern itself with the incompetence of the administration, or if jokes were in order. In deference to the two men in uniform, humor was chosen as more fitting, which gave the general an opportunity to distinguish himself as a raconteur. Peter, too, was called upon for a story, but at the risk of putting Uncle Newell out of sorts he had to apologize for not being able to think of anything amusing at the moment. Fortunately it was not long before Uncle Newell broke up the gathering with his invariable comment under such circumstances: "The ladies can't get along without us."

Peter took advantage of the regrouping of the guests to withdraw for a while. He went upstairs and stepped out onto a small balcony from which he could see the lights of downtown Philadelphia.

The November sky hung low over the city. It was cold, but Peter felt no need for a coat. The air was sharp and dry, and its freshness did him good. The reflection of the neon signs gave the heavens a yellowish-red coloring that almost suggested the sky over Paris. Peter breathed deeply. He thought of Maria. He had been thinking of her constantly, but for that very reason it was as if he no longer was aware of her absence. She went with him along the streets, her face was on the paper as he wrote, and in the mirror when he looked at himself. But now there was something more; as he put his hand on the cold railing of the balcony, he felt as if he were laying his hand on the warmth of hers.

She had spoken of the temptation that he would encounter here —of the laughter and the fullness of life and the lights. But as he looked out at the nervously twitching lights of the city, he felt only a desperate, tearing longing for the dark streets of Munich, for the black sky over Berlin, yes, for the frightening silhouettes of Braunschweig as they loomed before the window of the prison. The fault is in me, he thought, not in the lights. What business have I to be here? The light that I can turn on here is one among millions. But over there I can try to turn on the first lights. Here it's impos-

sible to reach deeply into the lives of people. They are not looking
for help, not seeking a way. Here everything is taken for granted;
over there everything is new. America was called the New World
once. But America has become old, he thought. A safe, settled
world. A tired world too—weary of its own good fortune and
wealth. The neon lights danced. He thought, the little nurse at
Camp Homerun was right. He understood now what she meant by
saying that the GI's had fallen in love with European girls because
the European girls were hungry. Or something like that. One could
fall in love with being needed.

The outlines of the Philadelphia office buildings stood out
against the illuminated sky. But he was remembering how deeply
he had been moved by the sight of the first scaffolding for a new
house in a suburb of Berlin. How he had watched in Munich as
each day a new store opened for business in the Kaufingerstrasse
and Neuhauserstrasse—a tailor shop with nothing to sell, a beauty
shop in the rubble, a cinema in a bombed house. He recalled the
wretched little circus that pitched its tent on the town square, and
the incredible pleasure of the men and women who streamed into
it. He thought of a butcher shop that he had passed every day,
anxiously scanning the show window to see if one sausage or two
would be on display. All that was his concern, it meant something
to him, to him personally—the circus and the sausages and the
beauty parlor in the rubble.

Philadelphia had been for him a city like many others, a city
where, by chance, he had met Patricia. Now, however, he thought
of Philadelphia in a different way. He thought of Benjamin Franklin's print shop, of the hall where the Declaration of Independence
was signed, and of Philadelphia as the birthplace of America's
official declaration of democracy. The lights of Philadelphia are not
important, but the light that went out from Philadelphia is. It was
to have been a light to brighten the world, but over there, in
Europe, it was feeble. Hitler was able to extinguish it. How could
one love both Europe and America, his thoughts went on, without
wanting to bring the brightness and the freedom and the laughter
and the greatest light of all from America to the people over there?

He must have stayed thus on the balcony for a long time, for
when he returned to the drawing-room several of the guests had

left. But Patricia's brother Bob had appeared. In civilian clothes he looked even younger and more carefree than he had in Bad Nauheim, where Peter had last seen him.

"Hello, Peter, old boy!" said Bob, shaking hands. "Glad to see you. What's this about you going back? Hell of a note. Still, when you've got hold of something good you hate to let it go, eh? What's new over there? What are the Fräuleins up to these days?"

Patricia stood behind Bob, leaning on the piano. Peter had the feeling that she was watching him attentively as she talked with the young man who had come with the governor's daughter.

"How are you, Bob?" Peter answered. "The Fräuleins are fine. They send best regards."

The young man at the piano, who had a face that seemed to have been drawn by a clumsy child, broke into the conversation.

"I'm sorry to hear you have to go back, Major," he said. "It must be pretty bad over there."

"Yes. It's pretty bad."

The young man turned to Patricia. "I wouldn't let him go back if I were you," he said.

"He has work to finish over there," Patricia replied quickly.

Peter was almost grateful to her.

"Let them stew in their own juice," said the young man. "That's what I always say."

Shortly afterward the family was left alone. Barbara Draper, Patricia, Bob, Uncle Newell, and Peter lingered in the drawing-room, and Peter wondered whether the time had come for a reckoning with the assembled family. He still could not tell whether Patricia had told her mother of the failure of their marriage.

As little as Barbara Draper liked being left alone, she liked intimate family gatherings less. Being with her family when no outsiders were present meant running the risk of having to deal with personal problems, and her aversion to personal complications was as deep as that of her daughter. Such matters were almost always unpleasant, tedious, and a waste of time. It therefore behooved such members of the family as were invited to Barbara Draper's dinners to take their departure afterward in the same way as other guests. Even Patricia, when she spent the night in the house on Rittenhouse Square, retired with the words, "Thank you, Mother, for a lovely party." So it was something out of the ordinary when

Barbara Draper seated herself again in the drawing-room after the last guest had gone.

"Let's have a quiet bottle of champagne before we go to bed," she said.

Watson brought a bottle of Mumm Cordon Rouge, and for a few minutes the discussion centered on the recently departed guests. Barbara Draper opined that the governor's daughter and her fiancé made an ideal couple. They were both, it seemed, crazy about tennis. Then she turned to Peter. "It's really too bad you can stay only for such a short time. I hope you and Patricia will at least have as much fun as you possibly can."

Before Peter could reply, Patricia said, "We're going to New York tomorrow. Peter wants to see all the new shows."

"Why don't you go to Florida for a week?" Barbara Draper asked. "The house is empty. You can have it."

"Peter would rather stay in New York. It's so long since he's been home. We want to visit all our favorite spots—Twenty-One and Voisin, and so on. Anyway, it's almost impossible to get train reservations."

"You could take my plane," said Barbara Draper, for whom railroad tickets were no problem.

"I'll fly you down personally," Bob offered.

"No, thanks," said Peter curtly.

Patricia turned to Peter. "When do you have to be in Washington?"

"Friday afternoon."

"Then we could give a dinner party on Thursday," Patricia continued. "It's pretty short notice, but I can telegraph the invitations. Do you think you could come up, Mother?"

"Thursday? No. Unfortunately I've asked Gallardi to dinner. He's guest conductor at the symphony here."

"It's so hard to get steak in New York," Patricia said. "In time for Thursday, I mean. And Peter must be starved for steak."

Steaks were no problem to Barbara Draper either. "Talk to Watson, Patricia," she said. "He can send somebody to New York with all the steak you'll need."

What's going on here? Peter wondered. He looked at his wife. What was Patricia's purpose in chatting about dinners and theaters and visiting their favorite restaurants? Did she believe that he had simply been talking nonsense that first night? Did she want to build a bridge over which he could come back to her? Or did she believe that the atmosphere of the Draper mansion, the prospect of social activities and amusements, would make him forget tomorrow what had seemed so important yesterday? Is she capable of overestimating so greatly what her world has to offer?

It would not be surprising if she were, Peter thought. Even Maria had believed in the seductive power of the world he was encountering. Why shouldn't Patricia, accustomed to buying everything else, believe that she could buy him too? The price she was offering was, after all, not small—it was all of America. But, he thought, maybe it's even simpler than that. Perhaps it's only that Patricia does not want to acknowledge that her marriage has failed, that it is painful for her—painful or merely uncomfortable—to talk of divorce. Until the night at the Walter Clarks, Patricia had never told him that Barbara Draper had opposed their marriage. If Patricia had nevertheless married him, defying her mother for the first time, then the marriage had to be a success. Patricia could not admit that her mother had been right this time too, without becoming shackled more firmly than ever in her slavery to Barbara Draper.

Not that divorce was something extraordinary; it was almost fashionable. Everything depended on the part one had chosen to play in society. Patricia had obviously assumed the role of the happily married woman. She had, indeed, hesitated four years before divorcing Luce Holborn. Society did not take kindly to abrupt changes and deviations; happily married women were expected to remain happily married. Marriage, furthermore, was a contest in which one had to retain the upper hand; it was permissible to rid oneself of a husband, but not to be discarded by him. One's value as a woman had to be rescued out of every wrecked marriage, and that was not possible unless one could demonstrate that while it was the husband's fault, you were the one who wearied of the marriage first. It would be easy to demonstrate that Peter was to blame in the affair, but Patricia had neglected to let her friends know in time that she was tiring of him. So one of the essential factors in a conventional divorce was lacking—and one had no right to surprise one's friends in these matters.

The conversation droned on. Peter could hardly understand how he was able to take part in it, but he talked, asked questions, and even smiled from time to time. It all seemed remote, a matter of complete indifference, almost unreal. Whatever the intent of Patricia's play-acting, it repelled him that she could go through with it. What was she proving? All she proved was that she had good nerves, perhaps better than his. Steady nerves were not what he admired in women. The thought came to him as a relief. It was easier to fight against steady nerves than against love.

➻ 41 ⤺

THE letter that was waiting for Peter in New York was eight pages long. On the first page Maria wrote of her inconsolable loneliness without him, of the first hours after his departure, and of the first black days. But there was no word of complaint on this page, only a breathless affirmation of her love. The letter continued:

And now, dearest, something that I know will make you laugh. I can see your dear good face as you try to make it look grave, but I can also see the beginning of a little sarcastic smile that you can't quite suppress. Never mind. Go ahead and smile. I know how you feel about "competent" women.

Yesterday afternoon a delegation from the village suddenly appeared: Mayor Pichler, Steinhäusl the apothecary—do you remember him? We met him in the village one day—and two farmers named Rüdenheimer and Schlögel. Rüdenheimer is an old man of seventy who hardly ever leaves his farm any more. Schlögel is only twenty-two, and he had never been to my place before. I knew at once that something special was afoot. All of them looked very solemn, and Steinhäusl had even put on his dark Sunday suit. For at least ten minutes they sat around and talked about the weather and the harvest and how their children were doing in school. I had no idea what they really wanted. Finally Steinhäusl gathered up his courage, cleared his throat, and made a long speech.

You will never guess why they had come. Steinhäusl explained that the Mayor had resigned the day before. You know that the Mayor was in a concentration camp for five years, was persecuted all through the

Hitler period, and is a splendid fellow. But he couldn't get along with the Americans. He has his own ideas about democracy and they have theirs. And somehow their ideas didn't seem to agree. An open break came when the Military Government ruled that Gross, the teacher, would have to be removed because he had been a member of the party, although we all know that Gross was anti-Nazi and often risked his job by urging the children to go to church instead of attending meetings of the Hitler Youth. He had to join the party so as not to lose his position. The Military Government put Teacher Hahn in his place. Hahn had just been released from an American prisoner-of-war camp. He spent the whole war, from Poland on, in the Wehrmacht, so he never joined the party. But he is an enthusiastic Nazi and turned in several local Social Democrats to the authorities. The Military Government, which naturally has to follow directions from higher up, could not alter its decision and Pichler would not give up his opposition. So he resigned. So the committee of four came to ask me in the name of the community to take over the duties of Mayor! (Can you imagine me as a lady mayor?)

Oh, Peter, it's so silly of me to write you everything in such detail. All this must seem terribly petty and ridiculous to you now, as you look out of your window at the skyscrapers. Perhaps you have just put aside one of your wonderful fat newspapers in which the whole world is mirrored. And here I come telling you about Teacher Gross and Teacher Hahn and Mayor Pichler. (That reminds me: don't forget to cut out the fashion advertisements and bring them along for the village dressmaker.) But that's the way I am, dearest. I want to come running to you with every trifle, and ask your advice, and do what you suggest, for you see everything so clearly and know what to do so much better than I. I would have preferred to tell my four fine visitors to sit and wait for a while—not long, just four or five weeks, until I could get an answer from you. Then I could make up my mind.

But then, dearest, I thought of our talk—do you remember, it was when we came from visiting the old seamstress? (She always sends her best to the *Herr Major* every time I see her. I think you made a great impression on her, but, after all, she's almost eighty, so I don't mind.) I thought of what you said about the pioneers, how they had begun in a small way with very little. I thought of how little I myself know of America, and of how the people live there, and of how they manage things so as to be free and remain free. But as I listened to old Steinhäusl I realized that, even so, I know more about democracy than these villagers, even though they are honestly concerned about it. The old gentleman was very solemn and a little comical as he said, "Frau Hoffmann, I know that we can trust ourselves to your leadership." I answered immediately, "Herr Apotheker, what we need is not so much leadership as confidence," and I thought of you, and whether you would be pleased with me, and it was clear to me at once that I couldn't say no. So I accepted.

Peter, dearest, I wish you had been here, because I don't know if I did the right thing. I know that women who do things that are really man's business are abhorrent to you, and sometimes my heart almost stops when I think what you will say about a "lady mayor," and whether it is possible for you to love a "lady mayor" at all. But if you can feel everything that happens to me across three thousand miles— just as I can divine every thought you think, see every cloud that crosses your brow—then you know that I am trying to fill the great void you have left behind. That I am trying to carry on as best I can until your good strong hands are here to support me again, and until I have nothing to do but lie in your arms, in the deep assurance that everything is right if you want it so. The pioneer women, I'm sure, also defended their homes until their men came back from hunting or fighting, and the women could be women again. This may all sound like big words, but you understand what I mean.

In my heart there is only a great boundless yearning to be with you.

Your Maria

⇒ 42 ⇐

THINGS had gone smoothly at PW Camp Special B since the court proceedings, but the quiet that settled over the prison community was only superficial.

On November 12 Colonel Stroud—he had been promoted to lieutenant colonel three or four days before, much to his surprise— was shaken out of his sleep at five o'clock in the morning. Lieutenant McClintock was standing by his bed.

"I had to wake you, Colonel. A hell of a thing has happened."

Stroud dressed hurriedly while the Lieutenant, who was Officer of the Day, gave him a brief account of what had occurred.

"We just found one of the prisoners murdered," said the Lieutenant. "We don't know who he is yet. One of the sentries found him hanging from a telephone pole in the north area. He hadn't been hanging there for more than an hour, apparently, because the sentry passes the spot about once every hour. You know that section of the camp, Colonel. No barracks. Just some workshops and the coal dumps."

"I know," said Stroud, ready to follow the Lieutenant. "But what makes you think the man was murdered? It might be suicide."

"He was dead when they strung him up," the Lieutenant explained. The Lieutenant was a young officer whom Stroud had brought along from his old battalion. He had a huge Irish head firmly planted on a bull neck, and a chest like a wrestler. Wounded four times, Lieutenant Patrick McClintock of the United States Infantry was not the man to be terrified by the sight of death. Now he was pale. His hand shook as he opened the door for the Colonel.

"How do you know he was dead first?" Stroud asked.

"You'll see, Colonel."

"Hasn't he been cut down?"

"I wanted you to see him first."

"Did you tell the doctor?"

"Yes. Captain Miller's on the spot. He said to leave the man there until you came."

They crossed the barracks area on the double. It was still pitch dark; only the searchlights swept the camp at regular intervals. The men felt small and helpless when the searchlight beams caught them. It was cold and damp. Snow might begin to fall at any moment.

"Why didn't the sentries on the guard towers notice anything?" Stroud asked.

"The searchlights don't reach that far," the Lieutenant answered. "There aren't any prisoners in the area."

"How did the man get there then?"

"Nobody knows," said the Lieutenant, out of breath. He could barely keep up with the Colonel. "He must have been murdered in the afternoon while shoveling coal."

"That still doesn't explain how he came to be strung up."

A narrow path led from the last barracks at the north end of the camp to a group of workshops and the coal dumps. The area was dirty with coal dust. Their flashlights revealed piles of coal to right and left, discarded shovels, and here and there scattered wheels and spokes.

"How was the man killed?" Stroud asked.

"You'll see, Colonel," the Lieutenant replied, avoiding a direct answer. "Anyway, there he is."

At the end of the path, not far from the high wire fence that separated the camp from the outside world, the glare of about a dozen flashlights appeared. In their light the Colonel saw a spectacle that made him understand the Lieutenant's pallor and trembling hands.

Between one of the workshops and a coal dump was a telephone pole, from which the body of a man was suspended. Several strands of strong, cutting telephone wire were tightly bound around the neck. But it was obvious that he had not been hanged; his tongue did not protrude. From the mouth, swollen and distorted by repeated blows, a thin trickle of blood ran down over the chin. The nose was a spongy lump of red pulp. The swelling around the left eye made it appear to be partly closed, but the eyelid had been torn away, and where the eye had been there was only raw, pulpy flesh. The other eye was undamaged. Wide open, it stared straight ahead, unmoving but horrifyingly alive.

Beams from the flashlights of the soldiers, who had recognized the Colonel at once, now passed slowly up and down the full length of the body.

The dead man was wearing his soldier's tunic and shoes, but no pants. The body had been so grossly mutilated that Stroud, who had seen death in a hundred forms, could not restrain himself from momentarily turning away in revulsion. The man's genitals had been hacked at by some instrument not quite sharp enough to cut them off entirely.

The murder must have been committed several hours earlier, for the blood was frozen and adhered to the man's body and legs in large brown blobs. The horror of the spectacle was heightened by a detail on which all eyes were riveted: fastened with a small piece of wire to what was left of the man's genitals was a piece of white paper on which were a few typewritten words that could not be read from the ground. And as if the murderers had intended to bring the ghastliness of the scene to its most intolerable pitch, the body was black from head to foot. It had apparently been hidden for hours in a coal pile.

Stroud gave orders for the body to be taken down after Lieutenant McClintock assured him that photographs had already been taken.

It seemed to Stroud that he had recognized the face of the victim from the first. He tried to suppress his inkling of the truth and postpone identification of the corpse as long as he was able. But as the body lay before him on a stretcher with a dozen flashlights turned on the face, the last doubt vanished. The murdered man was Hans Honegger, the prisoner who had acted as prosecutor in Emil Teitinger's trial. On the slip of paper were only three words: "Warnung an Verräter!"—"Warning to Traitors!"

Stroud turned the atrocity over in his mind on the way back to his office. There was, of course, no doubt about the motive and the perpetrators. Hans Honegger had been murdered by the same group of men who had committed the still unsolved poison killings because of his valiant prosecution of Emil Teitinger. The murder had doubtless taken place before dark, probably some time during the previous afternoon. One man could certainly not have overpowered the young and robust Honegger; it must have required at least three or four men to subdue and mutilate him. It was not too difficult to devise a plausible reconstruction of the crime. Every prisoner was required to take his turn at shoveling coal, and the murderers had evidently waited until it was Honegger's day to work in one of the dumps remote from the barracks area. They had, most likely, overpowered him as he shoveled, beaten him unconscious and castrated him. They had then hidden the body for several hours under a coal pile. One or two of them, Stroud assumed, had stayed behind or, having left their barracks on the pretense of going to the latrine, had returned after dark to climax their crime by stringing Honegger's body up on the telephone pole.

Back in his warm office, Stroud stood looking out of the little window, pondering. Dawn was breaking. Snow had begun to fall from the heavy, sullen sky. The lamps glowed bright and cheery in the office. Stroud felt that events were pressing in on him, were coming to a climax.

He returned to his desk, and his glance fell on the slip of paper he had brought with him from the murder scene. As he read it again, he knew that with their three-word message the murderers had made the mistake that criminals almost invariably make. They had been too careful. If they had printed their message by hand in block letters, it would have been virtually impossible to find the writer among eight thousand men. But the camp typewriters were accessible to only a limited number of prisoners, and a test would quickly establish which machine had been used; this would further reduce the number of possible prisoners who might have typed the note.

Stroud ordered black coffee and had Parker roused from sleep. By seven o'clock he had dictated orders that sentries be assigned to every barracks, and that the prisoners be kept rigidly confined to their quarters; that a check be made as to which typewriter available to prisoners had been used in writing the note, and which prisoners had recently had the opportunity of using the machine; that a list be compiled of the names of all prisoners who had left their barracks for any reason the night before; a special list to be made of those prisoners, if any, caught sneaking back into barracks after having left them without permission; that it be determined which prisoners had been assigned to work at or near the coal dumps on the day before, or had been seen in that vicinity at any time during the day; and finally that Lieutenants Horvath and Jones form two groups of investigators to go through the barracks and search all prisoners and their belongings, looking particularly for traces of coal dust or blood on the persons of the prisoners or on their clothes. Any prisoners caught attempting to leave the barracks or to hide or destroy clothing or personal objects were to be brought to the camp commandant at once.

It was eight-thirty before Stroud had an opportunity to look at the clock. He was again alone in his office. It's time to strike a balance, he thought. The primary purpose of the camp is not to make good democrats of these Germans—that's not possible in the length of time available. The purpose is to find out how Germans react to democratic institutions. Five men who had openly declared themselves on the side of democracy had been murdered—three poisoned, one stabbed, and one brutally beaten and mutilated. Was all this conclusive evidence of the impossibility of planting the seeds of democracy in Germany? Stroud admitted that he had not even come close to finding the answer, one way or the other. Democracy, he thought, is in the last analysis a sense of security—the consciousness of protection against injustice, against the "insolence of office," against the domination of one class or group, against the arbitrary will of individuals or cliques. Freedom itself, so often confused or identified with democracy, is secondary to this feeling of security. Anyone who lives with the assurance that his merits, and his merits alone, count; that he cannot be persecuted on account of his opinions, his ancestry, or his station in life—in other words, anyone who has been liberated from fear, except for fear of the law, feels like a free man and will speak and act like a free man. Freedom without security, Stroud thought —and the idea had never seemed so vivid to him before—is not democracy, but anarchy. I have tried to give these people freedom, or at least something that approached freedom. But did I give them the law without which democracy is a mere shell? Did I give them a constitution that governs laws and duties? Didn't my own police stand outside the rules and conditions of the community they regulated? Did I give them protection and security? Or only the dubious protection of barbed wire and nocturnal patrols?

Toward ten o'clock he decided to call General Lowell. He lifted the receiver and talked to Parker. "Sergeant, please put me through to Berlin. General Lowell."

"Maybe you'd better hold it a couple of minutes, Colonel," Parker answered. "Lieutenant Horvath just called. He's on his way over with three prisoners. He's sure they're connected with the murder."

Stroud sat quite still, waiting for an inward sign. Then he was sure that this sudden development, welcome as it was, could not be the event he was anticipating. He knew only that when the event took place, a bell would sound within him. The bell was silent.

It would be something else.

IN THE ensuing days developments came so rapidly that Stroud found it impossible to leave Munich for so much as half a day. As often as he was able he called for Wanda and drove with her through the snowy countryside for an hour or two. He had become accustomed to discussing everything with her, unburdening his mind, listening attentively to her comments.

They had been driving for half an hour through the woods leading to the Starnberger See. Stroud was at the wheel. Wanda was more silent than usual.

"The minute I saw the body hanging from the pole," Stroud was saying, matter-of-factly, with no triumph in his voice, "I knew that we were on the way toward uncovering the whole organization."

"What made you think so, John?"

"I don't know exactly. Brutality always reaches a point where it loses control of itself. Maybe it has something to do with divine justice, or maybe it's just something in human nature. Not all criminals are mad, but crime often leads to madness."

"How many prisoners took part in the murder?"

"If only I knew! So far we've locked up seven men. They're all directly connected with one or more of the murders. But how many others there are, we don't know. Seven or twenty or fifty? If that's all there is to it, then I don't think the conspiracy amounts to much. A terroristic minority can be dangerous and has to be fought. But you can't generalize from it. But if the organization extends throughout the camp, then my whole conception of the situation goes to pieces."

"You still believe in 'good' Germans, don't you?"

"In 'good' people of all nationalities."

She was silent again. For the first time he felt that her silence denoted that her mind was elsewhere. She seemed remote. When he saw that she was not going to reply, he said, "Didn't I convince you in one case at least?"

"Maria?"

"Yes, Maria."

"I'm fond of Maria. I appreciate how fine a person she is, but—"

"But what?"

"Why should a good minority prove any more than a bad one?"

They were driving through soundless woods. The first heavy snow lay on the pines and firs. Stroud thought of Christmas. Will I still be here at Christmas? he asked himself. Only five more weeks. The realization came to him with a shock. He tried vainly to tell himself that, after all, December 25 was a day like any other. In Spokane it was by no means a day like any other. There the first signs appeared at least five weeks before. The stores on Riverside Avenue began to be jammed with shoppers, Christmas decorations appeared in the show windows, and soon Christmas trees would go on sale in open-air markets on vacant lots. In the courthouse the talk would be of plans for the holidays. Emily and Eleanor would whisper together like excited schoolgirls; Jim would keep his closet locked and accuse Eleanor of spying; and he himself would act as if he had not been made privy to the individual and collective secrets of the others. Soon the whole house would be pervaded with its Christmas smell: a mixture of the fragrance of wreaths and the odor of polishing wax. As he thought of it, Stroud could smell the Christmas fragrance of his home as surely as if he were sitting in his easy chair at home. He was startled when he heard Wanda's voice next to him.

"John, could we go back to Munich now?"

"Already?"

"Yes. I have to do something there."

It was unusual that she would have an engagement to keep in Munich, but there was more than that in her tone.

"What do you have to do in Munich?"

"I've got to go to the doctor's."

"The doctor? Are you sick?"

"No," she said.

He suddenly guessed the truth.

"You should have told me," he said. He was looking straight ahead, as if the icy pavement were occupying his whole attention.

She spoke softly but hurriedly, as if what she was saying was of no great importance.

"I really didn't want to say anything about it, John. And maybe it's silly to mention it even now. But I discussed it with Maria. She thinks I ought to tell you. Even though there's nothing certain. In fact, it's all quite unlikely. It's probably just female hysteria."

He still did not look at her. "Have you already been to the doctor?" He was not sure of his feelings as he asked it. It was only as if ice-cold water were streaming down over his chest from his throat to his heart.

"Yes," she answered. "Maria sent me to a doctor. He's making a test. I'm to call for the result today."

He had turned the automobile around. On the ice-covered road the heavy command car made slow progress. A lonely raven here and there hopped across the snow: a doleful, shifting patch of black.

He struggled for a word, a gesture. He waited for an emotion to surge over him. He did not know what kind of emotion—something strong and overpowering that did not need thinking about, that would move him automatically to the right word and gesture, that he could follow with assurance like a great signpost showing the way. But nothing happened. It was as if a thick, opaque sheet of ice had formed over his soul.

She laid her hand gently on his right hand, which rested on the steering wheel. "Dearest," she said, "I'm sorry. I shouldn't have told you. But don't worry, everything is all right."

He did not answer. As they approached the city she told him the doctor's address. Then he said, "I'm going in with you."

She protested. "No, there's no need for that."

"There's plenty of need for that. I want to talk to the doctor."

He would not be dissuaded. Together they went up the stairs of the crumbling old house where Dr. Markstein had his office.

An old lady wearing an untidy apron opened the door. She recognized Wanda, but scrutinized the American with a sharp, distrustful look.

"Sit down for a moment," she said. "The doctor will see you shortly."

She left Wanda and Stroud alone in the little reception room. It was not an inviting reception room. One could tell immediately that the doctor not only practiced, but also lived, here. The furniture, covered with cheap flowered material, was worn and rickety. On a little table lay old magazines and travel folders; in the center of the room was a large, old-fashioned table, evidence that when the patients were gone the reception room became a dining-room. A tiny iron stove standing before the large tile oven and connected with it by a little pipe labored mightily to heat the room. Fifty years ago the room had probably exuded an air of comfort and inspired confidence. Now it aroused Stroud's anxiety.

"Does Maria know this doctor?" he asked.

"Oh, yes, darling. They've been friends for twenty years. During the war she hid him from the Nazis several times. He was in a concentration camp four or five times. He's a Jew."

"An amazing woman," said Stroud, relieved. "I'm always learning something new about her."

"He has just recently resumed his practice," Wanda continued. "The Nazis took his home and his practice away from him, of course. He found this little place and is beginning all over again."

They sat silently on the sofa. Stroud took Wanda's hand. In a doctor's waiting-room, he thought, every minute is an hour. But here the minutes seem to stand completely still.

The door to the doctor's office opened.

"Fräulein Komarnicki!" said the man in the white smock. He had silky gray hair, worn somewhat long over the ears. His face was white and drawn. Behind his thick horn-rimmed glasses were eyes that were benign and intelligent. Stroud felt at once that Dr. Markstein belonged to that vanishing category of doctors who treat human beings rather than organs of the body.

"Dr. Markstein," said Wanda, introducing him to Stroud. In her uncertain German she added, "The Colonel wanted to meet you."

The two men shook hands. It struck Stroud that Wanda had avoided mentioning his name.

Then he was left alone. He sat down and made an effort to quiet his twitching nerves. He reached for the magazines. They were of the Hitler period and showed such standard scenes as the Führer reviewing a parade in Berlin, heroic Knight's Cross aviators who had bombed London, and Italian widows being decorated by Il Duce. The pictures gave the effect of hooting mockery. Stroud turned to the travel folders. They were from health resorts that seemed identical in every detail, with their carefree promenaders, horse-drawn carriages, and the same bright advertising sun beaming down on all of them. The travel folders were as unreal as Hitler and Mussolini.

Stroud put the folders aside too. He tried to examine his thoughts. He felt neither joy nor pain, not even solicitude for Wanda. He felt only the absurdity of the situation. He had not known before that a sense of one's own ridiculousness could be stronger than joy or pain. Maybe I'll become a father and a grandfather at the same time, he told himself, not without bitterness.

He suddenly felt the weight of his fifty-three years as if they had not accumulated one by one, but as if he had become fifty-three years old overnight. Ever since he had met Wanda he had been more or less conscious of his age. He took no pleasure in the reawakening of his own youthfulness; when he felt youthful he also felt ridiculous. He had, as he now admitted, attempted to be frivolous in order not to be absurd. A man of fifty-three in love with a girl of twenty-two was ridiculous—but not so a man of fifty-three indulging in an affair. So time and again he had tried to convince himself that Wanda, after all, was just such an affair. He was perhaps ashamed of being involved in an affair, but it saved him from appearing laughable in his own eyes. Now the pretense was over. This was no longer an affair, and the inescapable paradox arose: the more seriously he regarded his relation to Wanda, the more ridiculous he seemed to himself.

The confusion of his thoughts and emotions was mounting when the door to the doctor's office opened again.

"Please step in, Colonel," said Dr. Markstein.

The office was painfully clean and brightly lit. Wanda was sitting on a little white stool. She looked up for a moment when Stroud entered, then lowered her eyes. Dr. Markstein sat down behind his white desk, which looked as if he had painted it himself. He took off his horn-rimmed glasses and put them down.

"I have examined Fräulein Komarnicki," Dr. Markstein began. He spoke rapidly and smoothly, with a practiced detachment designed to purge diagnosis of its terrors. "I gave her the Friedmann test, which we now employ instead of the Aschheim-Zondek method. The Aschheim-Zondek method was once widely used, but the newer Friedmann procedure has many advantages over it. Errors are out of the question under the Friedmann test—that is, as far as anything can be said to be out of the question in medicine.

Especially in the earliest stages of pregnancy, which is what we are concerned with here, the Aschheim-Zondek method would have been by no means conclusive." He broke off, confident that he had contrived to convey his message as tactfully as possible.

Stroud did not know what he ought to say. He said, "I'm much obliged to you, Doctor, for your trouble."

"Not at all, Colonel. What we have to do now is decide on the next step." He interrupted himself to ask, "Would you prefer to speak English, Colonel?"

"Fräulein Komarnicki would certainly prefer it." Stroud was aware how awkward it sounded when he said "Fräulein Komarnicki." He felt like a schoolboy. He thought, five minutes ago I was feeling like an old man. He pulled himself together and said, "I'd be grateful for any advice you may care to give, Doctor."

"We are living in unusual times, Colonel," Dr. Markstein began, as if to submerge the unconventionality of the present situation in the general disorder of the times. He was now speaking slowly and laboriously, in precise English, which, one felt, he had learned largely from books. "I understand your position, and I especially understand the predicament in which Miss Komarnicki finds herself. I know what it means to live in a *Lager*—a camp. At various periods I have spent six years in concentration camps."

"How did you manage to survive, Doctor?" Stroud asked.

Dr. Markstein smiled. "All my friends ask me that. Many Jewish doctors survived."

"The Nazis needed doctors, I suppose?"

"That also. But I believe something else was of even more importance. We were probably the only prisoners who could help the others. Sometimes I think there is no greater selfishness than to want to help others. I, at least, know of no better way of making an unbearable existence bearable than by helping others for whom it is just as unbearable. And even so, the help I was able to give was of relative worth only. I have delivered hundreds of mothers of children who were gassed the following day. Life and death were so close to each other that one could hardly mark the boundary between them."

They were silent for a moment. Stroud offered a cigarette to the doctor, who accepted it and laid it aside.

"Don't you smoke, Doctor?"

The sad, shy smile played around the doctor's mouth again. "Yes," he replied. "After dinner. When a cigarette comes one's way these days, it has to be hoarded until after dinner."

Stroud tried to give the conversation a more agreeable turn. He asked, "Was it the Americans who freed you, Doctor?"

"No. I was hidden by my friends during the last four months of the war. Almost two months of that time by Frau Hoffmann. You are acquainted with Frau Hoffmann, I understand. She is a great woman. I am very deeply in her debt."

Stroud looked at him. Was there any special significance in the way the doctor emphasized the last sentence?

But Dr. Markstein continued, "Frau Hoffmann also gave shelter to my wife and mother in Berlin. That was earlier in the war."

"Is your family with you now?"

"No. They were burned to death in Ohrdruf. I was there at the time. I could not help them."

Before Stroud was able to say anything, Dr. Markstein returned to his role as medical consultant. "I have given Fräulein Komarnicki a thorough examination. She is healthy. A little undernourished, but then we all are. A weakness of the heart could be established." He ran his long, thin fingers through his gray hair. Stroud saw that his hand was trembling.

Wanda looked up. She had said nothing until now. She asked, "What do you mean, Doctor?"

Dr. Markstein did not answer at once. Without thinking of what he had said a moment before, he quickly picked up the cigarette and lit it. He said, "I mean that I understand you completely, Fräulein Komarnicki."

Stroud looked at the girl. What had she said to the doctor? How much had she told him? A thought that had been lurking in the back of his mind for several minutes now asserted itself. Was that the reason she had consulted Maria and gone to Dr. Markstein without telling him? Had she, thinking it all over in her own cool, practical, and youthful way, chosen this solution? I ought to be grateful to her for taking this way out, Stroud thought. But he was not at all grateful. It was as if the sheet of ice under which his emotions had been slumbering began to break up, and he was now able to look into his own depths. What he saw was a love that had nothing to do with a casual affair, and the face of a child that looked like Wanda, and a strange joy that was shadowed by fear but stronger than fear. And out of these depths there arose an offended wrath against this girl who had, without asking him, gone to the doctor and reached her own decision on something that concerned him as much as it did her.

Dr. Markstein sought to bridge the silence. "I understand the special circumstances," he said. "In this very early stage, it would be possible to—" He began to lose himself in a medical explanation.

Wanda broke in, "I am afraid you have misunderstood me, Doctor," she said with a smile. "I want the child."

She said it calmly, without emphasis, and she looked at Stroud and the doctor with great, glowing eyes as she said it.

The men were silent—the doctor surprised, Stroud overcome with a feeling of wild happiness and a sudden sense of humility.

When no one spoke, Wanda began to laugh. It was the sound, healthy laughter of an unworried young girl.

"Don't look so stupefied," she said. "Excuse me, my dear Doctor, but you really don't look very intelligent at the moment. Is it actually so surprising that a woman wants to have a baby?"

Stroud stood up and went to her. He took both of her hands in his. He no longer had to grope for the right gesture.

Dr. Markstein remained seated behind his desk. He played awkwardly with his glasses. He said simply, "My child, you have removed a great weight from my heart."

Then he stood up and went to his instrument cabinet. He took out forceps and scissors and put them into a sterilizer. He tried to give his visitors the feeling that he was paying no attention to them. After a while, when the man and girl kept standing wordlessly opposite each other, the doctor went up to Stroud.

"Perhaps my behavior seems strange to you, Colonel," he said apologetically. "You are an American. With us, the past twelve years have destroyed all ethical concepts. Perhaps that was Hitler's greatest crime—that his ideology wrecked the ethical standards even of those opposed to him. You would not believe how often one comes to accept the morality one fights against. Infection can come through opposites too."

He paused, a little embarrassed, like a man who fears that the intensity of his feelings has betrayed him into sentimentality. He continued as rapidly as his laborious English permitted, "To obtain a hospital room is difficult, but I am head of the Hospital of Our Lady. You may be sure, Colonel, that everything will be done for your"—he stumbled again—"for the young mother," he went on. "We will find a room for her, and I will call in my best obstetrician, Professor Hofer. The hospital is pleasantly situated. Most of the rooms look out over the Isar. The food is satisfactory. Expectant mothers receive two thousand calories. And Frau Hoffmann will no doubt be able to provide us with some milk besides." He looked younger as he spoke. Color came into his sallow, sunken cheeks.

Stroud extended his hand. "I am very grateful to you, Doctor."

"Thank you, Colonel."

At the door Stroud asked, "And when, do you think?"

"June, probably. In summer, thank God!"

"Yes," Stroud repeated, "in summer—thank God!"

⇒ 44 ⇐

PETER spent only a few hours in New York. A telegram from the OSS was waiting for him when he and Patricia arrived early Tuesday He left for Washington at noon, attended a conference in the Q Building that afternoon, but found it impossible to return to New York in the evening. He arrived back in New York late Wednesday afternoon.

A cocktail party was in full swing when Peter entered the Fifth Avenue house at about six o'clock. He went unnoticed to his room and instructed the servant to tell Patricia he was home. A few moments later she came in.

"Hello," she said. "I'm glad you're back again."

"Let's dispense with the formalities, Patricia," he replied. "The house is full of guests again. I'm not going downstairs to the party. I'm tired. I suppose you also invited a dozen people for dinner. All right. I'll be there. But we are going to have a talk today, Patricia, even if it has to begin at two in the morning."

"I don't know why you're being so unpleasant," she said, obviously taken aback. "I've invited only friends of yours."

"For instance?"

"Senator and Mrs. Norden."

"I've met them three times in my life."

"Chandler Wright and his fiancée."

"I don't know them at all."

"Mr. and Mrs. Reginald Fitzpatrick."

"The most boring couple I know."

"And your publisher, Vernon O'Brian. I hope you're not going to tell me you only met Vernon yesterday."

"No. I'll be glad to see Vernon. But I don't need a whole dinner party for that."

"I thought you'd be happy to get together with some of our friends. Uncle Newell and Cousin Shirley are coming too."

"I've already told you that these people are no friends of mine. But it wouldn't make any difference if they were my most intimate friends. For days you have been avoiding a discussion with me. Today we're going to talk."

Her hand was on the doorknob. As she left the room, she said, "You'll have to excuse me. I have guests."

The dinner went off without incident. The Republican Senator J. Arthur Norden was a man who never spoke unless he had something weighty to say. Whenever he opened his mouth it was as if he were reciting an editorial. The words "decency," "dignity," "integrity," and "our way of life" recurred in his conversation like the same costumes on the stage of a provincial stock company. Chandler Wright was a young man from Philadelphia, the sole heir of the Donald Wright chewing gum fortune. His passion was South America. To the dismay of his mother, a Bostonian by birth, he had become engaged to the daughter of a former Brazilian ambassador. Mrs. Wright was under the impression that all Brazilians had Negro blood. She was somewhat mollified when her son's fiancée turned out to be white. Mr. and Mrs. Reginald Fitzpatrick owned one of the few remaining Fifth Avenue mansions. Their names were in the Social Register, but the most resourceful society reporters were unable to find anything more remarkable to write about them than to record from time to time that they were staying at this hotel or that. The Fitzpatricks were always present "among those present," though nobody would have noticed had they been absent. They were the kind of people whom maîtres d'hôtel regard as especially elegant on account of the smallest tips given over the longest period of time.

The only breath of youth and vigor in the gathering was supplied by Vernon O'Brian and Patricia's cousin Shirley. Shirley belonged to the impoverished branch of the Vanderwoort family. Her father had recently died in Hollywood, where he had been a bit player specializing in characters who were supposed to represent people like the Vanderwoorts. The family had ostracized him, but the beautiful, twenty-one-year-old Shirley had, strangely enough, become a family pet in spite of earning her living as a model. Vanderwoort women who worked for a living at least had the charm of eccentricity; the men had no excuse whatever.

The after-dinner conversation turned to an appraisal of the new President. Peter preferred not to take part, not only because he usually avoided political controversies while in uniform, but also because he feared that a lively discussion might prolong the stay of the guests. Senator Norden, however, wanted to draw Peter into the conversation. He asked, "And how was the news of President Roosevelt's death received at the front?"

"I was in the northern sector then," Peter answered. "We were fighting in the outskirts of Bremen. The war was nearing its end. In one week we took two hundred and fifty thousand prisoners, if I remember correctly. The war gradually began to lose its deadliness. Our own losses were negligible. Whole cities were captured by handfuls of soldiers. The news came at about six in the morning. I don't know how, but the whole front seemed to know about it in a few hours. The war stood still. I mean it literally. I saw artillerymen standing behind their guns, forgetting to load them. Soldiers crawled out of their foxholes and ignored enemy fire to go over to another foxhole where they could talk to friends, or just be near some. The infantry didn't march that day. It was simply paralyzed. The officers of our small detachment took their meals in a little suburban house outside of Bremen. That morning we sat waiting for more than an hour for breakfast. Finally I went out to the kitchen to see what was wrong. Our cook was a swarthy little fellow from New York. Of Greek descent, I believe. He was sitting in the kitchen, crying. When I asked him if he had started to cook anything, he only looked at me and said, 'My God, Captain, you ain't going to eat anything at a time like this, are you?' "

Peter felt the mounting coolness with which his story was being received. He knew that Patricia was trying to catch his eye. The others remained silent, as if their host had tactlessly said something insulting to one of his guests.

After a while Chandler Wright said, "Were all the soldiers New Dealers, Major?"

"My own Colonel," Peter replied, "is an influential Republican from Tennessee. I believe he is going to run for Congress when he gets back. He was the first to hear the news over the radio. He woke me up. He could hardly speak. It was the only time in the whole war that I saw tears in his eyes."

"Well, I can understand that," said Senator Norden, manfully attempting to retrieve the situation. "After all, Roosevelt was the Commander-in-Chief of these boys."

"Whom he promised never to send overseas," Uncle Newell interjected.

Peter ignored Uncle Newell. "That wasn't it at all, Senator," he said. "Where tears are involved, titles don't mean anything. It was something else, something that is not easy to explain. Our Army was the best in the world, Senator, not because we had better equipment than any other nation. And not only because our soldiers were courageous. But because we all had a feeling of assurance, a feeling that somebody was looking out for our best interests—"

"It's a good thing the boys didn't know what was going on in the White House then," said Mrs. Fitzpatrick, as if referring to some disgusting occurrence which all present knew of and which she did not care to describe more fully.

Peter did not look at her or make any other sign of having heard what she said. "The Germans," he continued, "sacrificed lives in order to save material. We sacrificed material to save lives. We all know that the war could have been won with fewer cannon, fewer planes, fewer machine guns, fewer shoes, and fewer OD shirts. But we know that this superfluity of everything, this willingness to squander material, if you like, this difference between what was absolutely necessary and what was too much, had the purpose of saving human lives. To die in a war is natural. But to be needlessly sacrificed is frightful."

"Our young friend," observed Mr. Fitzpatrick, "talks as if Roosevelt paid for all that war equipment out of his own pocket. As far as I know, the money came out of the pockets of the taxpayers."

There was general agreement. Only Vernon O'Brian and Shirley gave Peter encouraging looks.

"You're quite right, Fitzpatrick," the Senator said. "And don't forget—the House of Representatives and the Senate had something to do with it."

Peter could feel Patricia's insistence that he say no more as surely as if she had spoken aloud. He said, "That may be, Senator. But I'm afraid that over there, during a war, nobody worries much about the taxpayers. What gave us the feeling of assurance, of being looked after, was the spirit of Franklin Roosevelt. Every little GI felt instinctively what it meant to have a great moral force at the head of the State."

He paused. He felt a deep and perverse satisfaction in the knowledge that the guests were becoming increasingly uncomfortable and hoped that he would stop. He continued, "And I recall something else. A minor episode, but significant. It was in Normandy. I happened to be the first soldier to enter a little town. A hellish bombardment had driven the Germans out. The town seemed totally lifeless. Then I saw a young woman with a child in her arms. She came crawling out of a cellar. The house was smashed. She came toward me hesitantly. When she was sure that I was an American soldier, she held out her child toward me in greeting. Then she asked, 'How is the President?' She didn't know the President, of course. Nobody in Europe knew him. But all of us were aware of the tremendous trust that oppressed Europe had in him. Wherever you went you felt it—the confidence that helped millions of Europeans endure the horrors of war and German occupation."

There was a pained silence. The Senator could not resist saying what all of them wanted to say. "With all due respect to your opinions, Major," he said, "I doubt whether you are qualified to speak in the name of all American soldiers."

Uncle Newell spoke up for the honor of the house. "I doubt it too," he said.

The Senator nodded, like a man accustomed to acknowledging well-earned applause. He continued in a patronizing, didactic tone, "We Americans, Major, have never exaggerated the importance of individual men, as Europeans do. That is part of our democratic outlook. It seems to me that the tendency to idolize Roosevelt is a typically European manifestation. After you have lived in America longer, Major, I am sure you will come to agree with me."

Shall I explain to him what I mean? Peter asked himself. That democracy does not exclude great men, nor admiration for great men? What it excludes is the illegal assumption and holding of power against the will of the people. But he did not feel like making a reasonable argument. Senator Norden and Mr. Fitzpatrick and Uncle Newell wouldn't understand him anyway. But Senator Norden, probably without intending to, had raised a personal question, and Peter was glad of the chance to take up the challenge. "Senator, don't you believe that I have a right to speak as an American?" he asked sharply, more sharply than he intended.

"Of course, Major, of course," the Senator replied. "I only mean that you need to acquire a greater understanding of the American people."

"Senator," Peter replied quietly, "learning to know people is not a matter of time, but of circumstance. You can live with a woman for twenty years and not know anything about her. Then something happens. You lose your money, or your position, or your leg. And in one day you learn more about her than in all the twenty preceding years. My understanding of the American people derives from Salerno and Cherbourg and Bastogne. All European cities, but important testing grounds of the American nation."

The Senator wanted to get back to Roosevelt, but the ladies had meanwhile decided to bring the controversy to an end. Mrs. Norden broke in, "I don't know why men always have to quarrel when they discuss Roosevelt. I thought the eternal bickering about him would stop when he died. But no. Even after his death he keeps right on spoiling every party."

"Anyway, he spoiled the Democratic party," said the chewing gum heir.

This witty sally momentarily relieved the tension.

Peter felt again how fruitless it was to attempt to tell the truth to these people. There were times when he had regarded people like the Nordens and Fitzpatricks as interesting specimens for

study. He lived among them like an explorer in a strange land. It
wasn't mere chance that attracted me to OSS work, he thought. I
like to parachute down behind the lines. A writer is a parachutist
behind enemy lines. I jumped behind the lines of this society;
I found out what it thinks, feels, how it acts and what motivates
it. They did not know I was observing them—like the Germans
in Naples, the Italians in Palermo, and the Arabs in Marrakech.

His patience was at an end because his interest had evaporated.
He knew that he would never write about these people again; he
was now too indifferent toward them. More and more Peter longed
for the ordinary people of the little Bavarian village, for John
Stroud and their discussions about the prisoners, for the soldiers
he had known in Italy and Normandy, for the boy who had carried
him to safety when he was wounded at Anzio, for Dirty Thompson
and the shortsighted little tailor in the Berlin cellar. Good and
bad, friend and foe: over there they were all alive. Here men and
women sat around like plants in a conservatory. He heard Senator
Norden working himself up over Eleanor Roosevelt, but he did
not listen to what was being said. Senator Norden was merely
a potted palm in a hothouse.

⋙ 45 ⋘

AFTER seeing the last guest to the door Peter and Patricia returned alone to the drawing-room. Patricia sat down. "Your
behavior was impossible," she said.

"I know."

"What did you hope to gain by being rude?"

"Nothing special. I had simply had enough of the nonsense they
were talking."

"You wanted to drive my friends away."

"Perhaps."

"After all, they were your guests too. Good manners are the least
they could expect of you."

"Good manners get tedious after a while. Besides, I can't seem to get used to the idea that speaking well of Franklin Roosevelt is a social error."

They were silent for a while. Then Patricia said, "You wanted to talk to me. What have you to say?"

"I have already said everything."

"What do you want then?"

"You haven't given me an answer yet."

"I have no answer to give," Patricia replied

"What does that mean?"

"That means that I have no intention of giving you a divorce."

"I don't understand," he said without heat, "why you want to make an issue of it. I had hoped that we could part in friendship."

She laughed unpleasantly. "In friendship? No. I have no friendship for you."

"Then why do you want to go on living with me?"

"I don't want to live with you."

"I'm afraid I don't understand you."

"I don't want to live with you," she repeated. "I have tried to. I've given you every opportunity during these past few days to come to your senses. I did everything to make you feel at home again. I said nothing to Mother. I invited your friends. I thought of all sorts of things to amuse you. You rejected everything. Tonight you went so far as to offend my guests. You behaved like an ill-bred child. I have no intention of living with you. But I also have no intention of doing you any favors. If you want a divorce—just try to get one! Just try to prove something against me. Do you imagine I've been unfaithful, perhaps?"

"No. I accept all the blame. I love another woman."

"But you're married to me."

"You've mentioned that before." He sighed. "It's quite true. But does that mean we both have to be unhappy?"

"I'm not unhappy."

"Do you realize what you said just then, Patricia? What you said was an admission. If you had ever loved me, you would be unhappy now."

"Is that what you want?"

"Certainly not. But I can't understand what happiness you can possibly gain by holding a man whom you do not love, and probably never did love. You are not keeping your hold on him, Patricia. You are keeping your hold on marriage."

"That, too, is my right. And anyway, what you say is not true. I did love you. I proved it often enough."

"How?"

"First of all, by marrying you. What did you have to offer me? You had no money, no social position. You wrote books. Hundreds of men write books. My family did everything possible to prevent my marrying you. I never even told you. I almost broke with my mother."

"Why did your mother object to me?"

"She said you were a foreign upstart. That you wanted to worm your way into American society. I forced you on Mother. I introduced you to society."

"What of it? What did your society have to offer me?"

"Apparently nothing. We don't expect to gain advantages from the society to which we belong. We simply belong to it. My friends accepted you courteously. No one asked where you came from."

"I would have been glad to tell them."

She paid no attention. She spoke like one who at last is giving vent to words long suppressed.

"During the war I went around talking about your heroic feats."

"I know. You talked too much."

This time she looked up at him. "What do you mean?" she asked.

"All your stories sounded as if you were trying to justify me."

"What are you driving at? What if I really did want to prove that you fought just like an American?"

"I am an American."

"A uniform doesn't make an American."

She expected a retort, but he could not speak. In his mind he saw a picture more vivid than the reality that surrounded him. The drawing-room, the furniture, the lovely blond woman opposite him seemed to fog and blur before his eyes, like a scene dissolving on a screen, to be replaced by the dim room in the half-ruined jail where an old man stood, collarless, his face contorted with malice. "A uniform doesn't make an American," the old man had said. Now it was as if he were repeating Patricia's sentence like a contemptuous echo, or as if she had repeated his. He could not tell; the two voices imitated each other, mingled with each other, clashed against each other. The sentence resounded from the walls, multiplying itself over and over—"A uniform doesn't make an American."

His face was white but his voice was steady as he said, "You are trying to make me lose control of myself. That isn't going to happen, Patricia. If you want to fight, I will fight."

Patricia passed over his remark. She said, "You never loved me. Why did you marry me?"

"I did love you. But I did not know you."

"And when did you get to know me?"

"Slowly, day by day. But that wasn't your fault. Every woman changes after marriage. Very likely it's impossible to know a woman without marrying her."

"Is that why you want to marry your German?"

"That's a little cheap, Patricia."

"And what was it you learned about me—day by day—that changed your feelings?"

"I've already told you all that, Patricia. I also told you that I don't hold anything against you. I simply don't understand you, just as you don't understand me. We don't speak the same language."

"It's up to you to learn my language. I was born here."

"You have pointed that out to me repeatedly in the past few days."

He lit a cigarette and poured himself a glass of cognac. He felt tired and hopeless. He sat down.

"The truth is that from the beginning you hated everything that was dear to me," Patricia said.

"For instance?"

"My work. Why did you hate my work?"

"Because you were never honest about it, among other reasons."

"Another of your accusations—without proof."

"Proof?" He gave a little sigh. "I wanted a child. You did not. I don't know why. Maybe you were afraid a child would chain you to your home. Or that you would lose your figure. Or that a child would simply be too much trouble. You never had trouble, Patricia, and you were more afraid of it than ordinary people. I don't know. But a few years later you threw yourself into the care of convicts' children. You don't love children. A woman who loves children wants one of her own. Your friends admire your unselfishness. I don't admire it. The tragedy of most American marriages, Patricia, is that wives don't do what lies close at hand, but what is far-fetched. They go to a hospital three times a week as volunteer nurses, but they don't even have a thermometer at home to take their husband's temperature when he's sick. A little more selfishness, Patricia, would mean a little more happiness. If more women worried about their own children, there would be less need for visiting ladies. These children of strangers mean nothing to you. They are just a thrill for you, and a thrill without risk, at that. Besides, they bring you a great deal of publicity which you pretend to shun, but which you love."

"How dare you!" she said. "How dare you! You're just trying to alibi yourself. Every word you say tells me that you always hated me. Why didn't you say so? Did you have to wait until you found another woman before having the courage to speak out?"

"I loved you, Patricia, if that's of any importance now. But perhaps it is true that I ceased loving you long before I admitted it to myself."

"But you kept up the pretense?"

"No," he continued, still without raising his voice. "I was captivated over and over again by the riddle of your personality. You aren't the only woman who has sought to hold her man by remaining a riddle to him."

She smiled for the first time, a self-confident, somewhat ironic smile. "I'm not one of these tedious European women, that's all," she said. Then, suddenly, with the look of a little girl, "When I married for the first time my mother said to me, 'Men soon get tired of women that they can see through. A wife must know how to keep her husband in suspense.' You're not offending me when you say that I kept you in suspense."

"I know that you're proud of it. But the moment came when I no longer wanted to live with a riddle, but with a human being. The day comes when the suspense flags—"

"And another woman comes along," she ended. "It's getting to be comical, the way you heap all the blame cn me. You talk of having a child, after not mentioning the subject for years and years. And you accuse me of hypocrisy! What it all comes to is simply that you're a European who expects a woman to give up her own personality and spend her time drudging in the kitchen." She lit a cigarette. She seldom smoked. She puffed with the edgy greediness of the non-smoker.

"I didn't want to speak of any of these things," he said. "I wanted to talk about the divorce. You want to maintain our marriage to avoid the unpleasantness of a divorce, the court action, the questions of your friends, perhaps the bother of new visiting cards. But I'm involved here, too, Patricia. I know what happiness and unhappiness mean. I'm not afraid. I've found happiness. I know what it is worth, for I've been very unhappy. I'll fight for it if I have to." He sat forward, his hands on his knees. His knuckles were white.

"Good," she said. Her lips were compressed, as if she were drawing a line under a reckoning with them. "You want to fight. I will annihilate you! I know ways and means of annihilating you. You want to go back to Germany. Who knows the real reasons why you want to go back? It may interest the War Department to find out. On account of a woman? I doubt it. You've probably taken up your former connections there. Once a German, always a German! The Germans are still our enemies. The enemies of America, not yours. You know what happens to an officer who conspires with the enemy. You also know what it would mean if Barbara Draper voiced the suspicion that her son-in-law was a spy. And your war record? A trick to win our confidence. So you'd be sent to Germany, where you could contact your friends again. You probably never lost contact with them. Whether I can prove it or not makes no difference. They'll listen to me. I was born here. I mean something here. You don't understand me, you say. An American major who denounces his own wife for behaving like an American! The War Department will be interested in that too. And so will the FBI!"

She stood up. He also got to his feet. He was white. They measured each other for a moment in silent fury. Then she went to the door. In the doorway she turned around. She spoke softly and slowly, emphasizing every word, taking care to give her voice an intonation of deepest contempt. "A divorce? You'll get your divorce, perhaps. But you'll regret it. You dirty foreigner!"

She slammed the door behind her.

Peter had left the house on Fifth Avenue immediately after his quarrel with Patricia. He had paced restlessly for hours around the little room at the Plaza, which a friendly clerk had managed to find for him after prolonged negotiation. Toward six o'clock Peter had thrown himself on the bed, fully clothed, and instantly had fallen asleep.

The telephone woke him at ten. Through a fog of sleep and exhaustion he heard Patricia's voice.

"Good morning, Peter," she said. "I'm down in the lobby. Would you like to have breakfast with me?"

"I'll be down in ten minutes."

They sat in a deserted corner of the breakfast-room. Patricia, wearing a plain but becoming black suit and a jaunty little hat of dark gray, looked radiant. There was no trace of last night's agitation in her face. She looked younger than at any time since Peter's return. She smiled at him as she sipped her coffee. "I've come to apologize," she said. "I'm sorry for what I said last night."

Peter mumbled something unintelligible.

"Of course, I'm willing to give you a divorce," she continued matter-of-factly. "Who is your lawyer?"

"I haven't thought about that yet," Peter answered, bewildered. "Vincent Slater, I guess."

"Gray and Gray will represent me. I talked to Parker Gray this morning. It would be best if the lawyers got together as soon as possible." Patricia spooned her soft-boiled egg. "Where will you live when you come back from Germany?"

"I haven't given it much thought."

He had not yet recovered from the shock of her about-face.

"I'm leaving for Springfield this evening," she went on chattily. "Naturally, I called off the dinner party. I hope I'll see you again before you leave."

"Of course," he replied. He had a firmer grip on himself now. He smiled at her. "You'll always be a riddle, Patricia. What happened since last night?"

"Oh, nothing special," she said. "I changed my mind. It's all in the way one looks at things."

He had been married to her eight years, and now he was a little
ashamed that he had not been able to foretell what would happen.
He should have known. He should have been able to picture precisely what took place after she left him in the drawing-room.

Now he knew. She had gone to her room. She had listened there
to see whether he would come up. She had heard his footsteps as-
scending the stairs. Probably she had waited for the running of
water in his bathroom. Then, suddenly, she became aware that he
was packing. It became clear to her that her threats had not frightened him. She must have awakened to the disturbing realization
that one could not always have what one wanted—not through pur-
chase, nor intimidation, nor as a natural tribute to one's position
and personality. She must have suddenly sensed that power is nothing but a convention maintained by those who want to be dominated. The man in the next room had broken the convention.

If she had loved him—loved him as he understood love—she
would have tried to block his way out of that house. With tears
and kisses and self-abasement, if there were no other way, she
would have tried to transform her defeat into victory—a victory of
love in which triumph and defeat mean nothing, in which personal
pride is sacrificed to the happiness of being together. Patricia was
confronted with only two ways to escape defeat: to hold her husband through a sacrifice on her part, or to give him up without
humiliation. In the struggle to hold him—Peter should have known
—she had to emerge victorious, or pretend that she had not struggled at all. As she listened to his bags being strapped and locked in
the next room, both ways were still open to her. But she would not
have been Patricia if she had chosen a struggle that meant giving
up something of herself, and of whose outcome she could not be
certain.

It was imperative that she instantly change her strategy. The
scandal with which she had threatened him was no solution. No
matter how she went about involving him in a scandal, she would
have had to acknowledge that she was putting up a fight against
his departure, that it was he who was leaving her. She feared the
opinion of the world, but she feared herself even more. If she
wanted to continue deceiving herself with the illusion of her own
power, then, paradoxically, there was only one way open: to relin-
quish her claim on him. Retreat could be made to look like vic-

tory in her own eyes and the eyes of the world. The important thing was not to admit that one had been defeated.

He was listening to her now with divided attention.

"I talked with Mother last night," she was saying, as if following his thoughts to a logical conclusion. "It was something of a shock for her of course. But she agreed with me that there was no point in creating a scandal that would do nobody any good."

"Of course not," he said absently. "I'm glad that we can remain friends, Patricia."

"I never imagined we would be anything else," she replied. She was under the compulsion to forget last night, not because she regretted what she had said, but because she had set out in the wrong direction—the direction of a struggle whose outcome was uncertain. She added quickly, "You know I'll always be fond of you, Peter."

"And I of you," he replied politely.

She looked at herself in her compact mirror and powdered her nose. Meanwhile she said, "I can't go to Reno, of course. You know how I dread publicity."

He thought, has she no shame? Didn't she talk about the FBI yesterday, or isn't that what she calls publicity? But, at the same time, he understood her too. She had disavowed the events of last night to herself. Why shouldn't she disavow them to him?

He said, "Naturally, you'll choose whatever method is most agreeable to you."

"I'd like to get everything over with as soon as possible," she continued casually. "Would you mind calling Mr. Slater and asking him to get in touch with Gray and Gray today?"

"Of course."

She sighed. "I must run along now. I have to order a few rags. I haven't been to Mainbocher for months. I want to go away for a while. It's time I thought of myself a little. I've been working too hard."

He fell in with her pretense. "That's what I've always said."

She stood up. "Well, Peter—" She held out her hand to him. Then she turned and left before he could accompany her.

Alone in his cramped, small hotel room, he sat down, tired out. He felt none of the relief he had anticipated. The tension of the past few days still tautened his nerves. Years with Patricia—one could not blot them out from one hour to the next. Did the finality of it frighten him? When a chapter of one's life, good or bad, comes to an end, he thought, there always remains a sense of uneasiness, of anxiety. And this chapter had begun well—now one could think of that again. But he knew that it was not this natural sentimentality which made him uneasy. He was like a pilot who breaks through a cloud bank, but instead of finding clear weather, discovers another fog bank ahead.

As long as his struggle with Patricia had continued, Peter had hardly given a thought to whether it was compatible with his conscience to return as an American major to an enemy country which, only a few years ago, he had ceased to regard as his fatherland but which he now intended to make his own again. Now the imminence of his problem swept over him. He had made up his mind to arrange a private conference with the General, and offer him his resignation, when the telephone rang.

A voice he recognized at once said, "Hello, there, Peter. What are you up to here?"

"Colonel Whimsley!"

The Colonel laughed. "So you recognize my voice. Good. I'm down in the lobby."

"When did you get in, Colonel?"

"Yesterday. I called your home and they said you were here. Come on down and have a Martini. I'll be in the bar."

Peter found Colonel Whimsley in excellent spirits.

"I was really lucky," the Colonel said. "The General was going to fly to Germany next week. But then something came up. Between you and me, he's about to resign. He's fed up with Army politics. If he has to be a politician, he'd rather be one outside the Army. Anyway, he wanted to talk to me. Day before yesterday I got a cable. Yesterday I was in Washington. Today I'm here. Tomorrow I'm going home for three days. Then back to Germany."

He waited for Peter to say something. When Peter made no comment, the Colonel said, as if by the way, "It would be nice if we went back together."

"My leave isn't up yet."

"I know. But when I found you weren't living at home I thought you wouldn't particularly want to stay any longer." He sipped his Martini slowly.

"We're getting a divorce," Peter said.

"A friendly agreement?"

"Yes. A friendly agreement."

The Colonel ordered another Martini. It irritated Peter a little that Colonel Whimsley never opened a conversation with the topic he really wanted to speak about. Even with friends and colleagues he used the elementary FBI method of talking about the weather when the purpose was to find out something about a murder. Colonel Whimsley had not come to visit him just to drink cocktails in the Plaza bar.

"There's nothing like a Martini mixed by an American bartender who knows his business," the Colonel observed. "I could sit here for hours. Have you time, Peter?"

"Of course."

"Good. I have something to discuss with you. But not here. Too many people. Let's take a walk."

It was a cold but sunny November afternoon. The sky above Radio City was clear and blue, as if reflecting the skating rink at Rockefeller Plaza.

"The General," Colonel Whimsley was saying, "didn't have me fly over for the fun of it. The situation in Germany is by no means as rosy as it looks on the surface."

"The political situation?"

"Call it what you like. The Nazis are far from dead. They were a little stunned, but they are coming to life again. In the last few weeks we've gotten on the trail of three separate Nazi organizations. They are little, unimportant cells. But we don't want to make the mistake of overlooking little, 'unimportant' cells again."

"That's a job for the Counter Intelligence Corps, isn't it?"

"We work together, of course. But the CIC is a police organization. What we're interested in is the political significance of the new Nazi movement. You see, Peter, the situation is extremely complicated. The men behind the new Nazi activity are mostly people with blameless records. I'd call them neo-Nazis."

"Who are they?"

"Disappointed Germans, among others. Hundreds of people who at first greeted us as liberators. Then they came up against our fatal non-fraternization policy, which did not discriminate between Nazis and anti-Nazis. That offended the best elements among the Germans, as you know. More and more they are turning into our enemies. And they are doubly dangerous because there is nothing in their records that we can hold against them. Many were in concentration camps or were otherwise persecuted. In addition, these people are greatly respected by their fellow Germans because they are obviously not self-seeking opportunists. They are advocating National Socialism at a time when doing so is anything but advantageous."

"Have there been many arrests?"

"No. We are not dealing merely with a concrete organization that can be rounded up and destroyed. What's involved here is something much worse—a state of mind. It's like the Fifth Column in France in 1940. Opposition has gotten under the skins of the people. They don't have to form a conspiracy."

Peter still did not know why Colonel Whimsley thought it necessary to tell him all this. The admission that the non-fraternization policy had been disastrous was surprising, coming from the Colonel. But Peter knew that there was some other reason for their stroll besides the delivery of a political lecture.

After a short silence the Colonel grasped Peter's arm. "Just the same," he said, "we have made an important discovery." He lowered his voice. "We have run down the complete membership record of the National Socialist party. You know what that means."

"I should say I do!" said Peter, astounded. "Where is it?"

"That's a whole story in itself. There's a paper mill in Freimann operated by a man named Hans Huber. He was given the task of pulping the index cards—sixty-five thousand kilograms of them. He couldn't do it on account of lacking coal to run his machines."

"We're guarding the mill, of course?"

"Yes. It's being secretly watched. The attempt to destroy it is set for a week from this Saturday."

"If the mill is well-enough guarded, the Nazis will never try it."

"We want them to try it. We want to kill two birds with one stone. We're going to let the Nazis make the attempt. We'll arrange it so that the records are absolutely safe, but at the same time capture the Nazis when they try to burn down the mill." With the suddenness that always characterized his most important announcements, the Colonel said, "I've proposed to the General that you be put in charge of the operation."

The Colonel expected an enthusiastic response, but Peter merely said, "I think I need another Martini, Colonel."

They had turned east on Forty-second Street to Madison Avenue. They entered a small café that was almost empty. Only two or three men stood silently at the bar.

When they had seated themselves in a dark corner of the badly lit room, Peter drank his Martini at one draught. He said, "I'm flattered to be offered the assignment, Colonel. But I don't think I can accept it."

"Why not?"

"I don't want to go back to Germany. At least, not right away. And not in my present position."

On the Colonel's thin, impassive face, which seldom betrayed emotion, there was now an expression of surprise. "I don't understand, Peter. After all, you're only on leave."

"I know. But I have plenty of points. I can ask for my discharge."

"I understand that even less."

"I don't want to deceive the OSS and the Army, not to mention the United States."

"What's that supposed to mean?"

"It means that when I do get back to Germany I don't intend to return to America."

"I'll be damned if I get it. A minute ago you were saying you didn't intend to return to Germany."

"I'll try to explain. You see, I believe that my future is in Germany. It would take too long to go into all that now. But I feel an obligation to return to Germany—an obligation to Germany as well as to America. I feel that those of us who love America and also know Europe have a mission to fulfill."

"And what's keeping you from fulfilling it?"

"That's what I want to explain. Europe, not only Germany, is a tremendous challenge to me. Missionaries in darkest Africa or darkest Asia used to spend ten or twelve years teaching the alphabet to the savages and curing their snake bites before they could begin preaching the Gospel in earnest. Europe today is darkest Africa—but with a magnificent culture behind the ruins. Maybe the people over there have become savages—but they know the alphabet. One can talk to them. And since one can talk to them, one must talk to them."

"That all makes sense, Peter. But I don't see what's bothering you."

"Well, I am a missionary, but I'm one of the savages too. I know that I belong over there. And that's where my problem begins. Anyone who goes to Germany as an American officer can be called back, his work can be interrupted at any time. Besides, I don't believe that the Germans can be educated from the outside." He lit a cigarette. "You understand, Colonel. A man can't be an American officer and at the same time work for Germany, even if his work in the last analysis is in the interests of world peace. I want to go back to Germany—as soon as possible. But I have never sailed under false colors."

The Colonel thoughtfully munched potato chips. He did not say anything for a while. When he did speak, Peter had the feeling that he had considered well what he was about to say. "I don't want to talk you into anything, Peter. I appreciate your sincerity. But you're wrong. You look at the American and European problem as two separate problems. That's just what you shouldn't do. You contradict yourself. You say that being a good American means being a good European too. Or words to that effect. But you yourself draw a distinction between the two. We are still in the midst of a battle. It will be years before nuances get to be important."

"Nuances?"

"Differences of opinion over occupation methods, and so on. And there's something more essential too. It will be years before you can afford the luxury of feeling or acting like a German. It will be years before I can permit myself to feel like an American. Don't you think I'd rather go back to Tennessee to live? What business have I got in Germany? But Germany or Tennessee—for the time being they're both hallucinations. The evil that we have to fight reduces all such geographical concepts to one common denominator. Everything else comes later."

"Colonel, you're a remarkable man," said Peter sincerely.

The Colonel smiled and was briefly silent again. Then he said, "Just wait a while, Peter. In one or two years, when the worst is over, we'll have a good talk about the question of Americans and Germans. But more immediate issues are at stake now. Nazi cells. A Fifth Column."

Peter smiled with a sense of sudden relief. For the first time he seemed to be breathing freely again. "How would it be, Colonel, if I called you tonight and gave you my decision?"

"Fine!" said the Colonel. "And meanwhile I'll arrange for our passage back."

⇒ 47 ⇐

AFTER notifying Colonel Whimsley that he was willing to return to Germany, Peter had three days left in the United States. He had sent several telegrams to Mrs. Thompson, Dirty's wife, none of which was answered. He decided to fly to Chicago and see her personally.

It was about five in the afternoon when he stepped out of a taxi before the Thompson apartment on Yorkville Street on Chicago's South Side. The building had apparently been constructed around the turn of the century, and it looked exactly like a thousand other lower middle-class dwellings he had seen in other unfashionable suburbs in America. It had the same dirty red brick, the same narrow stairs, the same high, narrow windows and incongruously elaborate lanterns on either side of the entrance. Peter could not tell just why, but the building reminded him of a mangy dog that is losing its hair and is badly in need of a scrubbing. Several unkempt children were playing drearily in the street; on the stairs a little boy sat thoughtfully picking his nose.

Under the bell were several nameplates, one of which read "Ralph D. Thompson." The name, so completely civilian without "T/5" or "Dirty" preceding it, moved Peter. He rang the bell and shortly afterward heard the repeated clicking of the lock. Mrs. Thompson was at home.

As soon as he opened the door and stepped into the dark corridor, a woman's voice came from above, "Who is it?"

"Major Olden," Peter answered. "Is Mrs. Thompson at home?"

"Come on up." There was surprise and uneasiness in the voice.

He went up the creaking stairs. On the third floor a door was standing open. He walked in.

Peter found himself in a neat, roomy kitchen. Two young women, who were sitting at an oilcloth-covered table, stood up. He could not tell which one was Doris. Both women were about twenty-five, small, and had chestnut hair and blue eyes. Only after he had looked closer did he see that the two women did not resemble each other at all. One had a fresh, healthy complexion and wore little make-up. Despite a somewhat too wide mouth and thickish lips, she did not look common. The other was glaringly made up, had scarlet finger nails, and wore a large brassy looking clasp in her hair. Peter was relieved to learn, through a stumbling introduction, that Mrs. Thompson was the one with the attractive skin and little make-up. The other was her friend Jane.

"I am Major Olden," he said. "I got back from Europe. Your husband asked me to bring you his greetings. Didn't you get my telegrams, Mrs. Thompson?"

"Yes, I did," Doris answered haltingly, obviously embarrassed. But she added with a show of firmness, "I just couldn't come to New York." She exchanged glances with the other girl.

No one spoke for a moment.

"How's Ralph?" Mrs. Thompson asked finally.

"Very well," Peter replied.

He took from his pocket the little package of perfume that Dirty had bought for his wife at Guerlain's. He handed it to her. "He sent this to you. A present from Paris."

She said "Oh!" a little breathlessly and took the package. She did not seem to know what to do with it. She put it down unopened on the table.

Peter was still standing in the middle of the room. Now he looked pointedly around, leaving little doubt that he would like to sit down.

"Please have a seat, Major," Mrs. Thompson said, pulling up a chair for him.

"Thank you." He sat down and they were silent again. Jane lit a cigarette, crossed her legs, and gave herself over to smoking as if that were an occupation in itself. She looked at Doris and Peter; both of them seemed to amuse her.

Peter also lit a cigarette. He said, "Mrs. Thompson, I'd like to have a talk with you. I have various matters to discuss concerning your husband."

"Go right ahead, Major."

Peter saw her press her lips together. It was odd how those lips, childish and sensuous at the same time, could thin out into one hard line.

"I would like to talk with you alone," he said.

"Jane and I have no secrets from each other," she said defiantly.

I know that tone, Peter told himself. It made him laugh inwardly to think how much the peremptory tone of Mrs. Dirty Thompson reminded him of Patricia's voice when she was asserting herself.

"Ralph has told me a great deal," he said. "Ralph was my driver during most of the war. But he's more than that. He's my friend."

"That's nice," said Doris. "But what's that got to do with me?"

"Ralph doesn't want to give you a divorce, Mrs. Thompson," Peter said as amiably as he could. "He loves you."

"What do you mean, he doesn't want to give me a divorce?" she asked. Her face flushed. "Does he want me to be unhappy the rest of my life?"

"Of course not. That's just what he doesn't want. He would like to come back and start a new life with you."

"It's too late for that, Major."

"I don't know all the circumstances, Mrs. Thompson. But it is never too late to start a new life when two people have the good will to do so. I know that Ralph has it."

"I couldn't live with Ralph any more," said Doris. There was a tinge of impatience in her voice.

"Why not? Don't misunderstand me, Mrs. Thompson. I am not asking out of mere curiosity. I'm going back to Germany. I would like to know what to tell Ralph."

"I've already written him."

"He doesn't seem to understand what has happened."

"Ralph always was a little slow catching on," Jane interrupted with a sneer, intended as much for Peter as for Ralph.

Peter ignored her.

"I don't know why he's being so obstinate," Doris said. "Ralph and I could never live together again."

"Why not?" Peter felt obligated to make an attempt at least. "Weren't you happy together? Didn't he provide for you, do everything he could for you? And didn't you love him?"

She shrugged. "Possibly," she said. "But that's all over."

"Why don't you give him another chance?"

"Ralph never understood me. And it's been so long since we've seen each other."

"That's no reason, Mrs. Thompson. Hundreds of thousands of soldiers were separated from their wives for years. After all, Ralph didn't become a soldier because he wanted to."

"He could've gotten a war job here," Doris replied.

Jane interrupted again, "I'll bet anything that Ralph had a wonderful time over there. You men all have the same idea. Women are supposed to sit home on their fannies and wait for you guys to come back. Hooey. Most of 'em that come back from Europe act real peculiar too. Ain't that right, Doris?"

"How?" Peter asked.

"Just like they did over there, probably. Big shots. Nothing's too good for 'em. Women are just servants. They expect you to shine their shoes. Europe went to their heads, that's all."

Peter again turned to Mrs. Thompson. "You know Ralph, Mrs. Thompson. Europe didn't go to his head. Otherwise he wouldn't have asked me to come and speak to you."

Doris looked nervously at the clock. It was a large, white kitchen clock, and it hung on the wall behind her. She had to turn around to look at it. She made no effort to conceal the fact that she was looking at the clock.

Peter knew she was expecting someone. He made no move to go. At least I'll get a look at the man, he thought. He settled back in his chair.

They sat in silence for several minutes. The clock ticked loudly. Then Peter said, "I will tell Ralph all you've said. But I can't promise that he will consent to a divorce."

Doris gave a start. "He promised me," she said. "He always told me he would never stand in my way."

Jane stood up.

"For God's sake, Doris, why don't you tell the truth and get it over with?" she said.

Doris flushed. She got up and walked over to the kitchen cabinet.

"I don't know why Doris don't tell you," Jane said to Peter. "She's expecting a baby. My brother's the father."

Peter involuntarily got to his feet. He considered a moment what he should say. Then he asked, "Shall I tell Ralph that, Mrs. Thompson?"

Doris, her back turned, did not answer.

"Why shouldn't he tell Ralph?" Jane asked. "Maybe that'll bring him to his senses. Or maybe he'd like to come home and take care of the kid himself." Peter said nothing, and she went on, "Doris could've done what other girls do, you know. She could've asked him to come right home, and then have a seven-month baby. Plenty of women are having seven-month babies these days."

Doris turned around. "It's really no use, Major," she said. She went to the sink and turned on the water.

Peter did not know whether she was doing it out of nervousness, or whether this was her way of showing that the visit was at an end. He also did not know why he did not pick up his hat and go. Poor old Dirty, he thought. He could picture him, his collar open and his sleeves rolled up, sitting at the oilcloth-covered table, contentedly reading the comics. Peter felt as if he were visiting the home of a dead friend.

He stood up. "I'm going now," he said. As he said it he heard footsteps on the stairs.

The man who pushed open the door was a good head taller than Peter. Though he was wearing a broad-brimmed hat, which he made no move to take off, it was apparent that his hair was black and curly. He had a broad flat nose and heavy lips.

"Hello, honey," Doris said. Between the "hello" and the "honey" there was the fraction of a pause.

The man looked questioningly at Peter, who said, "My name is Peter Olden."

In the man's dark little eyes something flickered. It was clear that honey knew what was afoot. He responded to Peter's self-introduction with a grunt.

"I am Ralph Thompson's commanding officer," Peter continued. "I have brought greetings from him to his wife."

"Okay," said honey. "Don't let me keep you." He threw his hat on the table and took off his coat. Doris hung it on the back of a chair.

Peter sat down. "I'm pleased to meet you, Mr.— I'm afraid I didn't catch your name," he said politely.

"Never mind about my name."

Peter pretended not to notice the words or the tone of voice. "Ralph and I," he continued, "were together several years over there. We're friends. What concerns him concerns me."

They were sitting opposite each other, the little kitchen table between them. Honey now leaned back, balancing himself on the rear legs of his chair. He put both feet on the table and then slowly and carefully let the two front legs of the chair down to the floor, his feet sliding forward on the table until his shoes were almost under Peter's nose. "So everything that goes for Thompson, goes for you, eh?" he said. "In that case, you can kiss my ass too."

Peter's face remained completely unchanged.

"That kind of talk won't get you anywhere," he said. "I'd like to know what you're doing here. What business have you in Ralph Thompson's home?"

He could not have explained why he spoke as he did. He did not even know why he had stayed. He knew only that he did not want to leave this apartment—where Ralph D. Thompson, called Dirty, had lived and been happy and for which he still yearned—without taking along something for his friend: a scrap of hope, a little satisfaction, or a final bitterness.

Honey teetered back and forth in his chair. He looked over to the two women who were standing together in a corner, Doris visibly frightened and Jane uneasy but curious. Honey laughed. "How do you like this guy?" he asked the women. "Some hot-shot major, eh? Ralph's commanding officer, he says. And he thinks he can pull that 'commanding officer' stuff around here too. Thinks he's a big wheel because he's got all that fruit salad on his chest." He looked at Peter. "Listen, Bud. If you think you're impressing anybody around here you're nuttier than you look, see? For all we care, you can take that fruit salad and stick it." He got to his feet. "And what's more, if you don't haul ass out of here pretty goddam quick, I'll send you back to your pal Thompson in pieces. By air mail."

"Take it easy," said Jane to her brother. "Don't hurt him." The contempt in her voice infuriated Peter more than the insults of the man.

Peter remained seated. I'll make one more attempt, he told himself. He said, "It's not much of a trick to take away a soldier's wife when he's overseas, you know. Ralph loves his wife—"

He got no further. The man stepped up to him and grabbed him by the collar. He was about to yank Peter to his feet, probably with the intention of throwing him downstairs.

But Peter, the instant the hand touched his collar, leaped to his feet and at the same time slammed his left fist into the man's stomach. The man doubled over, and Peter swung his right hand in a short arc to the point of the chin. The man wilted into a heap on the floor and did not move.

The women screamed but did not dare to step forward. Peter picked up his hat. At the door he said, "That was a little greeting from Ralph. By air mail."

The last thing he noticed before he left the room was the little package from Guerlain's, still unopened on the table.

Outside, it was night. The cold Chicago wind whined through the deserted streets. Peter buttoned up the collar of his trench coat. A fistfight, he thought, a little ashamed of himself, is no argument. But he had to admit that he felt much better.

⋙ 48 ⋘

A FEW hours after Stroud received Peter's cable, he was on his way to Oberndorf. Maria was in the village when he arrived, and Helga, her daughter, received him.

"Please sit down, Colonel," she said. "Mama will be right back. Have you any news of Peter?"

"Yes. He's arriving in Bremen next Friday."

"That will make Mama happy."

Stroud sat down on the little bench around the tile oven, and leaned back against it. The girl sat near the window, a pile of linen next to her on the floor. She was busy mending kitchen and hand towels. Stroud observed her silently. Helga had few of the features of her mother. The blond hair, the dark eyes, and the little snub nose suggested Maria, but while Maria could have been a Czech or a Russian, Helga could have been nothing but a German. Maria's features were coarsened in her daughter. The girl's eyebrows were too thick, her lips too fleshy, and her feet too big. She was pretty and she had an attractive, dimpled smile, but one knew by looking at her that she would not remain pretty long. All that was lovely about her resulted from the freshness of her seventeen years.

The girl looked up from her sewing. "Do you think that Mama will be able to travel to Bremen to meet Peter, Colonel?" she asked.

"That can probably be managed. Would you like to go along?"

"No. I think it would be better if Mama went alone."

While Stroud was thawing out from the ride through the cold November afternoon, he considered how best to engage the girl in conversation. This child, he thought, was barely four years old when Hitler came to power. What does she think and feel? And, above all, how does she regard the strange man who suddenly turned up in an American uniform to intrude himself into the life she had been leading with her mother? Since nothing else occurred to him, he decided to be frank and ask her.

"Do you like Peter, Miss Helga?"

"Yes," she said without looking up. "I think I like him."

"Aren't you afraid he will take your mother away from you?"

She laughed. "No. Why should I? Mama will be happy with him."

"How do you know?"

"She waited so long."

"Would you marry an American?"

She still did not look up. "Of course."

"Do you know the one already?"

"I know many Americans. There were Americans in the village for three months. A new regiment is supposed to arrive tomorrow."

"Has one of the boys pleased you especially?"

"Yes. He was here just yesterday. He's stationed in Munich now. He has a farm in Iowa. His parents, that is. Do you know Iowa, Colonel?"

"Yes. A wonderful state."

"That's what Fred says."

"Would you like to go to America, Miss Helga?"

"Yes. As soon as possible. Anything to get out of Germany!"

"Why?"

She looked up. "I can't bear the people here, Colonel. They're so mean and selfish and sad."

"People aren't terribly happy anywhere, Miss Helga."

"I know. But still, the Americans are quite different from us. It was wonderful when they were here. You only had to look into their eyes, and you had such a free, happy feeling. Our men are so heavy and depressed."

"That's no doubt a result of the defeat."

"No," Helga replied earnestly. "They were always that way. As long as I can remember, at least."

"I guess that's part of living under National Socialism," Stroud speculated. "In a National Socialist state everyone had to live for a cause. With us people simply live. They don't have to live for anything."

Helga nodded. "That's what I mean."

"I wonder," Stroud continued, "whether many young Germans feel as you do. There must still be a lot of Nazis among the young people."

"Not among boys and girls of my age."

"Of what age, then?"

"Oh, say, twenty to twenty-two or three."

"That's odd. Boys and girls of your age are just the ones who grew up under Hitler. They don't know anything else. It might be different in your case. Your mother certainly told you about the world outside of Germany."

"Mama often did. But that wouldn't have been necessary. I hated the Hitler Youth and the League of German Girls and all those other organizations. And of course the Labor Service."

"What made you hate them?"

"We wanted to be free, just like the boys and girls of other countries. But they would never let us."

"Did you know what freedom meant, to begin with?"

"Yes. A thing like that doesn't have to be taught."

"But how did it happen that older boys and girls didn't long for freedom, as you say you did?"

"I don't know. They were too unhappy before Hitler came. Unemployment and inflation, I suppose. Afterward things went better for them."

"On account of the rearmament?"

"They didn't worry about why it happened. They just knew that it happened."

"May I ask you something frankly, Miss Helga? Please don't take it amiss. Didn't you hope all through the war that Germany would win?"

She pondered for a little while. "Oh, yes," she said. "I hoped so. And that is perhaps the only thing that sometimes came between Mama and me. Mama prayed for an Allied victory, and I for a German one."

"If Germany had won, then everything would have continued as before—the Hitler Youth and the League of German Girls and the Labor Service?"

"Yes," she said. "That's true. It's probably illogical. But just the same, one prays for one's country to win."

Stroud looked at the clock. "Do you think your mother will be here soon? After all, I could go and leave the cable here for her."

"Oh, no!" Helga protested. "You must give her the great news yourself."

"Your mother must have a lot to do these days."

"Yes, she has. She's busy all day long. Yesterday she didn't get back from the village until ten o'clock. But you'll be amazed to see how well Mama looks."

"She's happy, I suppose."

"Mama is always happy when she can be helpful. And besides, for several days she has been quite certain that Peter would soon be back." She said it naturally and openly.

"You are probably very busy yourself," Stroud said. "All the household work falls on your shoulders, doesn't it?"

"I like it. It's wonderful to be able to do something for Mama for a change."

"What would you like to be, Miss Helga? I believe your mother told me that you wanted to study medicine."

Helga stood up to put the linen away. "It's too difficult now," she said. "If Mama gets married, someone will have to look after the farm." She looked at Stroud and laughed. "Are you surprised that I speak of Mama's marriage, Colonel? Mama tells me everything. We have no secrets from each other."

"Don't you want to get married, Miss Helga?"

"Oh, yes," she answered. "I want to get married. But Mama's turn comes first. And anyway—"

She was interrupted by Maria, who came bursting breathlessly into the room. Her cheeks were red from the winter air, and there was frost on her hair. As she gave her cold, firm hands to Stroud, he hardly recognized her. She looked ten years younger than on the day he had brought her news of Peter's wound.

"Colonel Stroud!" she cried. "I'm all out of breath! I saw your car outside. Have you news of Peter?"

"Yes." Stroud smiled. "And I don't always bring bad news. This time it's good. Peter arrives at Bremen Friday."

She had given him both her hands, and he had held them while they spoke. Now she withdrew them. He saw that the emotion that overcame her was more than she could control. She sat down on the bench. She tried to say something, but no word passed her lips. Two large tears were in her eyes. She did not try to find a handkerchief, but let the tears roll slowly down her cheeks. She smiled.

In the car going back to Munich, Stroud sat silently next to his driver. He was filled with an emotion new to him. Envy. For Peter was a man who had burned his bridges behind him.

➤➤ 49 ◀◀

THE plan of Colonel Whimsley and Peter to return to Germany together was frustrated by the Army administration, which ordered the Colonel to fly from Washington to Berlin, while Peter had to take a ship. Peter was, in fact, grateful for the sea voyage, which gave him eight days in which to settle his thoughts, ponder events of the recent past, and plan for the future. From the beginning of the voyage he experienced again the feeling that had first come to him on Broadway, the sense of being involved in a common destiny with the strangers who surrounded him. In the war men had lived through wildly disparate experiences and yet were bound together by the war itself. Now they were all members of the brotherhood created by the war's aftermath, in which their individual lives were submerged and swallowed up. Men who long had hoped, consciously or unaware, to escape the overpowering collectivity of war now discovered that they were unable to find their way back again to the loneliness of an individual destiny.

Almost all the passengers on the ship that took Peter back to Europe were officers and soldiers who had re-enlisted after being mustered out. There were certainly some among them who deliberately chose the comforts of occupation life in preference to the struggle for a livelihood at home. But the more he talked to officers and men, the clearer it became that most of them were returning to Europe not out of fear of being jobless, but of being homeless. What they dreaded was the loneliness of Sundays, the grim emptiness of furnished rooms, and the closed circle of those who had remained at home, into which they could not break. They loved America with a love that was boundless and fanatic, and Europe had not been able to impair their affection. But Europe drew them back because it was too foreign and remote to be able to disillusion them. Few of them loved the real Europe with its ancient twisting byways, its cathedrals and castles, its grimy coffee houses and melancholy people. But America, like a desirable beckoning woman, had proved herself cold and capricious. Sometimes Peter was almost inclined to believe that many soldiers returned to Europe only for the purpose of making America jealous and thus winning her back.

Not many of them, Peter learned, were returning to specific women in Europe, but most of them cherished the memory of some girl in France or Germany, Belgium or Luxembourg, who in a few days' time had made a home for them, had tried with her few shabby garments to make herself beautiful, who seemed to be receiving more than she gave, but who actually gave more than she received.

As closely as Peter felt bound to these young men, he nevertheless recognized the great danger implicit in their return to Europe. Since most of them were disillusioned, they could not be successful ambassadors of America. They were not going back to spread the gospel of democracy; most of them had given little thought to democracy at all. Many were young, inexperienced, uneducated: they knew as little of what America meant as they did of Europe. Unknowing or unhappy—how could these peacetime soldiers become missionaries for democracy? The more he came to understand them, the more certain he was that he had done right in returning to Europe.

A hundred times on the way over he had asked himself whether

Maria would be waiting for him in Bremen; a hundred times he had pictured to himself what their meeting would be like. It was all the more remarkable, then, that their reunion occurred exactly as he had imagined it.

She was standing on the pier. Dirty Thompson stood a few paces behind her.

The December morning was gray with fog. Bremen first became visible through its ruins. Like all ruins, these, too, had their own personality. These were theatrical. They made Peter think of a stage setting in which a miniature ship is pulled along behind the scenes. Here the effect was reversed: the ship was real, the approaching city the stage setting. The architecture of the old Hanseatic city, although it no longer existed as buildings, still had a baroque, operatic grace. The shadowy outlines of what were once patrician homes emerged by degrees from the fog, forming elegant façades behind which there was no life. Then there was the lighthouse. Then the breakwater. And then Maria.

He discovered her at once. She was wearing a gray fur coat but no hat. She must have been standing at the pier a long time, for her face was reddened, and as the ship was slowly warped into the dock Peter saw that she repeatedly took out her handkerchief to blow her nose. The wind fluttered her hair. From time to time she turned to say something to Thompson.

Then she saw him. She raised her hand and waved. The gesture made Peter realize how different the identical motion can be when it signifies parting and when it is meant for greeting. He recalled the picture of her as she had stood before her house when his car had pulled away. Her waving hand was then a stricken bird falling to earth. Now it was a lark that soars upward, singing.

He was one of the first down the gangplank. Only when he stood opposite her did he remember that he was in Germany, an American officer for whom a German woman was waiting. She did not embrace him. She only gave him her hand. He seized it silently. Thus they stood facing each other in the rubble of the half-wrecked harbor, amid the hubbub of military commands and the shouts of GI's, without being able to embrace. And thus they would have remained standing, absorbed in each other, jostled by soldiers and sailors, if Dirty Thompson had not finally intruded.

"Welcome back, Major," he said.

Peter smiled and shook hands. "Hello, Thompson. It's good to see you again."

"Good to have you back."

They stopped at a little hotel on the road to Hanover, in the English Zone, where the non-fraternization law had been completely revoked. While Maria went to her room to make herself more presentable, Peter and Thompson sat down at a table in the taproom on the first floor and ordered kirsch.

"How was America?" Thompson asked.

"It was all right," Peter answered. And because he knew the question that burned on Thompson's lips, he added, "I was in Chicago, Thompson. I saw your wife."

"Yeah?"

"It's no use, Thompson. That is, if you want to hear the truth."

"That's what I want to hear, Major."

"I saw the man too."

"What is he, a lady killer?"

"By no means. He's a typical pimp. I don't know if that's any comfort to you."

"No," said Thompson dryly. After a short pause he added, "Doris couldn't love a man like that."

"Don't you believe it! It's amazing what kind of men women can love."

"But she'll never be happy with him."

"Probably not." Peter hesitated. "Look, Thompson. I promised to be frank with you. And you promised to take my advice. My advice is: try to forget it. Most of all, try not to think about whether Doris will be happy or not. Just think of your own happiness. That's more important now."

"Should I give her a divorce?"

"Yes."

Thompson drank down his kirsch in one gulp. "I didn't expect anything else," he said. "But just the same, it's a shock."

"What are you going to do now, Thompson? Do you want to go back to America?"

"No. I'm staying here."

"How long?"

"At least three years. I'm going to re-enlist."

"Have you thought it over carefully?"

"Yeah. What've I got to go home for? I asked Mrs. Hoffmann whether you're goin' to stay over here. She said you probably would. Do you want to keep me on as your driver?"

Peter reached over and patted Thompson on the shoulder. He smiled. "Of course. How can you ask? But I didn't re-enlist. I may be out of the Army in a year. You have to take that into consideration."

Thompson shrugged. "Somethin' will turn up before that," he said. He tried to appear indifferent, but he could not refrain from asking, "What did she say, Major?"

"Not much. The man's sister was there."

"So she couldn't say much, eh?"

"I don't think she wanted to say much. I don't think she knows how much she means to you. But it wouldn't be any different if she did." He leaned over the table. "Don't imagine for a minute that you're alone in this. I heard of a dozen cases like yours every day over there. I don't think most of the women knew what they were doing. So they don't regret it yet."

Peter was attempting in this way to give the conversation a general application, but he did not succeed.

Thompson seemed hardly to be listening. He asked, "What was she wearin'?"

"I don't remember exactly. I think she had on a gray dress with blue sleeves."

Thompson drank a second glass of kirsch. "I don't know that one," he said. "Must be new." Then, after a pause, "Were you out to the apartment?"

"Yes."

Thompson's broad face creased into a slow smile. "Did she show you my garage? Behind the house? I built it. I've got a workbench and all my tools there."

"No, she didn't show me that."

Thompson cleared his throat. "And the guy? How did he look?"

"Like a pimp. I've already told you."

"Did she go to the station with you? Were you in the city with her?"

"No. Listen, Thompson. Don't keep asking questions. Not now, anyway. Maybe sometime later. Doris didn't go to the station with me, and Doris wasn't very friendly. But that isn't important. The important thing is for you to begin to put it out of your mind. A man should look at everything as if it had happened a year ago. He should ask himself, how will I look back a year from now on what is happening today? Will it still be important? Will I cry over it a year from now or smile about it? Will it have changed the course of my life or will I have almost forgotten it? Time does wonders, you know, but you can help it along a little too. The way to live is as if life were a memory." He broke off for a moment and then repeated, "It will all look different in a year."

Thompson stared steadily ahead. "And she didn't give you a letter for me either?"

"No. No letter and no message," Peter answered harshly. "Only that she wants a divorce."

"Did she say I should write to her?"

"No. And you shouldn't, either. You've got your own life to lead. There's more to life than just Doris."

They said no more until the tavernkeeper appeared and took Peter's order for dinner. Then Peter left Thompson alone.

The little hotel room was unheated. Maria and Peter did not notice. They sat close together, pressed against each other. Peter was trying to give a chronological account of his stay in America, but poured out his story so hastily that he soon lost track of the proper sequence of events and his narrative became confused.

Finally she interrupted him with a laugh. "You don't have to tell me everything today, darling. We have plenty of time."

He caught his breath. "We have plenty of time." No other sentence could have moved him so deeply.

She saw that he gave a start. "What's wrong?" she asked.

"You said, 'We have plenty of time,'" he replied. "And suddenly I realized what that means. To have time, for the first time in my life. My whole life has been like a race. My childhood was a long effort to outdistance my own weakness. Then came the compulsion that drove me from my home. Then the discovery of my own ambitions against the shadow that was falling over Germany. The feeling of being under constant pressure to accomplish something before it was too late. I remember how it was when I wrote my first book. I was completely absorbed in my plot and characters. But when I went outside and bought a newspaper I was overwhelmed with the feeling that I had entered into a race with the swiftest runner of all. And I was beaten. Time defeated me in every contest. The book was never finished, because while I wrote, everything around me was engulfed in the deepening shadow. And then America. I thought at last that I would be able to stand still, but I had to keep running. I was like a man on an escalator. Even when I stood still, I moved. I had no time; time had me. I made a name for myself, but I was a stranger without roots and therefore I had to hurry on to show this foreign world that I could make good what I had promised. And again time took a hand. I thought perhaps the war wouldn't reach me, but the war closed the gap I had put between it and myself. I wrote a new book, but meanwhile Hitler marched through Poland. He stormed into Belgium and France. I ran, but history was rolling in high-speed tanks. Everything I wrote, everything I did, suddenly seemed insignificant, as remote and small as a stage seen through the wrong end of opera glasses. What was more important, to talk or to act? That, too, was a race: between the writer and the soldier. The soldier won. I had to act, tormented by the conviction that the proper function of the writer is not to act, but to write. And then I found you again, darling, and again I was overpowered by the frightening realization that here was another fight against time."

She had listened intently. She said, "Now I'm not so sure I was right when I said we had plenty of time, Peter."

"Why not?"

"As I listened to you I had a feeling of guilt. All the plans you have in Germany—the village, and education for the Germans, and teaching them about America—aren't they tasks imposed on you by time, and in a measure by me too? Wouldn't it be better if you kept yourself aloof from all that and devoted yourself to your books?"

"No," he answered. "That's something else. You are here and my work is here. It may be two or three years before I can sit down to write again. But the competition with time is over. Time is passing, but that's not important any more. Up until now time not only dictated the tempo of my life, but my life itself. Now there is nothing into which time forces me. Now everything is of my own free will and of my own choosing."

He took her hands and kissed them. She laid her cheek against his hair.

"Strange," she said. "Time—it seemed as if these weeks would never end. And now it seems as if you had never been away."

"That's the way it was when we saw each other again for the first time in twelve years."

"Yes. Exactly."

Later, after they had eaten and returned to their room, they began talking of Stroud and Wanda.

"I don't know what will come of it all," she said. "Wanda is expecting a child."

He was about to pour himself a glass of kirsch, but he froze with the bottle tilted in midair. "What is John going to do?"

"I don't think he knows exactly," she answered. "I'm sure he's not evading the responsibility, but—"

"But he is going home?"

"Probably, when the time comes."

"What does the poor girl say?"

"She's not a 'poor girl,' Peter. That's just it. She wanted the child. She wanted it, even though she knew that he would go home."

"I don't understand that."

She smiled. "That's why you're a man."

"But what will she do? She can't bear a child in a DP camp. We must do something for her."

"That's just what I thought, dearest." There was a note of gratitude in her voice that he did not understand at once. "Would you object if I took her in with me?"

"Of course not. But can you? I mean, will they release her from the camp?"

"If she agrees not to hold the Military Government responsible for her transportation back to Poland."

"That means that she can't get back to Poland."

"For the time being, yes. But for the time being it makes no difference. She must give birth to a healthy child. Then we'll see what comes next."

"Does she want to live with you?"

"Of course. And I think she'll remain in the village. At least until she feels that she can return to Poland."

"Wanda living among Germans? Has she changed that much?"

"No. How could she? But I think that the same thing has

happened to her as has happened to so many of us. The possibility of starting again from the beginning has captivated her too."

"I still don't understand how it's possible that now she wants to help Germans."

"She just wants to help people, and in doing so she forgets they are Germans. At any rate, I'm sure she'll do the village a great deal of good. The people there know only Poles who plunder. So far they have never met a Polish woman who has suffered such injustice and is ready to forgive."

"But is she?" Peter asked.

"In time she will forgive," Maria answered.

He took Maria in his arms. "If you want it that way," he said. "Do you know that you are a great sorceress?"

She nodded. "I must be, if I've bewitched you."

He became serious again. "Do you really mean that she knows John will leave her, and she is not upset? Doesn't she love him?"

"Oh, yes. She loves him very much. She always knew that some day he would have to go away. Now she is certain of holding on to a part of him. A part that will come to mean more to her than he does himself. Her life is no longer hopeless, Peter."

He did not seem to be convinced. He said, "Poor child!" And Maria could not tell whether he meant Wanda or the child that was about to be born. He lapsed into a thoughtful silence.

She freed herself from his embrace. "I'm cold," she said.

He looked at the bed. She nodded and began to undress slowly. He watched her without moving. He could not explain the charm that each of her movements had for him, but perhaps it was the mixture of solemnity and coquetry that attracted him, the utter absence of shame, and the matter-of-factness, the provocative assurance with which she could repeat the same gesture in the same light a hundred times, always in the certainty that it would have its effect.

"I was a little afraid," she said, stepping out of her skirt as if she were stepping out of a bath, "that everything would be different when you came back. That maybe we needed the fear of losing each other."

"No," said Peter, "we don't need any fear."

PART V

PART 2.

CHRISTMAS of 1945, the first peace Christmas, was white in Germany. It had been snowing for days. The snow disguised the harshness of the prisoner-of-war enclosure almost completely. The barbed wire, coated with white, lost itself in the whiteness of the surrounding countryside, and it was difficult to tell where open ground ceased and the prison area began.

Guards stood only on every other watchtower. The vacant towers created the illusion that the prison camp had been abandoned. On the towers that were manned, Stroud had ordered little Christmas trees set up. Prisoners had worked for weeks to install the electrical connections for the colored lights. At night the trees were outlined against the dark as if suspended in the December sky, and the guards in their heavy overcoats and turned-up collars seemed to be stationed on the towers only to see that the lights did not go out.

Stroud would have arranged for a complete traditional Christmas for the prisoners had not the recent murder strained the atmosphere of the camp and necessitated a sterner regimen than he was accustomed to imposing. Nevertheless, he could not refrain from allowing a number of liberties in keeping with the season. The civilian authorities in Munich had sent out four or five roasting ovens for chestnuts, which were erected in the alleyways between the barracks. Prisoners took turns tending the fires in the tubby little stoves, and others gathered around them. The chestnuts crackled merrily, and a lively traffic went on between the barracks as prisoners came and went, carrying off the finished chestnuts in improvised paper bags. Stroud also tacitly permitted any suitable festivity that the men saw fit to arrange for themselves within the confines of their barracks.

Since Stroud could not leave the camp, Peter, Maria, Helga, and Wanda were to celebrate Christmas Eve in his quarters. Maria and Helga came to Munich by train, and Peter met them at the station. Then Thompson drove them to the DP camp, where Wanda awaited them.

It was about six-thirty as they drove through the city toward the prison camp. It was still snowing. The streets were full of life and activity. People were hurrying toward their homes, quickened by anticipation of the holiday, just as if they did not live among gaping ruins, in dimly-lit cellars and in unheated rooms. Shop windows were illuminated, and their total emptiness suggested that they had been plundered by enthusiastic shoppers; one forgot that the windows had been empty all along. Men and women hastened furtively out of the stores, each carrying off something wrapped in newspapers. What had they bought, where there was nothing to buy?

The command car moved slowly through the deep snow as it passed the City Hall. Here the fragrance of Christmas was so strong that they all breathed deeply. On the City Hall square there was a Christmas tree market, and now the last delayed shoppers were carrying away, on their shoulders or in pushcarts, the scrawny, left-over trees. The doors of the miraculously undamaged little church were open, revealing to passers-by the worshipers crowded inside. The faithful were kneeling in the middle aisle leading to the altar, and the altar itself radiated light from dozens of candles. The odor of incense came through the open doors, mingling with the fragrance of the fir trees.

"We must go to midnight Mass," said Maria.

Peter nodded.

The farther they traveled from the center of the city, the more they were enthralled by what they saw.

Here and there a lighted Christmas tree gleamed in the window of a devastated house, often from the window of the only habitable room left in the building. It was as if great illuminated Christmas cards had been pasted on the charred and shattered walls. Trees twinkled even from cellar windows. These windows extended only a little above the ground, so that nothing but the tips of the trees were visible, and where there was a row of such windows it looked as if handfuls of stars had fallen from the sky and had been strung along the edge of the sidewalk like a necklace of pearls.

Children appeared everywhere among the ruins, pulling little sleds behind them. Many of them climbed to the tops of snow piles that had accumulated on the ruins and went sliding down, plunging from a height of two or three stories over snow-covered rubble, broken furniture, and probably buried corpses, into the streets. Some were arrayed as pilgrims to Bethlehem, with golden crowns of paper on their heads and carrying tiny cardboard stalls in each of which a candle burned. The children went carefully through the snow, clambering gingerly over the wreckage, lest their candles go out. The streets were in total darkness, since lamps were not yet working on the outskirts of the city, and the little processions made pockets of light among the ruins, the wavering candles giving a gleam of genuine gold to the paper crowns and throwing long, weird shadows on the mountains of debris through which the Bethlehem pilgrims wended their way. Here the sharp, corrosive smell of conflagration left behind by the bombs that had destroyed the houses still lingered in the air and intruded itself into the subdued, homelike odor of Christmas.

On the last square that the command car passed before leaving Munich, a gigantic Christmas tree, ablaze with electric lights, had been set up. In America, or in the peaceful countries of Europe, such trees for the homeless and poor would themselves have been deserted and abandoned on Christmas Eve; no one in those countries was so poor and homeless as to be forced outdoors for light and companionship on the night before Christmas. Here men, women, and children gathered in the open to wish each other *Fröhliche Weihnachten* and even to exchange meager gifts wrapped in newspapers. The crowd did not seem sullen, depressed, or hopeless. In the light of the common tree, everyone appeared to share a common buoyancy and exhilaration.

When they reached the camp and entered Stroud's living quarters, all four—Thompson too had been invited to share in the Christmas dinner—were greeted by Sergeant Parker.

"Please make yourselves at home," he said gallantly to the ladies. He could not suppress a shout of welcome as he saw Thompson. "Well, look who's here!" he said. "Santa Claus himself. What did you bring me for Christmas?" Peter was about to take off his coat, when Parker stopped him. "The Colonel's taking a look around the camp, Major. He ought to be over in Barracks 8 about now. He wants you to join him."

Peter crossed the big, deserted courtyard of the camp and headed for Barracks 8. As he approached, he heard the sound of music. Strong, full-throated voices were singing "Stille Nacht, Heilige

Nacht." He paused outside the barracks and listened, singing the carol softly to himself.

The door opened and Stroud came out. He saw Peter at once. "Hello, there," he said. "Merry Christmas. Good to see you."

"Merry Christmas, John," said Peter.

"I'm not much of a host," Stroud said. "I don't even greet my guests when they arrive. And I still can't celebrate. I have to take another look around the camp. Do you want to come along?" He added anxiously, "I hope our turkey doesn't burn meanwhile."

They went slowly through the alleys between the barracks. From time to time Stroud stopped and looked through the windows. "Everything seems to be going all right," he said, but there was a vague anxiety in his voice.

"You sound depressed," Peter observed. "Is something wrong?"

"No, everything seems to be in order," Stroud replied quickly. "If anything's wrong, it's with me. I'm not used to celebrating Christmas among prisoners."

He looks old and tired, Peter thought. "You probably wish you were home celebrating with your family," he said.

"Perhaps," Stroud replied meditatively. "Perhaps not. I don't know, Peter. The older I get, the less sure I am of anything."

They were now walking along the barbed-wire barrier around the camp. When they passed one of the manned watchtowers Stroud shouted a greeting to the sentry. He knew almost all of them by name.

"Merry Christmas, Kelly," he called out. "When are you being relieved?"

"In fifteen minutes, Colonel."

"Good. There's a second serving of turkey in the mess hall, you know."

"I know, Colonel. Thanks."

"Are all your lights burning up there?"

"All but one, sir."

"Well, good night, son."

"Good night, Colonel. Merry Christmas."

They turned and went toward Stroud's quarters.

"When is the camp being closed down, John?" Peter asked.

"They're talking about the end of February. I'm working on my final report. It'll probably be finished the end of next month."

"Any new arrests in the murder case?"

"No. Just those seven, up to now. They're being taken to Berlin day after tomorrow."

They stood for a moment in the center of the courtyard. The singing now came from all sides. And as the strains of the "Hallelujah" resounded through the camp, one chorus intermingling and clashing with another, Peter had the feeling that there was something ominous in the sound. Can't these German soldiers sing even the "Hallelujah" without making it sound like a battle song? he asked himself. Their Christmas anthems ring out like "We're Sailing Against England." But he said nothing.

As they neared Stroud's quarters the Colonel stopped again. "Wanda is here for the first time since the day I met her," he said. "How many months ago is that? It was summer. Almost half a year." He turned suddenly to Peter and gripped his arm. "Whatever happens to me," he continued, "I know you'll never leave her in the lurch. I'll always provide for her, Peter. But I don't know what I'd do if you two weren't here."

Peter tried to smile reassuringly, as if everything were quite simple.

"Don't worry, John," he said. "She's in good hands."

Neither of them was wearing a hat. Large sparkling snowflakes covered their hair.

"We're beginning to look like snow men." Peter laughed. But again it struck him that Stroud looked like an old man.

⇒ 51 ⇐

PETER had looked at the clock a few minutes before. It was exactly ten when the first shot rang out.

They were all a little tired, especially the women. Wanda, Maria, and Helga were not used to heavy meals. There had been tomato juice, consommé, turkey with mashed potatoes and gravy, cranberry sauce and peas, a salad, ice cream, cake, and coffee. Stroud had embellished the feast with several bottles of excellent Moselle.

After dinner they had turned on the lights of the Christmas tree that stood in Stroud's office. Each had packed his gifts so that they looked as numerous as possible; since there was little of any worth to be bought, quantity had to take the place of quality. Nevertheless, Stroud had managed to ransack the PX for suitable gifts for Wanda—a bright, patterned sweater, a pocketbook, a scarf, and a variety of candies, which he had saved from his ration for weeks. Peter's gifts were more lavish, since he had been able to make purchases of clothing and trinkets for Maria and Helga in New York. The men were not left empty-handed either. In the past two weeks Maria had traveled repeatedly to Munich under every possible pretense and had searched for hours for any trifle that could pass as a gift, returning triumphantly when she had found something and locking it up as if it were precious booty. One afternoon Maria had taken Wanda to Mother Nebenzahl, an old woman who dealt in antiques, and had persuaded the old lady not only to part with a silver tobacco box, but also to let Wanda carry off several rare and obscure maps, which became prized additions to Stroud's collection. From America Peter brought a wristwatch for Thompson, while Thompson, to everyone's merriment, also surprised Peter with a timepiece. It was an automobile clock that Thompson had "liberated" somewhere and which he had paid a Munich artisan to build into a wooden casing so that it could be used on a desk.

The women were as sleepy as children after the excitement of distributing the gifts, and Thompson was so drowsy that he dozed off while playing blackjack with Parker in the next room.

The table had been cleared off, and the three women, Stroud and Peter sat in the Colonel's living-room. They listened to the radio and spoke little. The women opened and reopened their packages, taking the gifts out to fondle and examine as if they were rarities of fabulous worth.

"I've got a bad conscience," said Wanda, working the shiny catch on her new handbag. "I should be in the camp with the others. Very few were invited out for the evening."

"It must have been a sad celebration," Maria said. "I'm sure the prisoners here in camp are having a much better one."

Wanda gave a little sigh but said nothing.

Peter looked at the clock. It was a few minutes before ten.

"We'll have to leave here at eleven if we want to get to midnight Mass on time," he said.

"Too bad we can't all go to Mass in the village," Maria remarked. "It's so pretty—the little church in the snow, and the farmers and their wives in their best costumes."

At that moment they heard the first shot. Nobody spoke. They all sat up rigidly and listened. It had sounded like the cracking of a whip magnified a hundred times. It was now so quiet that the heavy breathing of Thompson in the next room could be heard.

"What was that?" Stroud finally said, standing up.

He had not reached the door when the second shot came. After a pause that could not have lasted more than five or six seconds, a whole series of reports rang out. It sounded as if the shooting was coming from all sides.

Stroud hurriedly strapped on his revolver. "Stay here with the women," he said to Peter and went out.

The noise increased. Thompson came into the room and yawned. "Who's doin' all the shootin'?" he said, stretching.

"Somebody's having fun," Peter answered. He took Thompson aside and whispered, "Better get out your pistol, and keep your eye on the door."

"Right!" Thompson nodded. The whole thing seemed to please him immensely. He turned to Parker, who stood blinking in the doorway between the living-room and the office. "Hey, Parker. Get that M-1 I saw in the next room. Maybe you'll finally get a chance to shoot a gun. I never did see one of you typewriter jockeys with a gun in your hand."

"Horse feathers," said Parker. "Somebody's just trigger-happy." But he went and brought back the rifle, just in case. "A couple of the guards must've gone and gotten themselves stiff," he muttered petulantly.

Peter immediately took up the idea. "Too much Christmas punch," he said. But he knew that the shooting could not be accounted for by drunken sentries. The noise increased steadily. At least a dozen rifles were being fired.

The women were standing together in a corner. They were pale but had themselves under control. Helga, who had been opening a box of candy, was pressing the box to her breast. She was like a little girl afraid that her doll would be broken.

"Have you got a revolver for me?" Wanda asked Peter.

"There's a .45 in the top desk-drawer," Parker answered. "Can you handle a .45?" He talked no more of drunken guards.

Wanda did not bother to answer, but got the gun from the next room. She released the safety catch. She knew exactly what to do with a .45.

Peter said as calmly as he could, "I'll go outside a moment and see what's happening."

Maria took a few quick steps to his side. He smiled at her reassuringly. She said nothing.

As he stepped out into the cold the shooting seemed to die down. For a few minutes it was still.

"Somebody's run out of ammunition," said Thompson, who had followed him out.

Parker, upholding the valor of the Army clerks, soon joined them. "Maybe somebody thought we needed fireworks for Christmas," he said.

Instantly a renewed burst of firing broke out, stronger than before. Until now the shots had come from a distance and only the report of the rifles was audible. Now the shooting was coming closer, and the whistling of bullets could be heard.

Peter went back into the room.

"Get away from the windows," he said. "Down on the floor."

He turned out the light. Thompson felt his way into the next room and put out the lamp there also. It was almost pitch dark in the room; a little light came through the windows from outside.

Peter knelt down next to Maria for a moment. He took her hand and pressed it. "Don't be afraid," he said. "It will be over soon."

"What's happening?" she whispered, trying to hide the trembling of her voice. She spoke as if Peter must surely know the answer to any question she might ask.

"I don't know," he replied. "A little row of some kind."

The lights of the camp that had been coming through the windows went out. Now nothing could be seen.

Then they heard a voice outside shouting, "Major Olden!"

Peter went to the door and opened it cautiously. He made out the white helmet of an MP and stepped outside. "Here's Major Olden," he said. "What's up?"

"The Colonel wants you to come," the MP said. "He sent me over with two men to stand guard here."

"Where is the Colonel?"

"Just to the right of the main entrance. They're having trouble over there. Somebody turned the prisoners loose."

Peter did not understand at once.

"What prisoners?" he asked.

"The seven who killed that guy and strung him up."

Peter stepped quickly back into the barracks. "Everything's all right," he said. "John is having some trouble, but it will soon be over. He's sent a guard of MP's. The barracks are well protected now. I'm going over to help John."

"Has something happened to him?" Wanda asked. She no longer lay on the floor, but stood next to Peter. Her voice shook.

"No. He's okay."

"Can I come along?"

"Don't be foolish, Wanda." He turned to Parker. "Give me the M-1. You take my pistol."

As he opened the door to go out again, he felt somebody next to him. "Where are you going, Thompson?" he asked.

"Hell, I'm goin' along," said Thompson. "You ain't leavin' me behind to miss all the fun, are you?"

"Okay. Come on."

They ran across the courtyard. Thompson said, "That's all we need in this rumpus—a Polish Wac yet. As if our own Wacs ain't had enough."

"Duck," said Peter. "Never mind the chatter."

"Anyway, the searchlights are still workin'," said Thompson a moment later.

"It can't be so bad," Peter said. The searchlights were again sweeping the area at regular intervals.

"Where's the shootin' comin' from?" Thompson wanted to know.

It was hard to tell, but the shots were evidently not directed at the courtyard. Only a stray bullet whined past.

The two men ran along the barbed wire. The lights in the barracks were all out.

"The fighting seems to be going on at the main entrance," Peter said.

"Our car is there," Thompson remarked. "The Krauts'll shoot holes in my tires, sure as hell."

They came out from behind a row of barracks and reached a point from which the main entrance was visible. To the right of the entrance a jeep was burning. Behind it crouched two MP's, firing into the darkness. Peter and Thompson, coming up behind the MP's, could not make out what they were firing at.

Before they reached the jeep Peter saw Stroud. He was standing with two other officers next to the gate.

"John!" Peter called.

"Over here, Peter," Stroud shouted back.

Stroud had a rifle in his hand. His face was drawn.

"They've liberated the murderers," he said. "They overpowered the MP's and probably killed them. They must have plenty of weapons. Now they're fighting their way through the guards toward the gate. They want to break out. They ought to be here any minute."

"How many of them are there?" Peter asked.

"At least four hundred."

"The sons-of-bitches," Thompson commented.

"Altogether I've got forty men here," Stroud said.

"Have you phoned for reinforcements?"

"All the telephone lines are cut. They learned just which ones to cut while they were working on the wiring for the Christmas trees. But I've sent two jeeps into the city. We ought to get reinforcements before long."

"Yes," said Peter skeptically, "if all the boys aren't off celebrating Christmas somewhere."

They spoke no more. The rebellious prisoners seemed suddenly to materialize from all sides.

Peter hastily attempted to estimate the strategical situation. Only a comparatively small space separated the gate from seven or eight rows of barracks. The mutineers appeared in the passages between the barracks in groups of six or seven at a time. They must have come from the inner area of the camp, slinking along the walls of the barracks. It was curious that they did not shoot, although they obviously had weapons. They made their way toward the entrance slowly and deliberately. They moved forward in a peculiar, snaking like rhythm, warily bent over, almost like a group of dancers waiting in the wings for a cue from the orchestra leader before bursting out onto the stage to join in a sweeping ballet.

Peter recognized this movement. "They've either got hand grenades or flame-throwers," he said to Stroud. "I wonder what they're waiting for."

Stroud, whose appraisal of the situation was similar to Peter's, replied, "They're probably waiting until the first one of each group reaches the last barracks."

In the distance, from the inner area of the camp, shots could still be heard.

"What are the women doing?" Stroud asked softly.

"Everything quiet when I left," Peter told him.

The shots inside the camp died out. The groups between the barracks kept snaking slowly forward.

And then an astonishing thing occurred. Almost simultaneously, as if at the signal of a stage director, dozens of barracks doors flew open. Out of them poured scores of prisoners who streamed toward the open space between the barracks and the gate. They carried neither guns nor hand grenades. They were unarmed. They simply left their barracks and walked at normal speed toward the open space. Many had their hands nonchalantly in their pockets. They almost seemed to be promenaders out for an evening stroll.

"Back in the barracks!" shouted the guards. "*Rein in die Barracken!*"

No one paid any attention. The promenaders kept coming as if they had not heard. But they gave no indication of taking any hostile action or of rushing the gate.

A little MP lieutenant next to Peter breathed in relief. "They've changed their minds about breaking out," he said.

Peter ignored him. He indicated the two watchtowers on either side of the entrance.

"Are there machine guns up there?" he asked Stroud.

"Yes."

"Then for God's sake, tell them to shoot!"

Stroud turned and stared at him. "Shoot into that crowd? Why?"

"I know that maneuver," Peter answered. "That's a street-fighting trick, German style. Don't you see what those men between the barracks are waiting for? They've sent that crowd out first, relying on you not to shoot into it. As soon as the crowd is thick enough, all hell is going to break loose."

"I'm not sure of that," Stroud said. "I can't order machine guns to fire at random into unarmed men."

"For God's sake, John!" Peter tried to control himself. "Can I mount the tower, in case of trouble?"

"Yes," said Stroud. His voice was now hard and sharp, that of an officer in complete command. "But there'll be no shooting without orders from me, understand?"

"Yes, sir," said Peter, furious.

The guards kept shouting "Back to the barracks!" in English and German, but the mass of prisoners in the open space grew steadily larger. Not one turned back to the barracks.

His foot on the ladder, Peter called to Stroud, "Can I at least threaten them, Colonel?"

"Yes."

He climbed to the top of the tower and looked around. It struck him as incredibly bizarre that the lights of the little Christmas tree on the platform were still burning. The tree, he thought, must be on a circuit of its own that had been overlooked. He took out a knife and cut the wire.

"It's not necessary to provide targets for sharpshooters," he said to the sergeant huddled behind the machine gun. "And take off that white helmet. Let's not make it too easy for them."

From the inner camp the sound of firing was renewed. Peter peered into the dark. Battle and duty and heroism suddenly seemed to him as peculiar and out of place as the white helmet of the sergeant. What am I doing here? he asked himself. Why did John ask me to come? Whose camp is it, anyway—his or mine? Where was Stroud's barracks? How close was it to the shooting? He felt a cramp around his heart, and sweat trickled from under his armpits. I should have stayed with her, he thought.

He cupped his hands around his mouth. "Get back into the barracks," he bellowed in a Prussian accent. "Anyone remaining outside will be shot."

A few of the prisoners hesitated and turned back. Encouraged, he shouted again, "Zurück in die Baracken! Alles zurück!"

His last words were drowned in a sudden fury of noise. Th

groups that had been lurking between the barracks burst out into the throng, and hand grenades exploded among the MP's deployed around the gate.

Peter hesitated for only a moment. He tried to call down to Stroud, but he saw that the Colonel was engaged in rallying his men to keep the gate under steady fire.

Orders or no orders, Peter thought. He turned to the guard. "Let's go, Sergeant! I'll shoot. You handle the belt."

In an instant the open space was under machine-gun fire.

After two or three minutes Peter paused. The insurgent prisoners had taken the tower on the other side of the entrance under rifle fire. They were barely a dozen yards from the gate. He lifted his head cautiously. Still lying on his stomach, he tried to peer over to the other tower. During a momentary silence in the explosion of the hand grenades he could hear that the other machine gun was not being fired.

"Damn!" he said. "With both towers firing we could command every foot of the entrance." The noise below broke out again, and he could hardly hear his own voice. He shouted into the sergeant's ear, "Can you handle this alone for a while?" The sergeant nodded.

Peter climbed rapidly down the ladder. A bullet went buzzing past his ear. On his stomach he crawled across the entrance toward the other tower. In the grenade smoke he caught a glimpse of Stroud and Thompson kneeling side by side and firing. Good old John, he thought. Good old John, who doesn't want to shoot any innocent men.

Halfway up the ladder Peter called up to the soldier in the tower, "Fire! Start shooting!" Then he lay behind the gun, and the soldier took the belt.

"Christ!" said the soldier, feeding the belt into the gun. "I been waitin' for the word to fire. I been itchin' to let those bastards have it."

The two machine guns kept firing steadily for five or six minutes. Peter listened. Silence had come suddenly. Then Peter knew that the battle had been won. The insurgents had found it hopeless to try to get through the cross-fire of the two machine guns, reinforced by the rifle fire from the MP's on the ground. They had begun to retreat. The leaders of the break, once they were sure that nobody was going to get through the gate, apparently realized what it would mean to be captured on the battlefield. There ensued a frenzied scramble to get back into the barracks before it could be determined who had taken part in the revolt.

The rebellion, skillfully planned and coolly executed until the last moment, disintegrated into chaos. Rifles and hand grenades were tossed aside in the rout. The prisoners jammed the alleyways between the barracks, crushed each other against the walls, stumbled, and fell. Others trampled on them or leaped across them with gymnastic or dancelike movements of involuntary grace. They surged against the doorways as if storming the barracks; their bodies blocked the entrances, and door casings splintered and cracked under the pressure. They fought among themselves to get inside, to force their way between the protecting walls of the barracks, which, a few minutes before, they had been risking their lives to escape.

Then there spread over the camp a silence that Peter recognized. He greeted it as a familiar friend. It was a silence known only to those who have participated in battle. This quiet was the more profound because it still held the after-echo of explosions, the hint of whining bullets, and the suggestion of dying groans. It seemed to Peter that even the snowflakes were now falling more softly and cautiously, as if not to disturb this deep and solemn peace. No sound broke the stillness until, from a distance, there came the approaching scream of the sirens of the riot platoon from Munich.

"Well, how is it? You all right?" Peter asked the soldier next to him. He had not seen the boy's face until now.

"Nothin' wrong with me. How about you?"

"Okay."

"A nice Christmas the bastards gave us," said the soldier as Peter prepared to descend the ladder.

Right, it's Christmas sure enough, thought Peter. The tricks death plays with time. Something else that nobody knows unless he's been through it. Wherever death comes close, it breathes a breath of eternity on the lives it doesn't end. Even those who stay alive die a little. Those it doesn't kill, it ages; and that has nothing to do with the fear of death either. Those it approaches but does not touch think of yesterday as years ago. Christmas? It seemed to Peter that the Christmas celebration in Stroud's quarters had taken place in the remote and half-forgotten past. Only the urgency to see whether anything had happened to Maria made the present seem important and alive.

At the foot of the tower he drew a long deep breath. He was warm. In the air there was a wholesome, cold freshness. Somebody seized his arm. Stroud was standing next to him.

"Sorry, John," said Peter. "It had to be done."

Stroud said only, "Thanks."

Peter could not see his face clearly. How many years has he aged in the last few hours? he asked himself. He looked at his watch. It was not yet midnight.

"Peter," Stroud said, "something pretty bad has happened. Come with me."

"Maria!" Peter cried in instant terror. His voice sounded as if two strong hands were closing around his throat.

"No, Thompson," Stroud said. "I don't know if we can pull him through. The hand grenades. He was next to me. He covered me when one went off, almost as if he were inviting death."

They began to run toward the barracks. They paid no attention to the armored cars of the riot platoon that came roaring through the gate.

Thompson lay on a bed in the first barracks to the left off the open space opposite the entrance. An infuriated MP had herded the prisoners into a far corner of the barracks and was keeping them there at gun point. Captain Miller, the camp physician, was bending over Thompson.

Peter kneeled next to the bed. He asked softly, "Can anything be done for him, Captain?"

"Yes," said Captain Miller. "We can hang the rotten sons-of-bitches who killed him." He covered Thompson's face with a GI blanket.

Peter remained kneeling at the bed for a moment with folded hands. Then he stood up and painfully pulled back the blanket. The doctor beamed his flashlight into the dead man's face.

Dirty Thompson, Peter thought. Dirty Thompson. He repeated the words over and over to himself, as if the derisive nickname could somehow call his friend back to life.

But the man who lay there in the rumpled uniform covered with powder stains and blood was not Dirty Thompson. His face, in which creases and crinkles used to make labyrinthine patterns, was completely smooth. The broad, heavy mouth had undergone a refinement. Around it there seemed to play a smile, good-natured, understanding, and a little mocking. It was as if Thompson had nothing whatever to complain about, except perhaps the blood that came from a corner of his mouth. The blood was still trickling slowly down his chin as if intending to live on after the body was cold. There was something ghastly about the living blood on the dead body.

Peter took out his handkerchief and wiped the blood away. As he did so, the full realization that Dirty Thompson was dead came to him for the first time. Until now he had half expected that Thompson would move when touched, that he would grumble, or say "Thanks," or simply turn over and go on sleeping. There was something desperately docile, defenseless, and unnatural in the patience with which Thompson allowed Peter to wipe the blood from his face. Thompson lay there and let it happen—but being alive meant not letting things happen to oneself. Why don't you move, Thompson? thought Peter. Why don't you mutter something about those bastards, those sons-of-bitches who hurt you, those goddam Krauts? It's high time you began cursing, and if you'd only curse properly you'd be alive. Come on, Thompson. Why don't you swear, now, when it's so necessary?

Thompson did not curse. There was a gentle, friendly peace on his face. It was as if he wanted to say that the dullest of the dead was cleverer than the brightest of the living. As if he wanted to say, Don't worry about me, Major. I'm okay.

From outside came the rumble of the armored cars, the sound of running footsteps and bellowed commands. Peter looked up, startled. He said, "I'd like to ask permission to take Thompson with me."

Stroud nodded.

Outside, in front of the barracks, the doctor took his departure. He had much to do.

"Sorry I couldn't do anything for him, Major," he said. "He must have meant a lot to you."

"Yes, he did."

The Captain had already started to go, when he turned to Peter again. "By the way," he said. "Just before he died he was talking deliriously about some woman. Dora or Doris, some name like that. Maybe his wife."

'Yes," said Peter. "Doris. His wife."

➤➤ 52 ◄◄

ALL through the auto ride Stroud had been silent, and Peter did not want to intrude on the brooding of his friend. They were on their way to an ancient castle on the Starnberger See which served as headquarters for General Aldington. News of the revolt in PW Camp Special B had reached General Lowell, who was spending a brief Christmas leave with his friend Aldington. On Christmas morning Stroud and Peter had received orders to report at once to the castle.

They were driving through the snow-laden forest. Stroud's silence, which had lasted almost an hour, finally became intolerable to Peter. He knew what was going on inside his friend. He said, "There's no sense tormenting yourself, John. It wasn't your fault."

"Seven dead and thirty-two wounded," Stroud said. "Four MP's and Thompson killed, and eleven others wounded."

"That's war."

"The war has been over for eight months."

"That's just the mistake. The brass thinks the war is over. America thinks so. But the war goes on. It will go on for years."

"Still, I can't figure out how it happened. On Christmas Eve!"

"On Christmas Eve the ovens kept burning at Auschwitz and Ohrdruf and Mauthausen and Buchenwald too. Did you expect piety from Nazis?"

"No, but the whole thing is inexplicable to me. What did they hope to gain by it?"

"They hoped to set the killers free, and they came within a hair of doing it too. I don't see anything remarkable about that. There's hardly a prison in the world that the inmates haven't tried to break out of at one time or another. And these prisoners had little to lose."

There was a note of irritation in Stroud's voice as he said, "You don't understand me. Even you don't understand. You talk about the camp as if it were an ordinary jail. That's the whole point. My camp was no Alcatraz or San Quentin."

"A prison is a prison. Wherever there's a barrier between you and freedom, that's a prison. It makes no difference whether the barrier is barbed wire or stone walls twenty feet high."

"I must admit you've said that right along."

"The important thing now is whether Military Government is willing to learn from the revolt. Willing to learn the right lessons, I mean. I'm afraid MG will draw only the obvious conclusion."

"That the Germans are incorrigible? It's hard to come to any other conclusion."

"Yes, if you use the test-tube method of judging people. If you believe that American democracy can be exported in cans. Democracy is a fruit that grows out of the ground. Dehydrated, it tastes sour." He cupped his hands and bent over to light a cigarette.

"Funny," Stroud said meditatively. "Do you remember Langhoff, the prisoner I told you about? He once said the same thing to me."

"And you didn't believe him."

"I never regarded democracy as something to be exported in cans. I understand democracy better than that." He was trying to suppress his agitation, but his long fingers drummed nervously on his knee. "So there just isn't any way," he said. "Your method failed once before, after World War I. We tried then to let the Germans build their own democracy, and look what happened."

Peter sighed. "Those eternal historical parallels!" he said. "As if there were any such thing. Conditions are by no means the same now as they were in 1918. Then the Germans fought in France. Germany hardly knew what war meant. She did not feel her Army had been defeated in the field. The question of guilt was only touched upon, never disposed of. The Germans believed their country had been conquered, but not their ideology. I could give you dozens of differences."

Why did I begin talking about Germany and democracy and MG policies? Peter asked himself. We're on our way to an extremely painful session with the General. He admired Stroud for being able to carry on a theoretical discussion at all, under the circumstances. "I'm curious about what General Lowell will have to say to us," Peter speculated.

"I know what he'll have to say."

"What?"

"He'll tell me I'm going to be court-martialed."

"He can't do that."

"Why can't he?"

"Because you're not to blame. Security was up to requirements. The prisoners were guarded. The searchlights were functioning, and there were guards on the towers."

"Those are logical arguments," Stroud said wearily. "The Army isn't logical. The camp was the General's idea. Now it may cost him his head. He needs a scapegoat."

"If that's the case, John, you'll just have to put up a stiff defense. After all, you did everything you could and everything that was required of you. You suppressed the revolt."

"Let's not fool ourselves. You suppressed the revolt."

"Nonsense! In five more minutes you would have done the same thing."

"Five more minutes would have been too late."

Stroud's hands now rested quietly in his lap. He succeeded in smiling. He said, "It's become a habit with you to rescue me, ever since the day we met. And still, I'll never understand you completely."

Peter grinned. "Why, I'm the simplest fellow in the world."

"Hardly," said Stroud. "I think I'll have to make a confession."

"You'd better hurry. We're almost there."

"I've always suspected you of being sympathetic to the Germans. You understand what I mean. I never believed that your sympathy for the Germans kept you from doing your duty as an American soldier. But just the same—well, I don't have to explain. And then, last night, you mounted the tower and fired a machine gun into that mob of German prisoners."

"John, you don't know enough about my youth," Peter answered pensively. "I spent my youth in Germany, remember. I learned that there is no answer to force but superior force."

"But that flies in the face of every principle of our democracy. It offends our deepest convictions."

Peter made a gesture of dismissal. He asked, "Do you think they've heard of Maria being in the camp?"

"I have no idea."

"That could make a lot of trouble for you. Be sure not to say that you invited her. I simply brought her along."

"I'll say nothing of the sort. I asked her, and I'll take the responsibility for it."

"John, don't act like a hero. They can't do anything to me. I can always find an excuse. But you're in a spot."

"How about Wanda?" Stroud asked. He could not keep the anxiety out of his voice. "I had a woman in my quarters when the revolt broke out—"

"Wanda is a Pole. You had a right to invite her."

In the distance the outlines of the castle became visible.

Peter said quickly, "The important thing is that you know what you want, and insist on getting it."

"But I don't want anything."

"Oh, yes. You want to deliver your final report and then go home. In four weeks you can be back in civilian clothes. In two weeks. Think of everything that's waiting for you there—your family, your profession. Compare your case with mine. The big difference is that you have a second line of defense—the most important thing in life."

"I'm afraid I don't understand."

"I haven't time to explain now. We'll talk about it later if you like."

The road made a bend out of the woods, and suddenly the tremendous mass of Ludwigs Castle loomed above them. It was more of a fortress than a castle, with immense stone battlements, soaring towers, steeply slanted pinnacles, and jagged crenelations. For all its massiveness, it recalled those toy castles that children play with in nurseries. Numerous kings of Bavaria had resided in it, and here the mad King Ludwig of Wittelsbach had lived until the day he walked out into the lake and drowned himself. Now Brigadier General Aldington was lord of the castle.

Nobody was quite clear as to why General Aldington should be living in the remote fortress on the lake. In the winter the road to Munich was snowed under, and ice made the last stretch, which ran along the edge of the lake, dangerous to life and limb. Trans-

porting fuel and supplies to the castle presented prodigious difficulties. But General Aldington was from a small town in Missouri
and had never recovered from the fact that he was not a West
Pointer. Upon being graduated from an obscure military academy
in the Midwest, he married a schoolteacher, who even then looked
like a general's wife. It had probably always been General Aldington's secret dream to be master of a castle, and no opportunity as
favorable as this would come again. He seized it. The innumerable
servants, the deep red rugs, the ancestral portraits, the crested
porcelain, and, not least, a superbly stocked cellar gave a feeling of
regal eminence to the professional officer who, before the war, had
been a lieutenant colonel stationed at a cavalry school in Kansas.
He was a leathery and granite-faced old soldier who treated his
officers as if they were privates and he himself a first sergeant.
Behind his back he was called "Ludwig" Aldington, although there
was nothing of the Bavarian Ludwig about him but his castle. It
was an ill omen that General Lowell heard the news of the prisoner
revolt as guest of the first American Ludwig.

General Lowell let the two officers wait a long time. They were
alone in the long, gloomy salon. Before the fireplace was an enor-
mous Christmas tree whose colored lights were the only illumination in the great room. Through the high gabled doors leading to a
balcony the wintry lake could be seen in the twilight of the dying
afternoon. Fog swirled high up as if trying to make its way into the
room. Over the house, over its brocaded tapestries, its pictures of
warlike petty princes and their ugly princesses, hung the holiday
stillness that comes only after a riotous night. The castle seemed
to be sleeping.

The silence of the two men, an oppressive, heavy silence, was
broken by a drowsy captain who summoned Major Olden to General Lowell. Stroud, who had gotten to his feet, sat down again.
First they'll examine the witness, then the accused, he thought.
He was left alone.

The memory of the day on which General Lowell had summoned him to the castle in Verdun came to him. That had been
in September. September, October, November, December—a year
and three months had passed since then. It did not seem like
fifteen months, but like fifteen eternities. It seemed to Stroud that
he had aged more in those fifteen months than in the preceding

fifteen years. Time, he thought, cannot be deceived. If the experiences of ten years are compressed into one, it isn't surprising if a man ages ten years too. Living and existing are two different things, he knew. A man could exist for a hundred years and acquire no skill in living. I, he thought, was unskilled in living. Peter would not have aged; he was on familiar terms with life. A man can't begin to get on familiar terms with life at the age of fifty-three.

An hour passed before Peter returned. It was now dark and chilly in the salon. The early moonlight that came in through the balcony doors was cold, as if its beams had traveled over miles and miles of snow. The moonbeams slanted through the room like endlessly long icicles. The princes and princesses seemed frozen in their frames.

As Peter entered the warm light from the next room flooded into the salon. Peter was alone. "Why are you sitting here in the dark?" he asked.

"I've been dozing."

"The General wants to talk to you." He lowered his voice. "It's not so bad," he said.

General Lowell received Stroud in Aldington's study. For a moment Stroud thought that Lowell was alone, but then he saw that General Aldington was seated at a little table in the background. He had a magnum of French cognac on the table before him and was smoking a long pipe with an elaborately carved ivory bowl. He did not get up when Stroud entered.

General Lowell indicated a chair that stood in front of the heavy old desk on which his papers were spread. Stroud sat down.

"I received your report this morning," the General said. "Since then I've had additional information from the provost marshal. I have also taken a statement from Major Olden. Have you anything further to add to your report of this morning?"

"No," Stroud answered hesitantly. "My report of course deals only with yesterday's events. I might, perhaps, want to add something relating the uprising to what has occurred in the camp during the past year."

The General coughed. "That doesn't interest us at the moment," he said. "So far nothing in our reports indicates that you were at fault, Colonel. That is naturally not final. The incident will be thoroughly probed. The investigation is not in my hands. General

Aldington has been assigned to gather the evidence and draw up recommendations."

General Aldington puffed on his pipe and said nothing. Stroud also remained silent.

"Tomorrow afternoon," General Lowell continued, "I will hold a press conference in my office. I would like you to avoid any possible mistakes in your answers. I think you understand me."

"Not entirely," Stroud said dryly.

"We must see that the press understands the significance of what has occurred."

The questioning look remained on Stroud's face. He saw that General Aldington was watching him.

General Lowell stood up, as was his habit when discoursing. He was always in motion while speaking. As he neared the end of his remarks, he also approached nearer and nearer to his chair. When he sat down, it was like putting a period at the end of his final sentence.

"This camp," he said, "has performed a great service. It has demonstrated to the world the urgent necessity for the continued occupation of Germany. The German people are not capable of self-government. Those of us who created this camp have been aware of this fact for some time. We had to prove it to the public. Unfortunately this proof has cost the lives of five American soldiers. But it can be said that these soldiers died in a worthy cause, when one considers what the consequences could have been, and the lives it would have cost later had this proof not been forthcoming. I believe that this view of the matter is clear and unassailable. We can so present it to the press."

Stroud hesitated a moment before he said, "I agree that it would be gratifying if the American public were made to realize that we must occupy Germany for a long time to come. Nevertheless, I believe that the conclusions to be drawn from yesterday's uprising are not so simple—"

"The conclusions are simple," General Lowell interrupted. He emphasized the "are."

"The press will want to question me not only about the uprising, but also about my experiences at the camp through the past year," Stroud pointed out. He was no longer inclined to give up without a defense.

"Your experiences were likewise quite simple," General Lowell said. "Poison murders. A fatal stabbing. Acquittal of a killer by his fellow prisoners. The mutilation and murder of an anti-Nazi. And finally the uprising."

"All quite true," Stroud agreed. "But also, an authentically democratic newspaper. Excellent instruction and attendance at lectures. Democracy preached from the pulpit on Sundays—"

General Lowell interrupted again. "All calculated to lull us into a sense of security. Nothing more. We were not deceived. I will make that clear to the public." His tone brooked no contradiction. Stroud felt that any further argument would be futile.

The General was walking up and down again. "The camp," he said, "will be closed down immediately. The prisoners will be turned over to the French Military Government authorities. We have received a request for fifteen thousand prisoners. The French need them for the Saar mines. How many have you in the camp?"

"Eight thousand, one hundred twelve."

"Good. They will be shipped off before New Year's."

"Is this intended as a punitive measure?"

"Naturally." The General's tone was brusque.

"Not all the prisoners participated in the uprising. About fifteen hundred were directly involved, another fifteen hundred indirectly," Stroud said. He was surprised himself that he had the audacity to offer these facts.

General Aldington, who had been sitting silently in his corner, stood up. He came up to the desk with a glass of cognac in his hand. He had a squat, bullet head and a Prussian haircut. A network of tiny blue veins clearly visible in his reddened face gave it the appearance of a colored detail map. He walked with the stiffness of an old horseman who does not bandage his gout but tries to ride it off in the saddle. He stood before Stroud.

"General Lowell is a patient man," he said. "I hear he is a friend of yours, Colonel. I am not a friend of yours. I don't think I'd care to be. And I am sure that I have no interest in your political views. Is that clear?"

"Yes, sir," said Stroud.

General Aldington smiled. His smile was more unpleasant than his anger. He went slowly back to his corner. With his back to Stroud he asked, "Have a cognac, Colonel?"

"No thank you, sir."

A prolonged silence followed. Finally Stroud asked, "May I go, General?"

"Yes," said General Lowell. He waited until Stroud stood up. "Naturally you are being relieved of your command, John. I have put Colonel Talbot in charge of the camp. He will take over from you this evening. If General Aldington has no objections, your travel orders can be cut the day after tomorrow."

Stroud considered whether he should make a reply. Don Quixote and the windmill, he thought. There's no sense to it. Shall I recall our meeting in Verdun to the General? Shall I remind him that back in Spokane he insisted I come to Europe on his staff? Oddly he had no hard feelings for the General. He felt almost sympathetic toward him. General Aldington had been put in charge of the investigation. Aldington had only one star, while Lowell had two. It was not a direct affront, since Aldington was not investigating General Lowell's activities but only the prisoner revolt. But Lowell nevertheless must know which way the wind was blowing. He was afraid of the Military Governor. He was afraid of Aldington. He was afraid of the press. Stroud felt that General Lowell was afraid of him too, afraid that Stroud would stand on their friendship, that he would remind the General of the past, of his own words when he put Stroud in charge of the camp. You don't have to be afraid of me, Joe, Stroud thought. He said, "Do you want me to retain my rank in the National Guard?"

General Lowell did not notice the ironic undertone. "Of course, of course," he said almost gratefully. "Why not?"

Stroud saluted. He was nearly to the door when he heard General Aldington's voice calling after him. "Would you care to stay for supper, Colonel? No offense, you know. Glad to have you."

The lord of the castle, Stroud thought. The stern but gracious lord of the castle. "No, thank you, sir."

Peter was waiting for him. They walked together to the courtyard. The night was huge and clear. In the moonlight the towers were ghostly white.

"I wonder if it's haunted," Stroud said.

"Only when General Aldington has house guests," Peter said. "Then he probably permits haunting from twelve to one, sharp."

They stomped through the snow to the car. When they sat back wrapped in their blankets, Stroud said, "They threw me out."

"What of it? Other people have lost bigger jobs."

The car went slowly over the twisting road that led to the lake. The lake lay there in the moonlight, dead and white, as if under a shroud.

Stroud said nothing. He was no longer thinking of the camp, the uprising, the interview with the generals. All that seemed long ago. Now there was nothing in him but an ungovernable desire for warmth, a warmth that he could not even define. He did not know whether it was the warmth of a room he longed for, or of a woman's body, or merely a warmth around his heart. Wanda seemed so close that he could reach out and lay his hand upon her breast, but he was not sure that it was she for whom he longed. Perhaps what he longed for was simply the warm security of his home in Spokane, for Emily's voice, for Jim's rambling stories of girls and flying. He ached to be away, it didn't matter where.

He heard Peter's voice talking to him. "It's high time you went home, John. Do you remember what I told you on the way here, about a second line of defense?"

"Yes. I remember."

"The most important thing in life, John, is a line to fall back on. All great captains know it. Even if they attack an unprepared enemy with hundredfold superiority, a line to fall back on is always part of the strategic plan. Only those who have no second line are crushed. All my life I've been on the offensive, without thinking of defense. For you that's not necessary. You've got a second line of defense."

Stroud had at first listened with wandering attention. Now there was interest in his voice as he said, "I think I know what you mean. My second line of defense . . ."

"Yes. Spokane. You can always fall back on Spokane." Peter's voice took on a bantering tone. "It was high time they threw you out, John. It was time you began a withdrawal according to plan, to the Spokane line."

Stroud made no reply. He looked out at the countryside. There was suddenly no longer any question as to what he had been longing for. All at once it was as if the car were winding its way through the Columbia River Valley. As if he were drawing closer and closer to Spokane. . . .

53

WANDA had been living in Maria's house for two days. Maria had made all the preparations to receive her before taking her from the DP camp. The second bedroom, which had served as a storeroom, was cleared out, cleaned, and painted. When she and Helga finished their work, the room had taken on a friendly, personal coziness.

She decided that at first Wanda would work in the barter mart. The girl who had been running the mart had gotten married and the vacancy had to be filled. The work was not strenuous and required no great mastery of German. Peter doubted the wisdom of immediately placing Wanda in a position that brought her in direct contact with the population, but Maria persuaded him. She argued that there was no point in trying to "hide" Wanda. It would be better for the village to learn at once that a Polish girl—no longer a DP, but simply a Pole—had settled there. And, in addition, Wanda would be an asset to the barter mart. The Germans would be ashamed to cheat each other in her presence. And how, Peter asked, would the village react to the fact that Wanda was pregnant? Maria had provided for that, she said. She had spread the story that Wanda was the wife of a Pole who had recently died in the DP camp.

During these days Wanda's pregnancy became visible. One saw it more definitely from day to day. Not only did her stomach grow rounder and fuller, but her whole body suddenly took on womanly contours. She did not, as many women do, carry a heavy torso on spindly legs. It was as if the child had taken possession of her whole body, as if she were not merely carrying it under her heart. Her face was transformed also. It not only assumed a fullness and color that she had lacked before, but it also became softer and more tender. The proud, challenging, and often melancholy look vanished from her eyes. It was as if the child itself were looking out through her eyes, as if a second pair of eyes, livelier and merrier than her own, were smiling behind hers.

Stroud and Wanda were sitting alone in the "good" room. They had been together there for an hour. He should have left long ago, for his plane was to take off for Washington by way of Frankfurt the next morning. He had to return to Munich that evening. His things were not yet packed and he had not said farewell to his fellow officers at the camp. But he could not bring himself to go. They sat together in the fading light and were silent for a long time.

Finally he said, "I'll have to go soon."

"I know," she said.

She doesn't cry, he thought almost reproachfully, she doesn't make a scene. It's harder this way. Everything has gone too smoothly. His conscience would be more at ease if things had gone less smoothly. If she had reproached him—or at least herself. Or if he had to leave her behind in the DP camp, unprotected and alone. He did not understand why his conscience would then have been easier; it was less difficult, after all, to bear his responsibility with the knowledge that he had left her in the hands of good reliable friends. He had been telling himself for days that everything would go off well. He had counted on her not to make trouble. He had counted on Maria and Peter. It was easy to rely on other people's "behaving well." One behaved doubly ill when one relied on the good behavior of others.

"It is better that you go soon," she said. It sounded neither ungracious nor regretful. It was a simple statement.

"Will you write to me?" he asked. He realized that he had not asked her this before.

"No," she answered.

"Why not?"

"It would do no good. It would make everything harder for you. And for me."

"And when the child comes?" He found it hard to speak.

"Peter and Maria will write you," she said. "I have talked it over with her. But do not expect long letters about the child. I do not want them to write you long letters about the child."

"Why?"

"The child belongs to me," she answered.

He recognized her tone now. She was not exasperated, but she said "The child belongs to me" in the same way as she had once, in his office, asked him, "What do you know about Poles?"

"Do you think I'm a coward?" he asked.

He regretted having said it. Why had he asked? Did he want

her to absolve him? Did he want to make it even easier for himself? Or did he want to hear that she regarded him as a coward? Did he want to stand up and part in bitterness, or was it merely that he wanted to demonstrate that he was no coward, that he would not forget her and the child?

She smiled at him. "No," she said. "You are no coward. Just a man."

He took her hand and looked into her face for a long time. He knew that any emotion would be better than the one he was feeling. It would have been better had he loved her with a tearing, tormenting, annihilating love, if he had known that he could never forget and would never be happy a day without her. Or if he no longer loved her at all, if he could convince himself that she was only a passing episode, perhaps a little more serious than most such affairs but essentially no different from the experiences of other American soldiers in Europe. But it was neither the one nor the other. It was, rather, that he was sitting opposite a memory, something long past, a great and tender love, but a love that already seemed to lie years behind him and of which he held on to nothing but a fragrance, a few letters, a sudden picture of a hotel room or a rendezvous under chestnut trees. Her face was so close to his that he could feel her breath. But he was like a man attempting to recall a dear and vanished face after many, many years, laboriously trying to put together features that have become vague, to hold on to a picture that keeps slipping away. He no longer remembered how she looked.

"Do you think you'll be happy here in the village?" he asked, to break the silence.

"Yes," she said. Then she added, "Probably."

"How will you get along with the Germans?"

"As with other people."

"You never believed that they were like other people. And my experience seems to indicate you were right."

"No, it only proves you were wrong. You believe in everybody. I believe in only a few."

He gave a little laugh. "I always knew that you were older than I."

She said, "Only a few thousand years older. Only as much as Europe is older than America."

"You'll take good care of yourself, won't you?" he asked. He knew it sounded foolish.

"Yes," she said. Her tone was neither hearty nor indifferent.

All afternoon he had been shying away from what he now forced himself to say. "You must not stay here if you don't want to. You don't have to do anything you don't want to do. I have given Peter money and authorized him to act for me."

"I know," she said. She did not say thanks. She gently took her hand from his. She stood up. He, too, got to his feet. They stood opposite each other in the semidarkness.

Now he would have liked to say that he was coming back. He was conscious that most people try to dilute a parting with a promise because they lack the courage for farewells. They hold fast to every thread, as if life itself would snap with the breaking of a single thread. They fear death, too, only because of its finality. Everything would be simple now if he said, "I know that we will see each other again." But this was exactly what he feared: to make it easier for himself. It was intolerable enough that everything was so easy. So he merely laid his hands on her shoulders.

She took a little step closer to him. She glided into his arms; his hands involuntarily stroked her back. In a voice that was the voice of her best hours, she said, "Don't you want to kiss me?"

She bent her head back, and her lips, young, full and fresh, closed over his kiss. Then she released herself from his embrace. There were no tears in her eyes. Suddenly she said, "Do you want to feel him?"

Before he could reply she took his hand and placed it on her stomach. He felt the faint beat inside her body. It was like the beating of a heart, but deep under the heart.

"He kicks," she said, smiling.

"How do you know it's a boy?"

"I know," she said.

They were the last words she spoke before he stepped out into the shadows of the Bavarian night.

54

Aᴛ ꜰɪʀsᴛ he did not want to telegraph from Washington, but then he did so anyway. He wired the exact hour of his plane's arrival in Spokane.

It was a sparkling clear January morning. The plane circled the city lazily a few times. Stroud was used to flying, and even landings usually caused him no uneasiness. But for half an hour now he had felt as if the plane would suddenly nose over and plunge to earth. Something like dread lay rolled up in a heavy ball in his stomach. He had never been quite sure as to the exact location of his heart, but now he felt that he could draw an accurate circle around it. There was a rushing in his ears. He tried over and over to concentrate on his copy of *Life*, but the words meant nothing and the pictures were blanks.

They were over Spokane. He looked out of the little window next to his seat and waited for a happy sensation of recognition. Nothing happened. Whenever he arrived home by plane he played the same little game with himself. He would pick out the suburb where he lived, then the neighborhood, and then try to spot his house. Now it was as if he were afraid that he would find the neighborhood and the house. It almost soothed him that Spokane looked exactly like every other city he had ever flown over, a confusing sea of buildings, houses, squares, and lawns.

Emily and Jim were standing at the edge of the runway, waving. He saw them at once. He first embraced his wife, then his son.

"John! You look wonderful!" Emily said.

"You too, darling," he said.

"Welcome home," said Jim. He was in civilian clothes and looked like a high-school boy.

"Where is Eleanor?" Stroud asked.

Jim was carrying his bags, and Emily was hanging on to his arm.

"I've got a little surprise for you," she said. "Imagine! Eleanor is expecting a baby!"

"And you didn't write me!" he said, trying to simulate astonishment. He was glad he did not have to look at Jim who was walking a step behind.

"No, we wanted to surprise you." Emily laughed. "Isn't it wonderful?"

"Tremendous," he said. And, not to betray that he was neither surprised nor overjoyed, he asked, "What month is she in?"

"The seventh. That's why she didn't come to the airport. She feels miserable all the time, poor girl. But she's waiting for you at home."

Outside the airport stood his comfortable green Mercury, which he had bought just before the war.

Jim took the wheel, "The old heap still goes like new," he said. "You bought her just in time, Dad. There still aren't any new ones to be had."

"My old Ford is slowly falling to pieces," Emily said. As the car moved off, she again talked about Eleanor. "Isn't it thrilling news about the baby?"

"I should say so," he said. He was almost convincing himself.

"They're all having children now," Emily went on. "Eleanor plans to go to the hospital at the same time as Henriette. Imagine, they expect their babies on practically the same day!"

He tried to recall who Henriette might be. Obviously she was somebody he ought to know. He had a vague recollection of a brunet girl in a woolly sweater with pushed-up sleeves. He did not ask about her.

He looked at Emily as she spoke. Under her fur coat she was wearing an afternoon dress of violet. A tiny hat with violet feathers crumpled into a little ball was kept in place by a narrow band of velvet looped over the back of her head. There was no gray in her hair anywhere, but its blondness seemed somewhat tired and faded. She must have gone to the beauty parlor the day before. Under the hat her hair was set in row on row of mechanically molded curls. Stroud found himself touched by her wifely, Sunday-best appearance. From the first moment he saw her, he had sensed something strange in her features. Only now did he realize what it was. She was amazingly younger than she had been in his memory. In reality she was two years younger than he, but he had been picturing her as an old woman. Now she looked fresh and gay, almost youthful. There were no wrinkles around her eyes, no slackness in her throat. He had forgotten that she was still an attractive woman. It came to him suddenly that perhaps he himself was not as old as he thought.

A little pulse of gratitude made him press her hand, a gesture to which she responded without knowing what prompted it.

They were driving through the center of town.

"The traffic's worse than ever," Jim said. "The town has grown terrifically."

"Yes," said Emily. "I'm always glad when I don't have to drive into town these days. You'll have to leave the house ten minutes earlier to get to the office in time."

"Tony was sore as the dickens that he couldn't get to the airport," Jim reported. "He was tied up at the courthouse."

Tony, Stroud thought. Anthony Doughty, his law partner. He hadn't thought of Tony for weeks, nor answered his letters for months. "How is Tony?" he asked. "I'm afraid I haven't written him in ages."

"He's been complaining about that," Emily said. "He's tickled to death you're back. He says he couldn't have kept it up much longer without you."

"What does he say about the office? How is it going?"

"A lot of little cases, but no big ones," Emily replied. "Your political friends dropped away during the war, you know. But Tony's sure they'll come back as soon as they hear you're back."

Jim was concentrating on the thick downtown traffic. "But he wants you to take a good long rest first," Jim said. "He'd like to go up to his hunting lodge with you for a couple of weeks."

"No," Stroud protested, more loudly than he had intended. "I'd rather go right back to the office tomorrow."

"Tomorrow's Sunday." Emily laughed. "Tomorrow you sleep all day. In the evening we're invited to the Pattersons. You know, Rita Patterson was married."

"No, I didn't know."

"But I wrote you."

"Oh, yes. Now I remember."

The car went slowly along Riverside Avenue. Stroud looked silently out of the window. Nothing has changed, he thought. Through the big plate-glass windows of the Owl Drugstore he could see the soda fountain with the same adolescents bent over the same milkshakes. The Metropole must be showing a new film, but the title on the marquee and the names of the stars seemed unchanged. They passed the neighborhood delicatessen, and he remembered that he had once defended the owner's son in an embezzlement case and had managed to get him off with six months' probation. On the corner of Post Street was the same big Swedish traffic cop, looking as if he hadn't left the spot since Stroud went away.

He asked himself if he was happy to be back. He did not know exactly. The familiar scenes did not fill him with bursting joy, but they did not leave him indifferent either. It was simply as if he could not rejoice at seeing it all again because he had never been away. It was all like an experience he had had many times before: the picture of a past event would pop with unusual clarity into his mind, and he would discover that he had actually been thinking of this event for days. How could he celebrate a reunion with that from which he had never parted?

The oppressive feeling that had crowded his breast as he approached Spokane had vanished the moment he stepped out of the plane. But now, as the car turned into the suburban friendliness of the street on which his house stood, he again felt the cold contraction around his heart.

Eleanor must have seen him coming from the window, for he was still standing at the car to help Jim with the bags when she came toward him across the lawn. She moved clumsily. He hardly recognized the slim, athletic girl he remembered as his daughter.

She flung her arms around her father. "Welcome home, Daddy!" she said.

He kissed her. "What a surprise!" he said, laughing. "Making me a grandfather with no advance warning!"

Rosa, the Negro cook, greeted him in the doorway. "Good to have you back, Colonel," she said heartily.

"It's good to be back," Stroud answered.

Emily and Eleanor conducted him through the house, which had been put into gleaming order for his return. The floors had been waxed and polished until it seemed dangerous to walk on them. In their big bedroom, overlooking the garden, Emily had had new wallpaper hung. It was bright wallpaper with a somewhat too vivid chrysanthemum design. He said he liked it very much. The Christmas tree was still standing in the living-room, and the whole downstairs of the house was fragrant with the remembered smell of Christmas.

"We really should have taken the Christmas tree down day before yesterday," Emily said, "but I thought we'd light it up once more when you came."

He sat down for a moment in his small study. His books, pictures, and souvenirs surrounded him. The desk was cluttered with dozens of photographs.

"It looks pretty untidy," said Emily, nestling next to him on the arm of his chair. "But that's been my greatest pleasure lately— pasting your pictures from overseas in albums. I hope you brought some of the prison camp. You haven't sent any pictures in a long time."

"No," he said, "I didn't send any pictures lately."

"Eleanor collected all the newspaper clippings about you, too," Emily continued. "We were terribly upset about the fighting in the camp. Jerry called us from the *Spokesman-Review* as soon as the news came in."

"What did the paper say?" He listened only fleetingly as Emily answered. The camp seemed dim and hazy, as if it were not in Europe but someplace on Mars or Saturn.

Emily was saying, "Oh, they published your picture and everything. The one you had taken just before you left for Europe. They said you acted like a hero. We were all so proud of you, John. But now it's high time you settled down and we stopped being proud of you."

He smiled gratefully but absently. He went over to the desk on which lay all sorts of mementos from two world wars. An Italian dirk, which a sailor had given him in World War I; a little statue of Louis XIV from Valence, in France; a box of Adolf Hitler's stationery from the Chancellery in Berlin. He took up the Louis XIV statue. Valence, he thought, Valence, World War I . . . a little French girl in the Café Central on the town square. He no longer remembered how she looked; he only heard the tone of her voice, a soft, southern voice, that kept repeating "*Mon chou.*" It was like a stitch in the part of his breast where he now knew his heart to be. Will I someday remember no more of Wanda than that? he wondered.

Eleanor came into the room.

"How is Tim?" he asked.

"Very well, Dad. He'll be here later. He has an awful lot to do these days. He's going into an air-conditioning firm. Mr. Gordon has offered him a partnership."

"Is he taking it?"

"Yes. It looks like a good proposition."

"You can tell Dad all that later," Emily interrupted. "Dad probably wants to change now. Do you want to put on civilian clothes? They're all laid out."

He undressed slowly in the bathroom. He let steaming water run into the tub. He grinned to himself as he recalled Peter's remark that American civilization begins and ends in the bathroom. The bathroom actually was out of all proportion to the comfortable but middle-class house—the combination tub and shower, the profusion of monogrammed towels, the bath salts, the variety of lotions and talcum powders, the pink cover on the toilet seat, the bottles of mouth wash and the tubes of toothpaste. Well, he thought, maybe we overdo cleanliness, at that. But it wouldn't hurt Europe any to learn from us. He luxuriated in his hot bath.

He was not yet finished when there came a knock on the bathroom door. He heard Jim's voice. "Come in," he said.

"Excuse me for intruding," Jim said, "but it's the only chance I'll get to see you alone. Downstairs the women will be on your neck all the time." He was obviously embarrassed.

"What's on your mind?" Stroud asked, drying himself.

"Do you remember when I came to see you in Germany?" Jim began awkwardly.

"Of course."

"Well, I hope you didn't write Mom anything about it."

"You mean about your little French girl?"

"That's it."

"Not a word."

"Good. I wanted to ask you not to mention it." He broke off for a moment and then added firmly, "That's all over now."

Stroud took care not to smile. "And Marjorie?" he asked. "Everything back to normal with Marjorie?"

"No," said Jim. "That is, I see her now and then. She'll be here this evening. But she bores me, Dad. You know, once a man's been to Europe . . ."

"I thought our girls looked better than ever to you fellows, after Europe."

Jim ran his fingers through his stubby blond hair, which was still cut in GI style. "Heck," he said, "it's not that simple. The girls in general look better here than they did over there, but I can't seem to get fond of any one of them."

"What happened with the French girl?"

"That's a long story. I'll tell you some other time. You know, Dad, I don't think I want to go back."

"I understand," Stroud said. "Why should you go back?"

After the midday meal he went to bed. Usually he never slept in the afternoon, but now he was exhausted. He had not had a single restful night since Christmas Eve. He had been taking sleeping pills, but they helped him little. He slept restlessly. Throughout the war he had never had dreams of battle or death; now nightmares awoke him in the night. He dreamed of war, of the revolt in the camp, of blood and murder and of men who threatened him. Wanda drifted through his dreams, a miserable, ragged, persecuted Wanda—the Wanda of the DP camp and the Warsaw uprising. Once he dreamed that he was wearing an SS uniform and was attempting to rape her. Another time he dreamed that she came to him in the midst of the uprising, fell on her knees before him, and confessed that she was expecting a child but that the child was not his; it was the child of the pockmarked officer of the SS camp. He always awoke around four or five in the morning and could not fall asleep again. But now, in his old bed, he fell at once into a deep sleep. He slept dreamlessly until five-thirty in the afternoon. Then Emily came and woke him. She laid her hand on his forehead.

"Sorry, dear, but you'll have to get up," she said. "We're having a few people in for cocktails and dinner. All the friends you want to see, I hope."

He wanted to see no one, but he said he was pleased. He got up and put on a freshly pressed uniform. For some reason he did not have the courage to put on a civilian suit yet.

⇛ 55 ⇚

THE living-room was already full of guests when Stroud entered. The first to embrace him was Tony Doughty. Tony was at least ten years younger than he, but they had been working together for fifteen years. He had taken Tony in as junior partner and had soon given him a full partnership. Tony, nevertheless, still looked up to him as boss. He bore Stroud no grudge for treating him well; he forgave him completely for taking him up as a young man without particular prospects and advancing him rapidly. Tony had never acquired the look of an established lawyer; he had something of the air of a college boy more interested in the baseball scores than in the intricacies of the law. Actually, however, he was not only a shrewd advocate, but a reliable partner. He had guarded Stroud's interests in the law firm with the singleminded loyalty of a watch dog. It was good to feel the powerful squeeze of Tony's broad hand again.

The Johnstons advanced toward him through the living-room. The Johnstons owned a large hotel in the city. They were an exceedingly popular married couple and had a reputation for making parties lively. Mrs. Johnston, the former Jessie Stock, was fifteen years older than her husband. When they were married it was widely predicted that the marriage would soon end in catastrophe; that was twenty years ago. Mrs. Johnston was fat, gray-haired, and never wore a hat. Mr. Johnston was slender, elegant, and passionately fond of dancing. She never drank; he drank all the time. They were still so much in love that once, when she was sick, he did not leave the house for six months, but stayed home and told her jokes. She knew them all, and most of them she had told him herself. But she laughed herself back to health at his, and her own, jokes.

"The prodigal son is back," Mrs. Johnston shouted, planting two enthusiastic kisses on his cheeks.

Stroud embraced her with exaggerated heartiness. He had not given the Johnstons a thought for months, and Mrs. Johnston was really a great girl.

"When does my turn come in all this kissing and hugging?" asked Mrs. Troy.

"Helen wants to kiss you," Mrs. Johnston cried, stepping aside. "I can't bring myself to delay the great moment any longer."

For twenty years Mrs. Troy had been a favorite topic of conversation in Spokane society. She had divorced Judge Troy years ago in order, as gossip had it, to marry Judge Cavensham. Since then she never went out unless accompanied by Judge Cavensham, but she evidently had no idea of marrying him. She was still called "Helen of Troy," and voices were lowered whenever she was mentioned in the presence of the young. No one conceded that in the course of time she had waned and faded and had long since ceased being dangerous.

"Helen, you're more beautiful than ever," Stroud told her.

"And you're more of a flatterer than ever," Helen retorted, kissing him with the coy restraint of a woman who knows that her kisses can be dangerous.

"And I have to stand here and watch all this," Emily said, laughing.

The living-room was so crowded that Stroud wondered how all the guests found room for themselves. Emily was still greeting newcomers. I never knew that I had so many friends, Stroud thought, and he could hardly conceal how moved he was. A gratitude that he could not explain to himself welled up in him as Gustave Beckman pounded him on the shoulder—the pompous W. Gustave Beckman who for years had done nothing but look respectable and give the impression that he was a candidate for the Senate. Stroud had never been able to stand W. Gustave Beckman. But it was as if all these people had come to assure him that they had forgiven him.

Almost all of them had made plans for him.

"I know you want to be alone with your family," Judge Van Devlin told him, "but how about hopping a plane for the south and playing some golf with me as soon as you're settled?" Van Devlin, a graying bachelor, was Stroud's favorite golf opponent.

He had barely finished explaining to Van Devlin why he doubted whether he could make it, when Mrs. Bendel, the widow of attorney Jack Bendel and a cousin of Emily's, was insisting that he keep his calendar clear for dinner at her house on the following Saturday.

Then it seemed to Stroud that a fresh wind blew through the living-room. Marjorie came flying into his arms. Where she was concerned, at least, he had no guilty conscience; whenever he had thought of Jim he had also thought of this unspoiled and ebullient girl.

"It's grand to see you, you old darling!" she said, kissing him full on the mouth, and Stroud felt that she had really missed him.

It was almost as if she were telling him that she had been through a trying period and it was high time that he had come back.

Eleanor's husband Tim was, as usual, the last to come, but he arrived in time to hear Johnston urging Stroud to mix one of his celebrated Old-Fashioneds. "Not that we exactly died of thirst while you were away," Johnston assured him, "but there was a definite drought of Old-Fashioneds. Nobody mixes them the way you do, John. How about it?"

"Only too glad," Stroud said. "But I don't know if we have all the makings."

"Everything's ready in the kitchen," Emily said.

Stroud went into the kitchen. Tony followed him. He took an apron from a nail in the wall and tied it over his uniform. "Do you want to empty a couple of ice trays?" Stroud said.

"Sure thing."

Tony opened the refrigerator, removed two trays, held them under the hot-water faucet, and broke the cubes from the containers.

"Where's the bowl for the ice?" he asked.

Stroud laughed. "You probably know where it's kept better than I do," he said. "I've been away three years, my friend. Maybe you hadn't noticed." He wondered whether he himself was aware of it.

He reached down and opened a cabinet under the sink. There was the chipped yellow bowl they used for ice, in the same place it had always been.

"Look at that," Tony said. "And you're trying to kid me you've been away three years!"

While Stroud dropped half-cubes of sugar in the bottoms of the stubby little glasses, squirted them expertly with bitters, and then crushed them with a frayed wooden muddler, he asked Tony about the office.

"You couldn't have come back at a better time," his partner told him. "This Edwards case is just a little too tough for me to handle."

"What's the Edwards case?"

It was the third or fourth time since he had come home that somebody had looked at him in that puzzled, questioning way. He recovered himself at once and said, "Oh, yes. You wrote me about that. But give me a little briefing on it, will you?"

"That'd take too long now. It's the case of a seventeen-year-old kid who shot his sister and her boy friend. You know who the Edwardses are. The old man owns the Edwards department store."

"I think I know him," Stroud said. "Doesn't he belong to the Rotary Club?"

"Yes. The big, gray-haired fellow with the remarkably long nose."

"Is the boy all right mentally?" Stroud asked, slicing oranges.

"That's what the psychiatrists say."

"What do you think?"

"We won't get very far pleading insanity."

"Why did he do it?"

"God knows. The boy says he killed them to redeem his sister's honor. If you ask me, he was in love with his sister himself."

"Is there any possibility he was avenging the rape of his sister?"

"Hell, no. He found them in bed together. Besides that, he shot his sister first and then the man."

"What do his parents have to say?"

Tony was dropping maraschino cherries into the drinks Stroud had finished mixing. "That's just it," he said. "The parents are acting like nitwits. They don't know whose reputation is more important to them—the dead daughter's or the living son's."

"Have you questioned them?"

"By God, I've practically been living with them. But they're no help at all."

"Carry in the first batch on that big tray over there," Stroud said. "Do you think I ought to talk with the boy?"

"As soon as possible. The case comes up on the twenty-eighth."

Stroud took off his apron and followed Tony into the living-room, an Old-Fashioned in either hand.

His guests swarmed around him. Sipping their drinks, they bombarded him with questions, and he scarcely knew which one to answer first. Judge Cavensham wanted to hear his opinion of how the Nürnberg trials were going. Van Devlin was interested in how Anglo-Saxon usage was being reconciled with French court procedure at Nürnberg. Millard Cross, a retired banker who was commander of the local American Legion, was worried about black-market dealings in Germany and the consequent loss of prestige of American troops there. The seductive Helen lived up to her

reputation by asking about the *Fräuleins*, how they were dressed
and whether they had anything at all to wear these days. Beckman
wanted to know whether all of Europe wasn't wantonly being
thrown to the Bolsheviks. He was eager to embark on a long dis-
course on the communist danger, but Mrs. Beckman cut him
short. She always forbade him a second cigar, a second drink, and,
whenever possible, a second sentence.

Then Mrs. Johnston asked, "And how about the revolt in your
camp, John? The papers here were full of it. They made you out a
terrific hero. Let's not have any false modesty now. Tell us all
about it."

He really did not want to talk about it, not because of modesty
but for quite other reasons. But in order not to seem coy and
affected he began to speak, and it all came back to him stronger
and more vividly than he expected. Europe, Germany, and the
camp no longer seemed far away, on Mars or Saturn, but so near
and immediate that his comfortable living-room filled with familiar
people and familiar furniture seemed to fall away. It all came back
—not only Christmas Eve in the camp, the little Christmas tree in
his office, and the battle at the main entrance, but everything that
had gone before—Verdun, and the little tavern on the way to
Berchtesgaden, and the swim in the Starnberger See, and the first
drive through the snow, and waiting in the reception room of Dr.
Markstein, and Teitinger's murder trial, and the DP camp, and
First Sergeant Parker, and the parting in Maria's house. And, above
all, Wanda, who seemed so near that it was as if he could not
tolerate the people around him, but had to be alone with her. Or
if not with her, at least by himself.

He was surprised that he could continue talking. From time to
time his glance fell on Eleanor, who sat, wan and tired, in a corner
of the sofa. Only now did he understand why it had cost him such
an effort to speak lovingly to her. At first he had thought that he
was shying away from the idea of becoming a grandfather. But he
knew it was something else. It was merely that he had no interest
in whether his grandchild would come into the world in two
months or five months, whether it would be a boy or a girl. What
he wanted was to lay his hand on the swelling stomach of the
distant woman, to feel the life growing within her, to detect the
movements of the little hands and feet as they moved inside her

body. He wanted to lay his cheek tenderly on that tender body and listen again to the beating of the growing heart, the first heart-beats of his child. He did not want to look at Eleanor sitting there in the well-heated living-room, spoiled, moody, and steeped in anxiety, planning her trip to the hospital with her friend Henriette and thinking how nice it would be for both babies to be born on the same day. He closed his eyes for a moment. He could smell the special odor of wood that filled the little peasant house where he had last seen Wanda. A voice inside him cried out, where are you? what are you doing? He had to close his hands into fists to keep from stretching them out beseechingly across six thousand miles to the woman in the cold, snowed-in house in the Bavarian mountains.

Questions that interrupted his story brought him back to reality. He was sitting in his own living-room, drinking an Old-Fashioned he had mixed himself, talking with his friends, listening to what they had to say, and from time to time looking across to the other side of the fireplace at his wife, who was surprisingly young and excited to have him back.

Then his eye wandered to the farthest corner of the room. Sitting close together on a little settee were two people who had paid no attention to his narration. Jim and Marjorie were holding hands. Stroud looked at them for a long time. He smiled.

⇛ 56 ⇚

S TROUD made good his announcement that he intended to return to work immediately. On Monday he was back at his desk, and before the week was out he was as conversant with the affairs of his office as if he had never been away. For four weeks he allowed himself no time whatever for meditation. He was back in civilian clothes, arrived at his office at nine every morning, attended Rotary luncheons on Thursdays, and met with a group of former officers in the Davenport Friday evenings.

Only two things reminded him continually that he was not the same. He had a panicky fear of being alone. Almost every morning he tried to persuade Jim to drive into the city with him so as not to be alone in the car. On the way home he usually found someone to whom he could give a lift. No route was too round-about as long as it guaranteed companionship. When he found himself alone he invariably turned on the radio, which he had formerly detested. At night he read in bed much later than he was accustomed to. He feared turning out the light before he was tired enough to fall asleep immediately.

The second thing was waiting for the mail. He had arranged with Peter to have letters addressed to his office. The mail was distributed there at ten in the morning and at four in the afternoon. He often inquired for the mail three times between nine and ten. When he noticed that his impatience struck his secretary as peculiar, he took to walking casually past her desk to see whether she was holding the mail longer than was necessary. When he was busy outside the office during the afternoon, he called his secretary a few minutes after four and asked about the mail. Four weeks had passed and there was still no news from Peter.

During this time Stroud concentrated all his time and energy on the Edwards case, which Tony had turned over to him with a sigh of relief. Tony told his friends that Edwards was a fortunate young man. Never before had Stroud devoted himself to a case with such unsparing application.

The trial lasted three days.

The courtroom was packed as Stroud rose to make his summation at the end of the second day. Interest in the case was intense. The Edwardses were a prominent family in the city, the trial had brought to light a variety of salacious episodes and details, and there was universal sympathy for the parents who, having lost their daughter, were now faced with the possible execution of their seventeen-year-old son.

Young Edwards's prospects were by no means favorable. The district attorney, Gunnar Toernsen, had conducted his case with great skill and effect. He was one of the most gifted young men of the local bar and was regarded as unbeatable in cross-examination. He had anticipated and nullified most of the arguments of the defense. He had established the fact that brother and sister had been living two lives at once. With school companions and family friends they had conducted themselves like the well brought up children of respected parents which everyone took them to be. At the same time, however, they had indulged in sexual practices and perversities with a depravity beyond their years.

Stroud spoke for an hour and a half. He knew after the first ten minutes that he would triumph. He heard his own voice, and did not recognize it. It had become mellower, more persuasive, warmer. He had prepared his summation painstakingly, as he always did, but he did not follow his original plan. It was not only that the district attorney had demolished many of his arguments before he could use them; it was rather that after a few minutes he was seized with a kind of fervor in which a flow of inspiration supplanted all his carefully considered arguments.

He had always been a competent speaker, but never an inspired one. Now something swept him along, a power he had never known before, a will stronger than his own. He seized instinctively on the one factor that gave him a superiority over the energetic young district attorney: his experience of life, his understanding that life was not round and whole and smooth, but jagged and involute, that the pure are not always pure, that under a tranquil surface there is often an abyss, that those who have least reason to sin often sin most blackly, that temptation is never restricted to certain types and milieus, that no human being is simple, no matter how simple he may seem, and that each carries within him a secret that no man can unriddle.

While he spoke, a surging sense of happiness came over him. He looked at the handsome, self-confident district attorney on the other side of the room and suddenly he felt how good it was not to be young. The unconscious battle against age, which had been going on within him for years, ceased; with hot, streaming gratitude he sensed that exchanging youth for understanding was no bad trade. In the eyes of the jurymen he read that they were becoming aware of the great difference that lay between the crudity of the district attorney's approach to the case and his own subtler evaluation of it, that the difference between them was almost that between a butcher and a surgeon. As he spoke of the unnatural relationship between brother and sister and its effect on the mind of the boy, and as, in conclusion, he urged the jurymen to look beyond the actual events into the mysteries of the soul, which are as important as actions in judging men, he thought fleetingly of

Wanda and the camp and the Bavarian village. But now no feeling of guilt accompanied these thoughts; it was as if everything had happened only to teach him an ultimate wisdom, to instruct him in the subtleties of the surgery of the soul, so that from now on he could operate with the skill that would save the patient.

In the hush of the great courtroom he heard his own voice ring out, full, clear, and confident. So sure was he now of his theme and of himself, that while he was speaking he could study the faces of the judge, the audience, the reporters, and the witnesses; and from this fleeting observation he also derived new and unsuspected powers. While he spoke of young Edwards and his victims, it dawned on him that one single human being at home was of more importance than the mass of strangers to whom he had been devoting himself in the past year. The thought did not dismay him, because he knew that he could help the Edwards boy, whereas he had always been helpless in the face of the strangers overseas. Yes, he knew these faces. In them he could read approbation and abhorrence, shock and compassion, revulsion and sympathy, and what he was saying wove itself into the web of their reaction. Over there, across the sea, it was always as if one were speaking in an unknown tongue, delivering diligently and by heart a speech that could not be altered. Here the words one spoke changed with each occasion, and the thoughts also; and not only did something stream out from the speaker, but while he spoke something also returned to him from those who listened. Here one could help because the patient responded, and one was familiar with everything: with the instruments, the nurses, the operating room, the odors, and the light. As he sat down he did not know whether he had saved Edwards; but he did know, as he listened to the outburst of applause which seemed to reach him from a great distance and which the gavel of the judge could not quell, that once again he was back where he belonged.

The jury had retired to deliberate, and in the hallway a swarm of people surrounded Stroud to congratulate him.

Tony pulled him aside. "I've got to shake your hand alone," he said. "This old building never heard a summation like that before. What on earth have you been doing overseas? Fighting a war or perfecting your courtroom technique?"

"No," Stroud answered, "it's only that I came to see how much easier it is to be counsel for the defense than prosecutor. At least, for some people."

Tony seemed genuinely stirred. He was not a man who was easily moved. Stroud saw that there were tears in his eyes. Since the time Tony had lost his mother fifteen years before, nothing less than drink in considerable quantity could make him shed tears. This time he had not been drinking.

The father of young Edwards was the next to come up and press Stroud's hand. "My wife is ill," Edwards said, "but I shall tell her what you have done for us, Mr. Stroud. No one can know what I felt while you were speaking."

Stroud walked up and down the long corridor with Tony. To hide his embarrassment he said, "You know, it still gives me a peculiar feeling when somebody calls me 'Mister.' 'John,' that doesn't sound unusual. They called me that in the Army too. But 'Mister'!"

"You'd better get used to it," Tony said. "We're not going to let you go off to any more wars." Then he asked, "How long do you think the deliberation will take?"

"I have no idea."

Stroud looked at the clock over the entrance to the courtroom. It was ten minutes after four. He continued his pacing with Tony. He had forgotten that the mail arrived at four o'clock.

$$\text{\guillemotright} \; 57 \; \text{\guillemotleft}$$

MARIA had spent the last two days and nights in the hospital. It was now six o'clock, and another uneasy night seemed in prospect.

"Is Dr. Markstein worried?" asked Peter, who was sitting next to her in the reception room of the maternity ward.

"No," Maria answered. "He's not worried yet, but the child should have been born forty-eight hours ago."

"What does he intend to do?"

"He's going to wait another twenty-four hours. If the baby isn't born by then, he'll order a Caesarean."

"Will he operate himself?"

"No. Professor Hofer."

"How's Wanda?"

"Good. She's resting quietly."

"Do you think you can go down in the garden for a while? You haven't been out of the building for two days."

"All right. I'll just tell the nurse where she can find me."

They went down to the hospital garden, which stretched down to the Isar River. It was a tepid June evening. The air was heavy and soft, and one felt it on the skin like a stroking hand. The shrubbery along the little stone wall that separated the garden from the Isar was in full bloom.

"Have you had news from the village?" Peter asked.

"Yes. Helga was in the city on a flying visit yesterday. She had great news. The Minister President has announced that he will attend our town meeting Sunday."

"I hope you can be there," Peter said.

"I hope so too. But they'd get on all right without me."

"It's a great thing for the village that the Minister President is coming to your meeting, isn't it?"

Maria nodded, pleased. "You know what he said to me not long ago. He's curious to see the place that everybody calls a model village."

"And it is too," Peter said. Then, changing the subject, "Did Fred bring Helga into town?"

"Yes."

"Don't you think she's getting a little too fond of him?"

"What makes you say that?"

"I don't know," Peter replied. "I like him. He's a nice boy. No ball of fire, of course. A typical, solid farm boy from Iowa. I like him all right—"

"Well, then?"

"He'll be going home one of these days. Tomorrow or the next day or the day after that. I don't want Helga to think that the world has come to an end when that happens."

"He says he wants to marry her."

"Maybe he means it. I don't doubt that he does. But things will look different when he gets back to America. Not that one forgets what one has experienced over here. These boys have gathered a whole new set of impressions. Learned to know new women. Different women. But I know what will happen. They will try to change their women at home, not marry European women."

"Some of them are doing it though."

"Not very many."

"I have confidence in Helga," Maria said. "I don't think she'll lose her head."

"I'm not so sure of that."

She looked at him gratefully. And after a little silence, "Have I told you today that I love you?"

"No," said Peter, "you've neglected it entirely."

"It's so sweet, the way you worry about Helga," she said. "You're probably right in what you say about Fred. I have a false perspective—ever since my own man came back."

"That's different," Peter replied. "Which reminds me, I've had news from Patricia."

She did not look at him. "So?" she said.

"The divorce becomes final next week."

They walked for a moment in silence along the Isar, which murmured as it flowed sluggishly past. The river was still carrying off debris, broken furniture, parts of blown-up bridges.

"Soon the Isar will flow as smoothly as before," she said finally. "Look. It's not blocked very much any more."

"Yes," he answered. "Most of the wreckage has been cleared away."

As they turned back toward the hospital she asked, "Have you heard from Stroud?"

"I had a cable from him the day before yesterday. He wants to know how things are going with Wanda."

"Wanda will be all right," Maria said firmly. It sounded a little as if she were saying, Wanda will be all right, but that's no concern of his.

They went up the stairs to the third floor, where Wanda's room was. Maria said, "It's good the evenings are cool. The heat makes Wanda terribly uncomfortable."

"Did you bring her my electric fan?"

"Of course. She told me to thank you."

In the corridor they met Dr. Markstein. "The pains have begun," he said in passing. "We've taken her to the delivery room. You can wait in her room."

"Will everything be all right?" Peter asked with the uneasiness of men for whom every birth is filled with mystery and dread.

"Why shouldn't everything be all right?" Dr. Markstein asked, smiling.

They did not talk much while they waited. Maria stood up from time to time and adjusted the pillows on Wanda's bed. Now and then Peter went to the window and looked out. Over the Isar the night was falling.

Once Maria said, "You're as nervous as if it were your own child."

He was standing at the window as he replied, "It is our child, a little."

He looked at the clock.

"How long has she been up there?" Maria asked.

"About two hours."

"You'd think the nurse would come down and let us know how things are going."

"You're as nervous as I am," Peter said.

Thereafter they looked at the clock more often. Maria went out into the hall three or four times. It was quiet out there. Only a feeble light was burning. From the distance the crying of a child could be heard. They heard footsteps in the corridor. They held their breath.

The nurse came in. She was an old woman whom Maria had known for years. Her son had a farm not far from Maria's. She had a face like a sergeant in a cavalry regiment, but when she smiled she looked like a sergeant who has renounced worldly things. She was smiling now.

"Everything's fine," she said. "It's a boy."

She held back the door and fastened it so that the stretcher could be wheeled in. She adjusted the pillows some more.

"Did everything go smoothly?" Maria asked. Her voice was full of gratitude and relief.

"Smooth as silk," said the nurse. "The boy is fine. Almost seven pounds."

"What's the child doing?" Peter asked.

"He's out bicycle riding," the nurse answered, pulling back the bedspread. "What do you think he's doing? He's yelling."

Then the stretcher was wheeled in. Dr. Markstein and another doctor followed. "She's just coming to," Dr. Markstein said quietly. "A splendid boy."

"Our deepest thanks, Doctor," said Peter, shaking his hand.

Dr. Markstein, confused by his gratitude, mumbled something unintelligible.

Now Wanda was lying in the bed. She was still sleeping, but it was a light sleep that bordered on waking. Her features were suffused by a beatitude which Peter had never seen on the face of a woman. He wanted to fend off the thought, but the harder he tried the more vividly he was reminded of the faces of dying comrades in the field—the peace that came to human beings only in the instant before death. No, Peter told himself, hers is not the face of one who is dying. It is only that the margin that separates life and death is so precariously slim. He thought of Stroud.

Then Wanda opened her eyes.

⟫ 58 ⟪

THE child was born on Saturday evening, and Peter planned to spend the rest of the week-end in the village.

Dr. Markstein judged it unnecessary for Maria to remain at the hospital, and so they drove to Oberndorf the same night. They spoke little on the way. As they entered the house, Peter said, "I'm going to write a letter to John."

"Aren't you going to send him a cable?"

"No. I'd rather write."

"Shall I make coffee for you?"

"Yes, please."

He sat at the table near the open window in the living-room. Maria turned out all the lights except a little lamp on the table. She brought him paper and ink.

He wrote:

My dear John,

The child was born this evening at seven thirty-five. It is a big, strapping boy. More than six pounds. Wanda is doing well. She says the child is beautiful. I don't know. I was only allowed a fleeting glimpse of him, through a glass panel. To me he looks like all newborn babies. Like a little red ugly old man. But Maria insists that I understand nothing of children.

I have promised you, John, to report every detail. I will do so, although I have the feeling that I shouldn't. One should not act as if the ocean between us were not there at all.

Well, then. Wanda awoke in her own bed in the hospital. Maria and I were standing against the wall. She opened her eyes. The way she did it was very remarkable, John. She did not become conscious slowly and fitfully, but as if she had only closed her eyes for a moment. And she was not dazed or confused, but had clear, unclouded eyes. Her glance found Maria at once. Her first words were, "A boy?" And as Maria nodded, she asked, half smilingly and half distrustfully, "Are you sure?" Then she fell asleep again.

When, after about fifteen minutes, she opened her eyes again, she asked immediately, "Where is he?" Dr. Markstein tied a mask around her face, and the nurse brought in the child. She laid him next to Wanda on the bed. We could not see him because we were not permitted to come close. We could only see Wanda. She took the child in her arms. As long as I live I will never forget her gesture as she did it. It was as if she had had ten children.

Everyone in the room held his breath. The baby yelled. I don't know whether all babies cry that way. But I think your son yelled especially loud. A few minutes later Dr. Markstein asked us to leave the room. Afterward we were permitted to look at the child through a window. Dr. Markstein went with us. He told us again that everything had gone smoothly. Wanda would pass a restful night, he said. He has behaved wonderfully. He asked me to write you at once, but in a few days he will give me a detailed report for you. He promised me that he would keep Wanda in the hospital for fourteen days. As we left he said with a grin, "But she won't want to stay after the first week." He is a marvelous doctor and an excellent fellow.

What more should I tell you, John? Whatever I may say to you tonight would sound hollow, and probably in bad taste.

So I will only add that I know what you are feeling. All through the afternoon and evening, while Wanda was upstairs in the delivery room and we were waiting in her room, I felt over and over again that I was taking from you something that no man has a right to take from another. I worried about Wanda, and trembled over the child, and as she lay there breathing with difficulty, her mouth open, but with a peace that was more than human on her face, I folded my hands and prayed. I'm not sure that I have prayed since childhood, but all at once I knew all the prayers of my youth by heart again. At the same time I had the feeling that I was robbing you—robbing you of the worry, and the impatient hours, and the prayers. And I could not suppress the feeling that your son belongs a little to me too.

And this is, after all, the most important thing that I want to say to you, that we want to say to you, Maria and I.

Whatever you are feeling now is your own personal affair, and no one can help you with it. But there are two things you must not do: Regret that you went home. And be sorry for the child. You had to go home, John, just as I had to come back here. How often have I told myself that I was ungrateful to America because I did not stay there. And I know that many times you have said to yourself that you should never have left Wanda and the child alone. But the one is as false as the other.

Do not believe for a moment that I subscribe to Hitler's doctrine of "blood and soil." I wish that we could all shed the ties that bind us to our narrow homelands—and even immense America is narrow compared with the whole world. But in this struggling, gestating, self-doubting age of ours the important thing is for a man to do all he can—where he can do it best. We must try, each of us, to realize our own highest abilities, not out of pride but because our best is just barely good enough for the world in which we live. You often called me a cynic and an idealist. You could also call me an altruist and an egoist, for I believe that the world can move forward only if the individual ruthlessly strives to unfold his own capabilities to the full. Those of us who call ourselves liberals often believe that we are at home everywhere. But we are not at home everywhere. It is precisely our best faculties that wither first in foreign soil. Human beings, John, are not for export.

And they should not be either. If the finest people of every country left it to become missionaries elsewhere, then every country would go to ruin. The essential thing is not to make foreign people over in our own image, but to understand them. You and I have learned this in the past few years, and you have paid more heavily for the lesson than I. I wish that there were fewer disappointed missionaries in the world, and more people who have learned to improve their own immediate surroundings and to love what they do not understand.

I know what you want to ask now. The child. Where will he belong? Will he be European or American? A Pole, an American, or even a German? That is just what I wanted to say to you: Do not feel sorry for the child, but envy him! He will be able to do what neither you nor I were able to do, what we should never have tried to do. Do you know what Hegel calls the "objective mind"? It is everything that a child absorbs before it is born. The stored-up wisdom of the world. The sorrows of his father, the battles of his ancestors, the trials of his parents. Only superficially does a human being's path begin at birth. Birth is an incident, and not a very important one. Do you know what the little man possesses who was born today and whose resemblance to an old man is not, I insist, accidental? He is richer than you and I. In him is America and Europe, the old and the new, freedom and oppression, hunger and surfeit, safety and searching. In him is the sorrow of his mother who has known bondage, and in him is you, who were privileged to be a liberator. In him is East and West, village and metropolis, farm and factory, the earth of two continents, and the heaven that arches over all continents. In him, John, is the world toward which you and I strive, but which you and I could never achieve. He is the child of two victors. But at his cradle stands Maria. And, believe me, that too is good. For the world should not separate victory and defeat either.

But that is not at all what I wanted to tell you. I merely wanted to give you a first, hurried account, and to promise you that I would send reports on your son just as often as I can. You may rely on it that he will grow up as you would have him.

Maria sends you her fondest regards, I embrace you.

Your Peter

He put down the pen and looked up. Only now did he notice that Maria had been in the room all the time. From time to time she had poured coffee for him.

"It couldn't have been easy for you," she said.

"No," he said, "it was not easy."

He handed her the letter. She read it in silence. Then they both stood up and, as if moved by the same impulse, went out into the garden. They opened the gate and walked along the little path that skirted the brook, as they had done so often before.

The smell of earth and water and summer was warm and strong. Their hands entwined themselves. Their fingers grasped one another with a pressure that was almost pain.

"You are right," she said. "It is a most fortunate child." She pressed herself closer to him.

For a while they were silent; only their thoughts went on in unison. They thought of the child at whose cradle the whole world stood. And of the mother who had not even a homeland to call her own.

"Poor Wanda!" Maria said.

Now they walked faster. They were almost running. They were overwhelmed with a great thankfulness that they were permitted to be together. Running now, they still held hands. In the clasp of their hands there was love and hope, a glorious obligation, an unshakable promise. In it, too, was a ripe but unweary wisdom, and an almost shy salute to fortune.

Suddenly Maria stopped. She looked up at the sky. "June," she said under her breath. "The time for shooting stars. If a star fell from the sky now, we could make a wish for the child."

He smiled. Even in the darkness she could see his smile as he, too, looked up. He said, "No star is falling. On the contrary, I think I see one star more in the sky. . . ."